11-08

DATE DUE		
~~FEB 0 7 2009~~	OCT 1 1 2009	
~~MAR 1 3 2009~~	JUL 3 1 2010	

HECTOR LASSITER is a legendary crime novelist who writes what he lives and lives what he writes. But Hector frequently goes a step beyond, drawing friends and lovers into the tawdry and turbulent territory of his fiction. Now, the large-living pulp author has at last met his match in the ultimate performance artist: a phantom killer committed to the art of murder... a blood-thirsty provocateur who leaves a string of macabre tableaus modeled on famous works of surrealist painting and photography...

Against the vivid backdrops of a killer hurricane that nearly destroyed the Florida Keys in 1935, the Spanish Civil War, post-war Hollywood and the first days of the Castro regime in Cuba, Hector engages in a decades-long duel against a cabal of killer artists...

As in its Edgar®-nominated predecessor *Head Games*, history and myth merge, drawing on recent scholarship pointing to the existence of a dark underground of artists, photographers and art collectors that flourished in Europe and United States through most of the Twentieth Century.

In a blood-limned haze of love, deception, murderous metaphor and devastating betrayal, nothing is what it seems and obsession and creativity collide in a wicked and unexpected climax that will shake the art world to its foundations...

Also by Craig McDonald

Head Games
Art in the Blood

TOROS & TORSOS

Toros
& Torsos

CRAIG McDONALD

Bleak House Books
Madison, Wisconsin

11-08

25-

Published by
BLEAK HOUSE BOOKS
a division of Big Earth Publishing
923 Williamson St.
Madison, WI 53703
www.bleakhousebooks.com

Library of Congress Cataloging-in-Publication Data has been applied for.

ISBN: 978-1-60648-000-7 (Trade Cloth)
ISBN: 978-1-60648-001-4 (Trade Paper)
ISBN: 978-1-60648-002-1 (Evidence Collection)

12 11 10 09 08   1 2 3 4 5 6 7 8 9 10

Cover image © 2008, Banco De México Diego Rivera & Frida Kahlo Museums
Trust. Ave. Cinco de Mayo No. 2
Col. Centro
Del. Cuauhtémoc 06059
México, D.F.

THIS NOVEL IS FOR

DEBBIE MCDONALD, WITH LOVE

Dedicated to the memory of

Effie Pearl Lyon:

grandmother, teacher, poet

"*The more horrifying the world becomes,*

the more art becomes abstract."

— PAUL KLEE

PART ONE

THE BIG BLOW

(1935)

From official weather advisories:

(Saturday, August 31)

Advisory 3:30 p.m. (Key West wind direction = NW, velocity = 11 mph.) tropical disturbance of small diameter central near Long Island Bahamas apparently moving westnorthwestward attended by fresh (19-24 mph sustained) to strong (25-31 mph sustained) shifting winds and squalls possibly gale force (39-46 mph sustained) near center. Caution advised Bahama islands and ships in that vicinity. Norton NAR 3:40 p.m.

*"It is not only the deceptive calm
of the surroundings that is troubling
but the clarity of the
unreal and fraudulent character
of that which is seen."*

— SIDRA STICH

CHAPTER 1

NO GOOD DEED

"CAN I SIT with you for a time, sir?"

A silky voice — alto, but strained. The young woman said, "I think a man in this place may mean me harm."

Hector Lassiter looked up from his notebook.

She was twenty-three, maybe twenty-four. Pretty, poised and flustered.

Hector had seen her come in an hour or so before, when he'd looked up to check the weather, which was still strangely calm. Although Hector had at least a dozen years on her, he'd been attracted to her. Then he'd become absorbed in his writing...lost track of the young woman and of his interest in her while he wrote.

The crime novelist closed his notebook, capped his pen and slipped it into the pocket of his faded and striped fisherman's shirt. He gestured at the empty seat across from him and said, "Sit, please."

The short story he'd been trying to shape was showing every sign of being a dog, anyhow. He'd been trying to write the forecasted hurricane into the story, but it wasn't coming together.

Hector sipped his mojito, watching her. The woman sat down and Hector rose, walked behind her, and scooted in her chair. She was wearing a white dress that bared her shoulders and most of her back — more than a little sunburn there. He sat back down and gestured at his glass. Hector said, "Ever have one?"

"No," she said. "I mean, I don't think so. Not even sure what that is. Is that mint in there with the lime?"

"Mashed in, then some more as garnish." Hector raised two fingers at his bartender friend. He pointed at his nearly empty glass and then at himself and the woman. "You'll love this, trust me," he said. "Calm your nerves. Like my daddy said, 'You've got to find what you love and let it kill you.'"

She was blond. Blue eyes and long legs. The woman was bustier than most regarded as the vogue. But Hector never bought into the flapper physique and mystique. That aesthetic bewildered him: Hector liked curves.

"I feel I know you," she said. "I mean, as if I've maybe seen you before. I'm pretty sure I have…just yesterday."

Hector winked. "Sure. And likewise. Think I saw you come in on the steamship. I was out fishing with a friend."

"The man with the black boat? I heard that is Hemingway's boat."

"That's right," Hector said. "The *Pilar*. Now, this man who scared you…"

She nodded and fidgeted. "He's across the bar. He keeps staring and smiling at me. He has a big knife. He's been running his finger along the blade as he smiles at me. I mean, it's not so much of a *smile*…more of a…" She searched for the right word.

"A 'leer'?" Hector offered.

"Perfect — a leer. And he doesn't have so many teeth." She paused as the bartender placed her drink on the table.

Hector said, "Here, Josie," and slipped a couple of bills to the man. He raised his fresh mojito and extended his arm for a toast. "To new friends," Hector said.

She nodded distractedly and they tapped glasses. She sipped her drink and said, "It's delicious." She took another sip and said, "If I leave here alone, I'm afraid he'll follow me. I'm pretty sure that he will do that."

Hector was pretty sure, too. But he said, "Well you can stop worrying about that. I'll see you safely out of here."

She smiled. "Thank you so much, Mr. Lassiter."

He narrowed his eyes. "You know my name?"

She blushed. "I've been holding out on you a bit. I do know who you are. My friend recognized you. She recognized Mr. Hemingway first, and then you. She's read his books, and yours, too. I've read you as well. She loaned me one of your novels she had along — one I seem to have missed." She rummaged through her purse and pulled out a well-thumbed copy of *Rhapsody In Black*. "I checked your face against the photo on the back of the jacket. You look just like your picture, Mr. Lassiter. I love it. Your novel, I mean...although your photo is certainly very nice, too. It's gripping. Your book, I mean. It cost me sleep. I'm truly afraid how it might end."

Hector shrugged. "Figure on it ending darkly. They all do. And hey, please call me Hector. Now, what do I call you?"

"Rachel Harper."

He shook her hand and gave her his best smile — strong white teeth and dimples. "Okay then, Rachel. This man — where is he?"

"Is it a good idea to point him out? I wouldn't want to provoke him."

Hector nodded at the bar. "The mirror there behind you...I have the angle. I can see the whole room. So describe him to me."

"Not hard to spot," she said. "He's swarthy...maybe Mexican, or Cuban. He has a patch over his left eye. Very few teeth. He is perhaps six-feet tall, although I haven't seen him standing. But to me he looks rather tall. He's thin. There is a scar on his forehead above the eyepatch and also below it."

"He is a nasty looking piece of work," Hector said. "Any reason you can think of as to why he might be after you, Rachel?"

"None at all, Mr. Lassiter."

"*Hector.* Well, you're a very pretty young woman. That's too often reason enough in these sorry parts."

"Do you know him, Hector?"

He hesitated, then shrugged. "What makes you think I might?"

"Key West is so small, and you live here."

"Me and twelve thousand others. And God only knows how many tourists. Scads of sightseers. Boatloads of 'em, in and out, every day. They come in like you and your pal, on steamships and on ferries or on private yachts. They ride in on that damned crazy over-ocean train. This friend of yours, by the way — you indicated this friend is a woman?"

"Her name is Beverly."

Hector nodded, pleased. "You and Bev — there are hundreds like you two through here every day, bound from Miami or headed back there," Hector said. "Or they're headed for Cuba, intent on slumming in Havana."

Rachel's cheeks reddened. "Funny you say that. Beverly — Bev, as you call her — she met a man last evening. She's gone on to Cuba with him for a day or so. She left me here alone." She shook her head at her abandonment by her friend. "She left me here, alone," she said again.

Better and better. Hector sipped some more light rum and lime juice. He licked his lip and said. "Well, for now at least, you're not alone, Rachel."

"No." She half smiled. "I was a fool to let Bev talk me into this trip. And we weren't keeping up with the news. Never occurred to us, either, that August and September are hurricane months in the Atlantic. We didn't know about the big storm headed this way."

Hector frowned. "'Storm,' even 'big storm,' is understating it more than a bit. It's almost certainly a damn hurricane — maybe the worst we'll ever see."

She sipped her mojito…a savoring sip. Hector smiled. She seemed to like it fine. But her hand was trembling. "I'm terrified of this storm," she said. "I hear, only now of course, that if it hits Key West directly, everything here could be laid waste."

Hector reached across the table and squeezed her hand. She squeezed briefly back, so he was emboldened to leave his big and callused hand there, closed over hers. "Key West has never taken a direct hit from a tropical storm like the one you're fretting over," he said. "Many of these homes here on Bone Key pre-date the Civil War. The old Islanders believe Key West's position makes it impossible for a tropical storm to strike it directly. But that's not to say it can't still be very nasty." Hector felt Rachel's hand flutter under his own. But she didn't move to withdraw her hand.

Encouraged, Hector leaned in, smiling. "With precautions, we can ride these things out, please believe me. I've been through several hurricanes and tropical storms since I moved here years ago. I'm still standing, and so is my house."

"I suppose," Rachel said. "I mean, here you are to prove it, right? But I have no experience with these things, Mr. Lassiter. And alone and with that man watching me? It's almost too much to cope with. I really don't know what to do, Mr. Lassiter."

"Hector. Where are you staying, Rachel?"

"We're in the Colonial Hotel." At seven stories, it was the tallest structure on the island — Key West's lone "skyscraper." Approaching the island by boat from a certain angle, with the lighthouse and the three wireless towers at the naval base hidden behind, the hotel made the island look like it had a hard-on.

"Swanky digs," Hector said. "The island's best rooms and view. It's pretty solid, too. 'Cept for all those damned windows.

How high up are you?"

"Fifth floor, facing east."

"Then I'd urge you to consider checking out of there in the next few hours. Speaking just for myself, I wouldn't try to ride out a hurricane in that joint. And certainly not on that side."

Rachel stared at her hands, flexing her fingers…she was feeling the alcohol numbing them, Hector figured. She said, "If I check out of the hotel, where would I go?" He could hear the strain in her voice.

Hector said, "Well…I have a second bedroom. You could take refuge at my place until the danger has passed. I boarded up the windows this morning. I laid in my own provisions, and early. We'll probably be without phones and electricity for a few days, if not a week here on the island. And fresh water will maybe be scarce, too. But I've seen to that at my place. Just have some last minute shopping to do — makings for big fresh sandwiches and some more candles for late-night writing. More batteries for the short-wave. And the fixings for more of these." Hector hefted his mojito, grinning.

Rachel smiled, propping her head up on her hand, clearly a little drunk now. "You sound like a boy planning an adventure."

Hector smiled. "It's my way of coping with this damned blow," he said. "It's the strategy that has seen me through storms before. We can be scared, Rachel. We can be depressed, or fatalistic. Or, when it comes to us and this storm, we can be well-fed and pleasantly lit. I can spend my time writing to make some money and taking breaks to warm my belly with rum and my big Cuban sandwiches and good talk with you." He smiled again. "So, are you willing to share this 'boy's' adventure?"

"You know, you really didn't answer my question," she said.

"What question is that?"

"Whether you know that man who keeps looking at me while he plays with his knife."

Hesitation: "I do."

"So he is a local."

"Kind of."

"And you know him?"

"Kind of."

"Are you going to tell me more, Hector?"

"I don't want to upset you any more than you already are, Rachel."

"I want to know about him. You tell stories for a living. Do that now. Skip the worst parts of it if you have to, but let me know this man's story. Why would he be after me?"

Hector held up fingers for two more drinks. Hector had finished his mojito. Rachel was two or three sips from polishing off hers. "This man you've identified is an island character…or I suppose you'd call him that in a charitable mood," Hector said. "He's part Cuban. He goes by the name of Tito Castillo. He's reputedly linked to a revolutionary cell based in Havana. The Cuban revolutionaries have lately taken to grabbing gringo tourists for hostages. They release them in exchange for ransom money they use to fund their guerilla operations. They rob banks and businesses across the Keys to generate more money to buy guns and explosives — that sort of thing. Tito has a small boat and allegedly smuggles guns and rum and revolutionists between here and Cuba and back. But he's also got a reputation as a lady-killer. I mean that literally."

Rachel was ashen. "And the police have done nothing to stop him? I mean, if you know, and if the whole island knows…?"

"Proof, Rachel." Hector nodded at Josie as the bartender placed their fresh drinks on cardboard mats. "Gotta have proof, and old Tito is a careful one. He may not look like much other than a one-eyed, gangly rummy with bad teeth and skin, but he's probably one of the five most dangerous men on Bone Key."

Rachel said, "So what do we do, Hector? Do I sneak out the back and you meet me somewhere, or…?"

"Nothing so cloak-and-dagger," Hector said. "Please remember, I'm a crime novelist, not a mystery writer. So I tend toward the direct approach. You just wait here, sweetheart."

Hector rose and walked over to the table where the tall, swarthy man with the eye patch sat. As Rachel had said, he had a Bowie knife out, and he was dragging his callused thumb across the blade.

Hector pulled out a chair across from the man and smiling, plopped down. Hector winked and said, "*Hola*, Tito."

The man scowled and said, "I don't know you, do I? No, I don't think I do. Maybe have seen you around. But I don't truly know you." He held up his knife and grinned — most of the teeth on the left side of his mouth were missing. "I no looking for company, my pretty boy."

Smiling, Hector said, "Me either." Then he brought the heel of his work boot down on the top of the swarthy man's sandaled foot. The one-eyed man screamed and reflexively raised his wounded foot, his knee smacking the underside of the table. As Tito groaned at that second impact, Hector reached across the table, grabbed the man by both ears and slammed his head down against the tabletop.

Hector stood and stepped back from the table, surveying the results. He smiled at a slack-jawed Rachel and stern-looking Josie. "Out cold," Hector said. He took Rachel's shaking hand. "*Now we go.*"

Looking flustered, Rachel stood and smoothed out the pleats in her dress and grabbed her purse and copy of Hector's novel. Then she paused and drained her mojito and set it back down, the ice cubes tinkling in the now empty glass.

"He'll come looking for you, won't he," Rachel said, scowling, "I mean, come looking for you for revenge? You know what they say about 'no good deed going unpunished.'"

Hector shrugged, draining his own drink. "Not so sure sucker-punching some son of a bitch qualifies as a 'good deed,' Rachel.

And Tito lives on that boat of his I told you about. He's famous — or infamous — for riding out storms on that sorry crate. If this blow is half as bad as it looks to be, bastard'll likely be drowned before end of Labor Day weekend. So don't sweat it on my account, honey. If Tito survives the hurricane, I'll see to him myself. 'Retaliate first,' that's my motto. But now let's get out of here."

He took her arm and said to Josie, "Sorry pal." Hector smiled and shrugged. "But at least no damages this time, yeah?"

"Sure," the bartender said with a frown. "Those'll likely come when that son of a bitch comes to."

Looking contrite, Hector bit his lip and steered Rachel out into the muggy sun. They walked a few yards, then Hector said, "I feel bad about that — for Josie I mean. And I forgot to arrange delivery of our provisions."

Rachel frowned. "You mean that we're going back?"

"Just me," Hector said. "Just to arrange delivery of the liquor to my place, and to give Josie some money to have his boy, Carlos, maybe drag old Tito to the other side of the island. Likely best to let Tito wake up far from the scene of my crime and Josie's joint. You wait here, Rachel. You'll be safe, I swear. I'll be back in a jiffy."

Hector ducked back into the shade of the saloon, his eyes slow to adjust from the harsh sunlight. He blinked a few times and looked back over his shoulder to make certain that Rachel hadn't followed.

Josie was patting the swarthy man on the back and handing him a drink and a wet towel for his swollen lip as Hector sidled up beside him. The one-eyed man grinned with bloodied gums and a swollen lip. He said:

"It worked, Mr. Lassiter?"

"It worked *so* fine, Tito. You okay?"

"Yeah...hell yeah, Mr. Lassiter. Thanks for putting the damage on the left side. I'm trying to save what teeths left on the right so I have something to chaw with."

"I promised you I would make it the left side, Tito." It was the least Hector could do: their little scam to score tail for Hector was tried and true, and it had cost Tito several of those teeth now missing along the left side of his mouth.

Hector dug down into his pocket and pulled out his roll. He tugged off two tens and handed them to Tito. "There you go, as promised, old pal." Hector smiled at Tito, thinking, *Poor toothless goddamn rummy.* But Hector said aloud, "We're going to hunker down at my place until this storm passes, then she'll likely be getting back on the boat for Miami. Think you could stay to the other end of the island until after the Big Blow, Tito? Wouldn't want to send her off to the mainland thinking you're still stalking her, Teet."

"Can do, Mr. Lassiter." That terrible smile.

Hector smiled back and clapped the one-eyed man on the back and handed some more cash to Josie. "A fresh bottle for Tito here, Josie. Then, say in an hour, can you send Carlos to my place with some ice and makings for mojitos?"

Josie nodded, holding out his hand for more cash. "Sure. Gonna nail this skirt, you figure? She's sure enough a looker, Hector, that's for certain."

"Time will tell," Hector said with a shrug and a smile.

"Hell of a soothing way to ride out a storm," Josie said.

"The only way to do it," Hector said. Then he frowned and stripped off two more bills. "And send Carlos around to the jewelers. Have him pick me up a locket, or brooch. Maybe a bracelet. Something old looking would be best...something I could say belonged to my mother."

Josie shook his head. "Jesus but you're going to go to hell, Hec."

The crime novelist smiled, then squared his shoulders, set his mouth in a frown and stepped back out into the harsh sunlight.

Rachel was standing on the corner, her bare and proud shoulders squared, silhouetted against the sun...the outline of her thighs visible under the backlit cotton of her dress and sheer silk of her slip. Rachel held her purse in front of her and she nodded at Hector as she saw him step out of Sloppy Joe's. There was a worried look on her pretty face and she said:

"That man, Tito, he's still out cold?"

"Still is." Hector said. "Now let's get over to that hotel and collect your stuff and get you settled in."

"I can't thank you enough for all you've done, Hector," Rachel said. "Not that you ever want to confuse authors with their books or with their characters, but I have to confess, I didn't expect you to be so gallant. I never expected you to be such a gentleman."

"That's me all over," Hector said, wrapping an arm around Rachel's waist as they crossed the street. "I'm a regular Boy Scout."

"...in the 1930s...the most casual reader
of murder mysteries could infallibly detect the villain,
as soon as there entered a character who had recently
washed his neck and did not commit mayhem
on the English language."

— ELLEN GLASGOW

CHAPTER 2

CROSSED WIRES

THE PALM FRONDS were thrashing and the white clouds were being pushed out into the Gulf by the quietly mounting, east-to-west wind.

The wind kept Rachel and Hector something close to cool on their walk from Green Street to the Colonial Hotel.

Browned, wrinkled old-timers were out nailing boards over the windows of their cottages and shotgun shacks or securing storm shutters...carrying in chairs and potted plants that might become projectiles when the high winds reached the Keys. A few called to or waved at Hector, who smiled and waved back.

Hector pointed and they ducked into the tall white hotel, the overhead fans drying the sparse beads of sweat on their foreheads. Someone was trying to inject a little dubious culture: a copy of Max Ernst's "Anatomie als Braut" was hanging behind the front desk. Hector found the image deeply disturbing. While they waited for the desk clerk to finish with an older couple, Hector picked up a discarded art magazine and began to leaf through it. He paused at an ad for a Picasso exhibition to be held in December in New York.

The ad featured a new illustration Picasso had titled *Le Minotaure*. A bullheaded, naked beast with a hairy chest, bulging biceps and a creditable cock was attacking a screaming horse in a bullfighting arena. Hector caught Rachel looking at the illustration and saw her blush. He closed the magazine and gestured at the copy of Ernst's circa-'21 collage hanging behind the front desk. He squeezed her arm and said, "Modern art. So damned much and diseased crap."

Rachel nodded, still looking embarrassed. If she was truly this prudish, Hector was beginning to think getting Rachel in his bed might require a substantial investment of time. If he succeeded, getting her *out* of his bed and sending her on her way might be harder still.

Hector was close to rethinking his hurricane plans.

The clerk finished up and Rachel told the man she would be checking out shortly and asked for a porter to be sent up for her bags and steamer trunk.

"Everyone's leaving," the clerk said, frowning and haughty. "Even though this is probably the strongest structure on the island. All this safety for $6 a day — whatever are they thinking?"

Rachel shot Hector a look. The novelist shrugged and said to her, "And this is the 'structure' with the most windows on Bone Key." Hector said to the effeminate desk clerk, "We both know that if a hundred-mile-an-hour wind hits the side of your hotel that my friend here is staying in, all that glass is going to be imbedded in the interior walls of this 'fortress.' And in anything else that gets in its way."

"The glass is a real concern," the clerk said reluctantly. "Particularly since we can't really get out there to board or shutter the higher windows."

He frowned again and said, "I'll close out your account ma'am. Oh, and you have a cable. It arrived a bit ago."

Rachel frowned at the telegram. Hector read over her shoulder:

<pre>
                                    Aug. 31, 1935
    Miss Rachael Harper
    Colonial Hotel
    Key West, Florida

    Things going swimmingly   stop Am in love
    stop Be safe and see you after the storm
                                        Beverly
</pre>

"That's certainly good news for Beverly," Rachel said, her voice raw and her cheeks red. "Suppose we should finish your shopping." She moved to crush the wire and Hector closed his hand over hers.

"Wait," he said. "Let me see that again."

Rachel frowned and released her hold on the slip of paper.

Hector read the wire again and said, "That's strange. You said this man took Beverly to Cuba."

"That's right," Rachel said, looking up at him. "They were going to go bar hopping in Havana. They were going to get rooms at the Hotel Ambos Mundos. That's where she said I could reach her."

Hector smiled. *Rooms. Right.* But there was more falsehood than that one afoot. Hector said, "Did you meet this man your friend ran off with?"

"No."

"Got a name for this fella?"

"No. Why do you ask, Hector?"

"Because this wire was sent from Upper Matecumbe."

Rachel scowled. "Is that somewhere in Cuba? Bimini?"

"No, it's here in Florida, Rachel. Several islands north of here. Not much there to see, either. Just a place you pass by to get to other better places like this one."

Rachel looked at Hector a moment, biting her lower lip.

"Maybe their plans changed, that's all."

"Maybe." Hector reached into the pocket of his shirt for his cigarettes and shook one loose and was about to put it in his mouth. Rachel took the cigarette from his fingers with a shaking hand and put it between her lips. Hector fished his Zippo from his pant's pocket and lit her cigarette, then lit a second for himself. He watched Rachel smoke — she looked practiced. She was maybe more worldly than Hector had begun to fear. Hector's hopes for a carnal Labor Day weekend buoyed, slightly.

"Guess maybe Bev and me got our wires crossed," Rachel said. "I must have misunderstood."

Hector held the telegram back up where Rachel could see it. He said, "Maybe. But do you really spell your first name with an extra *a*?"

"No," she said. "*R-a-c-h-e-l.* You know — like everyone else does."

"Except for the person who wrote the text for this wire."

Rachel looked at her misspelled name and nodded. "Yes, I see. You think something's wrong?"

"Suspicious, anyhow. Let's go upstairs. Get you packed. I'll try to think of something."

"Could I get there," Rachel said, stepping into the elevator with Hector, "could I still get to Upper Matecumbe, I mean?"

"With this storm coming, I wouldn't recommend trying it," Hector said. He nodded at the elevator operator and flashed him five fingers to indicate Rachel's floor. "Road doesn't go all the way there…so you have to ride the train. Nobody competent or in love with life is going to take you north by boat with the storm this close. And like I said, there's not much there. Not much to see or to do, and nothing like real shelter. And that train, in this weather? You'd have to have a death wish to make that trip."

The eavesdropping elevator operator said, "You're right about that, brother." He held the gate for them as they exited and walked to Rachel's room.

"Alright. If it was your aim to alarm me, now I'm getting worried, Hector."

"It may be nothing," he said. "But all the same, let's do *something*."

"What?"

Hector took her arm and steered her toward her room's writing desk. "As I said, you go ahead and pack, Rachel. I'll spend a little time with this hotel stationary and my pen. I'll draft a reply to that telegram."

While Rachel packed her suitcases, Hector sat by the window, staring off at the horizon. The sky was still clear, but there was something wrong about the clouds drifting over the Atlantic. He thought a time, then wrote:

Bev, am staying with Hector Lassiter stop All is well stop Thought you were headed to Cuba so surprised to see you're in the upper Keys especially that one where Hector says there is nothing stop Will be weathering storm with Hector and Hemingway stop Hec says to come to Hem's place at Whitehead Street if you can get down from Matec. before Sunday afternoon stop Hector and Hem anxious to meet you and your beau and learn what he knows about that Key that they don't

— Rachel

Rachel read over Hector's shoulder. She said, "Should we misspell my first name?"

"I pointedly think we shouldn't," Hector said, capping his pen. "It's not much, but I'm hoping my reputation, such as it is — combined with Hem's — might at least throw some caution in this man who's with your friend. Just in case he's up to anything…well, untoward."

"You're worried, too, aren't you?"

Hector shrugged. She put her hands on his shoulders and massaged them. Hector rolled his neck, enjoying the sensation. His back and shoulder muscles were still tight from fighting marlin the day before. "You've sure got strong hands, kid," he said. "But to answer your question, I'm more worried because of where they are now. Those middle Keys are basically labor camps…populated by destitute vets building the next leg of that crazy highway. Rough customers, to a man. You'll see some of them in town tonight if we go out. They come into Key West for the weekend to drink their wages or to hit the sporting houses…to lose money on the cockfights. It's not a real weekend for these rowdies until one of them stabs or shoots another. They're riff-raff, mostly. And the Keys where they live and work are squalid. There are also the usual camp followers…gamblers and prostitutes. A few wives and kids. If this man had taken Beverly to Key Largo, or to Miami — or to Havana, like he said he was going to — I'd say he's just a wolf looking to show your friend a good and tawdry time. But to take her to Matecumbe? I honestly don't know to what end." Hector reached over his shoulder and took her right hand. He held and stroked the back of her hand with his thumb. He said, "You hungry? I'm hungry."

Rachel thought about that. She said, "I could eat a little."

"I'll go fetch my car so we can load your bags and trunk. Then we'll get an early dinner — before those damned vets get out of control. Honestly, between those fellas and the mosquitoes, it's been a rotten summer."

"Mosquitoes?"

"The little bloodsuckers are out of control this summer. That's another sign, or so say the old conchs, that we're due for a big storm."

Rachel nodded. "Where shall we eat?"

"I know a place."

5

Their blond, busty waitress said to Hector, "Papa was in this morning, sugar. He asked after you. He said this storm could be the one that swamps Bone Key. He's pretty down about it."

Hector half smiled. He said, "The son-of-a-bitching swain wishes, Karen. And that's our Hem — always the expert. Always the know-it-all." Hector perused the menu written on the chalkboard hanging on the wall and said, "Turtle steak and potatoes for me, I think. Rachel?"

She licked her full lower lip then bit it. For the first time, Hector noticed her slight overbite — he thought it becoming. She said, "I think I'll try the yellow tail and potatoes." The waitress, Karen, said, "Sure, sweetie." Once she was out of earshot, Rachel said, "Looking over the menu, it's kind of all seafood something and potatoes, you know?"

Hector nodded. "It's always 'seafood something and potatoes.' That's the price of island living. And it's almost always 'something' involving conch. Conch fritters…conch chowder. You're just lucky to hit this joint on a non-conch day."

Rachel smiled and looked around. "'The Electric Kitchen'…it's…curious."

"You'd be hard-pressed to find anything on this island that isn't 'curious.' We're hardly even in America. Hell, we're closer to Cuba than the mainland. It's like a border town surrounded by water, Rachel. A weigh-station and a retreat for mavericks and misfits. Or at least it used to be."

"Is that how you see yourself, Hector — as a maverick?"

He grinned. "Sure...makes me feel like a Romantic with a capital *R*. You know — in the Byronic sense."

Rachel smiled back. "Just how long have you been here, Hector?"

"I came here in the early '20s and bought my house. Then I skittered back and fourth between here and Europe for a few years. Long about '27, I really dug in my heels here. Paris was getting too touristy. Key West was remote and cheap — important selling points for a pulp writer. But it's changing now, not for the better, and more every day. It's going the sorry way of the Left Bank. In other words, the Key is on all the tourist maps now. Partly because of John Dos Passos and me, Hemingway came here. That bastard never left. Hem bought the best and stoutest house on the island — with his wife's family's money — and became some kind of mangy feudal lord. And he soon enough drew more tourists, like flies. And then along came goddamned FDR and his communist crew. Roosevelt and his New Deal cronies and their notions of turning Bone Key into a tourist attraction have just about ground out the last best qualities of this place. This crazy railroad they've helped to build...the damned overseas highway they're working on now. It's all slipping away. I think I'm truly starting to hate this place."

Rachel sipped from a glass of iced tea. "Are you thinking of leaving?"

Hector blew two smoke rings. "More and more, I do think of leaving. I'll maybe always keep the house as a retreat of sorts. A last hideout. But it is feeling like time to move on, yeah."

Rachel reached across the table and took Hector's hand. He smiled and squeezed back. She said, "Where would you go?"

"Hard to say. Maybe just across the Gulf. Maybe to Galveston. I was born in Texas, you know. Or maybe to Seattle, or to Vancouver. Puget Sound. Have me a notion they may be the next good places. Need to get there before they get overrun like Paris and Key West."

The pretty blond waitress put down their plates. Karen said, sotto voce, "Did you hear about the murder, Hec? Some woman was killed. They found her near the lighthouse. They say she was cut into pieces. They say—"

Scowling, Hector held up a hand. "Jesus, Karen, enough! You're going to put me right off eating."

But an old Conch, eavesdropping from the next table, growled, "Poor bitch. I've heard about it, too. Least she won't likely be crossing over alone. Not with the storm headed our way." The man dragged a scarred, tanned hand through his tangled white hair. "This morning I was down at the point. The crabs were crossing from the Atlantic over to the Gulf of Mexico side. Critters only do that for the biggest blows. And Toby Duke, he said the tarpon are all running westward through the Keys — like bats out of hell."

Hector gave the old man a sour look and chewed his turtle steak. He smiled at his dining companion and said, "Ignore that crazy old coot, Rache. We'll be better than fine."

"Everything in this world has two handles.

Murder, for instance, may be laid hold of by its moral handle...

and that, I confess, is its weak side; or it may also be

treated aesthetically, as the Germans call it —

that is, in relation to good taste."

— THOMAS DEQUINCEY

CHAPTER 3

IN YONDER ROOM

HECTOR WALKED with his hands in his pockets, feeling the wind against his back, drying his damp shirt. The wind still wasn't particularly strong...just strangely steady. The gulls and herons and pelicans were all heading out west into the Gulf — racing to outrun the storm. Rachel slipped her arm through his and Hector smiled. She brushed her windblown hair back from her face and said:

"This murdered woman they were talking about at the restaurant..."

"I think I know where you're headed with this," Hector said. "It's a crazy thought, but I had it, too. If you're really concerned about it as a possibility, I can check with the police. But I'll need a description of Bev."

Rachel sighed and shook her head. "I can't believe I'm even allowing myself to entertain this notion. It's quite mad, you know — terrible and sick. And probably pointless. I pray it is."

"All the same," Hector said, "it's your instinct to check. When we ignore our instincts, we suffer."

Rachel seemed to think about that. She wrapped her other arm around his, squeezing his bicep. Hector resisted the urge to tighten it.

She said, "Beverly is about my height: five-seven. Maybe twenty pounds heavier than me. She has black hair and dark eyes. She has…well, her nose…well, her name is Beverly Rubenstein. She has a mole on her left cheek. Oh, and a few years ago, she met a man at Coney Island and got a little tight. So now she has a small red heart tattooed on the inside of her left thigh, just above the knee."

"How…scandalous," Hector said, winking.

"It was certainly scandalous enough in South Bend. That's where we're both from."

"Any distinguishing marks along those lines of your own that you want to tell me about?"

Rachel frowned. "*No.* And no, there aren't any like those. I hate tattoos."

"I'm clean, too," Hector said. "Well, there are scars aplenty, but no body art."

"A man's not a man without a few of those."

Hector thought, *Hm.* Then he said, "I can drop you at my place and check with the police, but we're only a block away from headquarters. You could wait in the lobby and I could talk to the sheriff now — find out one way or another, fast like."

"You know him — the sheriff?"

"He knows me," Hector said. "And once in a while, he gets a call from me to check something — some detail or procedural thing — you know, research stuff, for a story or a novel."

"I'll wait in the lobby, then," Rachel said. "I want to know and know now if there's been some trouble."

5

"It's a terrible bloody fucking thing," Jack Dixon said. Jack was Monroe County Sheriff…another veteran, but one of the increasingly rare ones who'd landed on his feet.

Hector offered Sheriff Dixon a Pall Mall and the cop nodded and leaned in to Hector's flickering Zippo. Hector lit his own cigarette and blew smoke out both nostrils. He said, "Karen, over at the Electric Kitchen, she said this woman was cut up."

"That makes it sound like butchery," Jack said, waving a big hand. His middle finger was missing at the second joint. He stared at his cigarette. "That makes it sound like some crazy son of a bitch went off his head and just hacked the poor bitch to pieces. But it wasn't like that at all, Hec. In some ways, she was dressed out like a deer — utterly gutted."

"Hollowed out, eh?"

"Yeah, but for the cogs and the flywheels."

Hector narrowed his eyes, his lip curled. He must not have heard right. He said, "*What?*"

"No shit, Hec, this bastard scooped her hollow and filled her up with metal: gears…a bicycle chain…even a propeller from a small outboard motor."

Hector felt his own disbelieving smile. He said, "You're pullin' my leg."

"Christ, I wish."

"My friend's friend…she's a Jewess," Hector said. "Dark hair, dark eyes. We in the ballpark in terms of what you've got on ice out back?"

"Not at all," Jack said. "This one's got dirty blond hair…blue eyes."

"No tattoos? Say, on the inner thigh?"

"Your friend's friend sounds like a wild one. But no, no tattoos."

Hector nodded. "That's a load off." Then he said, "No shit? This woman was gutted and her organs replaced with machine parts?"

"No shit, Hec. Could I make that kind of stuff up? Hell, in your darkest study, and three-sheets-to-the-wind, I doubt even you could make that kind of thing up. Have you ever heard the like?"

"Heard? No," Hector said. "But seen? Maybe. On canvas. In Paris, in the '20s."

"What?"

"Let me back there to the ice house," Hector said. "I want a look at her."

"We've already established she's not your lady friend's friend."

"Right, but I may be of help to you. Based on what you've said, I'm getting notions. Let me see that body."

"It'll mess with your head, Hec. Trust me on this."

Hector waved a hand. "My head's so messed with, it couldn't do me any real harm. Let's have a look at her. Based on things you've said, I've got me a wild hair of a notion."

დ

Hector was sitting in the Silver Slipper with Rachel, slamming back the mojitos. It seemed that Rachel had also been to Paris…toured the museums and studied painting herself before moving back to the States as the '20s wound down. Her father, she said, had stayed on in the City of Lights a few years longer before settling in Los Angeles in late '34 — convinced Hollywood was "the next great frontier for artists."

When Hector described the state of the corpse he'd seen — the area between the woman's sex and her breasts that had been laid open and packed full of carefully arranged cogs and wheels — Rachel had confirmed Hector's own surmise: "It sounds like Magritte's *L'age des Merveilles*," she said. "A woman with clockworks in lieu of organs." She shivered despite the heat. "But it wasn't Beverly?"

"No, the murdered woman was fair. A real blond." Hector winced. "Sorry. You'd never know I write for a living. I could have put that much better."

Rachel half smiled and squeezed his hand. "It's alright, Hector. You're shaken up by what you've seen."

She picked up his pack of Pall Malls and shook one loose. She looked at his Zippo, running her fingers across the inscription:

To Hector Lassiter:

'One true sentence.'

— E.H.

Key West,

1932

She said, "A gift from whom I'm thinking?"

Hector nodded and flicked his Zippo open with one hand and lit Rachel's cigarette. He noticed his hand was shaking. "It is."

She said, "What's it mean? The engraving, I mean?"

"Little game Hem and I still play from time to time. One of us writes — or really, speaks — a few words. Perhaps the start of a sentence. The other one tries to give it the best finish — make it a clear, true sentence. A kind of writing exercise."

Rachel nodded. She said, "Your color is coming back, thank God. I can't imagine what you just went through for me. I'm in your debt."

Hector waved his hand — it was steadier now. Rum — the great stabilizer…until it becomes its own problem. "Nah, hell no. You don't owe me a thing. I've seen worse. Just not…odder." Trying to make light of it, he said, "What's your thought on this? You think maybe René Magritte or Salvador Dali went off their heads, came down to Key West and decided to take the concepts of surrealism and *trompe l'oeil* to new and heady heights?"

"Is that what you think, Hector?"

"Frankly, having seen that sorry woman? Yeah…I nearly really do."

Rachel squeezed his hand. "Based on what you've described, I think I do, too."

Hector drained his drink, then began fishing his rear pocket for his wallet. Getting the signal, Rachel finished her Cuba Libre.

Hector nodded at her glass and said, "That made like you like 'em?" He'd told the bartender to go light on the cola.

"Yes, it was yummy."

Hector smiled and threw a few bills on the table. He dipped his head at the bearded, bronzed man behind the bar. "Later Tone — after the Big Blow."

Rachel slipped her arm through Hector's. She tipped her head back into the breeze. Between the various forms of rum and the rise and fall of tension regarding the potential fate of her friend, Rachel seemed obviously and pleasantly numbed. Hector said, "What now, sweetheart? Any shopping to be done for items you might need for my place? Provisions you want? Some Coca-Cola to go with our rum supply, since I know now that you're a Cuba Libre fiend?"

"No, Hector. Maybe just a walk back to your place. I could use a shower, if that's okay…freshen up for dinner tonight. Maybe call over to the hotel after — while the phones are still working — to see if Beverly responded to my, or rather, your cable."

"Sounds like a plan," Hector said. "I could use a shower myself." He couldn't get the scent of formaldehyde and the combined odors of dead flesh and oil from the machine parts jammed into the woman's body cavity out of his mind.

A voice behind them — a masculine tenor with a slight speech impediment that made his individual *i*'s and *r*'s sound a little like *w*'s: "Jesus, Lasso, where you been hiding this one?"

Hector smiled and shook his head. He turned around, saying before he even saw him, "Rachel, meet Ernie, from Oak Park. Hem, this is Rachel Harper, of South Bend, and now, the prettiest girl in Key West."

"Usually you talk a lot of crap, Lasso, but this time…" Limping up to them, he stuck out a hand. Ernest was just under six feet — a couple of inches shorter than Hector but broad-shouldered and deep-chested. Ernest carried himself like a taller man, and somehow to Hector, they always seemed about the same height. Hemingway's dark hair was already receding into a widow's peak and his skin was dark brown. His teeth were white and straight in contrast to his bluntly cut moustache and he had four days' growth of beard. Ernest's legs were covered in old scars and now bore a few fresh bandages. He had a rubber brace secured around one bronzed knee — just visible under the fraying cuff of his khaki shorts. His black polo shirt was stained with dried fish blood. He smelled of sweat and whiskey and fish. Yet Ernest's smile was infectious. In Hector's experience, his famous friend's smile was always winning in the first minute or two, even when you knew Ernest well and knew what that smile could hide.

And if it was your first time meeting the famous writer?

Hector smiled and shook his head at Rachel's expression — star-struck.

Ernest said to her, "Jesus, you're sure beautiful for a blind woman. I mean, you must have eye problems to be with my buddy Lasso, here."

"I like Hector fine," Rachel said, shaking Ernest's hand and smiling. "And he's clean, Mr. Hemingway...well-groomed and smells nice." Hector suppressed a smile.

Ernest's own smile didn't ebb. "Christ, I know I stink to high heaven. Been on the boat all afternoon; hauled a big one alongside to lash it fast to try to outrun the sharks. Haven't been home yet to shower — kind of a last blast before the storm. Just secured my boat in the Naval Station's submarine basin...tied her up fast."

Rachel pointed at the bandages on Hem's legs. She said, "Mr. Hemingway, what happened?"

Ernest shook his head. "Christ. A while back, we had a shark alongside the *Pilar* and I tried to shoot it. The fish lashed out and hit the gaff hook in my mate's hand and the gun in my other hand discharged. The bullets hit the brass rail of my boat, fragmented, and then hit me in both legs. Just wrote about it for *Esquire*."

Ernest's admission about his self-inflicted wounds — and his willingness to write about them — pleasantly surprised Hector. Ernest rarely publicly placed himself in less than the most flattering of lights. He *never* made himself the brunt of his own jokes.

Hector hadn't witnessed the shooting accident, but John Dos Passos had and had told him about it. Dos had said his wife, Katy, a childhood friend who knew Ernest longer than any of them, had been so offended by Ernest's "stupid" and "reckless" actions she hadn't talked to Papa on the trip back into the harbor. She'd remained tight-lipped even as Ernest lay bleeding and groaning on the deck of his own boat. She thought he was lucky not to have shot and killed someone else.

Clearly, it had been a stupid accident resulting from a cruel and senselessly destructive act. There could be no good way to spin it for the *Esquire* essay.

Ernest said to Hector, "Hard to say what the next few days may bring. Pauline is edgy and bitchy and wants a party to lighten the mood. So 'we're' having a few people over for drinks tonight. What about you two kids coming by? It's mostly going to be Pauline's friends. I could use you there, Lasso — someone to drink and talk with. I mean really *talk* — not have to play 'author' to impress Pfife's goddamn artsy friends."

Squinting against the sun, Hector glanced over at Rachel. "What do you say, Rache?"

"Sure, sounds wonderful. What time, Mr. Hemingway?"

"Papa," Hem said. Hector resisted rolling his eyes. His nickname-mad friend had been making heroic efforts the past year or so to hang that patriarchal handle on himself. "Say eight."

Rachel said, "It works for you, Hector?"

"Aces," Hector said. "Eight it is." He slapped Hem's thick bicep. "Tonight then."

"Tonight." Hem was about to shove on, then held up a finger. "Lasso, you hear the news about this woman they found over by my place—?"

"I've *seen* that news, up close and personal," Hector said quickly. "Tell you more about that tonight. What should I bring this evening, Hem?"

"Suit yourself. Just make sure you bring this beauty." He winked and pointed at Rachel.

Hector chewed his lip. So it was going to be that kind of a night.

From official weather advisories:

(Saturday, August 31)

Advisory 9:30 p.m. *(Key West wind direction = NW, velocity = 4 mph.)* the tropical disturbance is central tonight near or over the northern end of Long Island Bahamas moving rather slowly westnorthwestward attended by strong shifting winds land squalls over a considerable area and probably gale force near center. Indications center will reach vicinity of Andros Island early Sunday. Hoist northeast storm warnings 10:00 p.m. Fort Pierce to Miami. 220631 Norton NAR 10:10 p.m.

"[I]f any human act

evokes the aesthetic experience of the sublime,

certainly it is the act of murder."

— JOEL BLACK

CHAPTER 4

ANATOMY AS A BRIDE

RACHEL HAD TAKEN the first shower, but she was still primping when Hector emerged from his bedroom, combing back his still-damp, dark brown hair. He'd dressed in white pants, white deck shoes and a white shirt — open at the collar and its long sleeves rolled up above each elbow.

Rachel was wearing a sleeveless black dress and flat, black sensible sandals. She was tall enough, even standing next to Hector, that the flats flattered her. Her sunburn from her time spent in the afternoon sun was already fading to golden brown.

She said, "I've been thinking about that murdered woman some more."

"Me too." Hector couldn't get the twisted image of the woman's corpse out of his mind.

Rachel stroked his cheek with the back of her hand. "You have the bluest eyes, Hector," she said. "They're almost wasted on a man."

Hector didn't have a reply to that, so he wrapped an arm around her waist and hugged her close.

"That man earlier this afternoon — Tito, I think you said his name was." Rachel laid down her brush and brushed a comma of hair back from Hector's forehead with her slender fingers. "You said Tito was a 'lady-killer.' Do you think that maybe he was the one who—"

"No," Hector said quickly. "Tito's a thug. But this thing with this woman — that's way out of Tito's line. It's far too bizarre. Diabolical. Whoever did this, well, Christ, I don't know how to begin to classify or to characterize this one. This goes well beyond murder."

"What about the police, Hector? Do they have any idea or clue as to who might have done this?"

"*Nada.* So I guess we better all hope that it's a one-off and that whoever did it has pushed on. The cops think the body had been there perhaps a day before it was discovered — plenty of time for the killer to have reached the mainland or to be deep into Cuba."

Rachel had the radio on low — "Red Sails in the Sunset." That song ended, and Marlene Dietrich's recording of "Something I Dreamed Last Night" began. The German actress had just released the sixth of her films with Josef von Sternberg, *The Devil is a Woman.* John Dos Passos had done some tinkering on that film's script. The guilt-stricken lefty was deeply ashamed to have taken Hollywood money, which amused Hector, who had since been ribbing "Dos" mercilessly for "selling-out."

Hem himself recently made Dietrich's acquaintance on his ocean-crossing back from Africa. He'd gone down alone for dinner and overheard Marlene balking at joining a party of twelve — afraid of being the unlucky thirteen. Hem had gallantly offered to be the fourteenth party at the table.

After recounting that story, Hem became bitter and crestfall-en when Hector confessed that he'd also known Dietrich since crossing paths with her in 1932. They'd met when Hector had undertaken some reluctant, but lucrative last-minute script work for her picture, *Blonde Venus.* Hector, at least, resisted boasting to "Papa" that he'd bedded Dietrich several times during his several days' stay on the set.

"You look very handsome tonight, Mr. Lassiter," Rachel said, holding out a hand. He took her hand and they danced together in his living room to Dietrich's song. That tune ended and a second by Marlene followed, "Falling In Love Again" — one of her signature songs. They danced through that one, too.

Smiling, Rachel said, "You keep surprising me."

"And surprising myself," Hector said. He hugged her to him again, smelling her hair and perfume…savoring the sensation of her breasts pressed firmly against his chest. Then he let her go and checked his pocket watch. "We should be going — there's still just enough time to be fashionably late."

Rachel said, "Damn, I forgot to check at the hotel…to see if there was an answer to my — our — wire to Beverly."

Hector disappeared into his bedroom. He called back, "It's on our way. We'll stop and check there in person."

When he emerged from the hallway he was wearing a pale sports jacket.

Rachel frowned. "A little warm for that, don't you think?"

Hector smiled. "Sure. But necessary on a Saturday night in Key West."

He took her arm and guided her toward the door. Then, remembering, he snapped his fingers and walked back to the kitchen. He opened a cabinet door and pulled out a bottle of Rioja Alta. "Hem's favorite wine," Hector said. He handed Rachel the wine bottle to hold while he locked up, then took the bottle in one hand, holding it by its neck, and wrapped his other hand around Rachel's.

It was already dark and the mosquitoes were scarce — a striking change from recent evenings inland…and another ominous sign the storm was drawing closer. The past few weeks, the bugs had become so thick that the rummies and homeless fisherman had taken to sleeping on the docks and piers and jetties, bunking out over the water where the little winged vampires wouldn't venture.

Hector and Rachel made their way to Duval Street and she said, "Curious, I don't remember there being streetlights last night."

Hector smiled. "For good reason. They can only pay to turn them on Saturday nights...mostly to help with arresting the vets. The Keys are broke, Rache. Deep in the red. But that didn't stop the Key West town council from buying two new traffic lights the island can't afford, even though there's hardly any car traffic on an island small enough to walk side-to-side and end-to-end. But the goddamn politicians see that highway construction pushing on and I reckon they envision eventual traffic jams." He shook his head. "Fools to a man. Course that's true of all politicians."

Rachel was quiet on their walk to the Colonial Hotel and Hector respected the silence...watching darkened corners and recessed doorways for menacing vets or marauding Cuban revolutionaries.

They ducked into the hotel again. Hector's gaze was again drawn to the horrible collage hanging behind the front desk — but now he saw it in the context of the surreal cadaver he'd viewed a few hours before.

In Max Ernst's black and white collage, a figure, vaguely female, lay in a large, rectangular metal washtub. "Her" face was formed from the combined images of a genderless wooden dummy, a real woman's eye and left nostril, and pieces of tin, riveted and curved to form the left portion of the figure's skull, mandible and chin. The throat appeared to have been cut and spread open, and rounded, gray-scale shapes that suggested organs were punctuated with a piece of tubing that descended into a mottled mass that extended from the collarbones down to a truncated waist. That was the other disturbing aspect of the collage — the figure was bisected, as if it had been cut in half just above the pelvis. The left arm was missing. The right arm began as the flesh of the woman who'd been photographed, but just below the shoulder, it became the tacked-on arm of a wooden mannequin. *Anatomy as a Bride*, Max had dubbed his work.

To Hector's mind, it looked like one of Victor Frankenstein's rough drafts.

Rachel said to the night clerk — this time a younger man with close-cropped yellow hair and a high-pitched voice, "I was staying here the past day or two, in room 510. I'm checking to see if a friend of mine perhaps sent a wire?"

"Your name?"

"Rachel Harper."

The clerk checked mail slots, patted around his side of the counter and lifted sheets of paper, then shook his head. "No, nothing."

Hector gestured at Max Ernst's collage. "Where in God's name did that damned thing come from?"

"A gift to the hotel," the clerk said. "Something a guest gave the manager. I guess the guest is a collector of surrealist art. This is just a print. But the guest stays here often and convinced the manager he needed to smarten up the lobby."

Smarten up? Jesus. Hector said, "This guest's name?"

The clerk said, "Haven't a clue. Just the owner's friend."

"So go fetch your boss, boy."

"He's not here."

"Where's he live?"

"In town. But he's in Bimini, on a fishing holiday. With the storm coming, I don't expect he'll be trying to get back for several days."

Hector rapped his knuckles on the marble desktop. "No, I don't reckon he will."

Outside again, Rachel said, "Guess we're thinking the same thing again…seeing that piece of 'art' in light of that murdered woman's body."

Hector wrapped his arms around her bronzing shoulders and said, "Yeah. But now let's try to forget that for a few hours. Let's try to have a good time." He smiled. "Sure hope you've got a world-class liver, Rachel. You'll be running with the bulls tonight."

"...if murder can be experienced aesthetically,

the murderer can in turn be regarded as a kind of artist —

a performance artist or anti-artist whose specialty

is not creation but destruction."

— JOEL BLACK

CHAPTER 5

MANIFESTO

AS THEY APPROACHED the big stucco house at Whitehead Street, Hector heard Rachel catch her breath. She said, "My God, it's beautiful."

"The wall is a new touch," Hector said. "Used to be a wire fence." He explained that the high, rough-hewn wall had been recently completed by one of Hemingway's cronies. "First wall the fella ever built," Hector said, slapping the cool brick. The wall was taller than Rachel's head.

"Impressive work," she said, "if a bit crooked."

"Hem was angry because the New Dealers put out a tour book — nearly fifty alleged 'highlights' to be viewed here on Key West. Hem's house is number eighteen in the tour guide." Hector gestured over his shoulder at the lighthouse. "That sucker's number nineteen."

Rachel considered that. "Is your house on the list, Hector?"

He hesitated, then said, "Nah. I'm off the bastards' radar. They don't care about crime writers. Crime writers don't go on safari. Crime writers don't write thick, nonfiction books about bullfighting. Slick magazines don't pay crime writers exorbitant sums to write about their trivial day-to-day activities or expensive hobbies that Mr. Depression-Era Middle America can't afford to indulge. Crime writers don't court publicity and schmooze with columnists like Leonard Lyons."

Hector immediately hated himself for that bitter diatribe. It stank of jealousy and well-nursed resentment.

Rachel said, "So what do we do? Is there a hidden bell we ring so some dwarf can mount the ramparts?"

"No, we goddamn holler," Hector said, smiling. Then he bellowed, "Hemingstein! Open the goddamn gate."

As they waited, a butterscotch-colored cat slipped between the bars of the iron gate and curled around Hector's leg, purring. The place was lousy with cats — mutant pussies with extra toes. Hemingway's attachment to felines threw Hector, who regarded cats as a lonely woman's pet...maybe the companions of fey men. Hector liked dogs...*big* dogs.

Something screeched from behind the wall — an inhuman sounding scream — and Rachel grabbed Hector's arm. "What in God's name was that?"

Hector said, grinning, "Just the peacocks."

A slender woman emerged from the house. She unfastened the gate and kissed Hector on both cheeks. "*Bonsoir*, Pauline," he said. "This is my new friend, Rachel Harper. Rache, this is Pauline Hemingway."

Pauline, a few years older than Ernest and more handsome than pretty, gave Rachel a once-over and shook her hand. "A pleasure." Hector handed Pauline the bottle of red wine and closed and locked the gate. He said, "How are things?"

Mrs. Hemingway shrugged her shoulders. "You know how he is after turning a manuscript over to Max — Papa's at loose ends. Dangerous to himself and to others. Especially those closest to him. He and Dos are apparently on the outs again."

Hector nodded. Hem had recently completed a nonfiction account of his African safari. He'd written a prefatory note explaining the book could be read as a work of fiction if one chose, and it was indeed written in novelistic fashion. Hector had read the book in typescript. It was marred by bitter passages in which Hem had determined to settle scores with critics and enemies — chief among them, Gertrude Stein.

In Hem's manuscript, the lines between author, character and public figure were blurred with almost Dadaesque zeal.

Hector had privately told Pauline he fully expected a bloodbath when the critics got their shot at Hem's book. Pauline had confided similar fears.

Death in the Afternoon, Hem's bullfighting book, had taken a similar drubbing, as had his most recent collection of short stories, *Winner Take Nothing*.

Hem's editor, Maxwell Perkins, was pushing for another novel, but so far as Hector could see, there wasn't another on the horizon.

Hector held the heavy screen door, then followed the women into the big, two-story house — perhaps the only truly hurricane-proof structure on the island. It was constructed from material quarried from the coral bed upon which it rested. It was also one of the rare houses on the Key with a basement. Wrought iron pillars supported a second-floor porch and canopy that ran around all four sides of the house. All the lights were on and the ceiling fans were spinning at top speed, but they were doing little other than pushing around the muggy night air. The ceilings were high — fifteen feet, to Hector's estimate.

The Hemingways' youngest son, Gregory — the spitting image of his mother — was wearing one of Pauline's hats and a boa and holding a rolling pin as if it was a microphone. He was singing some cabaret number called "Mister Cellophane".

Pauline frowned and snatched her hat from Gregory's head. She said, "Time for bed, Gigi."

The boy ignored her, clutching the rolling pin up close to his mouth, belting out his off-key song.

Pauline said, "Bless it, children are made to be seen and not heard. Upstairs right now, and to bed."

Gregory continued vamping. Pauline looked at Hector in exasperation. The lanky crime writer knelt down in front of Gregory and tousled the boy's black hair, messing up his crookedly cut bangs. Hector pulled out a silver dollar and held it up. "Avoid an argument, what do you say, Gig? The coin for cooperation? It'll buy a fair amount of ice cream...a pulp magazine or two."

The boy snatched the coin from Hector's hand and bolted up the steps. As Gregory's footfalls faded up the stairs, this creaking, plodding thump came down the other way.

Hem had shaved and showered. He wore a white shirt and white pants cinched with a black belt. As was his custom, he'd foregone shoes and opted for house slippers. Beaming and stepping off the last step and onto the landing, Hem said, "There's my girl!" He gave Rachel a bear hug and she gave him Mayfair kisses back.

Pauline smiled taughtly. Hem's wife had only recently let her hair go black again. She had dyed it blond through most of '34, driven to do so — or so was island conventional wisdom — by her concerns regarding the striking Jane Mason...Hem's Cuba-dwelling, younger and very blond presumed mistress.

The second Mrs. Hemingway's hair had darkened back to its natural shade of charcoal black, but now her hair was shot through with strands of silver.

Hem slapped Hector's offered hand away, then saw the bottle of wine Pauline was holding. He took it from her and said, "Let's start with this son of a bitch...lay the firm foundation for the harder stuff. Come on Lasso, help me rustle up a corkscrew."

Hector followed Hemingway through the house to the kitchen. "Where'd you find that one, Hec?"

"Rachel more or less found me, at Sloppy Joe's," Hector said. "She was in some trouble...being followed by a man."

"A vet?"

"Probably," Hector lied. "She came down here with a friend. The friend supposedly met a man, then went off with him. Last Rachel heard, they were headed down to Cuba. But earlier this afternoon, she received an apparent telegram from this friend. The wire was sent from Upper Matecumbe. And Rachel's first name was misspelled."

Ernest grunted and the cork made a "pop" as he wrenched it from the bottle. "Troubling. Sounds like something from one of your goddamn books." Hem poured four glasses of wine — one a bit deeper than the other three, and drank from that one. "On that note, this murdered woman, the one found across the street, by the lighthouse..."

Hector told Hem about the state of the woman's body and about his and Rachel's shared notions about the surrealist painting that the corpse had evoked.

"Christ, but that's a sick thought," Hem said, sipping more wine. "At least it wasn't your friend's friend." He smiled, his teeth grayed a bit by the dark red wine. "Sorry you had to see that, Lasso...particularly since it's too strange to use, even in one of your crazy books. What good is an experience when we can't write about it, am I right?"

That was pure Papa: The ex-journalist rarely posed a direct question — at least not since becoming successful. Instead, Ernest phrased all his questions as he had that last one — a statement or assertion demanding affirmation...all Hem's "questions" lately ended in, "Am I right?" or "Tell me I'm not wrong."

"For our purposes, some things are too real to be good," Hector said. He picked up one of the glasses of wine for Rachel and headed back toward the sitting room. He asked over his shoulder, "Who else is coming?"

As he looked back over his shoulder, Hector saw Ernest pour some of the wine from Pauline's glass into his own to top it off. Ernest said, "Pauline's friends, like I said. People Pfife knew from Paris — you know, before she and me…"

When they reached the sitting room, Hector saw that a tiny bald man was sitting on the divan next to Pauline. The man wore a black suit and starched white shirt with French cuffs. His shoes were highly polished and an ebony cane rested against his right leg. One of Ernest's trophy heads — a water buffalo — glowered down from the wall behind the dandy little man. Pauline said, "Hector, you must meet Bishop!"

Hector smiled and handed the second glass of wine to Rachel. He shifted his own glass to his left hand and took the little bald man's offered hand. "Bish, this is the author Hector Lassiter I've told you about," Pauline said. "Hector, this is the very fine painter, Bishop Blair."

"I've certainly heard of you," Hector said. "Unfortunately, I've been on this tiny rock for so many years, I'm out of touch with the art world. I'm afraid I'm not familiar with your work."

"Or I with yours," the little man said smiling. His entire head was shaven and the light glowed on his veined and spotted scalp — many liver spots there. Hector guessed the little painter must be in his late fifties or early sixties. Bishop said, "I have to confess that I only read nonfiction."

The man's handshake was damp and weak. Hector said, "You must be looking forward to Hem's latest, then."

"Of course," Bishop said, releasing Hector's much bigger hand. Hector resisted the urge to drag his now-damp palm down the side of his trousers. "What do you paint, Bishop? Cubist, Dada…what's your cup of tea?"

"Surrealism," Pauline offered.

Hector arched an eyebrow. He felt Rachel's and Hem's gazes. "Now I'm placing your name, Bishop," Hector said. "Think I may have seen something or another of yours in the magazine *Le Minotaure*." That seemed to catch Bishop's attention. "Ah! You're a subscriber?"

Hector shook his head. "No. I was leafing through a copy earlier today…in the lobby of the Colonial Hotel. The hotel seems to have gone surrealist, of late. They have this enormous print of Ernst's "Anatomie als Braut" hanging behind the front desk."

"Indeed?" The little painter ran a hand back across his skull, damp with perspiration. It was still in the mid-eighties, three hours after sunset. "I suppose I chose the wrong hotel, then," he said. "We're staying at the La Concha."

Hector said, "'We're'?"

"Yes, my wife and me. And here she is." The little man rose and extended both hands.

A little woman, no more than five-three, Hector guessed, emerged from the back hallway where the restroom was located. She looked to be sixty-five, perhaps older. She was certainly older looking than her husband. She came and stood next to the little man. She was dressed in a long black dress and black pillbox hat. Her hair was dyed an unconvincing shade of black. Black gloves ran up both arms, stopping just three or four inches short of her bared and rounded shoulders.

Hector thought, *Sweet Jesus, don't let her be his model.*

She stood next to her husband, beaming — two little doll-like people, dressed in black. The painter introduced his wife, "Harriet," and she smiled and curtsied when introduced to Hector. She spoke thickly-accented English.

Hector wondered, *Albanian?*

She said, "I'm a tremendous fan of yours, Mr. Lassiter. I read all of your novels. Yours, and Holly Martins' — I just finished his *Lone Rider of Sante Fe*. It's amazing how you both keep up that peppy pace. *Trés Americain.*"

Hector smiled, ignoring Ernest's snort from the other side of the room, as well as Papa's under-the-breath muttering of "'Peppy'...*Chee-rist.*"

She said, "I was particularly taken with your first, *Rhapsody In Black*. What a brave way to end a first novel, and—"

Hector winked and held a thick finger up to his own lips. "Careful now — Rachel's just reading that one, and she hasn't finished yet."

The elderly woman smiled and pretended to lock her own lips with her gloved hand, and then to throw away an invisible key. "Mum's the word," she said, winking back.

Another shout from outside: "How the hell do I get in there?"

"That must be Quentin — he's a very fine critic...visiting from Paris," Pauline said for Rachel's sake. "He's been running late, everywhere he goes, for days...running up and down the Keys for a piece he's writing on island folk artists. I'll go and let him in. Please excuse me."

Hector leaned in close to Rachel and said, "Quentin would be Quentin Windly, critic from the Left Bank...a jack-of-all-trades-style critic. Music, art, writing. He's tried, and failed, at all of them himself. So he's a bitter bastard. So now he makes money critiquing the ones who can do what he can't. Meager money, but he's doing just fine. He's a trust-fund baby."

"You sound bitter," Rachel said.

"No, Quentin doesn't stoop to critique the stuff that I write," Hector said. "And he gives Hem's stuff a wide berth, too. Probably to avoid alienating Pauline. He also has a reputation as a ladies' man, so please, don't let him steal you away tonight."

Rachel smiled and stroked Hector's cheek. "Guess that'll depend on you, Hector," she said. "How willing are you to fight for me?"

"To the death."

She squeezed his hand again and sipped more wine.

Hem had his back to his guests, studying the painting hanging there on the wall — Joan Miró's *The Farm*. Ernest had admired the painting during his younger and hungrier time in Paris. Though he really couldn't afford it, he'd nevertheless purchased the painting — with the help of Dos Passos — ostensibly as a birthday present for his first wife, Hadley. Somehow Hem had wrested the painting back from Hadley and gotten it to Key West. Now it hung with paintings by André Masson and Juan Gris' *The Guitar Player*.

"You should collect some of Bishop's work, Ernest," Mrs. Blair said.

"Sure, swell," Hem said "You have anything at hand?"

"I'll send you a catalogue when we get back to Montparnasse," she said. Then she said, "You seem to know art as well, Mr. Lassiter. Do you collect?"

"Not very much," Hector said. "Not like I wished I could have when I was in Paris many years ago. Hadn't the money then. Just a couple of pieces by Nick Hart. One tiny Picasso. A Matisse I picked up from the estate of Bertram Stone. And now I'm here, where there is no art worth buying."

"I'll send you a catalogue, too," she said. "My Bishop's not yet priced himself out of the market."

"That's great," Hem said, his back still to his guests. He said, suddenly, "What do you think of Magritte, BB? I'm thinking particularly of *L'âge des Merveilles*."

Hector shot Ernest's broad back a glance. The hair was standing up on the back of Hector's neck.

"That was about '25 or '26, if I'm remembering correctly," the bald little artist said. "I think it had the most profound influence on Dali. The cutaways in the torso, particularly. And with the machine parts and cogs, well, I've definitely seen much of that imagery in Man Ray's photography from roughly the same period."

Rachel said, "So much of the surrealists' work seems to reflect a kind of hatred toward women. Almost what you would call an 'Irish hatred' of women. I mean, all of their bodies cut into pieces or, as you describe them, just cut *into* — segmented and hollows and compartments carved into their thighs and torsos. And speaking of Man Ray…all those photos of women laying naked and dead…"

The little painter scowled. "Dead? Why do you say dead?"

"Their eyes are always closed…they look naked and dead," Rachel said.

"No, no, dear," Bishop said. "That's a convention of surrealism. Their eyes are closed to indicate 'the dream state.' They are nude and sleeping. Dreaming really. Although there is one photograph, in particular, which you might be thinking of. Man Ray called it "La Prière". It's a self-portrait where he's pressing his cheek to the hip of a nude woman. She appears to have a bullet hole just under her left breast." He turned to Hector and said, "It's a dark-haired woman, laying on a bed and the photograph, is, of course, black and white. But Man's colored in a stream of blood with red ink, trailing down the torso and pooling on the mattress by her side. Man is embracing the nude's body, looking as if he shot and killed the woman in the picture."

"You also seem to know a bit about art," Mrs. Blair said to Rachel.

"I spent a couple of years in Paris," Rachel said. "Studied for a time there. I concluded that I don't have the talent." She said it matter-of-factly.

"Maybe you just haven't unlocked your talent yet," Bishop said, smiling. "Perhaps you should experiment in my medium — surrealism. It may be the key for you. As André Breton said, in his 'Manifesto of Surrealism', 'There is every reason to believe that surrealism acts on the mind very much as drugs do; like drugs, it creates a certain state of need and can push man to frightful revolts.'" He smiled again. "Perhaps it can push you to realizing the full extent of your own painting talent, Miss Harper. It's hard to deny the field is dominated by men. We're well past time for a female surrealist to come to the fore."

A deep voice, from behind them: "*Argh*, fucking shoptalk. Thought we'd skip discussion of fucking art for one night."

Ernest limped over to the tall, blond man standing in the doorway. He said, "Hey, Wind — what are you drinking, my foul-mouthed friend?"

The critic looked at the nearly depleted glass of wine in Hemingway's hand. "Why waste time with that swill? Cut to the chase — whiskey, neat."

Ernest slapped the man's arm with real relish, "Why not… asshole. Fetch 'fucking' Wind here a drink, Hec, won't you? If I make it, I might be tempted to stir in some cyanide."

"The simplest surrealist act consists of
dashing down into the street, pistol in hand, and firing blindly
as fast as you can pull the trigger, into the crowd."

— ANDRÉ BRETON

CHAPTER 6

LE CADAVRE EXQUIS

DINNER WAS MUSSELS in peppery cream broth, *bouillabaisse de Marseilles* and Châteaubriand.

Pauline had cautioned everyone to save room for Key Lime Pie. Hector and Hem had finished their main courses first. Hem was drinking whiskey and Hector had made himself a mojito. The crime writer sat back in his chair, smoking a cigarette and watching Rachel eat. Pauline was watching her too — Hector was increasingly aware of that. Pauline didn't seem to regard Rachel as some threat. It was not at all like he'd seen Pauline act around Jane Mason or other younger women who brazenly made clear their interest in — or availability to — Ernest. No, this was something else that Hector couldn't put his finger on.

Seemingly oblivious to Pauline's scrutiny, Rachel pushed away her plate and sipped her Tavel wine. She said, "I've seen Hector's cigarette lighter, Papa. He told me of this game, or 'writing exercise,' that you two engage in…'One True Sentence,' he called it."

Hem savored his whiskey and said, "That's right, kid. One of us starts a sentence, and the other finishes it, best he can. Rules are it has to be short and sharp and as close to true as we can come under the gun." He grinned and said, "Here, Hector, catch this one. 'The old man died—'"

"'—illusioned and therefore disappointed,'" Hector replied.

"Not terrible," Hem said. "Your turn, Lasso."

Hector thought a moment, then said, "'The drunken priest, awaiting execution—'"

"'—wished that one of his fellow prisoners was a whore.'" Ernest grinned and slapped the table. "I should use that somewhere…get under old Max Perkins' skin with that." He drank some more whiskey and said, "'You know how it is Sunday morning on Duval Street,—'"

Hector thought about that and finished with, "'—the rummy vets propped up out cold against the walls, their pants stained with their own piss.'" Hector made a face. "Christ's sakes, I'm sorry all, that was a bit much," he said, "particularly over dinner."

"But stark and real," Mrs. Blair said, her old face very serious. "Authentic. I admire that."

Ernest had this strange expression on his face. "I *could* maybe use that one…"

Bishop Blair, tittering, spilled a little wine on the lapel of his black jacket. He wiped it off with a burgundy linen napkin. He said, "You writers' game reminds me of one we used to play in Paris — we artists, I mean. Same concept really, but different métier, obviously."

Hector, blowing smoke out both nostrils, said, "Elaborate, please."

The little artist fished the interior breast pocket of his black suit jacket and pulled out a long, thick Cuban cigar. He tore off the cellophane and then cut the end off with his own cigar cutter. Bishop leaned across the dining table and picked up a candelabra and held the flame of the candle under his cigar with one tiny hand while he rolled the cigar, getting it started. He blew a few smoke rings and then said, "Oddly enough, it actually started life as a writing game, not too much unlike your own. A poet was present at one of our gatherings one night, and he wrote a few words down, folded over the sheet so the words couldn't be seen, then asked someone else present to write a few words down to finish his unseen sentence. The result was something like dark, surrealist poetry. As we were all visual artists, the game soon enough vaulted into the realm of the 'seen.'" He smiled and winked. "But by way of the unseen."

Quentin, the critic, lasciviously eyeing Rachel, said, "I know of this game. *The Exquisite Corpse*, it was called."

Hector suppressed this little chill. He reached across the table and took Rachel's hand, brazenly rubbing the back of her left hand with his thumb. Marking territory. He said, "A damned ghastly name."

Bishop Blair shrugged. "That comes from the writing game that inspired it. The poet who wrote that first, partial sentence had written, 'The exquisite corpse…' The title stuck."

Hem was sprawled back in his chair, one hand shoved down his pants behind his belt — up to the second knuckle, or so. He said, "But you said the game evolved."

"Into a drawing game, yes," Bishop said, smiling. "One of us would take a long slip of paper, and in the upper portion, we would draw the top portion of a figure, say, the head, shoulders and perhaps the upper torso. Then we would fold the paper to obscure what we had drawn — all but the very lower-most portion so that the next artist could pick up the lines where the previous artist left off. The second artist would then draw everything from about the breasts or pectorals down to the genitals. He, too, would then fold the paper, hiding 98 or 99 percent of what he had drawn. The third artist finished the drawing by sketching in the legs and feet…or whatever else his mind was inspired to supply. Then we would all unfold the slip of paper and see what our 'blind' collaboration had resulted in."

Hem nodded, considering the surrealist painter with his warm, sharp brown eyes. He said, "A woman was murdered across the street. They found her body earlier today — just behind the lighthouse."

Hector paused, his next cigarette hanging unlit between his lips. Pauline looked mortified. Mrs. Blair raised a gloved hand to her mouth. Rachel looked surprised that Ernest would just toss it out there, naked.

Quentin's expression Hector couldn't read…mocking…surly…either was as close as Hector could come to characterizing it.

Bishop Blair scowled. "For money; passion? Why was she murdered, I mean?"

Hem sat up straighter in his chair, relishing the focused attention. "That's the thing," he said. "It wasn't like any of that. Hector saw the body. He said the woman was naked. She was gutted and dressed out like a deer — her internal organs all removed."

Pauline was furious. She said, "Ernest!"

He held up a big hand. Hem said, "No, it gets stranger. And this audience? Here we have gathered some that might really have some useful thoughts toward a solution."

"A sex crime," Bishop Blair said. "Something like, oh, Jack the Ripper?"

"Nothing so…straightforward as that," Hem said, stroking his thick dark moustache and glancing at Hector. "Hector thinks this was a surrealist killing."

Slack-jawed expressions, all around…except for Hector and Rachel — those two stared at one another, increasingly stunned by Hem's brazenness in putting it out there, cold.

Bishop Blair licked his lips. He stroked the rim of his wine glass. "Why? Why surrealist?"

Hem gestured at Hector. "One true sentence, Lasso. Lay it out for Bish."

Hector blew smoke. He said, "The woman was gutted, as Ernest has described. Where her organs should have been, the killer inserted cogs…fly wheels…a bicycle chain and discarded machine parts. Even the prop from a small, outboard motor."

A wineglass spilled. Flustered, Mrs. Blair tut-tutted, excused herself and righted her goblet. She began dabbing at the white linen tablecloth — patting at the stain from her spilled glass of Valdepeñas, now insinuating itself into the crisp cotton like a fast-spreading bloodstain.

"Forget it, please, Harriet," Pauline said. "It's nothing."

Bishop Blair looked stricken. He sat back in his chair, his cigar clutched in one hand, and his napkin in the other. "It's what you said, Papa — *The Age of Marvels*."

Hem winked. "That's just what Rachel and Hector thought. And I agree."

Quentin Windly shot Hector a glance. "So, a hack writer who claims to know surrealist art. Wonders never fucking cease. Or did Miss Rachel fill you in on art, 'Lasso'?"

Hector held his tongue. Anything he might say was going to lead to an inevitable conclusion — Hector likely beating the handsome critic near to death.

"And the police?" The now-paler Bishop Blair sipped some more of his Tavel, as if white wine could supply the false courage of, say, whiskey…perhaps of Pernod in the near term, if one had not sampled absinthe.

The critic said, "Were the organs found?"

Hector bit his lip. Looking at his drink, he said, "Leave it to the likes of you to pose *that* morbid question, 'Wind'. But, no, they were not. The sheriff's boys put the body on a set of scales they use to weigh marlin and swordfish. With all the metal, the woman's corpse came in just under 275 pounds. The body of even a small, comparatively light woman is a lot for even a strong man to transport across any kind of distance or terrain. So the sense is this woman was murdered and…prepared…just where she lay. Where she was found…displayed."

"Then there may still be clues to the killing around — perhaps the discarded organs are close by." Quentin was focused on Hector.

Hem rose, beaming. "I've got flashlights."

The little surrealist artist stood, straightening his lapels. "I'll come, of course." Mrs. Blair held a hand up to her mouth again — like some over-acting silent film star. The little painter grabbed his wife's gloved hand. He urged his wife's hand from her mouth and patted its back. "I'll be fine, my dear. I'm in stout company."

Hector rolled his eyes. He felt like he'd just lurched into one of Dame Estelle Quartermain's damned locked-room mysteries with all their exaggerated British civility and stilted dialogue. Before he could check himself, Hector said aloud, "Jesus fucking wept."

Rachel just looked at him, this drunken and disbelieving smile on her pretty face.

Scowling, Pauline said, "For the love of God, go with them, Hec — this is your bloody field. And I hold you responsible for keeping them all from abject embarrassment or accidental drowning."

"The artist must work with the thought
that the spectator can understand things half said,
not completely described."

— ANDRÉ MASSON

CHAPTER 7

MINOTAURE

HECTOR WAS LOITERING in the kitchen with Pauline and Rachel.

"Utterly fruitless," he said, grimacing. He was balancing on his left leg and massaging his right ankle...wondering how the hell one-legged vets coped with limb loss. Hector had wrenched his ankle when his foot found a sinkhole. Wincing, he said, "It's just too far in any direction to reach water in order to pitch anything into the ocean. Blocks and blocks to get to Negro Beach, or to South Beach, to the east. To the southwest, you have the military reservation, and nobody's going to go sneaking through there hauling body parts. To the west? Well, you're nearly walking the width of the island with a bucketful of guts. Not going to happen."

Rachel stood in the middle of the kitchen, her arms crossed. "So what do you think happened to the organs?"

"Buried likely...not far from where the body was found," Hector said, shrugging. "Might want to watch what your cats drag in for the next several days." He put his foot down and put a little weight on it, frowning through the pain — he refused to baby it. He said, "Unfortunately, the intrepid sleuths Mrs. Hemingway sent me out with didn't bring shovels. Hell, maybe the killer burned the innards. But that's all a colorful diversion, anyway — dwelling on process and technique is like racing into a cul-de-sac."

"Because the work is the thing?" This sultry, mocking half-smile on Rachel's face, she said, "*Chacun à son gout?*"

"The *insanity* of the work, yes," Hector said, smiling back. "Here are the real questions. Who on this goddamn rock truly knows surrealist art? Who disdains it or resents its practitioners so zealously as to mock it in this bloody way? Who hates women so much as to do that wicked thing to one? Those are the questions to seek answers for. Supply those answers, and you find your killer."

Pauline, looking slightly nauseous, sipped her wine. Hector wasn't sure how much she'd had, but she seemed a good bit tighter than when he and the "boys" had gone on their hideous scavenger hunt.

Bishop Blair cleared his throat to announce his presence. He said, "My wife is very tired...and a bit overtaxed by events, Pauline. I'm afraid we must go. Now."

"It's too late to call for a cab," Pauline said. "There's only one on the island and, frankly, Ross is usually quite drunk by this hour."

"We *could* walk," the old artist said less-than-convincingly.

"No, La Concha is too far to walk to from here," Pauline said. "And it's Saturday night — the vets will be out and they are their own kind of menace. So I'll have Ernest drive you." She looked at Rachel and smiled. "Have you seen La Concha, Rachel?"

"No."

"Then you should go, too," Pauline said. "Go with Ernest. It's really quite beautiful, particularly at night, with all the lights on. You should see it before the storm perhaps damages or destroys it."

Rachel frowned at the old man. "Don't you fear staying there?"

The painter said, smiling, "If it looks like Key West is to take a direct hit, Pauline and Ernest have promised us safe haven here."

"There's another reason I want you to go along, Rachel," Pauline said, "but you can't mention a word to Ernest. His night vision, it isn't so good, though he'll never admit it. So, I'd feel much better knowing there's a sharp pair of eyes with him. I'd be quite grateful for you to ride along."

Rachel nodded. "Alright. Are you coming Hector?"

One glance at Pauline's stern face told Hector he was to stay. He said, "A murdered woman's body was just found less than fifty yards from here, Rache. Go see the pretty hotel. I'll stand sentry here over Pauline and the boys." He smiled and picked up a half-empty bottle of rum. "I'll guard them, and this soldier…"

Quentin, the art critic, wandered into the crowded kitchen, yawned, and stretched. "I'm staying at the Concha, too — a nice change from the Matecumbe Hotel," he said. "I'll ride along, as well." He smiled and winked at Rachel. "If it's too crowded, you can sit on my lap, dear."

"In that event, I'll take the rumble seat," Rachel said, pure ice.

"Why don't you strike poses on the running board, Quentin," Hector said. "Maybe the goddamned real wind will blow you off the car and out to sea."

Rachel said to the critic, "You were recently staying at the Matecumbe Hotel?"

"Yes," Quentin said.

"Why?"

"Working my way down here…car, boat — I don't trust that train," Quentin said. "I missed the last ferry and had to spend a night on Matecumbe. What a shithole." He looked at Rachel again and frowned. He raised a finger and was about to say something when Pauline called loudly, "Ernest, find your keys — you need to drive our guests back to the hotel."

5

Pauline leveled a skinny finger in Hector's face. "I can't *believe* that you brought that woman here, Hector!"

Flustered by her angry tone, Hector scowled and said, "Rachel? What in God's name is wrong with Rachel?"

"She's a reporter! How could you bring a journalist into this house — and unannounced? Ernest could well shoot you for this."

Hector was reeling. "Journalist? What the hell are you talking about?"

"Rachel Harper — she's a correspondent for *Parade*," Pauline said.

The second Mrs. Hemingway was a college graduate with a journalism degree and clip file spanning several daily newspapers. Pauline had been working for French *Vogue* about the same time she met Ernest and took him from his first wife. Despite Pauline's own reporting credentials, Hector said, "I don't buy it."

Fuming, Pauline beckoned Hector to the sitting room. She leafed through a stack of magazines, then pulled out a copy of *Parade*. She flipped through pages, then held up a spread on European fashions, by-lined "Rachel Harper."

"You know I covered fashion for *Vogue* back in Paris in the '20s," Pauline said. "Even in this tropical hell hole, I like to try to stay a little current, Hector…see what's in style in places where style still matters. I recognized that woman's name as soon as you said it."

Hector waved it away. "It's a fashion piece…a bit of fluff, Pfife. I'd hardly call it 'journalism.'" The former Paris *Vogue* correspondent's brown eyes flared. Hector shrugged. "I mean by that, it's not the kind of journalism to threaten us, or Ernest."

"But you didn't know she was a reporter, Hector. She kept it from you. What else might she be keeping from you?"

"I'm not sure it's fair to say she 'kept' it from me, since I haven't asked her what, if anything, she does for a living." Hector said sheepishly, "I haven't asked her much about herself, to be honest. Only met her a few hours ago, Pauline. It didn't come up."

Pauline's smile hardly qualified — more in the neighborhood of a sneer. She said, "Oh, something came up alright. Your mind, and your other parts, were too focused on that pretty face and body of hers. You're such a...man."

Hector said, "I'll confront her later this evening, Pauline. I'll make sure she's not on the clock for some newspaper or magazine — make sure she's not thinking of using any of this evening for some profile or the like. No sweat."

5

Rachel kissed Hector's cheek. "Miss me?"

"Of course." His hand strayed to the small of her back. Hugging her to him he said, "That damned critic didn't get fresh did he?"

"No, I sat up front with Ernest and Mrs. Blair."

Hem strolled in, hefting a bottle and grinning. "Say one thing for your friend Bish, P.," he said. "He knows the way to my hard black heart." Hem held up the dark green bottle. "Can you believe it? Absinthe, children!"

Rachel said, "Isn't that illegal?"

"Terribly...everywhere but in Spain," Hector said.

"Bish smuggled in three bottles for us in a hidden compartment in his steamer trunk," Hem said. "These, and a couple of banned books by some guy named Miller."

Pauline said, "You're not thinking of drinking that poison? That wormwood? Not with your stomach, Papa? You're still ill. And that can damage your brain...your nervous system."

"Not in the quantities we'll be drinking it," Hem said. "Gotta ration this precious stuff...stretch it out, because there'll be no more. And that's all bullshit about it hurting your brain. It opens the mind and that's important for creative types like me and Lasso." He winked at Rachel. "You'll have some with us too, won't you, Harp?"

Hector knew then that Rachel had made it into Papa's inner circle — nicknames were always the badge of merit with Ernest.

Rachel smiled uncertainly. "Of course…"

"Gotta rustle up some things to do this properly…or improperly, since it's illegal as hell, as Hector points out." Hem smiled at his frowning wife. "You'll have some too, right? Boys are asleep, so it's time to be fun, yes?"

Pauline nodded shallowly. "*Of course…*"

Hector lit a cigarette and stared at its glowing end. He'd never cared for the bitter, vaguely licorice-tasting dark green spirits. In Hector's limited experience with absinthe, the liquor didn't 'open' his mind so much as assault it from all angles. But he'd be damned if he'd shame himself in front of Hem by deferring the potent mixture of anise and wormwood.

As Hem set up the drip glasses and spoons — arranging sugar cubes on each spoon — he said, "Bishop was teaching me and Rachel all about the Minotaur myth as it relates to surrealist art. It seems to be a central image or motif for the surrealists…hence their naming of their magazine *Le Minotaure*. Bish said Picasso made an image of the Minotaur by juxtaposing a bicycle seat with a set of handlebars…he made a kind of metal bull's head."

"Picasso called it *Tête de Taureau,*" Rachel said, carefully watching Ernest's preparation of the absinthe. She was looking increasingly apprehensive. Frowning, she said, "Picasso also seems to be going through some period now of producing illustrations of Minotaurs and bulls raping women."

"Well, at base, Picasso's always been a woman-hater," Hector said. He made a face at his first taste of the absinthe. "You can never be ready for it," he said. It numbed his tongue and burned his throat all the way down to his belly.

Hem said, "Lasso! One true sentence: 'Absinthe tastes—'"

"'—like regret,'" Hector said.

Rachel said, "Probably the most famous Minotaur image in the surrealist movement, at least so far, is a photograph by Man Ray called "Minotaure". You know it, Hector?"

"Huh-uh. He licked his numb lips. "What is it — some snap-shot of a bull like out of Hem's *Death in the Afternoon?*"

Rachel made a sour face after her first, hesitant sip of the absinthe. She let it settle, then sipped some more. It seemed to agree with Rachel as much as it didn't agree with Hector. Her voice a little raw from the liquor, she said, "It's a nude woman's torso, taken against a field of black. It's the expanse of her body between her navel and shoulders. No head is visible — it's cloaked completely in darkest shadow. Her arms are raised, like this." Rachel raised her own arms over her head. "Like horns — the horns of the Minotaur, you know? The model's breasts are the eyes of the bull, and the concave portion of her belly — the model is very skinny — is in heavy shadow, evoking the mouth and muzzle. Man Ray, using crops and shadows, has made this naked woman's body suggest the head of the Minotaur."

"Vividly put," Hector said, narrowing his eyes. "You talk — or describe — like a writer, Rachel." Hector could almost feel Pauline's gaze drift his way.

Rachel hesitated. "No, I'm no writer like you two. Nobody for you two writers to worry about," she said, pointing at Hector and then at Ernest. "In terms of competition, I mean."

Hem, savoring his absinthe, said, "*Writers*...like me and Lasso?" There was an edge in his voice. Hem clearly resented being assigned peer status with Hector. Or so Hector suspected. Hem confirmed it: "Oh, hey, Lasso — driving back from the hotel me and Rachel saw your fellow mystery writer." Hector frowned at the word "mystery." Hem continued, "You know, Jonathan Latimer."

Hector knew Latimer well enough, he supposed. Jonathan was a recent arrival on Key West...a journalist turned pulp novelist. Latimer's stuff verged on the comic and downright deranged. Locals were always confusing Latimer and Lassiter's last names. Hem said, "Of course the son of a bitch was stinking drunk, like most pulp writers." He glanced at Rachel and winked. "And journalists."

"Of course," Hector said, hoarse from the absinthe. "Drink is an occupational hazard for all crime writers. For all reporters. And for all so-called literary writers, too. Drink, and sodomy for that latter class."

Ernest smiled crookedly at Hector. It was stupid to provoke Hem, but tonight, the grand man wasn't to be baited. Hem asked, "Ladies, how's the absinthe? Does it make the heart grow fonder? I mean, for ugly sons of bitches like Lasso and me?"

"A little goes a long way," Pauline said. "Time to stop this before we're all driven mad, Papa. It's past late."

"It is," Hector said, rising. He stretched and yawned, then offered a hand to Rachel. He drew her up into his arms. "The main brace is well and truly splashed," he said. "Time to head back into port and batten down."

 ໑

Hector thought he could smell the rain on the wind now. It was bit cooler and the wind was still steady. He said, "How are you doing Rachel? Okay to make the walk?"

"I'm a little drunk," she said, hanging on his arm and walking with her head resting on his shoulder. "I'm a little drunk," she said again. She laughed. "Well, maybe lotsa drunk."

"Good — the state of least resistance."

She looked up at him with sleepy eyes. "Oh my — what are your intentions toward me, Mr. Lassiter? What's on your mind?"

"For the moment, satisfying my own curiosity," he said. "When did you mean to — or did you *ever* intend to — tell me that you're a journalist?"

She nodded once, deeply. "Oh." She sighed. "Wasn't ever going to say," she said. "Though I did confess it to Papa on the drive back from the hotel. Mostly because I saw a copy of a magazine with one of my articles in their house."

"Yeah, Pauline made you, like that," Hector said, snapping his fingers. "She was a fashion journalist, herself. What did Ernest say when you confessed to him that you're a reporter?"

Rachel shrugged, watching their shadows. "Hem laughed. He doesn't put much stock in fashion reporting — that was clear enough."

"Hope he doesn't tell Pauline that."

"Well, anyway, Papa's very disdainful of lifestyle reporters."

"Yes," Hector agreed. "Probably puts them just a notch above crime novelists. Only reason he tolerates my company — he can look down on me as a writer."

She said, "I really like your books better. You understand women in ways Hem doesn't."

"You know the way to my heart," Hector said. "But when were you going to tell me that you're a journalist?"

"I told you — never," Rachel said. "Or probably never. It's irrelevant. I'm not here as a reporter. I'm on holiday, that's all." She squeezed closer to him, her head on his shoulder again. "Still mad?"

"No," he said. "I was never mad. But there is one thing — you're hanging on my gun arm."

Rachel smiled mischievously. "Is that some of kind of euphemism?"

"No, sweetheart, it's a literal statement of fact. We're headed toward some strife, Rache. Casual-like, but swiftly, switch sides with me — take the left-hand side."

Looking confused, Rachel drifted to Hector's left arm.

Two men stepped from behind a big old Banyan tree, blocking their path.

Hector stopped and urged Rachel behind himself.

The two men were skinny. Both looked to be in their mid-thirties. They were clearly drunk...unshaven and dressed in badly patched clothes. Vets on a tear. One was missing an eye; the other had a hook where his left hand should be.

The one-eyed vet hefted a metal pipe. "Your wallet, her jewelry and her purse, lickety split." He pointed the pipe at Hector and said, "That means *right now*."

Hector said, "Move on boys. Because you're fellow veterans, I'm giving you the chance to walk away before I maim you more."

The one-handed man turned his hook back and forth so it glinted in the light. "Maim us? How'd you like one of these yourself, slick?"

Hector shook his head. He reached under his sports coat, cocking on the draw.

The vets' eyes widened at the sight of the antique Colt. "Seventy-three Peacemaker, boys. Ready to sleep forever? If not, best drop that pipe and get on with you. I want to see asses and elbows all the way down Duval."

The vets backed away, the one stooping to drop the lead pipe.

They half ran, half fast walked down the well-lit street, headed toward Negro Beach.

Hector holstered his gun and Rachel said, "So that's why the sports jacket. That's what you went back for earlier this evening — your gun?"

"I usually keep it under my pillow," he said, still watching the retreating vets. "But Saturday night in Key West? Like I said, danger city, baby."

As they passed the Colonial Hotel, Hector held up a finger. "You check with the front desk — see if there's been an answer yet to our telegram. While you do that, I'm going to pinch their copy of *Le Minotaure*."

"A masterpiece...

may be unwelcome, but it is never dull."

— GERTRUDE STEIN

CHAPTER 8

ACHUCHÓN

"NIGHTCAP, RACHEL? Some coffee? Maybe aspirin?"

She tossed her purse on his couch as Hector checked the locks. He'd closed most of the windows earlier in the day and secured the storm shutters, but he'd left two windows open on either side of his house — the windward side and one at the other end — in order to keep a cooling cross breeze. Hector turned on the electric fans to help draw in more of the cooler night air and he again smelled rain. He dropped his stolen copy of the surrealist magazine *Le Minotaure* on the coffee table — it was all they'd gotten at the hotel. Neither Bev, nor her alleged "suitor," had responded to Hector's telegram.

Rachel kicked off one shoe and then the other, tipsy enough that she lost her footing. Hector caught her arm. "Easy there."

She smiled up at him, sloe-eyed. "Again to my rescue — that's what, two, three times today?"

"I'm not counting, and neither should you," Hector said. He stroked her cheek with his knuckles. She turned her head to kiss his hand.

"I should get your room ready," he said.

"Let's drop that pretense," she said, her hands clasping the back of his neck, urging his face down to her waiting mouth.

co

They'd kicked off the sheets and chenille bedspread — far too sweltering for those. The oscillating fans were no real help, either. Hector had left the venetian blinds cracked and bars of inky shadows criss-crossed his bed. The darkened room reeked of sweat and sex.

Hector didn't know if it was the absinthe and the other liquor, the threat of the storm, or just Rachel's own nature, but she was utterly abandoned — completely giving herself over to him. Her damp hands were clutching the now-slippery bars of his bed's brass headboard, her legs wrapped tightly around his waist. Rachel pushed hard against him, groaning loudly and causing the head-board to squeak as her sweaty palms gripped the bars for purchase — seeking counter-leverage to his thrusts.

He was above her, propping himself up off her body so he could see her better, his weight on his hands as he plunged into her, over and over.

Rachel's face was obscured in shadow and more shadows gathered in the valley between her rib cage and parted thighs. The scant light through the window fell squarely on her generous, heaving breasts.

In the throes of their rutting, his mind warped by the absinthe, Hector was suddenly seized by a terrible vision — seized by the notion that he was fucking Man Ray's masterpiece.

Rachel's slender, sweat-slicked torso had become the "Minotaure". Her strong, well-defined arms, reaching above her hidden head, were now the horns of the bull. Her splendid, hard-nippled breasts were the bull's accusing eyes, and the dark hollow between her rib cage and vagina was the muzzle of the bull — its mouth devouring his cock.

The demented image edged Hector over and Rachel must have sensed it and have been taken along with him.

They screamed together, their bodies racked by tremors.

After a time, settling half atop her, he said, "I'm sorry, I meant to pull out before…"

Rachel's trembling hand stroked the small of his damp back. She said, smiling, "Frankly, I'm more concerned what the neighbors might think."

5

They never truly slept — talking into the small hours of the morning between bouts of raw, enthusiastic sex. After one episode Hector said, "This thing about you being a journalist and me not knowing…it reminds me I don't really know you."

"You know me…biblically," she'd said, kissing her way down his torso to take him into her mouth.

After, the taste of her and them together on his tongue, he said, "I really don't know you. You're Rachel Harper from South Bend, Indiana. You're a would-be painter turned fashion reporter. You've got a friend named Bev who has gone missing. You're magnificent looking naked and and you're splendid in bed. That's really all I know."

"For some men that last would be enough," Rachel said, smiling.

"But not for me. Tell me about old South Bend."

"A nothing little place with less nothing than most nothing places have," Rachel said.

Hector laughed and said, "Jesus, you been reading Gertrude Stein?"

She smiled again and reached across his torso to the bedside table. She picked up an ashtray, cigarette and Hector's Zippo. She arched an eyebrow and Hector said, "Sure, for me, too." He sat up and propped a pillow up against the headboard. He was getting a bit of a chill with the fans now cooling his sweat and he pulled the sheet over his thighs. Rachel balanced the ashtray on his belly. She rested her head on his shoulder and they smoked their cigarettes.

Hector tried again: "Tell me about your folks."

"My mother died when I was twelve," Rachel said. "Some kind of congenital heart defect. My father was never quite the same after that. He'd always nursed artistic ambitions — photography. But he'd been the dutiful provider and instead channelled everything into business...became a banker. When Mother died, he'd amassed a pretty good amount of money. He decided to retire and chase his dream. So we packed everything, and my father, me, and my younger sister, Alva, moved to Paris. He was intent on pursuing art photography. He was there less than six months when he had his first showing. Studies...of me and my sister."

Hector said softly, "What kind of studies?"

"Nudes," she said, so softly he hardly heard it. "He still — well, when we cross paths, he still tries now and then to get me to pose." She sat up and searched Hector's face. "It's not like you're thinking."

He nodded, then said, carefully, searching her eyes, "I haven't said what I'm thinking. It's...a bit libertine, make no mistake. I mean, I'm just an old boy from Texas. But Man Ray's lost muse, Lee Miller — I've seen similar naked pictures taken of her by her father. So there are precedents." *So far so good*, Hector thought. But as was too often the case, he didn't know when to shut up. "Some of the nudes shot of Lee by her father are fringing creepy, but that doesn't mean the pictures taken of you by your father..." He trailed off, lamely.

Rachel stubbed out her cigarette and scooted back down the bed, her cheek pressed to his chest so Hector could no longer see her expressions. "Anyway, that's how I got to Paris," she said. "How I...got caught up — you know, in the art scene."

"And this sister, Alva?"

"She met a man, a Spaniard, and got married...got away. She wasn't as comfortable with posing naked for Father as I guess she guessed I was."

Hector said, "Rightly or wrongly guessed?"

Rachel said, "Anyways...Father's still in Paris. He moves back and forth between there and Los Angeles, I hear. He does some studio work for the motion picture industry — shooting publicity portraits and the like. Glamour shots of the stars."

Hector said, "I'd like to see some of your own artwork sometime, Rachel. Maybe buy a painting or two."

"It doesn't exist like that," Rachel said. "I never did anything worth keeping."

"We're trapped here a day or two, Rache. Tomorrow, I'm going to go to the general store and buy a couple of canvases and some paint. I'm not letting you off this rock until you paint me something to hang on my wall."

She kissed his belly. "It's a nice sentimental gesture, but unneccesary, Hector. You've already done enough for me. And do we have to talk about me leaving already?"

"It wasn't meant like that," he said. "Not at all. I really want to see you at work, painting. I want something of yours to hang on my wall. And I'm not thinking of you leaving." He moved the ashtray to the sidetable, then cupped her chin in his hand and urged her back up the bed. She turned, her thigh sliding over his lap and her breast pressed tightly to his chest. He kissed her, slow and hard, his tongue exploring hers...the taste of her mouth a heady mix of rum, absinthe, cigarettes and sex. She said, breathily between kisses, "Where have you been all this time?"

"Here I suppose. Hell, I'm always around."

From official weather advisories:

(Sunday, September 1)

Advisory 10:00 a.m. tropical disturbance central short distance south of Andros Island moving westward about eight miles per hour attended by shifting gales and probably winds hurricane force small area near center. Indications storm will pass through Florida Straits late tonight or Monday. Caution advised vessels in path. Northeast storm warnings displayed Fort Pierce to Fort Myers Florida. NAR 10:22 a.m.

"A creator needs only one enthusiast

to justify him."

— MAN RAY

CHAPTER 9

TABLEAU VIVANT

HECTOR AWAKENED at four in the morning, as he always did. He slid quietly from the bed, careful not to disturb Rachel. He picked out some clothes and closed the door softly behind himself. He padded down the hallway to the bathroom. He was careful washing himself down there — rubbed raw in some places. Smiling to himself between winces, he wondered what damage he had done to Rachel's body — wondered if she would even be able to walk when she awakened.

After showering, Hector dressed, started some coffee, and sat down at his Underwood.

For the next two hours, the crime writer worked at his novel, a book he was calling *Wandering Eye*. Hector was about a quarter way through the first draft and making it up as he went along. He always started with a notion of an ending and just had to pick his path to get his Florida Keys-based investigator, Jim Drake, to the doom-laden denouement his creator envisioned.

Some authors had confessed to Hector that they always wrote with a particular reader in mind — a wife, a lover…a brother or sister.

Hector wrote for himself — his own best audience and harshest critic.

Several years before, a magazine catering to would-be writers had polled Hector and several of his fellow *Black Mask Magazine* stablemates for their definition or summation of the dark school of crime writing they collectively embodied.

Hector had responded, "Character is plot. Obsession is motivation. The quest, whatever else it may appear to be, is always a search for self — a race against time to a blood-spritzed epiphany. When that lightbulb goes on, the world goes dark. No happy endings."

Hector kept his "definition" of his life's dark work pasted to the tray of his Underwood.

By six he noticed first light glowing on the cherry surface of his writing desk. He finished mid-sentence, knowing what was to come next, and how the sentence would end — his trick to ensure a fast and smooth start when he next sat down to write.

Terrible screeching erupted on either side of his house. From the bedroom, Hector heard Rachel call in a hoarse and husky voice, "What in God's name is that?"

Hector laughed and stood and stretched. He poured some coffee in a mug and took it in to Rachel. She sat up in his bed, coyly tucking the sheet into her underarms to cover her breasts. She ran a hand through her tangled hair, blushing. "Morning, Hector," she said, unable to meet his gaze. The noise from outside erupted again. She said, again, raising her voice over the din, "What in God's name *is* that?"

"Roosters," Hector said, handing her the coffee mug. "Fighting cocks, actually. Nasty, tough bastards. Blood sports are big around here in the Keys. And because of those fighting roosters on either side, I've never needed an alarm clock."

"It's truly terrible," Rachel said, smiling. She sipped her coffee and made a face. "Boy, that's bitter. It'd wake the dead."

"Cuban," Hector said. "I've developed a taste for it, but it is potent stuff. I'll fetch you some sugar and cream."

"No," she said, sipping more and smiling. "It's fine. It's good — help clear my mind. That damned absinthe…"

Hector said, "If I took advantage — I mean, that stuff does wild things to me, too — well…"

"No apologies, Hector," Rachel said. "And no regrets. I didn't need the absinthe or any of the other liquor to do any of that last night. It would have happened anyway, because I wanted it." She hesitated. "But if you, on the other hand, I mean, if the absinthe…"

"No," Hector said. "Last night had nothing to do with liquor for me, either." He kissed her hand. She was still blushing. She said, "I must look like a wreck…ravaged."

"And ravishing." Hector smiled and stood up. He rummaged through his closet and found his robe. He tossed it across the foot of the bed. "Place is all yours…shower, get dressed. While you do that, I'll go fetch something to eat and pick up the newspapers. Any special requests?"

"Your second book if the newsstand has a copy — I want to start it as soon as I finish the first one," she said.

"I have copies here. Hell, I'll give you my whole ouevre."

5

Hector found her brewing more of his Cuban coffee. She was dressed in white slacks, a white shirt and sandals. Her hair was scraped back into a ponytail. She looked poised and Nordic. She said, "I'm sore in places I never knew existed in me."

"Me too," Hector said, setting down his shopping bags. He reached into one and pulled out a smaller sack. "Chocolate-filled croissants," he said, "fresh fruit and some Cuban bread. We have to finish that last off today — they cook it fresh and without preservatives. Tomorrow, that loaf will be a weapon."

Rachel smiled and fetched some plates from the kitchenette's cabinets. She seemed to be finding her way around just fine. Hector was troubled to find that he didn't find that troubling. She said, "How are things?"

"Beautiful, but deceptive. The sky has a kind of coppery color you only see with the worst storms. But there's no wind to speak of, and no rain. Wouldn't go out on a boat though — the water is hellish rough…and the big birds are moving in greater numbers to the west — racing out to the Gulf."

Rachel set out dishes and silverware. She said, "I thought I heard typing this morning."

"Hope it didn't disturb you," he said. "I get up around four and go until six or seven…later if I'm really on a roll."

"I wish I had your discipline," she said. "Maybe then I could write more than just puff pieces on couture."

"You make the time," Hector said. "The thing that stands between most published authors and those who merely aspire isn't just talent, but self-discipline." Christ, he was starting to sound to himself like one of those how-to writing magazines he so loathed. He handed Rachel the newspapers — the *Key West Citizen* and the *Miami Herald*.

She said, "Which sections do you want? Sports…crosswords?"

"God, suddenly I feel like a married couple." Hector winked and shook his head. "I don't keep up with news much. And I ain't got no politics to speak of. The papers are for you. For my part, over breakfast, I mean to steep myself in some surrealism." He held up his stolen copy of *Le Minotaure*. Then he said, "Reminds me, while I was out, I hit the hotel again. There's still nothing from Bev."

Rachel nodded, biting her lip. "I guess I just have to hope that nothing doesn't mean something."

Hector nodded and sipped his coffee. He chewed on his chocolate croissant and began flipping through *Le Minotaure*.

It was a curious and often arresting mixture of image and text. Between collages of bulls and severed or disarticulated headless or legless women were bizarre tracts of poetry and essays on Greek mythology.

In one article, the writer had composed a skin-crawling recreation of an imagined conversation between Jack the Ripper and the Marquis de Sade.

An equally unsettling centerspread — titled *Poupée* in block letters — was a collection of photos depicting a naked mannequin shot at various angles. In many of the photos, the figure's arms were severed at the shoulders and the legs missing below the knees. The mid-section, just below the large breasts, was laid open and the organs replaced with bric-a-brac. The various poses of the figure, designed by Hans Bellmer, looked like nothing so much as morgue photos of a mutilation murder victim. The piece was subtitled, *Variations on the Montage of an Articulated Minor.*

Hector closed the magazine in disgust. "Alright," he said sourly. "I've seen enough. And seen enough to buy, 100 percent, that whoever killed that woman over by Hem's is working on surrealist models." He didn't know what he expected by way of response, but he figured Rachel would have something to say to that. He reached across the table and gently lowered the newspaper. She looked up at him with stricken eyes.

"Something terrible has happened in Miami," she said. Rachel read the article to him, and Hector sat back in his chair, shaking his head.

On Friday morning, a torso had been found sitting on a public bench at South Beach.

The still-unidentified woman's body had been disarticulated. The arms and head were missing, and the legs cut off just above the knee. The remains of the torso had been severed just below the breasts, and the two halves arranged, a bit off-center, on the public park bench, the breasts pointed out to sea.

"These things have to be related," Rachel said. "This woman in Miami, and the one you saw yesterday...they must have been killed by the same man."

"Yes," Hector said. "I'm sure the murders are linked." He also thought about the fact that between Miami and Key West lay Matecumbe and about what that might mean — or have meant — for her friend, Bev. He said, "This woman — what was left of her — was posed again. Who do you think the intended audience is...or was?"

Rachel shrugged. "Maybe just himself."

Hector nodded uneasily. "Suppose that could be true."

From official weather advisories:

(Monday, September 2)

Advisory 1:30 p.m. Hurricane warnings ordered Key West tropical disturbance central noon about latitude twenty three degrees twenty minutes longitude eighty degrees fifteen minutes moving slowly westward stop. It will be attended by winds hurricane force in Florida Straits and winds gale force Florida Keys south of Key Largo this afternoon and tonight. Caution advised vessels Florida Straits next twenty four hours: Northeast storm warnings remain displayed elsewhere Miami to Ft Myers. NAR 1:30p.m.

"Bullfighting is the only art

in which the artist is in danger of death

and in which the degree of brilliance

in the performance is left to the fighter's honor."

— ERNEST HEMINGWAY

CHAPTER 10

REVISTERO

MOST OF SUNDAY'S REMAINS and Monday morning passed much the same way. To preserve their hurricane supplies, Rachel and Hector dined in restaurants around the island and drank in various of Hector's favored watering holes. Between those trips out, they'd retire to his bedroom to make love, or to lounge together in a cold bath in order to cool off, drinking Hatuey beer and listening to the radio.

Hector was more attuned to the barometer now, and watching it fall, he began to think the better plan might have been to pack Rachel up in his Chevrolet sports roadster and make a run for a good Miami hotel. Maybe tool up as far as Tampa, just to be on the safe side. But any window to run had now firmly closed — they were fully committed, at this point.

But the phones were still working, so Hector called the Colonial Hotel again, checking a last time to see if Rachel's friend had surfaced, but it was still silence.

Hector was sitting at his writing desk, the candlestick phone heavy in his hand. Rachel massaged his shoulders and he was again struck by the strength of her hands. She was built athletically, with lean, graceful muscle tone, and, as she had said, she had no distinguishing marks on her long, sleek body…no birth marks, moles — perfect.

Rolling his head back and fourth as she worked the muscles of his neck with her thumbs, Hector said, "Probably our last chance to venture out, Rache. Any special destinations in mind…anything we want or need?"

Over her objections, Hector had purchased for Rachel two moderately-sized canvases, paints, brushes and an inexpensive easel. So far, she hadn't touched them.

But then, Hector figured he shouldn't complain about that as all Rachel's time had been spent drinking and eating with Hector…or with Hector inside of her.

Rachel squeezed the back of Hector's neck and slapped his shoulder. "How about if we return to the scene of the crime? Where we met, I mean? Just go there and have some of your mojitos and maybe some big Cuban sandwiches? Maybe some oysters."

Hector winked. "I favor this plan."

"Why shouldn't you?" she said, smiling. "It favors you."

5

It was quiet in Josie's joint.

To Hector's relief, old toothless, one-eyed Tito was nowhere in evidence.

The bartender smiled and nodded as they stepped into the darkened cool of his saloon. Hector pulled out a chair for Rachel and then scooted it in behind her. He strode up and put an elbow on the bar, one foot on the brass rail. "Two mojitos, Josie, and a couple of Cuban sandwiches and some fried plantains. And an order of oysters on the half shell."

"Done," Josie said. He winked and smiled meanly. "Jesus, Hec, that skirt looks like she's been gang-banged by a Hun regiment. And more, she looks like it agrees with her."

Hector shrugged, in no mood to make dirty jokes about Rachel. He took that as another disquieting sign that she was weaving her way into his heart and head…getting past all of his guards. Hector said simply, "She's a real sweet kid."

He returned to the table with two mojitos and they sipped those, using the rum drinks to wash down the cold, coppery-tasting fresh oysters that Josie had brought them on a bed of crushed ice. Rachel, teasing said, "Those are a start." She pointed at the oysters. "But maybe you should have some conch chowder, too."

Hector shook his head, grinning. "You're talking aphrodisiacs, honey. We don't need those. Stamina is looking to become more the issue for us."

She reached across the table and squeezed his hand.

Their Cuban sandwiches arrived, and as they ate, they heard the wind begin to play a bit harder across the roof of the saloon. Newspapers and severed palm fronds whipped by the open doors and the palm trees were beginning to bend in the wind. Across the street, an agile islander had shimmied up one of the palm trees with a machete to cut off the coconuts before the storm could turn them into cannon balls.

Hector heard a familiar, gruff voice. Ernest grinned as he saw Hector and Rachel. Hem spread an arm and stepped aside. Bishop Blair and his wife, Harriet, smiled and waved to the couple as they ducked into the cool of the saloon.

Bishop was wearing white deck pants, a short-sleeved, floral print shirt — untucked — and a ridiculous-looking white Panama hat. Hector said, "Going native, huh? It looks real good on you, Bishop." Except for the fact that the little painter was also wearing highly-polished black dress shoes and black socks with his tropical attire.

For her part, Mrs. Bishop wore a light blue print dress covered with erupting volcanoes and lush, exotic flowers. She had on big round black sunglasses and a huge, floppy white straw hat. Ernest was his usual slovenly-dressed self — khaki pants held up with a rope, a bloodstained Polo shirt and sandals. He still looked relatively clean though, his hair slicked back and just the hint of a five o'clock shadow shading his jaw.

Uninvited, he gestured at the two empty chairs at Rachel and Hector's table, then pulled up a fifth chair for himself. "How were the heads after the other night, kids?"

"Fine," Hector said. "Yours?"

"Not bad…slept the sleep of the dead. Then wrote a thousand words the next morning. A new story about the island, here."

Hector joked, "Not something I said, I hope."

Ernest gave him a sour look and said, "Based on the updated reports, we're playing it safe and moving Bish and Harriet into our place for the night. Sounds like the worst is going to be over Matecumbe, but us being seventy-five miles from the eye, gotta figure things are going to be plenty tough here, too."

"Plenty," Hector agreed. He smiled at the little painter and his wife. "Hell of a way to spend your holiday."

Mr. Bishop shrugged and said, "And Miss Harper, too. But we're treating it as an experience…not quite an adventure, but something akin to that."

"Me too," Rachel said.

Hem called, "Josie, two more of those mojitos for Harp and Lasso, and a daiquiri for me. Bishop?"

The little man smiled and called to the bartender, "*Highbalito con Aqua Mineral.*"

The bartender stared at Hem, uncomprehending, who replied, "He means a highball, Josie. Made with whiskey."

Hem said to Harriet Blair, "And yours?"

"Campari and Gordon's." Ernest ordered for her and said to Hector, "So, when do you think?" He gestured outside at the wind-driven debris whipping by.

Hector ordered another serving of oysters and said, "Midnight… or just after. Figure by five or six tonight, we'll all want to be indoors.

The wind and the rain should be fairly intense by then."

Hem said, "I plan to go out to the base tonight and see the *Pilar* through."

"That's nuts," Hector said. "You've got her lashed down. What happens, happens. You can't do anything for her, standing by. And if you tried to get out to her, you'd get yourself killed. Hell, you could get yourself killed being out in the storm when it truly gets here...one tree branch...a stray coconut...a piece of planking or some empty bottle discarded by a rummy...maybe a rummy himself, or what's left of him. You've got the safest house on the Key, Hem. Stay there with your wife and boys and guests."

"All the same," Ernest said. "Want to sit out with me?"

Hector looked at Rachel and back at Ernest. If she wasn't there, he'd probably be game for it. Just sit out all night in the lashing rain with Hem, getting drunk and trying to justify the craziness of being out there by kidding themselves it was something akin to research. They'd have themselves a high-old time or die trying.

"Hell no," Hector said. "I mean to be warm and dry and tight." He paused, then said, "What about that critic friend of Pauline's, Quentin? You throwing him a lifeline, too, Hem?"

"You mean Wind? Christ no," Hem said. He accepted his daiquiri and drained it by half at a pull. "Wind can go down with the goddamned Concha if the world turns that way. That said, the son of a bitch is supposed to be joining us in a few minutes." Hem drank some more of his frozen drink and then said, "Sorry, Lasso."

"It happens."

Hector lit a cigarette and said, "Bishop, I've been looking over *Le Minotaure* some more. What exactly is it with the bulls...the Minotaur thing? What's the significance to you surrealists?"

Bishop pulled out one of his own cigarettes and then fastened it to the end of a long, black cigarette holder. Hector lit the little man's cigarette with his Zippo and then lit another

for Rachel. Hem, a nonsmoker, scooted his chair around a little closer to Harriet, who also wasn't smoking.

"Partly, I think it's just a preoccupation of our times, driven in
no small part by this man, here." Bishop gestured at Hem. "First
with *The Sun Also Rises*, and now with *Death in the Afternoon*.
Hem has made us all fascinated with the myth and ritual of the
bullfight. And many of us in the surrealist movement are
Spainophiles and *aficionados* in our own rights. But it is also the
myth of the Minotaur that fascinates us and made us choose the
Minotaur to serve as our kind of surrealist emblem."

Hector said, "I'm just an old boy from southern Texas. My
Greek mythology is, well, it ain't great. I mean, I know it involves
something about a maze, or something, and some fella going in to
kill the half-human, half-bull who lived at the center, but..." He
shrugged. "But that's as far as I go."

Bishop said, "Harriet here is quite an avid folklorist. You tell
Hector, dear."

She smiled and blushed, her gaze darting around the table. It
was apparent the little woman was intimidated by her story-teller
company, but she pressed ahead:

"The story goes that Poseidon, the sea god, gifted the king of
Crete — Minos — with a white bull. Minos was supposed to sac-
rifice the white bull, and when he didn't, Poseidon retaliated by
making the king's wife, Pasiphaë, fall in love with and actually
couple with the bull. Their offspring was a hideous creature, the
Minotaur, a giant human hybrid with a bull's head. Minos then
hired Daedalus to construct the labyrinth to contain the
Minotaur. Once a decade, Minos sent seven men into the
labyrinth to their deaths — and to be food for the beast inside.
Finally, a hero, Theseus, volunteered to be one of the seven sent to
their deaths. Theseus was in love with Minos' daughter, Ariadne.
He planned to kill the Minotaur. Ariadne provided Theseus with

a long spool of thread, so that after he had killed the monster, Theseus could follow the thread back out of the labyrinth."

Hector blew a smoke ring and said, "Things went to plan, and then this Greek boy and the king's daughter, Ariadne, they lived happily ever after?"

"Oh no," Harriet Blair said, shaking her head. "Theseus abandoned Ariadne soon after. He was off on his next adventure."

"In that, it sounds like one of my books," Hector said. "But I see now — the myth, I mean. It's a psychological minefield."

Hector did a double-take. He suddenly realized Quentin Windly was sitting beside him. He hadn't heard the critic arrive.

Hector shook hands with the critic — at least the bastard had a firm grip. Hector signaled to Josie and asked, "What's yours Quentin?"

"Planter's punch," Quentin called to the barkeep.

Hector nodded slowly. "Exotic sounding. You may have to give old Josie instructions on making that brew."

Quentin winked and said, "So, you all were talking a lot of bull."

Hector let that one pass. "Minotaur stuff, yep. You into bulls, Q?"

The critic smiled and helped himself to an oyster. Swallowing, he said, "As it happens, I'm a recent convert. Been reading Hem's book and caught the fever. Soon as the weather clears, I'm headed across the Gulf. Going to start with the Mexican bullfights. Then, once I'm grounded, I'll move on to Spain. Think I'm going to spend a couple of years working as a bullfight reviewer...gather material for my own book on the bullfight."

Hector glanced across the table at Ernest. Hem looked vaguely nauseous...a twisted smile of derision on his face. But it was early yet, and Hem's alcohol consumption relatively light, so he was, so far, able to hold his tongue.

Bishop Blair, indignant, said, "Surely that book's been written. *Death in the Afternoon* is the final word, I think."

Rachel said, "You're a bullfighting enthusiast, Mr. Blair?"

"For many many decades now. Sometimes, when there's a particularly fine young fighter, Harriet and I will follow the circuit. But really, Quentin, what else is there to say after Hem's book?"

Quentin accepted his drink and sipped at it through the large paper straw Josie had provided, perhaps mockingly. The critic said, "Ernest had a hidden agenda. That book of his is as much about the craft of writing as it is about the bullfight. He used the matador as metaphor for the writer. Used the rituals of the bullfight as an excuse to explore his own beliefs about writing. And he used it to settle literary scores."

Hector was toying with scooting a bit away from the critic, not certain whether Hem would hurl something across the table, or maybe just flip the table aside to get his hands around the critic's throat.

But Hem was struggling to remain on best behavior, probably because the critic was one of Pauline's friends. Hem said, "You go to Mexico, Wind. Go see what passes for a bullfight there. Then, Wind, you go on to Spain. I'll give you some names of bullfighters who'll show you the ropes. Give you the insider's view. Sidney Franklin and the like. You'll love 'em, Wind."

Hector had to smile. Franklin was light in the loafers — one of an increasing number of *maricón matadors de toros*.

"But you should get your *ass* moving *now*," Hem said. "September is the month of the great *feria*. Get out of here in the next few days, and you might still make the subscription season in Madrid…in Jerez de la Frontera, Castuera and Tomelloso."

Quentin said, "Thanks, Hem — for the letters of introduction. That would be swell of you. And goddamn sporting."

Hem winked and raised his glass. "Anything for a fellow writer, Wind."

Surely Quentin couldn't have missed that sarcasm. But he just smiled and sipped his planter's punch. Impulsively, Hector said, "Q, you been to Miami lately? Must have passed through on your way down here…"

"I did," the critic said, smacking his lips. "But I didn't really stop for more than some fuel and a drink in a Cuban-run bar there that I favor."

"South Beach?"

"Yeah."

"I may know just the place," Hector said. "Was reading the Miami papers this morning. Authorities there are investigating a death that occurred a few days ago. A woman's naked torso was found on a South Beach park bench — posed, you might say."

"Like the woman here," Harriet Blair said softly.

"Yes, but worse," Hector said. "This would have taken some real effort and some muscle. The woman's head and arms were missing. Her legs cut off high at the thigh. And her torso was cut apart in the middle and then put back together, though artistically askew…going for the effect, you might say."

"I just can't believe this is happening," Bishop Blair said, wringing his hands.

Quentin said, "If you're trying to insinuate something, Lassiter…"

"I'm just inquiring, Quentin. You hear anything about it while you were there? The papers, necessarily, are a bit vague. I crave more of the true gen."

"Looking for more source material for your potboilers, Lassiter, is that it?" Quentin drained his drink. "Word's out on you, Lassiter — 'the man who lives what he writes and writes what he lives.' Shit. How long until Rachel here ends up between the covers — of your books, I mean — as one of your femme fatales or luckless round-heels victims?"

Hector couldn't check himself. He stomped down on the critic's foot, then, as Quentin howled, Hector got a handful of
Quentin's blond hair and drove the man's face down against the
table, making cocktail glasses jump. Still clinging to a handful of
hair, Hector lifted the critic's face up off the table and tipped his
head back. Blood was streaming from Quentin's nose.

Hem said, unperturbed, "Wind, in the bullfight game, they
call a move like that *tapando la cara con la muleta.* You'll want to
squeeze the bridge of your nose, Wind — to staunch that bleeding, I mean."

Hector was braced for a counter-attack, but the critic was
wadding up a napkin to his face. Quentin stood up quickly, turning over his own chair. "You're going to fucking regret that,
Lassiter!" Quentin was backing out of the bar, one hand pressed to
his nose, the other pointing at Hector.

Nodding — ashamed to look at the Blairs or at Rachel —
Hector sipped his half-spilled mojito and said, "I already do."

Hem, grinning broadly, said, "Set 'em up for everyone, and
pour one for yourself, Josie." Hem toasted Quentin's back with his
daiquiri. "So, it's gone with the Wind!"

(Monday, September 2)

Advisory 10:00 p.m. *(Key West temperature = 81, direction = NW, velocity = 34mph.)* Northeast storm extended north of Sarasota to Carabelle Florida and hurricane warnings north of Everglades to Punta Gorda tropical disturbance of full hurricane intensity but rather small diameter central 8:00 p.m. near Matecumbe Key moving northwestward accompanied by shifting gales and hurricane winds near center. Northeast storm warnings are now displayed from Titusville to Carrabelle and hurricane warnings from West Palm Beach to Punta Gorda. NAR 10:00 p.m.

"If there is a special Hell for writers
it should be in the forced contemplation
of their own works."

— JOHN DOS PASSOS

CHAPTER 11

STORM SURGE

"JUST FORGET ABOUT IT, Hector. It's over and you can't undo it. Besides, Quentin didn't even try to swing back."

Hector stroked Rachel's breasts, his fingertips wrinkled and slippery with the bath water. "He's not the kind to strike back directly," he said. "He's a critic. They don't fancy face-to-face confrontations. He'll more likely avenge himself in print."

Tipping her head back to search his eyes, Rachel said, "You really think he might be the one who's killing these women? Quentin seemed to think you suspect him."

"I'm not sure that I really do," Hector said. "Though I think I could mount a good enough circumstantial case against the bastard. Hell, he's a critic...nothing's beneath him. Bishop Blair, too, is certainly an odd duck and a logical enough character to have committed these crimes...if he weren't so frail."

"Character..." Rachel murmured. "Interesting word choice."

The wind was tearing along the roof now, and the palm trees surrounding Hector's house groaned and creaked in the wind. The rain lashed the windows and the electricity was flickering with the wind gusts. Rachel shivered against him. The rain pounded the tin roof, sounding almost like hail.

Hector had already set out and lit several candles in anticipation of a blackout. He said, "We should probably get out of this tub and get some clothes on."

Rachel sighed and drew her legs up under herself, her hands gripping the sides of the claw-footed bathtub, the muscles of her arms swelling as she raised herself up out of the bath water. Hector put a hand to the small of her back to help her up, then leaned forward and kissed her bottom.

He stood up behind her and began patting down her body with a big towel. He said, "We'll get the radio on...see what we can learn from that. Sounds like the wind's really picking up now. Time for us to be on the sharp."

Rachel looked back over her shoulder, frowning. "What for, other than the wind?"

Hector said, "Storm surge — just in case the weather bureau gets it wrong and the eye passes over or nearer to us. If that was to happen, it could push a water wall across Bone Key. We're not what you'd call much above sea level. A six- or seven-foot surge could be very bad news. And a twelve- or fifteen-foot surge, sustained, could put the whole Key underwater, perhaps for hours. Have to be prepared to move into the attic if that happens. I've got a shotgun stored up there, in case we have to blow a hole through the roof to get up on top of the house. If that's still not high enough, I've got life preservers stashed up in the attic. We'd lash ourselves together, then find ourselves a tall palm tree to cling to until the waters receded."

Rachel looked stricken. They were both still naked and Hector hugged her bare body tightly to his. He said, "Please don't worry, Rachel. We're talking worst-case-scenarios and never-going-to-happens here, darling. I'm just being that over-prepared Boy Scout, you know? More likely, the way we'll pass this storm is doing more loving damage to one another's most private parts."

5

The radio was mostly crackle and static. Through the pops and cracks, Hector determined the experts were still predicting the storm's eye to pass over Matecumbe.

He hoped the veterans' camps there had been evacuated in time. That Key was one of the lowest-lying in the chain of islands trailing down from the Florida panhandle southwesterly to Cuba. Matecumbe was also devoid of anything like real shelter other than the hotel and a few small houses…it was more Hooverville than town — a rag-tag collection of tents and shacks.

Hector checked the weather gauges hanging on his kitchen wall and shrugged off a chill. For the first time, he was truly concerned for Bone Key's welfare. The house was sweltering — almost ninety, but he couldn't open the windows with the rain coming down as it was now. He estimated it must still be in the low- to mid-eighties outside. But the barometer was what really unnerved him — it was at 29.392 inches and in free fall. Based on the falling barometer, if Key West was not in the storm's direct path, then the true eye of the storm must be devastatingly hellish — a true killing wind.

Hector put on a brave face and mixed two mojitos and handed one to Rachel. She was sitting on the couch, her legs curled up under herself, sorting through Hector's own hardcovers and bound pulp magazines containing his short stories.

Smiling, she took the drink from him. She sipped some and set it on the table by the couch. "You make the best ones," she said.

He sat down next to her and looked over some of the covers of his books: *Rhapsody In Black*…*The Big Siesta*, *The Last Key*, *Satan's Daughter* and *Border Town*. She picked up that last one and read aloud, "'Whores die hard.' Hard to stop reading there, granted," she said. "But do you really, to use Quentin Windly's phrase, 'Write what you live and live what you write'?"

"Isn't that what we all do? Us artists, I mean."

"Well, certainly it seems to be what you and Papa do."

"We use our lives as touchstones. But there's still plenty of invention there."

"I was reading this story of yours," she said. She began sorting through the pulp magazines he'd had bound into hardcovers. Here," she said, "*Black Mask Magazine*. The story is called, 'Hellcat.' In it, your 'hero,' if he can truly be called that, Tom Reed, he pays a man to scare a woman so he — *Tom* — can pick her up in a bar."

Uh-oh. Hector had written that story five years before…probably six or seven teeth ago, for Tito Castillo.

Hector searched Rachel's face. He didn't get the sense there was accusation there…maybe not even a recognition of the real possibility that Hector might have scammed her in just such a manner. He said, trying to look innocent and nonchalant, "Sometimes, and maybe more for me than others, life imitates art. I honestly don't know what else to say."

Rachel weighed that, then said, "At least you're no Tom Reed, so maybe I'll fare better than—" she scanned the yellow-ing pulp pages to refresh her memory, then said, "—than the luckless Becky Case."

"Yeah. She was a wicked piece of work…worse even, than old Tom, if I'm remembering the right story."

Hector closed the book, stacked it with the others, and sat them on the coffee table. As he did that, something hit the roof, hard, and Rachel clutched at him. The lights flickered again. There was another crash, the sound of splintered wood, and Hector saw that the glass pane of the window at the other side of the room was now fractured. "Something must have hit the storm shutter," Hector said. "Must have penetrated the wooden slats and put enough pressure on the glass to crack that, too. Probably coconuts — the damned neighbors probably forgot to cut them down before the storm. With any luck, that was the last of them going."

Rachel held him tighter as the thunder exploded overhead, rattling the windows in their cases and causing their drinking glasses to shake. "That sounds so close," she said. "I really hate storms...even little ones."

He could tell she meant it. Rachel was shaking out of proportion to the storm. The Big Blow was bad, but it was still nowhere near its peak, by Hector's estimate.

There was another crash, this time out back. Hector gently freed himself from Rachel's arms and flipped on the back porch light and cracked the back door, holding it tight against the buffeting wind. A lawn decoration from some neighbor's yard had crashed into a tree out back. Hector shook his head. His fool neighbors hadn't exercised due diligence and gathered up loose items that might be rendered killer projectiles by the big winds. Then Hector saw the dead fighting cock pinned to the palm tree — its beak driven into the trunk of the tree. Hector thought of Hem out there in the storm, standing suicidal watch over his beloved new boat, the *Pilar*, and wondered if he'd ever see Ernest again.

The lights flickered several times in quick succession, and now there was a strange, terrible howling sound, like a banshee or the soundtrack from some Universal horror picture. It was an inhuman, sustained screaming noise. Hector realized it was the wind. Something else crashed outside and struck the back door, nearly knocking Hector from his feet.

Hector saw that a pelican had been swept from some tree it had settled in and had been hurled against his back door. The pelican lay dead on his porch step, its neck twisted twice and many of its feathers stripped by the wind.

Another hard gust came and the door was torn from his hand. The wind blew through his house, extinguishing all of the candles just as the power failed again.

Hector felt frantic hands grabbing at him and turned to find Rachel, hysterical, tearing at him. "Make it stop," she pleaded.

He twisted around in her arms just long enough to get both hands on the back door's knob. He wrenched the door shut, struggling hard against the wind and blowing rain. He locked the door, brushed his wet hair back from his forehead and turned and opened his arms to Rachel. She hugged him close in his darkened kitchen. He felt her mouth close, her breath coming raggedly. She was on the verge of hyperventilating. She said, "Love me, Hector! Or *something* — do something to take it away."

He shook her once, then kissed her hard. She responded hungrily, her tongue groping for his, her hands tearing at his wet clothes. He swept her up and carried into the bedroom.

5

The wind was still a howling constant, but it had been so for hours — Rachel had at least adjusted to that aspect of the storm.

Panting, her legs wrapped tightly around his own, she said between ragged breaths, "You were right about my father...about what happened after my mother."

"I didn't saying anything like that," Hector said, his skin crawling to hear it, now, while there bodies were still joined...while he was still spasming softly inside her. "Never said what I thought."

"You thought it; I could see it in your eyes. Blue eyes don't hide much, Hector. You said it yourself, or rather, you wrote it, in *The Last Key*. I knew you knew. It was a week after the funeral. I was still just a little girl, really. He came to me, awakened me in the middle of the night from sleep — from a dream about my mother, oddly enough. He said it was time for us to comfort one another...that he'd show me how."

Hector was torn: the writer in him wanted her to push on and tell the terrible tale. Something he might be able to use. But the man who had come to care for Rachel, who was still inside her, needed the story to stop, right there. He said, "I can imagine the rest."

Her eyes glistened in the light from the candle by the bed. "I suppose that's true. You can probably imagine like few others ever could...writing the things that you do." She turned away from him, and away from the flickering candle's light. The wind was still a fierce scream and the house was shaking and vibrating with the wind and the hard, nearly sideways rain. "I don't remember much more than that," she said softly. "But I do know it was storming outside, during that first time. Not a storm like this one, not at all. I've never experienced anything like this — but a hard rain...thunder and lightning. Ever since, well, storms..."

"We'll get through tonight, darling," Hector said. "I'll see you through it, I swear. And in a few days, when it's quiet, we'll get ourselves on a boat and we'll make a run to the other side of the Gulf...start searching for my next good place. Maybe New Mexico. We'll look for somewhere it does little more than softly rain...and hardly ever even that."

She turned again to face him, her hands reaching up and pressing tightly to his face, holding his head in the half-light where she could see his pale blue eyes. "Are you...? I mean..."

Hector, surprised to find that he was hard again inside her, said, "No more words."

"A curious thing about atrocity stories

is that they mirror, instead of the events they purport to describe,

the extent of the hatred of the people that tell them.

Still, you can't listen unmoved to tales of misery and murder."

— JOHN DOS PASSOS

CHAPTER 12

PANIC

MUCH OF THE FIRST NEWS came by word of mouth. It came from those with battery-operated short-wave radios. It came from the few fisherman crazy enough to put to sea soon after the storm passed by Key West.

It came from gutsy pilots who'd flown northward over the Keys and seen the miles-long devastation wrecked on the overseas railway and the rescue train sent too late by dithering federal employees — dispatched tardily through the storm-swept Keys to pick up the doomed veterans. And the poor people who got on that too-late train? Most of them were equally doomed — the train cars swept out into the ocean and then swamped.

Only the train's engine remained sitting upright on the surviving stretch of tracks.

The first reports claimed that Matecumbe Key had been stripped down to its coral base and that everyone on the Key should be presumed dead.

The outside world heard tales of even greater devastation — with phone lines down, rumors ran rampant that Key West and many others of the Keys had been "blown away."

A lot of wild, insanely false rumors were started.

But in terms of the actual devastation and loss of life? That was still beyond exaggeration or comprehension, in Hector's initial estimation.

Later days only proved him right...at least to his own stricken mind.

They initially determined that the winds across Matecumbe had reached two-hundred miles an hour. The sustained tidal surge had been fifteen feet, and they figured that some waves might have climbed thirty feet above the norm. Hector couldn't conceive of that, or its likely results.

Whatever its actual depth, the high water was more than enough to drown nearly everyone on the Key.

And the winds that had come ahead of the storm surge would have been sufficient to drive sand at blasting force across clothing and skin — more than enough to strip someone caught outside and deprived shelter of their clothing. The wind had been strong enough to scour exposed skin and underlying muscle and soft tissue down to bone.

The barometer at Matecumbe had fallen to 26.35 — a new record low for the United States.

About five in the morning on Tuesday, Key West time, the barometer had finally begun climbing again.

The thrashing rain continued through much of Tuesday, but late that afternoon the rain eased and then stopped.

When it was finally safe to venture outside his house, Hector found that apart from the single, fractured storm shutter covering the sitting room window facing east, damage to his own cottage was minimal. There was minor scarring to the light-green stucco walls — apparently from the impact of coconuts, severed tree branches and dead birds. Most of the dead fowls were his neighbors' fighting cocks.

Palm fronds were strewn several inches thick across his backyard and in the street. But Key West seemed to have come through intact for the most part — mostly fallen trees and wind damage.

Yet there were already a few missing persons reports being filed.

Rummies and homeless bums had gone missing — maybe swept off the docks and piers where they'd slept off their last drunks...maybe swamped in the rickety boats a few called home.

Rachel and Hector spent Wednesday morning into afternoon in Josie's, eavesdropping on storm "war" stories that were pretty much the equivalent of their own and trying to forget the sound of the wind that had blown all Monday night through early Tuesday morning, so unnerving Rachel.

Early Thursday afternoon, having wrapped up his morning's writing and just stepping out of his second shower of the day after a late morning spent in Rachel's arms, there was a hard knock at his door. That voice:

"Lasso! It's Hemingstein! Put on some old clothes — something you can burn later. And gather some gear. We've been mobilized."

Hector frowned and zipped his pants and pulled on a T-shirt. He said to Rachel, "Best put something on." He called outside, "What are you talking about?"

"All able-bodied men," Hem yelled back. "We're ordered up to Matecumbe — the water's finally calm enough to mount a search-and-rescue effort."

Hector was almost sorry he'd answered Hem's call, now. He looked at Rachel. "I have to go."

"Of course you do," she said. "I'll be fine. Go and do what you can to help."

Hector said, "It's probably just for the day. Be back tomorrow afternoon at the latest. I'll get that pledge from Hem. *Mi casa es su casa*," he said. "There's an extra door key in the drawer to the right of the cutlery tray. I have credit at Josie's too, so run a tab if you want."

"I'll be fine," Rachel said, tying off the belt of his bathrobe, now gathered tight around her. "The weather is clear now." She kissed him hard on the mouth. "Tell me what you need and I'll help you pack, Hector. Those poor people, if they're still alive, have waited long enough."

Hector winked. "You've got a good heart." He called to Hem, "Meet you at your boat in twenty minutes." Then he held up a finger, remembering. He said to Rachel, "Something I want you to have, Rache." He opened the drawer of the table by his bed and pulled out a small, velvet box and opened it. She smiled at the gold bracelet. He said, "It was my mother's."

She held out her hand and he clasped it to her wrist. "Damn — a perfect fit," he said.

She gave him a long look. "It is. It is perfect." She frowned and hugged him tightly, then pressed her palm to his temple. "Stay strong, Hec. What lies ahead could be terrible to behold. Don't let it get inside your head, promise me?"

5

Hector stood with Ernest on the flying bridge of the *Pilar* as her master piloted her north, skirting the perimeter of Long Key.

"It sounds like murder, Hector," Hem said.

Ernest using Hector's given name was unusual, so he figured Hem must be badly shaken. "They delayed and delayed sending down the train, those cocksucker FDR flunkies," Hem said. "Federal government might as well have flown those poor bloody fucking vets out over the Atlantic and dropped them in to save a step. Fucking bureaucrats. Some cocksucking decision-maker was hankering to get down to Key West for his honeymoon to get his ashes hauled. Think that night of fucking was worth the deaths of half-a-thousand?"

"I've got no politics," Hector said.

"This isn't about politics, Lasso."

They plowed on through choppy water. As they approached the camp, they could smell the bodies. Many of the dead were floating in the waters around the annihilated ferry slip.

At first, Hem tried to steer the *Pilar* around the floating corpses, but they lay so thickly in the water, face down and bloated, that Ernest eventually gave up, setting an idling course for one of the remaining piers where they might be able to tie fast. In time, they both stopped flinching at the sound of the *Pilar's* bow bumping bodies.

5

Hector and Hem were both covered in sweat and each had vomited in front of the other several times. Their stomachs were empty now and they'd tied strips of their own shirts around their mouths. They had poured rubbing alcohol and coffee and any other pungent thing they could find across the surface of the fabric tied around their faces — anything that might meet or overmatch the smell of decay from the victims strewn around the Key. Eventually someone had handed them gas masks.

Their gloves were slick with blood and puss from the bodies they'd been handling. The stench was made worse by the rotting carcasses of the big birds and scavengers that might have been consuming the corpses if the birds themselves hadn't also fallen prey to the killer wind.

The Atlantic had swept over the Key for hours, and deep inland were the stinking, deposited remains of octopi and tarpon and barracuda…the twisted knots of dead moray eels and the remnants of Spanish mackerel, now being picked at by the surviving land crabs. The trees had been stripped of all their foliage.

The bodies had swollen so much in the sun that in several cases the seams of their dungarees had given way. Many of the dead were entirely naked, their clothes stripped away by the wind, and the portions of their nude bodies that had faced into that

wind looked like lovingly polished and posed skeletons in a muse-
um — everything scoured cleanly down to ivory-colored bone.

His voice cracking, Hem pointed to the bodies of two naked
women hanging in a tree and said, "Like something out of Bruegel
or Bosch," he said, "if Bruegel or Bosch had ever truly seen hell."
The women were twisted in the trees, their bodies swollen to twice
natural size. Their breasts were red and mottled and looked ready
to burst. Flies swarmed between their legs. Hem said, "They used
to run the sandwich shop over by the ferry. I liked them."

About 4 p.m., Hector found the first body of a
child...presumably the daughter of one of the vets who'd brought
his family down to the Keys to live with him.

Hector crawled off on all fours to try to vomit again, but there
was nothing left, not even bile. He felt Hem's naked hand on his
shoulder. "Come on, Hec. We've done enough." Hector nodded,
struggling up to his knees. Hem offered him a gloved hand and he
pulled Hector up to him.

"It's too much," Hector said.

"It is," Hem agreed, pulling back on his other glove. "It's like
you said the other day. Some things are too true to be good for the
purposes of fiction. But I mean to write about this...journalistically.
Ram it down that invalid President of ours goddamn throat."

Hector nodded, then frowned. A few yards away, behind a
stand of mangrove, he saw a shack, sheltered on three sides by
accumulated sand. The wind seemed to have been directed over
and around the shack by the storm-fostered sandbars.

Hem said, "Just in case, we should look in." He nodded back
over his shoulder in the direction of the dead young girl. "Maybe
this is where she came from, or was headed."

Hector said, "Just what I was thinking."

But it wasn't like that.

As bad as the rest had been — and it had been worse than
what they found in the shed — the sight Hector beheld in the
shack was the most appalling of all to him.

Later he would decide it was worse than the rest because this had not been an "act of God" or capricious nature.

The shack also smelled of death, and Hector could hear the flies buzzing inside before they even opened the door.

Standing back from the rough-hewn door, Hector edged it open with his work boot. There were two female bodies inside.

One was stretched out on a cot by the door. The woman was dark-haired and nude, and her body had been gutted. Her organs lay haphazardly discarded next to the cot. Inside the woman's torso, someone had tucked stray pieces of metal...discarded hand tools and fishing lures.

Hem said, "Just like the other, by the lighthouse."

"Yes and no," Hector said, breathing through his mouth and biting back his bile. "This is sloppy. Like somebody's first draft." He pointed at the other body. "Just like that one." The second body was also that of a nude woman, dangling from her wrists by a rope tossed over an exposed rafter. The woman was dirty blond, and her belly had been slashed open at the navel. Into the ragged incision, someone had tucked a dozen red roses, now wilted and browning.

Hem, wincing and pointing at the second woman said, "That another allusion to some fucking surrealist piece?"

"Yeah," Hector said. "Salvador Dali. *Les roses sanglantes.*"

"*The Bleeding Roses,*" Hem said softly.

"Just so." Hector frowned, his eyes searching the mottled thighs of the woman stretched out on the cot. Hector edged closer, his left hand held over his nose and mouth. He beat away the flitting flies with his right hand. He said:

"*Fuck!* No...!"

On the upper, inner portion of the dead woman's left thigh, just above the knee, was the distorted tattoo of a red heart.

Hector realized he was sitting down when Hem said, "Christ, you okay?" and helped him to his feet again. Hem said, "What is it, Lasso?"

"That tattoo — it's Beverly…Rachel's missing friend." Hector turned on heel, shrugging off Hem's hands. "I've got to get back to Key West. Tonight. Right now."

"Mistakes are almost always of a sacred nature.

Never try to correct them. On the contrary:

rationalize them, understand them thoroughly.

After that, it will be possible for you to sublimate them."

— SALVADOR DALI

CHAPTER 13

BLEEDING ROSES

IT SEEMED LIKE the whole of Bone Key's population was waiting on the docks as the *Pilar* idled back into harbor. The whole town, or so it seemed to Hector, was awaiting the verdict of the island's legendary man of letters…every man and woman ready to hang on each of Papa Hemingway's words about what he'd seen north of Key West.

Josie presumed to jump on board the *Pilar*. "It's not looking good here," he said. "Poor fucking Tito…they found his boat half-submerged over on the East End. When they towed it in, they found him drowned in the hold. Poor luckless rummy."

Hector felt freshly stricken. Josie seemed to have forgotten that Hector had banished the "poor rummy" to the far side of Bone Key to minimize the danger of him crossing paths with Rachel after Hector had used the one-eyed Cuban to finesse Rachel into his bed.

The fry-cook from the Electric Kitchen stepped on board behind Josie. He said, "Can't find my damned dog. And Karen's now among the missing."

Hector nodded distractedly. He said, "Hem, I've got to—"

"*Go.* I know." Hem slapped his back. "I'll check in with you in a bit, Lasso. My best to Rachel. And, Lasso, thanks for riding shotgun."

Hector licked his lips and nodded. "Sure. But I've gotta fly."

ↄ

Hector sprinted across the Key. When Rachel didn't open the door at his knock or to the sound of his voice, he fished his back-up key from a hook hidden behind a shrub to the left of the front door, just above the frost line.

Hector keyed himself in, calling again to Rachel. He was unsettled by the silence of his house.

He walked back to his bedroom and found the bed made…the drapes opened. But Rachel's bags were gone. Her travel trunk was missing.

Shaken now, Hector wandered back into the living room. He sniffed, scenting death on himself. But there wasn't time for a shower. He looked around, then narrowed his eyes. There was a fresh sheet of paper in his Underwood.

Hector was certain he'd left the typewriter empty.

A note had been typed and left in the machine:

```
Dear Hector:
   Sorry, my love, but word finally came from
Beverly.
   She is, she wires, on Tavernier, recovering
from injuries sustained in the storm.
   Her "friend," a Mr. Vale, is to meet me at
the ferry in a few minutes and take me to her.
   I'll get back down to Key West in a few days,
when I know Beverly is on the mend.
   Until then.

                                      Love,
                                      Rachael
```

Hector bit through his lip — that goddamned extra *a* in Rachel! He was tingling all over, could feel his pulse in his ears.

The doorbell rang, then emphatic pounding. "Hector, it's Papa...open up dammit!"

Walking clumsily backward, in a daze, Hector stumbled toward his door and said, "It's unlocked."

Hem stepped in...Sheriff Jack Dixon followed. Both men looked ashen. Hem said, "Hector, uh..."

"We found a body," Sheriff Dixon said. "It's a woman, nude, chained to a pier down at Negro Beach. She's, or she was, blond. We know that from her pubic hair."

Hem grabbed the sheriff's arm, holding up a hand to shush him. "It's exactly like what we found on Matecumbe, Hector. *The Bleeding Roses*. The woman's belly has been slit and a bouquet thrust in there. Only difference is, this woman's head is missing."

"We saw the rough draft," Hector said in a daze. "He's refining his craft. The killer is no longer content to copy the Masters...now he's executing elaborations on themes."

"The murdered woman," Jack Dixon said, looking bewildered, "well, she had no distinguishing characteristics...no birthmarks or blemishes. And, without a head... But we did find a purse discarded nearby, with some identification." The sheriff held out his hand with the missing finger. Something glittered in his mutilated hand. "We also found this...on her wrist. The only thing she was wearing."

Hector recognized Rachel's bracelet — his last gift to her. He heard himself scream.

Hem grabbed him tight. "I fucking led the cocksucker to her," Hector shouted. "I sent that bloody bastard a telegram telling him just where to find Rachel!"

The elder author held Hector tightly to him as the crime writer's misdirected rage and blows to Hem's back softened to sobs and then to shaking.

Several minutes later, Hector shook loose from Ernest's embrace. He staggered into the bathroom and splashed cold water on his face. The writer considered his hated face in the mirror, and then he smashed the glass with his fist.

Hector contemplated his distorted image in the fractured mirror.

His first work of surrealist art.

PART TWO

THE GOOD FIGHT

(1937)

"Man is, above all,

the plaything of his memory."

— ANDRÉ BRETON

CHAPTER 14

SPAIN IN FLAMES

THEY WERE DRIVING back from the front to their hotel — a disturbingly short distance.

The ground shook under their Jeep from the concussion of the shell strikes behind them. The film director and cameraman had gone ahead in a lorry; Hector, Hem and Dos were in the first of four trailing Jeeps.

"Fucking parched," Hem said. "What have you got, Lasso?" It was cold and Hem's breath trailed frostily from his mouth as he called out over the rumble of the Jeep's engine.

Hector rooted around through his knapsack and pulled out two bottles. "What's your pleasure, 'Stein? Whisky, or whiskey?"

"Let's go with the top shelf stuff," Hem said. Hem twisted off the cap and tossed it over his shoulder into the dust plume of their wake. "Now we're committed." He took a long pull and handed the bottle back to Hector, who took a deeper drink and then passed the whisky to Dos, who was sitting up front.

"Bless those fucking crafty Scots," Hem said. He dragged his sweater's sleeve across his mouth. Hem pulled off his dusty glasses, wiped them clean, then put them back on, tucking the curled arms of his wire-rimmed glasses behind each ear. "Some good stuff we got today, yes?" The Jeep lurched as they bumped up and off the dirt path and onto pavement, climbing the last hill to their hotel.

Hem had arrived in Madrid in early April as a North American Newspaper Alliance correspondent. Now he was also working with the Dutch filmmaker Joris Ivens to film a documentary — really a propaganda film — entitled *The Spanish Earth*. Hem and company were angling to use the film to raise American money to support the Republicans standing against the fascist insurgency of Francisco Franco.

Ernest was still working under the auspices of a correspondent's visa for the NANA. He had set up in the Hotel Florida — a too-short traipse from the front and within occasional striking distance of the Nationalists' artillery fire. The top floors of the hotel had been abandoned and lay mostly in ruins.

Nevertheless, a motley array of journalists, military advisors, dissolute bullfighters, soldiers-of-fortune and camp followers had set up in the surviving, lower floors of the hotel…a place to retreat from the front to sleep, eat, drink, write and fuck working girls and girlfriends.

Dos — slope-shouldered, pot-bellied and bald — handed the bottle back over his shoulder to Hector as they rolled to a stop by the shelled-out Hotel Florida. "Home again, home again, jiggedy-jig," Dos sing-songed.

"Home again, home again to fuck a fat pig, you Portuguese bastard," Hem said, surly.

The writers staggered out of the Jeep and Hector stowed his unopened bottle in his rucksack. He held the opened Scotch whisky in his left hand by the bottle's neck. With his free hand, he brushed dust off his leather jacket and corduroy slacks and ran a hand back through his hair, now, like Hem's, graying at the temples and along the nape of his wind-burned neck. Hem's hairline was continuing to recede. Hector was holding onto his hair, at least so far.

Bald Dos, still smarting from Hem's barb, said dully, "What'll it be tonight, boys?"

"Figure we'll gather in Hec's room for some more Scotch, say about four," Hem said. "Then, properly fortified, we'll head over to Casa Botín. Got some old acquaintances — loved and unloved — to meet up with. So until then…"

Hector shook his head: Hem was off to his own front with lusty young Martha Gellhorn.

Dos and Hector walked into the Hotel Florida together, stepping wide around some fresh rubble that had fallen from the increasingly decimated upper floors of the hotel. The smell of cordite and blasting powder and the sharp scent of violently upchurned clay-heavy earth permeated Madrid. Smoke seemed to drift through the streets, all day and all night, blown from elsewhere in the city — from some fresh devastation somewhere.

The writers walked the long, dimly lit corridor to Hector's room, 107, and deposited their bags on the floor. Hector fetched two glasses and poured more single malt for Dos and himself. Dos drank some of that and said, "He's becoming unbearable…at least to me."

Hector shrugged off his leather jacket and draped it over the back of a chair. "I know. But those who don't know Hem like we do think he's marvelous. They think he's exuding 'grace under pressure.' They think he's a good man to have around when the chips are down. And that's true enough, so far as it goes. But *Jesus*, we know it's been a downhill slide for Hem since his old man shot himself. That old bastard's selfish death may well have doomed our Hem."

Dos nodded slowly and said, "Hem says something similar about you, you know. Hem claims you've never overcome the death of that woman a couple years back…Rachel?"

"Rachel Harper." Hector shrugged. "I'm soldiering on, just fine, Dos. And anyway you slice it, near as I can tell, Hem didn't drive his father to suicide. And even if he had in some way, the final decision to put the revolver to his head and tug the trigger was nobody's decision but sick old Clarence Hemingway's. Rachel was different, Dos. Rache was an innocent who got killed because I got cute playing 'last-tag' with some killer who I never even laid an eye or a fucking glove on. I'm culpable in her death, every inch of the way. But that's history." Hector drank more whiskey and said, "Any new word on Robles?"

José Robles was a friend and translator of Dos Passos'. They'd known one another since 1916.

Dos, the committed social activist, had been among the vanguard of American writers and intellectuals to rush to Spain. Dos had arrived for the first time many months before, well ahead of Papa, and that was still a sore point between Hem and Dos.

Robles was a professor — an instructor at John Hopkins — and a Loyalist. But the Soviet "advisors" had gained control of the Madrid front in late December of the previous year and someone — some kind of "secret police" — had arrested Robles on unspecified charges. Robles' fate and whereabouts were still a mystery.

"No word," Dos said, somberly, "but I keep asking. I'll *keep* asking, Hector, consequences be damned, until I have my answers." Dos drained his drink and set it on the table next to Hector's typewriter. Weak-eyed, Dos pulled on thick glasses and read a few paragraphs there and said, "This is damned fine stuff, Hec. A bloody good beginning."

"I've got plenty of bloody good beginnings, Dos. It's the finishings I'm having trouble with, lately."

"But this is fiction, Hector. Not genre stuff. It's swell to see you're getting back in the swing — and reaching farther."

"It *is* crime fiction, Dos. If you actually read *good* crime fiction you'd know that."

"Okay. But you're not writing about this...?" He gestured at the window and presumably what lay beyond it.

Hector said, "Hell *no*. I'm no political animal. You know that. As regards subject matter, I have my rails and I run on 'em. And so far as Hem is concerned, the Spanish Civil War is his and his alone to write about. And his conversion to a political animal is startling. Guess I saw the first signs of that after the hurricane in '35. He wanted to personally kill FDR for what happened to the vets."

"Well *you* should at least feign some interest, or express some opinions about the conflict here," Dos said. "I mean it Hector, the paranoia runs thick in these parts. People are already talking about you. You're not here on a correspondent's VISA. You're not fighting...not attached to the Abraham Lincoln Brigade. And you also have an anti-FDR reputation that makes some think you are a mean-streaked conservative."

"Those are people who didn't or don't live on Key West," Hector said. "The ones who don't know what the New Deal has done to that island. It's ruined, now."

"Sure, for an isolationist like you. FDR made it accessible to the masses. That's what you hate. And Hem, too." Dos shook his head. "I guess what I'm really saying is, some people are beginning to talk here about you, Hector...to wonder about you. Some think that you're a spy, here on our government's nickel, snooping around for J. Edgar and the Republicans back home."

Hector shrugged. "I *am* here as a spy and that's no lie. I'm spying for Pauline on that son of a bitch Hem and that roundheels journalist he's screwing." Hem was deeply mired in a dubious love affair with a younger "journalist" and sometimes fiction writer named Martha Gellhorn. Martha was a pretty, strawberry-blond Midwestern woman with a foul mouth, extreme nicotine addiction and equally strong activist streak. Hem seemed drawn to the Spanish Civil War primarily by his lust for Gellhorn.

Hector had been in Madrid just under a week. He was still trying to get his bearings and, at the same time, growing increasingly eager to clear out. Hector had come to Spain because he was adrift.

He had also come at the urging of Pauline Hemingway, who wanted her husband protected from his own increasingly reckless self and kept away from randy Martha to whatever extent Hector could arrange to do that.

Two days in, Hector had determined the Hemingway marriage was doomed.

But Hector was equally sure that any union with Martha would be just as star-crossed and probably infinitely more turbulent. It didn't help that Martha was also the first of Ernest's women who was younger than Hem, and by several years. She was independent, feisty and a writer with her own streak of talent and ambition.

Martha embodied all of the things that Hem thought he wanted in a woman and that Hector knew Hem didn't need.

But you couldn't talk to Hem about any of that...Hector knew that, too. And Hector considered himself in no convincing position to dole out advice. Hector's own drinking was out of control. He smoked too much and stayed up too late.

At thirty-seven, he had several crime novels and scads of short stories under his belt. But after Rachel, and after the surprising success of *Wandering Eye*, Hector had found it impossible to find his next novel...starting and stopping a dozen different books...sometimes a chapter in, sometimes two-hundred or three-hundred pages along.

To keep himself in the money, Hector had been whoring in Hollywood to increasing extent...writing screenplays or polishing dialogue for various crime and mystery movies by lesser writers. He'd bedded rising and promiscuous young starlets and begun scouting possible West Coast second homes.

Dos winked. "Hem's being just discreet enough with Martha that some could dispute that charge."

"Right." Hector held a hand over his head. "I'm fucking up to here with Martha and her goddamn Bryn Mawr drone."

"Ditto,'" Dos said. "She clearly hates me. Well, I know you're here for your own reasons, Hector...for Pauline, sure, but also just to keep yourself stimulated, I suppose. But this isn't Key West, Hec. This isn't Chicago back in Prohibition. Not Cleveland during the bootleg wars. This is the dress rehearsal for Hitler and the next big war and it's treacherous as hell, Hec. You best step careful. Really, buddy, I don't want to be asking around after two disappeared friends."

Hector held up his whisky, turning the glass in the low light. "I'll be careful as cowardly mice, Dos — honest Injun. See you tonight, pal."

Dos left and Hector sat on the bed a time, drinking more whisky. His drunkeness hit him all at once…this stomach-churning sensation that the room was spinning.

It was an unwelcome, too-familiar sensation…actually tiresome, to his surprise.

Hector thought, *I don't want to do this anymore.*

He put a foot on the floor to impede the sensation of spinning. When that tactic soon failed him, Hector struggled up onto unsteady feet.

He shrugged back on his leather aviator's jacket. Hector looked at his unfinished drink, then opened the window and poured the expensive whisky into the dust.

It was funny how something just turned off inside him. He thought, *No more tears…no more beers.*

5

Chicote's management had piled sandbags along the side of the restaurant facing the front — heavy bags stacked flush with Hector's belt buckle.

The waiter recognized Hector — a fringe benefit perhaps of hanging with Hem and Hector's own penchant for over-tipping. The concierge led him to a table just inside the door, next to a partially barricaded window. A few, side-choosing "journalists" at adjacent tables eyed Hector, with intent, he thought.

He ordered iced-tea and a bowl of gazpacho. The cold soup and colder drink came quickly, and Hector sat ladling scoops of the peppery, vinegary soup into his mouth…at first savoring the tangy stew and then finding himself adding more and more drops of Tabasco and stirring them in. He just couldn't get it spicy enough to suit his tastes.

As he ate, Hector thought about what Dos had said about the loose talk regarding Hector and the suspicion on the part of some others that he had come to Spain as a spy. That suspicion wasn't to be taken lightly…Hector knew that. Several other American writers and college professors who presumably raised the hackles of the communists underwriting the loyalists were "disappearing" with accelerating ferocity, just like Dos' missing friend.

In the current charged climate, wagging tongues could kill.

Hector sipped more of his iced-tea, feeling sobriety return in steady increments. Finished with his soup, he ordered a double espresso. That sent him lurching back toward hand-shaking sharpness.

Wired, he sat up a bit straighter to see over the stacked sandbags on the other side of the window…people watching.

I should find a woman, Hector told himself.

That was the ticket — find some dark-haired, dark-eyed Spanish beauty with gypsy blood and lusty impulses.

A woman who would claw his back in passion. Hector suddenly craved a lover who would draw blood…and he promised himself he would savor her assaults, sober and clear-eyed.

Yes, that was what Hector needed — Hector needed a woman.

Outside, a cab slowed for a light.

A woman was in the backseat, her head turned away from Hector.

Hector saw short, sharply cut chestnut-colored hair and a defined jawline…the long promising curve of a slender neck.

The woman turned, looking incuriously at the façade of Chicote's.

Their eyes met. She stared back at him.

Hector felt this chill and then a terrible tremor of recognition. He said aloud, "*Rachel…*"

"Perhaps I am doomed to retrace my steps
under the illusion that I am exploring,
doomed to try and learn what I should simply recognize,
learning a mere fraction of what I have forgotten."

— ANDRÉ BRETON

CHAPTER 15

THE PERSISTENCE OF MEMORY

A KNOCK AT HIS DOOR: Ernest was alone.

"You're early, Hem," Hector said, closing and then locking the door behind his burly friend.

"Yeah? Well, I'm at a loss for diversions."

"Martha's afield, then?"

Hem nodded, pushing past Hector. "That's one way to put it." He beelined for the bedside table and scooped up a glass. He held it up to the light, grimaced, and poured himself three fingers of Highland malt from the bottle whose stopper he'd thrown away earlier. He added in a little water from the pitcher on the night-stand. "Martha has ambitions," Hem said. "I'll credit her that."

"Miss Gellhorn is archly ambitious," Hector said. "You should think hard about that."

Hem pointed at the bottle and one of the empty glasses. "You want?"

"Nah. I've drunk my fill for now."

"What do you mean about me thinking about Martha and her ambition, Hector?"

"She's a writer, Hem. She's got a lot of ambition, like you say.

She's young and passionate in every direction. The way we all are when we're young. But she's no *haus frau*, and, at the end of the day, you goddamn need a *haus frau*. You need a woman who'll bend to your whims, share your hobbies, give you structure and room to write. Martha offers none of those qualities. Not a damned one."

Hem shrugged. "I didn't fucking ask for that assessment. You think I don't know you're here, at least partly, because Pauline shamed you or begged you into coming? I know you're here to keep an eye on me…to report back."

Hector smiled crookedly and slumped down on the foot of his bed. "Everyone thinks I'm a spy."

"It's no joke. It's being talked about, Lasso. Dos raised the issue the other night. He doesn't believe it any more than I do — these notions you're here for the FBI. But others believe it well enough. You need to go home, Hec. Yesterday."

"I think so too. And I mean to do just that, and soon. But something has come up. I need to look into something first."

Hem wasn't hearing him; still focused on himself. "It's been over between me and Pauline for a long time, Lasso."

Hector nodded softly. "Yeah. And near as I can tell, from the outside looking in, it was never really there, Hem. I was there in Paris and Spain in '26 and '27. I saw."

"And you took Hadley's side," Hem said. "I remember. Should have fucking listened to you. But goddamn Dos…he led to Gerald Murphy…Murphy led to Pauline. Those rich bastards egged me on. Fucking Dos. Fucking pilot fish."

Hector's memory of all that was quite different from Hem's. Hector said, "Either way, now you have the life you have. And listen to me now. The life you have in Key West is better, or at least more stable, than anything Martha offers you. You didn't ask and you may tell me to fuck off for volunteering this, but my best advice to you, Hem, is that you throw yourself into this Civil War, here. Get all you need for a novel or a story and while you do that, you go right ahead on and fuck that tall blond out of your system. Fuck her and your own brains out. Then you get your ass back to Key West and your life there, Hem. Your problem, in so far as I can see it, is that you feel duty-bound to marry every woman you take to your bed. For you, love and sex are synonymous. Well, you need to disabuse yourself of that notion. Stop being a last-century man."

Hem poured himself another drink. "If any woman heard you say that, you'd never get a piece of ass again in this lifetime, Lasso."

Hector shook his head. "You're using yourself as a yardstick for all women, everywhere. And there are the things we know and the things we say. Remember? Some things are too real to use or to state. I remember a night in Paris, in '24, Hem. We were at Stein's salon, three-sheets-to-the-wind. You said something and I thought it was maybe the most honest statement of longing that I've heard from another man. I still think so. You said for you, heaven would be an enormous bullring with your own private trout stream running alongside and two houses close by — one with your beloved wife and children, the other with your nine mistresses. You thought there would be a good church between the two so you could confess while moving between houses. I thought that was a raw and real expression of an honest man's mind."

"Your mind maybe. Lasso, now who's using himself as yardstick for all the rest?"

"No good can come from this affair, Hem, not carried beyond this fucked-up country."

"You said something has come up…something that might delay your leaving here. What is it, Lasso?"

Hector guessed they were done talking about Martha Gellhorn. He said, "I saw a woman today. I know it sounds crazy, and her hair was different. But I swear to Christ, Hem, I'm sure I saw Rachel Harper this afternoon."

Hem hesitated, his glass halfway to his mouth. He shook his head and sighed. He poured himself some more whiskey. He took a shot of his single malt. "Dark fucking waters, this," he said, hoarse from the whisky.

That got Hector's attention.

Hem said, "I didn't bring it up because Madrid is crazy now — crowded and under fitful siege — and the odds of you two crossing paths seemed at best, remote. So of course you went and promptly fucking saw her. I know who you saw, but she's not Rachel. It's her sister, Hector. The woman is named Alva Taurino. She's Rachel's kid sister. I met her at a fundraiser a few weeks back. Smart lady…very serious. She's a dead-ringer for—" Hem made a face. "Sorry, bad phrasing. What I mean is, she's Rachel's sister to the nines. Darker — I mean the hair. She wears it short, too. But she's beautiful, just like Rachel was. A painter, too. Damned fine painter, if a little uninspired. I mean in terms of originality. But the execution is flawless."

Wringing his hands, Hector said, "Rachel mentioned this sister. Vaguely remember that name, Alva, too. Last name is a married name, I guess."

"Married to a college professor. Or she was. He went to arms for the Republic. He was killed last fall, or so she says."

"In combat?"

"Presumed captured and shot by Franco's bunch. Cocksuckers."

"She know about me? About me and Rachel?"

Hem drank more whisky. "Yeah. I don't think she's bitter or blames you, really. That said, I mentioned you'd be coming to Spain." He hesitated. "She didn't ask for an audience or even an introduction."

"Who could blame her?" Hector pulled up a chair close to the bed and sat down across from Ernest. "Hem, can you reach her? Invite Alva to Casa Botín tonight. Tell her I'd very much appreciate meeting her. To perhaps talk about her sister. I'll pay her way."

"You shouldn't chase ghosts."

"I'm not doing that. I'm just...closing accounts. Maybe, meeting her, I can—"

Hem quickly held up a hand. "Stop. Don't you fucking ever finish a sentence that trite."

"Sorry. But for Christ's sake, just get her there tonight."

"I can try, Hector. Can't guarantee she'll say yes, or if she does, that she won't put one between your eyes or behind your ear when she sees you. I just can't read this one. And I can't predict her attitude toward you when you meet."

"My problem, Hem. Not your concern. I want this. You're fully absolved of the consequences."

"I fucking wish it was ever that easy. But I'll try to lure her there tonight."

"Thanks. You succeed, and I'll owe you large."

"There's a fucking true sentence. And I do this, Hec, then after, you go home, yes? You go back to Key West. Tell Pauline whatever you want when you get there. But you get out of here before you end up shot or arrested by the son-of-a-bitching Communists. My bench of good old friends is getting sorrily shallow, Hec. Partly through my own fault, sure, but partly through bad luck, too. And your luck, Lasso? From where I sit, she's not running good these years."

"Agreed," Hector said. "I'll go home. But you also have to agree that you'll think about what I've said about Martha and the future."

"I'll think about it," Hem said. "You know me, Lasso — I'm a thinking fool."

"An original is a creation motivated by desire.

Any reproduction of an original is motivated by necessity.

It is marvelous that we are the only species

that creates gratuitous forms.

To create is divine, to reproduce is human."

— MAN RAY

CHAPTER 16

DOPPELGANGER

THE HUM of a hundred passionate, politically-charged conversations…clattering silverware and dirty dishes being gathered up to be bused back to the kitchen…corks being pulled.

The haze of cigarette smoke and the thick smell of wine and garlic burned Hector's eyes.

At the back of the restaurant, their own backs to the kitchen, a couple of gypsy folk musicians were performing, trying to be heard over the crowd. The man played piano; his partner, a woman, played the mandolin. The woman wore a ragged shawl and a scarf. It looked as if her hair had been recklessly cut down to the scalp. She was singing "Ring of Bone."

Hector first spotted Hem, his usual boisterous public self…laughing and talking and then pausing to accept an offered bota bag from someone at an adjacent table — perhaps from a dissolute and idled young bullfighter.

Hem held up the wineskin and shot some wine into his own mouth. Then, holding it higher, he squirted some more in the direction of Dos, who was clearly very drunk. Dos tried to dip his head to catch the wine in his mouth. Some went there, but most stained Dos' white shirt, making him look like someone had shot him in the heart.

Hem saw Hector, but stopped himself from calling out when Hector put his fingers to his lips as he approached the table. Hector stood behind a woman with a long, slender neck, proud shoulders and short-cut, dark brown hair. The woman said in a soft, clear, alto voice, "Of course the question remains, is it blood sport, or is it a form of art?"

She said this last to a blond man who also had his back to Hector.

The blond man said, "Of course it is a form of art, but built on a tragic model. The odds are all stacked against the bull and that precludes the possibility of any 'sport,' regardless of whether or not the occasional matador falls or spills his own blood. We have the layers of time-tested ritual and routine calculated to break down the bull…to bleed him…to weaken him. And then, at the last, to position him for the kill. But I'd liken it to a form of musical or theatrical art, rather than that of painting, or, as Hem tried to have it in his *Death in the Afternoon*, to writing. We have the three great movements: *los tres tercios de la lidia* — the so-called 'thirds of combat.' The first act is *suerte de varas*. This is when the bull first charges. Perhaps there will be the *achuchón*, when the bull actually bumps the man while passing by him, but it's as close as most bulls come to ever truly striking their nemesis. Then there is act two, *tercio de banderillas*, or the placing of the banderillas — stabbed into the muscles of the bull's neck — further breaking him down and forcing his head into the lowered position for the eventual kill. Act three is the actual death of the bull, *tercio de muerte*, itself divided into three smaller acts: the toast of the president, the use of the muleta or cloak, and then the final killing thrust of the sword, dropping the bull where it stands. It's not about the combat, or the risk to the man — it's an artistic ritual keyed to the death of the bull. It goes all the way back to Greece and the Minotaur."

Hector suddenly placed the blond man's voice. The *son of a bitch* — Quentin Windly...the critic turned evident *aficionado*.

It wasn't the best way to make a first impression — particularly on Alva Taurino. But Hector couldn't stay his tongue — a part of him still suspected that Quentin might have been the one killing all those women in the Keys two years before. The man who maybe murdered Rachel. Hector had gone looking for Quentin in the wake of the hurricane and Rachel's death...eventually picked up rumors of the critic having drifted down into Mexico, but nothing strong enough to allow Hector to follow at the time.

Hector said, "Now who's talking a lot of bull, Quentin?"

The critic looked up at Hector and frowned. The critic's nose was bent severely leftward. Hector smiled meanly — he thought it lent character to the bastard's formerly too-pretty face.

Hem said, "Lasso, it's swell you're here!" He stood up quickly and walked around the table and grabbed Hector's arm, pulling him away from Quentin. Hem held another hand out to the dark-haired woman now staring curiously up at Hector.

Hector realized that his lips were dry and his heart pounding. Jesus, but the woman looked like a brunette version of Rachel.

Hem pulled her to her feet and said, "I have another table reserved over here." He pulled Hector and Alva along. Hem signaled a waiter who rushed over with a bottle of Rioja Alta. Three generous glasses were poured. Hector was already determined to nurse his. Yet he felt his hand nervously stray to the stem of his wineglass. He thought, *Old vices, like whores, die hard.*

Hector couldn't take his eyes off Rachel's near twin.

Hem said, "Alva Taurino, this is my best and most trusted friend, Hector Lassiter — the best man to have at your back in any fight."

That was laying it on well beyond thick, but Hector was grateful for Hem's over-the-top endorsement. Hector held out a hand and the woman took it and shook it lightly. An indifferent handshake, but she was candidly sizing him up. She said, "Thanks for all you did for Rachel in Florida, Mr. Lassiter. For seeing her through the hurricane. For trying to help Rachel with the matter regarding her friend. And for all you went through as a result of knowing my sister."

"You know about the hurricane and her murdered friend, then?"

"Partly from Mr. Hemingway. Also from a letter Rachel wrote me…evidently the day she…well, you know. She was terribly fond of you." Alva sipped her wine and then unclasped her purse. She pulled out a gunmetal cigarette case and slipped out a cigarette. Hector fished the pocket of his tweed sports jacket for his lighter. She narrowed her eyes as the inscription on his Zippo caught the low light. She reached out again and took his hand, turning it so she could read the words on his lighter. Hector savored her touch. She said, "You two really do go back."

Hem said, "All the way to the trenches of Italy. And I see my other guest is coming. I'll leave you two to talk…but don't be anti-social, children. We'll be expecting you back to the party soon. Enjoy the wine. *In vino veritas*, am I right, daughter?"

Hem rose, and limping slightly, he dodged waiters and tipsy patrons to meet and embrace a tall, strawberry-blond woman in a heavy, silver fox fur coat.

Alva said, "I've read some of your novels, since getting that last letter from Rachel. I enjoy them."

"Enjoy?"

"Maybe not the right word," she said, half-smiling. "I'm gripped by your novels and I appreciate them," she said.

"Hem says you're a painter."

"I try."

"Hem says you go well beyond that, and he knows art."

She shrugged, smiling and staring at him.

Resisting the urge to squirm, Hector said, "I was very sorry to hear about your husband. Not to be indelicate, but what's keeping you in Spain, now, as it is? You're an American…you can leave.

Certainly go somewhere safer than here, which is to say, anywhere."

"Spain has been home for many years," she said, pausing to sip more of her wine. "It feels like home in ways the States never did. And to leave now would be…" she searched for words. She finally said, "To leave now would not so much be cowardly, or selfish, but maybe akin to a failure of character and artistic nerve in some way. Many painters are here now. Or they are in spirit. The surrealists, particularly, are using their art to help the Republic. Picasso, Miro, Dali…many more artists in Barcelona. They're using their art to oppose Franco. Some of them are creating propaganda posters…placing veiled statements against fascism in their paintings, and perhaps doing that at great personal risk." She sighed. "You're frowning. You disapprove? You're against the Republic?"

Hector didn't need to further undermine his foundering reputation in Madrid's politically charged milieu. He said, "No, it's not like that at all. I'm just always a bit leery of artists who inject politics into their works. I'm maybe not qualified to speak as to painting or sculpture or theatre. But putting politics into prose — I mean fiction — well, it nearly always destroys the fiction. Art, if it's good, endures. But the politics of the moment, regardless how fiery or worthy, are the most transient things of all. At best, injecting politics into a novel dates it. At worst, it mutilates it."

Alva nodded slowly. "A legitimate concern in some ways. Particularly if legacy or broad commercial appeal is what really matters to you. Sometimes, you have to give yourself over to something greater than yourself, Mr. Lassiter. I've truly come to believe that. For example, I don't think a fascist government would ever countenance the kinds of books you write. Much as I admire them, or even enjoy them, they're not what I'd call edifying."

"I'm not sure I even know what that last word means," Hector said, smiling.

"I'm sure that's not so, Mr. Lassiter."

"Hector, please."

"Hector. You lay on that Texas accent when it serves you, but you're your own kind of smart."

"Right. And is that what you're doing? Using your art to help the Republic?"

"Yes. At least I hope that I am. I've painted several posters — recruitment posters…pleas for money and donations to help the Loyalist cause."

Hector hesitated, then said, "I just want to say now, before I forget or don't get the chance, that your willingness to meet with me this evening — and to be so, well, gracious and tolerant toward me — it means very much to me."

"Why? Do you feel some sense of guilt, Hector? Do you think I should bear you some grudge for what happened to Rachel?"

"No, but under similar circumstances, some others might, regardless of the facts."

"From all I know, you did all you could to help my sister and to protect her. The man who did this to her — whoever he may be — him I hate. I would kill him myself. But by now, he might also be dead. I wonder if he isn't. I mean, in the years since, have you heard of more killings like those that happened in Florida?"

"No. At least, not around there."

"Elsewhere?"

Hector realized he was staring at Quentin Windly. "No," he said softly. "No, I've heard of nothing like them."

That wasn't true. A year or so before, while working in Hollywood, Hector had shared a dinner with Orson Welles, an aficionado of Mexican bullfights. Orson had told Hector of a string of strange murders of men around Mexico City that some were whispering seemed to echo some of the works of Remedios Varo — one of the rare female surrealists.

"It was so strange, as Rachel described it in her letter…and as Mr. Hemingway has described it." Alva exhaled smoke and stubbed out her cigarette. "Those murders, I mean."

"They were sublime and diabolical," Hector said.

She gestured at his goblet. "You're not drinking your wine."

Hector was naked about it. He said, "It's starting to feel like a problem. So I'm trying to taper off…had quite a lot of whisky earlier today. You know the old Catalan gypsy proverb? 'The man takes the drink, then the drink takes the man.'"

Hemingway suddenly called, "Hector, one true sentence: 'A man truly alone—'"

"'—has no last words," Hector called back. For whatever reason, they were evidently being summoned back to the main table by Hem — their old game was the signal — but Hector didn't want to go there yet.

Hem said, "Not your worst effort. Your turn, Lasso."

Martha Gellhorn, sitting next to Hem, was watching Hector carefully — one of the ones who didn't trust him. He didn't sense Martha regarded him as Pauline's spy — she saw Sidney Franklin as that — but rather as a spy in the deadlier sense. Hector put away his Zippo. Meeting Martha's gaze, he said, "I'm afraid I'm flush out of true sentences, Hem."

Hector stood and said, "I'm going to take some air." He extended a hand to Alva. "You up for a stroll — get away from the noise for a time?"

Alva took his hand. "It's too cold just to walk, aimlessly. But there's a little café around the corner that makes excellent coffee."

"Then let's go there."

"Max Ernst died on the 1st of August 1914.
He resuscitated the 11th of November 1918
as a young man aspiring to become a magician
and to find the myth of his time."
— MAX ERNST

CHAPTER 17

RETIRADA

THEY STOPPED at the coat closet and Hector turned in his claim tag for his longer, sheepskin-lined leather overcoat that reached just below his knees. Alva turned in her own tag and was handed a heavy, worn-looking sweater — hardly enough against the chill. She frowned at Hector, who was staring at her sweater, holding it up for her as she turned to slip her arms through. "Money is scarce for a time," she said, her back to him now. "I've been modeling to make ends meet."

Hector took that wrong. He said, "You're quite beautiful — many magazines must be after you."

"Not that kind of modeling. It's life modeling, at the art school…and privately for painters and photographers. That work is chilly, too." Hector nodded slowly, closing her sweater around her. He shrugged off his leather coat and wrapped it around Alva's shoulders. The coat's hem nearly reached her ankles.

"It looks much better on you," he said.

"But you'll be cold," she said.

"You said it's a short walk."

They stepped out into the dark — the streetlights were all turned off to avoid giving the fascists any assistance in targeting for their nighttime bombardments. Alva started to take Hector's arm, then stepped around to his other side, taking his left arm. "Papa says you're also staying in the Hotel Florida."

They had to step around occasional expanses of rubble and everywhere broken glass lay under foot. Some of the shelled-out buildings' still-standing façades moved in the wind, creaking and spitting bricks…sending Alva and Hector into the darkened, empty street.

"I think most of us are there," Hector said. "It's like a hive, with all that implies."

"But they're shelling the hotel," Alva said. "It seems very dangerous, even self-destructive to stay there." Their breath trailed frostily behind them as they walked to the café.

"Actually, they only occasionally hit the hotel," Hector said. "I'm told they're really aiming for the telephone exchange."

Alva said, "That man back there…Quentin, the bullfight reviewer — or he was until the fights were suspended here for the war — you know each other? And you hate each other too? It seemed so from the looks of things back there."

"He was in Key West in '35," Hector said. "He also knew your sister, however briefly. I broke his nose."

She looked up at him, scowling. "He tried to take liberties with Rachel? Is that why you hit him?"

"It wasn't quite like that." Hector reached out with a stiff hand and grabbed the brass handle of the café's door, wincing at the burn of the cold metal. He guessed it would soon be below freezing.

There were relatively few people in the café, just two or three couples — some probable journalists who gave Hector the eye, then shifted attention to Alva, giving her the eye, but in a different way. Their leers didn't escape Alva's attention. She pulled

Hector's coat back over her shoulders, shrugging off a little chill. They found a table by a stone fireplace that dominated the center of the café. Hector ordered two espressos, then pulled out his cigarette lighter and last pack of Pall Malls — he hated European cigarettes and was still trying to decide what brand he'd settle for.

Alva pulled out her cigarette case and Hector lit her cigarette. She took his lighter from him and weighed it in her hand. "Papa's worried about you, you know. He says what happened in Key West nearly 'swamped' you. I'm so sorry for that."

"Not your fault."

"He's freshly worried, too. He says you 'have no politics.' That you're here to look after him at the behest of his wife. But he also says that because you haven't taken sides — at least not sides anyone can detect — that people are talking. They think you're a spy. The Spanish, depending on their own loyalties, think you're spying for Franco, or for the Republic. Your countrymen think you're spying for your government, or the FBI."

"I've heard. I'm here like Hem said — as a favor to his wife, and to see a little of this for myself. They say in four or five years, tops, we'll be in the thick of a world war against fascism. Some think maybe that wider conflict can be avoided if Franco is stopped here, now."

"Do you think that, Hector?"

"I think there'll be plenty of wars for a very long time for those who care to go to them."

"You should leave, like Papa says. One of these people who suspect you would only have to denounce you to the authorities or the secret police, Hector. You'd be hauled off…possibly tortured. Probably killed. Once they have you, and they work you over for a time, well, they can hardly release you back to your own government. They can't risk the scandal of having falsely imprisoned or tortured a foreign national."

"So they kill them instead?"

"Yes. Make them 'disappear.'"

Hector sipped his espresso, staring at the end of his cigarette. "Well, as it happens, I'm thinking of leaving in a couple of days. Time to get back to Key West…warm up. Get back in fighting trim, wrestling those big fish."

Alva smiled. "Rachel wrote that your island is beautiful. She wrote that it is like a curious mixture of the Left Bank and a frontier town."

"Sounds about right. At least it used to be that way."

She hesitated. "She loved you. Did you know that?"

Hector sat back in his chair. He took a deep breath, then said, "She didn't say it. We had just a few days together. I knew so little about her. She…well, she told me how it was with your father."

"That bastard. Sometimes I think of going to Los Angeles — he lives there now — and killing him myself. What he did to Rachel…"

"And to you?"

"He never touched me. I wouldn't let him."

Hector winced and took a deep breath. That implied Rachel hadn't fought their father's advances. Alva said, "Did you love her, Hector? Did you love Rachel?"

Hector didn't have to think about it. "Yes, I fell in love with her. I miss her still."

Alva almost looked stricken. She bowed her head. "Is that guilt for what happened, or real affection?"

"Truthfully? Both."

"Of course. And even more tragic." She looked back up at him, her eyes wet.

"How are you doing, Alva? Since your husband, I mean?"

"Coping. I paint…try to help the cause. I'm able to maintain our apartment, mostly with the modeling. I'm still not really making money on my own painting."

"You live close by? You have some of your works there?"

She nodded, narrowing her eyes.

"When we finish our coffee, I'd like to see your paintings," Hector said. "I collect, modestly, but I collect. I have a Picasso, some Harts…a Matisse. I should have a Taurino."

"An 'Alva,'" she said, smiling. "That's how I sign them. But you don't have any obligation—"

"Desire. Not obligation."

"Interesting choice of words, Hector. I—"

"Mr. Lassiter! It *is* you!"

This small little black-clad man, leaning heavily on a cane, limped over to the table. He took off his beret to reveal a bald scalp covered with liver spots. Hector remembered then: Bishop Blair, the surrealist painter.

He took the man's tiny hand and shook it. The grip was still weak, but, having just come in from the cold, Bishop's handshake was at least dry this time. Hector introduced Alva and the little man appeared shaken as he took her hand and raised its back to his mouth. He said, wonderingly, "You could be your sister, Mrs. Taurino."

Alva nodded. "Everyone has said so. Being younger, and inheriting her clothes, her teachers…her friends' younger sisters, well…" She ran a hand through her chestnut hair. "I kept my hair dark, though it wasn't ever enough to avoid confusion."

Hector remembered Rachel's longer, blond hair, and the hair between her legs that the sheriff had relied upon to help identify Rachel's body. The "collar and cuffs" had matched…attention to detail on Rachel's part, Hector guessed.

Hector pulled over a third chair and gestured for the little man to join them. He said, "And Mrs. Blair?"

"Harriet died fourteen months ago — a terrible stroke, that left her paralyzed…hardly able to speak intelligibly. She survived another three months, then had a second stroke that killed her — a massive brain hemorrhage. You know, for those last few months, she liked me to read to her. I reread all of your books to her, Mr. Lassiter, including your last one, *Wandering Eye*, which brought Key West back to both of us so vividly. They were a great entertainment and diversion for us both. I'm a fan now."

Hector smiled. "I liked Harriet. And when I saw you just now, I wondered what in God's name you're doing here."

"At first I came thinking to reinvent myself," Bishop said. "Or, at least to reinvigorate myself. Many of us are here…painting to make statements…painting to generate propaganda and support for the Republic. The fascists would never let us paint what we want. Neither would the communists. So we fight in our own way — through our art, to protect our art. We share a studio a few blocks from here. We paint there…posters, handbills…some pure art, as well. By that, I mean works that aren't directed toward overt propaganda."

Hector said, "Then you and Alva should talk. She's doing much the same thing."

The little man smiled at Alva and handed her a card. "Our studio's address is there. Come by. Please bring some samples of your work."

Hector said, "Why do it here, Bishop? Why not work from Paris? At your age, and with your reputation, why expose yourself to all of this risk?"

The little man pulled out a Puro and Hector lit the cigar for him with his Zippo. "There was an American writer many years ago, an Ohio journalist turned novelist," Bishop said. "He was old and felt the world was leaving him behind. So he went to Mexico — to revolutionary Mexico. His stated intent was to find and meet Pancho Villa, but he had a second, highly idiosyncratic agenda."

Hector ground out the stub of his cigarette and lit another. "I know who you mean. Ambrose Bierce. I was in Mexico a few years after and heard the story — when I was part of the Punitive Expedition, chasing old Pancho."

"Then you remember what Bierce wrote in his last note, Mr. Lassiter?"

"Vividly. 'To be a gringo in Mexico — ah, that is euthanasia!'"

Bishop Blair puffed and waved smoke from his face. "Exactly. That's also why I'm in Spain."

Alva said, "You must keep painting, Mr. Blair."

"I miss my Harriet," he said. "I painted for her. She was my real audience."

Hector said, "Alva's husband was killed by the fascists last year. She knows loss, too. She's right, we push on. We soldier on. Hand some back to this bloody fucking world as we can."

The little painter stood up and leaned again on his cane. "I didn't mean to intrude upon you two, but I thank you for allowing me to. And thank you again, Mr. Lassiter, for the joy your books gave my Harriet."

Hector rose and squeezed the man's arm in farewell. "Don't let the bastards get you down, Bish."

The little man smiled, unconvinced, then stumped off into the cold night.

Alva said, "You should take your own advice to that old man, Hector. Put what happened with Rachel behind you."

Hector drained his espresso. "Yeah. But I'm too often a do-as-I-say, not-as-I-do kind of fella."

"I am responsible only to God and history."

— FRANCISCO FRANCO

CHAPTER 18

THE DENUNCIATION

ALVA MOVED around her apartment with a flashlight and box of kitchen matches, turning on oil lamps. She took a couple of spindly pieces of scrap lumberyard wood from a small pile and tucked the stingy slats into the fireplace and bent to light them.

Watching her, Hector said, "Excuse me a moment. I'm going to run down to the corner...getting low on cigarettes."

When he returned she frowned. Hector's arms strained under a stack of fresh-cut planetree logs. He said, "Don't look at me that way. And there'll be another delivery tomorrow. Enough to see you into mid-May and the warmer weather. It's the least I can do." Smiling, ignoring her frown, he bent to her fireplace and put in three of the logs, positioning them over the smaller fire. The frost on the logs cracked and popped.

Alva moved closer. She knelt beside him, holding out her hands to the growing fire. "You really shouldn't have done this, Hector. But thank you — it feels wonderful. I think I may sleep on my rug here tonight, by the fire."

She went to a gramophone player and cranked it and set the needle down: "Ciaccona" from *Bach's Partita No. 2 in D Minor.*

Alva smiled and walked to the kitchen. She opened a bottle of wine, then shook her head. "I'm sorry — I forgot that you're no longer drinking."

"No, it sounds wonderful," Hector said. "I don't think of wine as liquor. Wine is wine." God, he was sounding like Gertrude Stein.

She smiled and poured him a glass, then said, "It's Algerian. Cheap, but good." She paused, then said, "Unless you'd like to run down to the corner for more cigarettes as pretense to perhaps buy a bottle of Rioja Alta."

"I said I'm sorry for the wood."

"And I said thank you."

They tapped glasses. He said, "To what?"

She pursed her lips and wrinkled her brow, thinking. "To art."

"Right." Hector sipped and began roaming her loft. The furniture was big and worn but inviting — suede couches draped with throws...worn leather armchairs. Big armoires and bookcases lined one wall. Hector saw several of his own novels there — English and Spanish translations. But there was nothing particularly masculine in the room — nothing that might have belonged to her husband. There was no sign of him, not even a photograph of the man. Hector understood the urge — put away every reminder of the lost love and wait for all that hurt to finally go away.

The remaining three walls of the loft were covered with paintings. Hector was awed by them. As Hem had said, there was something not quite original about any of them, but they were beautiful and Alva's execution was indeed flawless. They were all Cubist and surrealist works...many of them homages, or elaborations — responses — to the works of male artists. And as the male surrealists used women in their art, Alva just as often used men.

But Hector was drawn most strongly to her paintings of other women. And somehow, the women in those paintings all looked a little like Alva.

She said, "Be honest — what do you think?"

"I think they're exquisite," Hector said. "I see at least three I want for myself. I also have a friend from Paris, and the old days. Libby is living in Cannes now, and she has a gallery there. I'm going to alert her to your work."

"Then thank you again."

Alva had returned to the fireside, her back to the flames. Her legs were silhouetted through the careworn, back-lit fabric of her dress. She had long legs, like Rachel, though a bit thinner. But Hector suspected that food, too, was in short supply for the pretty young widow. Properly nourished, he thought Alva would be just as curvy as Rachel had been. But she seemed fit...a dancer's body and carriage.

She said suddenly, "Okay, all is *really* forgiven for the firewood. It's heavenly."

Hector smiled and moved next to her. "I love fireplaces. In Key West, we don't even have interior heating — rarely gets that cold. If it does, you just start stacking blankets on the bed...coats and other clothes."

They stood there a long moment, neither knowing what to say. Hector felt like he was hanging around. He asked himself what he wanted — an improbable invitation to spend the night? He wasn't yet sure that his feelings ran that way, and her resemblance to Rachel was so pronounced he wasn't sure bedding Alva wouldn't be more unsettling than satisfying.

He could talk to her for hours, he figured, but Alva seemed tired...mellow past the point of small talk.

Hector made a show of checking his pocket watch and sighed. "I should head back. Hem will be bitter if I don't at least show up in time to let him think I helped him close the place down."

"Hem's still like a big, overgrown boy."

"Still?"

"I've always gotten that sense of him from his books and articles," Alva said. "And in person, despite his age, he comes across as strangely boyish at times."

Hector suddenly wondered if, at thirty-seven, he also came across as "boyish." Rachel had characterized him to be at least nearly so two years before.

He checked his watch again. He really needed to shove off. When Hector had suggested his leaving, Alva hadn't tried to talk him out of it and that fact wasn't lost on him. But Hector didn't want to leave without some kind of a commitment for another rendezvous. He said, "I'd like to buy you breakfast…discuss terms for those three paintings of yours that I want to buy."

She smiled. "Have you found a place that's good for breakfast?"

"Anywhere I set off to, I seem to end up at Chicote's. Say, nine?"

"Nine tomorrow morning it is." She hugged him chastely and gave him air kisses. "Thank you again for all you did — all you tried to do — for my sister. It's too bad for her it was too late, but Rachel found a very good man in you." She seemed very sad.

Hector smiled uncertainly and walked to the door. He saw his overcoat draped across the back of her couch but decided to leave it…to feign having forgotten it. It could serve as pretense for another visit. If the world didn't turn that way, Alva obviously needed it more than he did, anyway. Hector said, "Goodnight Alva."

ᘖ

Hector turned up the collar of his sports jacket and buttoned it across his chest. His eyes were already tearing and stinging from the cold. Snow was sifting softly down — already a thin cover of snow draped the rubble. His prospects of finding a cab during the sporadic, unpredictable night shelling appeared remote, so Hector began steeling himself for the long, cold walk back to the Casa Botín, or perhaps just back to his room.

Stamping his feet to keep warm, Hector shook loose another Pall Mall and lit it. As he closed his lighter, he heard engines gun and tires squeal.

Three trucks pulled alongside the curb and several men jumped out, holding rifles and handguns.

Hector's stomach rolled: Spanish Secret State Police. Some of them wore uniforms, but several were wearing long black leather coats and peaked black leather caps. Hector gestured with his cigarette at the black-clad men and said, "You boys look like ex-Cheka. You some of old Joe Stalin's flunkies?"

One of the uniformed men, a squat, thick-necked man with bad skin and a too-long moustache said in English, "You would do better not to joke, hombre, especially not to joke with those ones." He nodded at his black-clad comrades.

"Okay," Hector said. "What's going on here?" He already suspected the answer would be that he had been denounced. He could also guess who had done that denouncing. Hector's money was on Quentin Windly. The English-speaking policeman said, "You are Héctor Mason Lassiter of the Key West, Florida, yes?"

"That's right."

"I need your papers."

Hector made a show of patting his pockets. He fished some pocket change from his pant's pocket, gripping it in his right hand, then he acted as if he remembered and pulled his identification papers from the interior breast pocket of his sports jacket. With his left hand, Hector passed the policeman his passport. Then he took aim at one of the second-floor windows he guessed to be Alva's. With his right hand, Hector pitched the heavy coins at the glass.

His unexpected pitch drew the expected response: rifle barrels and Mausers were quickly trained on Hector's head and heart.

Somewhere, a dog barked.

A light came on in the window struck by the coins.

The window opened and Alva leaned out, frowning. In pitch-perfect Spanish she said, "What's going on? Why are you accosting my friend?"

"There has been an allegation," the big man who spoke English said. He responded to her question in Spanish. He said, "There has been a very serious allegation, *Señorita*." Hector also spoke fluent Spanish, but he didn't want the secret police to know that — at least not yet. If they took him into custody and didn't suspect he spoke their language, they might say something he could use to his advantage.

Other lights were coming on now in Alva's building. Other tenants were now peeking out their windows. When they saw it was the secret police, the neighbors quickly closed their windows or pulled shut their drapes. The citizens of Madrid lived in fear of nighttime visits of the secret police. The *madrileños* had even evolved a term for it: "The Knock of Death."

Alva said, "What is this allegation?"

"Murder, *Señorita*. Murder."

Now Hector was surprised, but he continued to play unilingual. He looked up at Alva, raising his hands in apparent confusion. Not that it took much acting: *Murder*?

"It's murder, Hector," Alva said.

Hector said, "Find out who's dead."

The policeman who spoke English said to Hector, loudly enough that Alva could also hear, "Many several. You go with us, now." He took Hector's arm and began pushing Hector toward one of the trucks.

Alva said, "Where are you taking him?"

"Seguridad headquarters. Unless he continues to provoke these others." He nodded at the men in black leather. "If he does that, then he may find himself in Lubyanka."

Alva looked stricken. She said, "I'll get word to Hem...he can call your embassy. I promise, Hector, I'll get help."

"That'd be real swell," Hector said.

One of the men in black coats punched Hector in the right

kidney, sending him to his knees, vomiting.

When he was finished being sick, three of the black-clad men grabbed Hector — two taking him under the arms, the other picking up his feet. They tossed him up and into the bed of the lead truck. They piled in behind him, taking seats along the sides of the truck and pointing their guns at Hector.

In agony from the kidney punch, Hector lay on the floor of the truck bed, nauseous and cold. In the distance he could hear the night shells coming over from the fascist side of the front. Sometimes he could hear the whine of the shell if it was passing close overhead, but each time, he could hear the concussion — some other part of Madrid blown to rubble...sending more smoke drifting through the ruined city.

Hector thought of José Robles and of Alva's missing husband.

He prayed he wasn't about to make it a trifecta.

"A great killer must love to kill;

unless he feels it is the best thing he can do,

unless he is conscious of its dignity and feels that it is

its own reward, he will be incapable of the abnegation

that is necessary in real killing."

— ERNEST HEMINGWAY

CHAPTER 19

MY ENEMY'S ENEMY...

THE CHIEF INTERROGATOR was dressed like a banker. At least he was dressed that way when he entered the room. He wore an old, well-cared-for business suit that was several seasons out of style. His thick gray moustache matched his hair, which was cut into a short, salt-and-pepper bristle. He wore wire-rimmed glasses.

He returned to Hector his nearly empty pack of Pall Mall cigarettes and the engraved Zippo lighter. "It's permitted to smoke while I change," the man said in English. "My advice is to savor this last cigarette."

Then the man walked to a cabinet, took off his suit coat, and hung it on a wooden hanger inside the cabinet. He next tugged off his tie and stripped off his shirt. He was wearing a T-shirt cut to expose his hairy shoulders and parts of his back. He kicked off his loafers, then slipped off his pants. Hector began to squirm. He got edgier when the interrogator said, "Hurry with the cigarette, please. When you finish, I'll need you to take off all of your clothes."

Two men were standing on either side of Hector. Each held a rifle pointed at Hector's head.

Not looking good.

The interrogator stepped into a bloodstained pair of overalls and shrugged the top on over his shoulders and then pulled the front zipper up from the crotch to his neck.

Stalling, Hector rubbed his burning kidney and said, "Was the beating really necessary? I was cooperating. If it'll keep me dressed, I intend to keep cooperating…enthusiastically."

The man blinked several times. "Beating? You were beaten?" He nodded gravely. "Was it one of these pigs? Do you wish to file charges?"

Hector exhaled smoke through both nostrils and shook his head. Given what looked to be coming, it didn't seem worth the charade, though his presumed torturer was clearly enjoying the dance. Hector exhaled more smoke and said, "Who the hell is dead?"

"Many, hombre. Many, and terrible deaths they were. Where were you three weeks ago tonight?"

Hector thought about that and said, "At sea. I was making the crossing from New York. A week ago tonight, I suppose I was on the night train from Paris. I've been in Spain for just about a week."

The man in the bloodstained overalls chewed his lip. "A week? Just a week in Madrid?"

"A week in Spain," Hector said. "More like six days in Madrid."

The torturer slammed his fist down on his desk. "Give me this bastard's papers."

He looked at Hector's identification and passport and then handed them back to Hector. "I am sorry. You can remain dressed." Seething, the interrogator looked around his desk. He picked up a chunk of ore — some rock he used as a paperweight — then hurled it at the head of one of the men standing guard over Hector.

Hector instinctively ducked. That was a good thing: the rock hit the guard in the head. The man's finger spasmed and he gut-shot Hector's other guard. Hector's ducking saved him from an accidental headshot.

The two guards fell on either side of Hector's chair. The torturer said to him, "Don't get ideas."

Hector held up both hands. "Not me, brother. I ain't movin'." Hector wet his lips. He said, "You've got some time troubles, I take it — making me for the murder, I mean."

"*Murders*. Yes."

The gutshot guard was rolling on the floor, groaning and bleeding hard from his belly. The torturer bent over him, pulling the man's hands from his stomach wound.

The head interrogator said, "That can't be fixed. So it's the gift of death for you." He picked up the guard's own Mauser and shot the man twice in the head. He walked over to the guard whom he had felled with the rock and put another shot behind that man's left ear.

Hector tried to look like he was taking it all in stride. Carefully, he lit another cigarette. He offered one to the interrogator, now standing with a smoking Mauser in his hand. The man nodded. "That would be very nice, yes."

He took the offered cigarette and Hector fired him up with his Zippo.

Hector said, "You got a handle, sport?"

"Handle?"

"What's your name?"

"Oh. Captain Rafael Barrera." He shook Hector's offered hand. "I'm doubly — no, trebly — sorry for this sloppiness tonight."

"It happens. Again I ask, who is dead?"

"Many. Mostly women, though a few men, too. Terrible murders. Bizarre. Things that defy description. They've been going on at least four months…maybe longer. They seem to echo works of art. The fact of the murders is bad enough. But they've also taken on political dimensions."

Hector said, "What do you mean? How are they political?"

"One victim might have a military medal clutched in one hand…a Soviet medal, as if, in her death throes, the victim had torn a medal from the tunic of her killer. A killer, that by obvious inference, we are to take to have been one of the Republic's Soviet military advisors."

Hector crossed one leg over the other, feeling chummy and nonchalant now — so long as he didn't look left or right to the floor. He said, "But that could be so. It could be just what it appears."

"But for the fact that some of the murder victims have also been found with evidence that would indicate their killer was a fascist, Mr. Lassiter. Many more of those than the other, frankly. These atrocities are being used to demonize the Nationalists."

"Are you a Nationalist?"

A shrug. "I'm a professional. I haven't the luxury of being a partisan. Not outside my head. What about you Mr. Lassiter?"

"I've got no politics. But I have some experience with killings like you describe."

"Yes, in Florida, in 1935. That's why you're here. There were such killings in Florida, where you lived."

"And now I'm here and you have these other murders, and yeah, I get the shitty logic." Hector blew smoke. "Who fingered me? Not that I truly need you to tell me."

"These things are confidential anyway."

"Sure. Well, let's approach it this way, Rafael. I'm not the only one currently in Madrid who was in Key West two years ago. There's Hemingway. I take it he's not a suspect."

"Of course not."

"There's also an old surrealist painter who could be taken out by a stiff wind. I won't give you his name, because I've eliminated him as a possibility…he's frail and harmless."

"You speak of Bishop Blair. Yes — he's not a suspect."

"And there is a man named Quentin Windly, the seeming bullfight critic."

"Yes, there is Windly."

"He's the one who should be sitting in this chair now," Hector said.

"Based on what I know now — because *you* are in that chair

— I concur. But I have no evidence. And he is an American and a journalist. Those things make it...complicated. Particularly because his family is rich and also has many Spanish business investments that cut to both sides of the war."

"You have pictures of any of these bodies?"

The man walked around his desk and pulled out a file folder. He handed several glossy black-and-white photos across the desk to Hector.

Gray-faced, Hector sorted and surveyed each of the photos. Apart from the new political dimension the killer had incorporated into his work — the apparent bid for anti-fascist propaganda — the killer was also combining elements of various surrealist works known to Hector. There were indications of some effort to synthesize the works of various surrealist artists.

Hector handed the photos back across the desk. "It's just like Keys. Of that I'm certain."

The police captain ground out his cigarette and put his feet up on his desk. He stared at the body of the gutshot guard. "So, Mr. Lassiter..."

Hector looked at the photos on the desk between them. He took a deep breath, thinking of Rachel. He massaged the back of his neck and said, "So I'll solve your problem for you, *Jefe*."

Rafael searched Hector's face. "Why?"

"Because this cocksucker killed a woman who was important to me."

The man shook his head slowly. "Then I will reward you for what you propose. There has been a second allegation against you. An accusation that you're here as a spy for your government. Normally, that would be grounds for summary justice. A bullet behind the ear, just like this rubbish either side of you."

"I need two days' grace," Hector said.

"It would take you that long to kill a man?"

"No. It might take me that long to convince a woman to go home with me after I kill a man."

"Ah, the pretty painter whose apartment you were leaving when you were arrested."

"That's right."

"Alright. For two days, I will 'lose' the second denunciation complaint. I'll find it when I hear you've crossed over into France. When I do, you may be *persona non grata* in Spain for a generation. Perhaps more. There may be a standing death warrant issued. But I will do this."

"That'd be swell of you."

"Just so. You're given your two days, hombre. For both our sakes, I hope you kill well and cleanly."

"I never paint dreams or nightmares.

I paint my own reality...

I paint self-portraits because I am so often alone,

because I am the person I know best."

— FRIDA KAHLO

CHAPTER 20

RECOGER

WHEN THEY SAW HECTOR turn the corner, Alva and Hem rose together. Hem, fairly drunk, kissed Alva on the mouth. "You see, daughter, I was right," he said. "You saved Hector."

Hector gave Alva a long hug. She squeezed back tightly and Hector, close to blacking out from the resulting pain, said, "Raise your hands just a bit, honey, won't you? My right kidney is pure misery."

Hem said, "I figured you for a dead man, Lasso."

"It sure enough could have gone that way," Hector said, wincing.

"Sure. Except for this one here." Hem squeezed Alva's neck. "She hauled your ass out of the fire."

Hector nodded. He hoped that Alva hadn't been needlessly suborned into some tawdry act — exploited by a horny functionary. But Hector wasn't about to disparage whatever gratuitous dirty thing she might have done to win him his already earned freedom. He hugged Alva again and said, "What did you do to save me, Alva?"

Meeting his inquiring gaze, she said softly, "I said we are lovers.

I said we were together, in bed, on several of the nights in question."

Hector nodded slowly. "That is a lot to have taken upon yourself for the likes of me."

Alva said, "I don't really have a reputation to destroy."

Hem, drunkenly exuberant, said, "To further the cause and to sell the alibi, I thought it best you spend the night at Alva's place. Dos and me packed for you, Lasso. He's getting your stuff moved into Alva's now. You can sleep on the couch or some damned thing. At least until we can get you on a train to Paris. You know — get your ass out of here before they change their minds."

And hustling Hector out of Hotel Florida left Hector in no position to "spy" on Hem and Martha.

"Well, Hem, it'll please you to know that I'm leaving day after tomorrow," Hector said. "But it's going to be a busy two days getting there." He cupped Alva's chin. He said to her, "I can find somewhere else to sleep, appearances or alibis be damned."

Alva said, "No, it's fine, Hector. Let appearances be damned. Besides, you paid for it…you should get pleasure from your wood, as I intend to."

Hem looked confused, but pleased, by Alva's words.

ဟ

Dos and Hem waved over their shoulders as their Jeep tore off back toward the Hotel Florida.

Alva had worn Hector's long leather coat to the station house. She said suddenly, "Oh, I should have given you your coat back — for the ride home."

Hector smiled at *home*. He said, "No way. I like it better on you and I have another leather coat — an aviator's jacket. That one is more manly. Besides, getting beaten by some bloodthirsty bastard in a long leather coat has turned my thinking on them — long leather coats for men, I mean. So you keep that one. Maybe we can get the shoulders and waist altered. Even if you don't do that, you look damn fine in it."

"It seems all I do is thank you, Hector."

"No, I have you to thank, Alva — for saving me from torture…from execution. For saving me from being 'disappeared.' Can't truly repay that flavor of favor, not ever."

"It wasn't a favor, Hector. It was a thing to be done. There was no choice involved."

"There are always choices, Alva. That's what passes for what we call our lives — just one long, unending string of goddamn choices, good and bad."

Alva considered that. She gave a last wave at the departing Jeep. "How does he get access to those vehicles — Papa, I mean? With the gas shortages and the rationing…?"

"He's Hemingway," Hector said, flatly. "Your war is Hem's oyster. Now, what do you say we get inside before someone else decides to denounce my sorry ass."

He followed her up the steep, narrow steps, presuming to put a steadying hand to the small of her back as they made their way up the dimly lit stairwell.

"You can have my bed tonight, Hector," she said. "I really meant it about sleeping by the fire tonight…I want to be warm. It's been a long time since I've been truly warm."

Hector didn't agree or disagree. He said, "We get in there, I'll get that fire going. No point in being stingy with the wood — like I said, there's more coming *mañana*."

Alva again went about her routine with her weak flashlight — moving around the room, lighting oil lamps. Hector made a mental note to buy her some fresh batteries. He shrugged off his sports jacket and draped it across the back of a chair set before a writing desk. Dos had placed Hector's Underwood there, opened — a hopeful gesture on Dos' part, Hector guessed. The writer checked his pocket watch — 11:50 p.m. He wound the stem a few times. If his body clock awakened him at 4 a.m., there'd be no writing.

Alva's drafty apartment was little better than one big room. In the cavern of her loft, Hector figured that his typewriter would sound like a machine gun firing.

Hector bent to work at the fireplace, stoking up a big fresh fire and then piling on an extra log or two. It had been colder upon their return and the draw of the chimney was quite strong.

Alva said, "With all you've been through, you must be very tired."

"More like wired," Hector said. "It's like walking away from a plane crash — there's a giddiness."

"Good. Good for me that you're 'wired' and awake. I was hoping to learn what exactly happened to result in your arrest for murder, Hector. Here," she said, coming up behind him and pulling his shirt from his pants. She lifted the tails of his shirt and he heard her sharp intake of breath as she examined his back. "That's a terrible bruise. You must be in agony."

That was true enough; Hector was also dreading the days of bloody urination almost certainly ahead of him. She said, "I could give you some ice, but I don't know what else to do for you."

"Time," Hector. "Just have to give it time."

"So tell me about the murders." She let go of his shirttails.

He slipped off his necktie and draped it across the chair over his discarded sports jacket. He unbuttoned the top two buttons of his shirt and rolled up his sleeves, two turns above each elbow. "It's perhaps a little late for that story," he said. "It's nightmare stuff, Alva."

"All the same." She smiled. "We left most of a bottle of wine untouched earlier. I destroyed the cork getting it out, so we should drink it now or have it be lost."

"Some wine would be nice," Hector said.

"I have some cheese, too."

"You see to that, I'll pour the wine," he said.

He kicked off his shoes and padded across the creaking hardwood floor to her kitchen.

They tapped glasses again. Alva said, "It's your turn to toast." He winked. "*Salud, dinero y amor... ¡y tiempo para disfrutarlos!*"

"Can't say no to any of that," Alva said, smiling. "You speak Spanish very well. After your arrest, I wouldn't have guessed."

She sipped her wine then picked up a plate piled with cubes of cheese and carried it to the couch close by the fire. "Put on some music if you'd like," she said. "But something quiet — the floors are thick, but…"

"The neighbors," he said. "And what they might think." He suddenly got this little chill up his back, but he couldn't figure out why. He said, "I don't think we need music."

He sat down on the couch, a cushion between them, and Alva pulled a throw from the arm of the couch and urged him to scoot over, closer to her and the fire. He did that and she tossed the throw over their legs and placed the plate of cheese on his lap. She said, "I keep thinking of what Bishop Blair said…about his wife being his real audience. And now his audience is gone, and so — or it at least it sounds this way — the rest of the world loses a fine painter."

"It does sound so in Bishop's case," Hector said. He was nursing his wine. "That's the risk of investing so much of yourself outside yourself. You have two hearts." He picked up a slice of cheese and paused, the cube halfway to his mouth. "I've known writers who say they write for a single person, just like Bishop said. They write for a wife, or for a sibling."

"Who do you write for, Hector?"

"I write for myself. Or so I tell myself. At least that way, when I stop, the writing stops. As long as I go on, there's the possibility I'll always have something to say." He sipped some wine. "After Key West, and that thing with the surrealists, I made quite a little study of surrealism. I came across a quote, by a guy named Yves Tanguy. Not sure why it speaks to me, but it does. He remarked, 'Very much alone in my work, I am almost jealous of it.'" He sipped more wine and nibbled some cheese and said, "Who do you paint for, Alva?"

"Myself, too, I suppose," she said. "At least at first. I'm not sure I really have a wider 'audience' — not such a defined audience — in mind."

"I notice the women in your paintings all look like you."

"I can't afford models," Alva said, shrugging. "So I have the mirror." She took a cube of cheese from the plate and held it to his mouth. He took a bite. She held the rest poised to her lips. "What about you, Hector, are you all of your own characters?" She popped the cheese in her mouth and sipped some more wine.

"I'm everyone I ever loved or have known," Hector said. "There's some of me in all of them — the ones I create."

"The murders, Hector. What are these murders that got you arrested?"

He took a deep drink of the wine and then set the glass on the end table before them. Cheap though it may be, the wine hit the spot, but with his damaged kidney, he knew he'd have to switch to water soon. "It's something I'm still coming to terms with. It's *déjà vu* all over again. It's Key West, and those murders, redux."

"What!"

"There have been many murders in Madrid, committed over a period of several months," Hector said. "Men and women. They were all killed in ways that evoke imagery from surrealist works of art — paintings and photographs."

"Just like Key West, as you said." Alva shook her head. "I can't believe it."

"Yet it's happening. The only difference is, the killer is now using the murders toward some end — a political end. He's working very hard to see to it that the fascists are blamed for the killings."

Alva said, "You don't think that Bishop Blair…?"

"Oh, God no," Hector said. "Bishop least of all. I'd make Ernest for the killings before I'd consider that old man to be a candidate for them."

"So who do you suspect?"

"Quentin Windly. He was in Key West. He was in Mexico. There were similar killings in Mexico last year…I kept that from you when you asked me if I'd heard of crimes like the ones in Key West. I couldn't quite bring myself to believe there was a connection until tonight…until I saw the evidence of the crimes here. Windly was in Miami when a woman was killed — her disarticulated torso posed on park bench on South Beach. He was in Matecumbe when your sister's friend, Beverly, was murdered. And he was in Key West. The last time I saw him, just before I broke his nose, he spoke of a plan to go to Mexico to study the bullfights there as preparation for a trip to Spain, to see and eventually write about the *Corrida de Toros*. Quentin accused me of the murders — denounced me. The secret police all but confirmed that."

"So the secret police will arrest him now, right?"

"Wrong," Hector said. "Politics preclude that."

Alva took Hector's hand and squeezed it hard. "If you truly believe he killed Rachel…well, he can't get away with that, Hector. *I'll* kill him."

Hector felt this shudder: he believed she meant it. He took her other hand and squeezed it back. "I've already arranged to do that myself."

Alva narrowed her eyes. She started to speak, once, twice…then she set her glass down next to Hector's. She brushed a comma of hair back from his forehead. She wet her lips, then her hand went to his neck, gripping at its nape. She urged his face to her own.

ᴑ

A savage coupling — hungry and desperate.

Still panting, sensing he hadn't peaked, at one point she rolled over and moved to all fours on the couch and said, "Like this, now."

It wasn't one of his favored positions, but Hector obeyed.

After several minutes, he still hadn't come and she rolled away from him.

Alva padded naked across her loft and dragged a thick bearskin rug over from the other side of the room and placed it by the fire and then stripped the bed of blankets and pillows and pulled Hector down onto the rug. She mounted him again. They rolled over and she gripped the bottom of the sofa for leverage, thrusting hard against him. She was a glistening, straining torso, her head hidden in shadows. Hector was suddenly seized again by a terrible vision of Man Ray's "Minotaure."

That did it.

As he came, he almost cried aloud, "Rachel." He thought maybe he started to say it, but it was lost under Alva's groans and cries of, "Fuck me, Hector…love me *harder*."

He'd been granted one wish — in her passion, Alva had bitten through his bottom lip. She clawed his back with her nails — just above his wounded kidney. As she came the last time, her teeth found his shoulder.

Stretched on his side, his heart pounding and his breath ragged, Hector's fingers drifted to his mouth. He felt something wet and held his bloodied fingertips up to the fire.

"If I'm to be punished,
I might as well be hung for a wolf
as for a sheep."

— COLLOQUIAL SAYING

CHAPTER 21

THE TREMOR OF INTENT

HECTOR CAME TO AT FOUR. He knew it was four because Alva had a grandfather clock that chimed on the hour. He awakened two minutes ahead of the clock's chime.

He was sprawled half atop her, still inside her. She tried to turn in her sleep. Her unblemished skin glowed orange and copper in the firelight. He traced the line of her jaw with his thumb. She smiled and turned again, her eyelids fluttering.

"I'm sorry," he said, "I truly didn't mean to wake you."

"It's okay." She stroked his cheek. "You really are a good man, you know."

"Why do you say that?"

"Why do you feel you have to ask? You don't think you're a good man?"

"I'm not sure there's any such thing. I'm not a believer in black and white. We're shades of gray...some grayer than others. I think I'm very gray." Hector's shoulder hurt a little where she'd bitten him. He could feel her nail wounds on his back.

Alva had surprised him with the raw level of her passion — she was much wilder than Rachel, who to that point in Hector's life, had been the wildest of them all.

But Rachel had been mostly inebriated with Hector…flying on absinthe…then made crazy by the hurricane and all it stirred inside her regarding her father.

Alva was like fucking a wild animal, and she had been that way relatively sober, in the confines of her drafty place where the neighbors might hear.

She raised her left leg and her calf moved back and forth against his thigh. She raised it over his hip, her thigh pressed hard against his waist, just under his bruised back. She began moving under him.

Stirring inside her, he said, "You should get on that train with me."

"You always like to talk while you make love?"

"This time, in this moment, yes," Hector said. "Not that I have much to say. I want you to come back with me."

"You've slept with me once and now you're in love with me? Is that it?" Alva smiled. "If that's it, well, it's very old-fashioned…very sweet, but…"

"I'm serious, Alva, get on that train with me," he said it, moving slow and hard inside her.

She groaned a little, half-smiling through nearly closed eyes. "What? Get on the train to Paris?"

"To there, yes. Then we'll take a ship back to America."

"We've made love — we're *making* love, Hector. It was wonderful last night and it feels wonderful now. But what of it? Do you propose to build a life together on a night and a morning of…fucking?"

The coarseness of the word coming from Alva threw him. It also excited him, a little. "More's been built on less," Hector said.

"I have my work here…for the Republic."

His elbows were carrying his weight now, and as he moved inside her she wrapped her thighs around his legs. She held his face in her hands so he couldn't look away from her.

"It's like I told Bishop — you can have your work in the States," Hector said. "You can do it all there, but from a position of safety. A place where trains run on time and you can go out for a drink or a meal and not worry about being blown to rags by a falling shell. A place where crazy allegations can't get you 'disappeared.'"

"But the war—"

"—was lost by the Republic before the first shot was fired," Hector said. "At best, the Republic is trapped in a holding action. Franco is backed by Mussolini. He's backed by Hitler. The other European countries haven't got the stomach or the will to stand against them yet. They think they can appease their own ways to safety. They think neutrality will buy them protection. As a consequence, the Republic is doomed. Spain will fall under fascist rule for a generation or more. The Loyalists talk of turning Madrid into a tomb for fascism. Brave talk. But they've only the got the first part right — moving through Madrid is like walking through a graveyard."

Breathy, building toward another climax, Alva said, "And you claim you're not political."

"I'm not, but I am a strategical animal. A pragmatist and survivor. And just because I'm not political, doesn't mean I'm not a patriot. And you, you're still an American by birth. You haven't renounced your citizenship, have you?"

"No," she said, her eyes dilating — the fire flickering in them.

"So come back with me to the States. Fight them from cover…at least until there are some real allies for the bigger fight to come. The one we can win."

"And where would that cover be? Would we live in that house in Key West where you and my sister loved one another? The place where you and Rachel were lovers? Doesn't that seem…very wrong?"

"No, not in Key West," he said, moving more quickly now, thrusting deeper. "I'm turning that house over to a rental agency. I'll keep it, but make money on it. I won't live there ever again."

"Where will you go?"

"I've found another place, out West. Puget Sound. Specifically, Whidbey Island. I've found an old Victorian house there. It's beautiful, Alva."

"Another island," Alva said. "Like Key West."

"As the war grows in the East, I run to the West."

"And to another island. You really are a loner in most ways."

"But I don't want to be alone."

"I'll think about it," she said, her nails digging in again. She was panting now. She kissed him, her tongue parting his lips. He cupped her chin in one hand, pushing her face back where he could see her eyes. "You'll really think about this?"

"I'll really think about it, Hector." She said, "Are you really going to kill this man?"

"I really am."

"Are you sure you can do it?"

Hector hesitated. "He wouldn't be the first."

She wrapped her legs tighter around his hips, her ankles crossed behind his thighs.

In the distance, Hector could hear shells falling. Each shell sounded like it was falling a bit closer to their building. The impacts sounded like rolling thunder. He felt her shudder under him as a shell struck outside the building, shaking the ground under them. He said, "You don't hear that back home."

"Doesn't mean you can't feel it," she said. "But I wouldn't miss not hearing it."

There was a terrible crash outside. He felt Alva's thighs tremble — felt her belly flutter under his.

She screamed then, wrapped tightly around him, taking him along with her.

"To me, a painter, if not the most useful,

is the least harmful member of our society."

— MAN RAY

CHAPTER 22

ART AS A WEAPON

LATE THAT MORNING, Hemingway came calling.

Hem was adamant Hector come with him for breakfast. Hem said, "If you're really leaving day after tomorrow then we don't have much time left together, Lasso. You know, in case something happens to me."

Hector nodded. So: Hem was in the throes of another of his increasingly frequent, fatalistic doldrums.

Alva had excused herself from the breakfast — sensing, as Hector sensed, that her company would be unwelcome. While Hem loitered, wandering her loft and looking at her paintings, Hector helped Alva pack a few of her canvases and some sketches into a big cloth portfolio valise. She had already wrapped the paintings in brown paper and twine, so Hector wasn't sure which she had selected. He said, "None of these better be the ones I want."

"No, I shipped those three you selected out to the States while you were showering," she said.

Alva found the card given her the night before by Bishop Blair and smiled, holding the business card up. "Wish me luck, Hector?"

"*Bonne chance*, darling," Hector said and kissed her. He wasn't enthusiastic — her call on Bishop, to Hector's mind, didn't bode well for the possibilities of Alva leaving her doomed, adopted country to return to the States to live in sin on Hector's new, good island.

Hector helped her on with his big leather coat and then pulled on his own aviator's jacket with its fleece lining and collar. He took the bag with Alva's paintings and led the way down the steep stairs from her loft to the street.

There was fresh debris strewn around the sidewalk in front of Alva's building from the night's bombardment. Hector looked up and saw the cornice had been blown off the facade.

"This is why you should come out west," he said softly to Alva.

Hem sat up front with his Jeep's driver and Hector and Alva sat in back. "Too far to walk to that joint," Hem had said, checking the card given Alva by Bishop. One thing Hector had to admit about Hem — the man had an uncanny sense of navigation and topography. Two days in any town and Hem owned it — knew where everything was and never forgot his way around. Hector figured you could drop Hem anywhere in Milan, certainly anywhere in Paris, and Hem would know just where he was.

They rolled to a stop in front of the studio. Hem helped Hector unload Alva's packaged paintings and said, "I'll send the car back with Hector for you in a couple of hours. Think that's enough time?"

Alva, who clearly had Hem's number, said, "You tell me."

"Two hours it is, daughter," Hem said, grinning.

"Until then, Hector." She kissed him again on the cheek. Hector squeezed her arm. "Good luck, Alva. I mean it."

"Anything comes up," Hem said to Alva, "you can try to ring us at Chicote's."

ຄ

"Sorry to tear you away from there," Hem said, talking loudly over the roar of the Jeep's engine. "Sorry to take you from the lady.

Looks like you two are living up — or is it down? — to Alva's alibi she supplied you."

Hector shrugged. The cold wind across his face was making his eyes water again.

Hem smiled. "Little strange though isn't it? I mean, you banged her sister, and now…?"

Hector shot Hem a look. Ernest raised both hands and said, "That was offside, yeah. If you're good with it, and she's good with it, well, it's nobody's business, right, Lasso? It's nobody's business who we're fucking, not any of us, is it, Lasso?"

"Right."

Hem slapped Hector's thigh. He said, "Look-it, I wanted you to hear it from me, Lasso. Me and Dos, we're quits for keeps."

Hector raised his eyebrows. "What happened?"

"I told that fucker the truth, Lasso."

"What truth?"

"The truth about goddamn Robles. That damned translator of Dos' that went 'missing' last year. Dos has been indomitable, roaming around, asking foolish questions, poking his nose in it any way and anywhere he can. It was putting us all in danger…casting suspicion on all of us. A lot like you, and all the loose talk about you spying for fucking Hoover."

Hector said, "You found out what happened to José Robles?"

"I have impeccable sources. I wasn't going to tell him. I was trying to spare that fucking Portuguese bastard's delicate sensibilities. Figured if a few months went by with no word, Dos would resign himself to the fact that Robles was likely dead and to be forgotten."

That was a belligerent misreading of Dos' personality, Hector knew.

Hem said, "So I finally told Dos today. Told him the truth. Robles was arrested and put in front of a firing squad for espionage shortly after the arrest. He's dead. End of story."

Hector heard the edge in his voice. "You break it to Dos, just like that?"

"What? I was supposed to dress it up?" Hem shrugged. "What? I was supposed to tell him something pretty and romantic with a capital R? I should make fucking Robles out to be Christ Himself on the cross?"

"Well, some would say *yes*, that a friend—"

"A friend isn't what Dos has been, not for a very long time," Hem said.

So, scratch Dos. Hem was right: his bench of old friends was getting sorry shallow. Hector wondered how long he had left to remain on Hem's roster of still-tolerated old friends.

Hector didn't want to hear more. He said, "This arrest last night…"

"Yeah, murder," Hem said, pretty clearly happy himself for the change of topic. "Who were you supposed to have killed?"

"Lots of people, Hem. It's happening again. Just like Key West — murders with the victims made to look like surrealist paintings and collages and photos. There's a mixture of works now, but it's the same damned thing."

Hem was visibly unsettled. "Christ, I can hardly comprehend that."

"Here's the other thing: This killer has evolved some kind of social conscience — a political sensibility. The murders are being staged to provide the possibility of anti-fascist propaganda."

"Least he picked the right side," Hem said, distractedly. "This reminds me of something I heard. Crazy stuff I dismissed at the time, but based on what you're telling me, it takes on a whole dark new light. They say that there are these hidden interrogation centers, mostly around Barcelona. Here's the thing Hector: They say they have evolved a new system of psychological torture that draws on the work of the surrealists…Bunuel, Klee and Dali and the rest of those women-hating bastards. The guy who pioneered this stuff is named Alphonse Laurencic. He's a kind of anarchist artist. They say he and a group of fellow artists invented this new form of psycho-logical torture that they call 'psychotechnic interrogation.'"

This was too much, even for Hector. He said, "This sounds like crazy talk."

"No, it's real enough," Hem said. "I believe it now, anyway. I've heard this stuff from more than one good source. Some of those sources are surrealists themselves. You know, like Blair, they were here to provide their painting talents for posters and the like. Then some of them got co-opted."

Hector said, "What do they do in these secret cells?"

"My understanding is that the rooms the prisoners are placed in are like something out of Escher. The beds are tilted at twenty-degree angles, so you can't really sleep on them. The benches are the same — plant your ass on one and you hit the floor. The cells aren't very large, and the floors are covered with bricks and geometric blocks — those make it impossible for prisoners to move around, to walk or try to get any exercise. The blocks also make it impossi-ble to sleep on the floors. The walls of the cells are curved and cov-ered with these wild patterns of shapes and lines and spirals and optical illusions. It's all forced perspective and counter-intuitive proportioning. The lights flicker and strobe in the rooms all day and night. They say nobody has survived, or at least stayed sane, for more than two or three days in one of these cells."

"So much for the Geneva Convention," Hector said.

"Rules in war are a joke, Lasso. We both know that. When you're in a war, there's only one thing to do — win the fucker any way you can. All the rest is shit and salve for the conscience."

"It's a lot to swallow — these surrealist torture chambers," Hector said.

"So are murders modeled after paintings."

"Touché."

Hem frowned suddenly, looking up. "Hear that?"

"What?"

Hem slapped his driver's shoulder. "Stop, *now!*"

Ernest grabbed Hector by the arm as the Jeep skidded to a stop. Hem dragged Hector from the Jeep and threw him on the ground and lay atop him. Hector almost passed out from the weight of the burly novelist on his hurting kidney. He wanted to crack a homo joke about Richard Halliburton or Sidney Franklin, but the pain was too great. As he twisted around under Hem for a view of the street, Hector heard it — the shrill, whistling whine of an incoming shell. Hector felt the ground move under them and the heat blowing under the Jeep. The Jeep lifted up onto two wheels. Hector was afraid they might be crushed by the Jeep as it rolled toward them, but it tipped back down onto all four wheels. Hem and Hector rose and saw that their driver had not left the Jeep. A piece of metal had caught him in the side of the head and he sat dead, both hands clutching the steering wheel, his eyes still open.

A woman was screaming.

The two writers turned together and saw a woman in a tattered dress and scarf holding a boy — perhaps of four — by one arm. The boy was dangling by his arm, his mouth open and eyes wide, staring at his own severed leg laying several feet away. The blast had severed the boy's leg just above the knee. Blood was pumping furiously from the boy's truncated thigh.

Hem, the son of a physician, began running toward the boy, stripping off his own coat and yelling back to Hector whose ears were still ringing from the blast, "His femoral artery is severed, Lasso. He'll bleed out."

Hem wrestled the boy from his mother's arms and laid him on his back. He wrapped his coat tight around the boy's stump and started applying direct pressure. Hector slipped off his own belt, wrapped it around the boy's thigh, a few inches above the amputation site, and cinched it tight.

Hem said, "That's damned good work, Lasso. That's got it." Hem lifted the boy and then said in ungrammatical Spanish to the boy's screaming mother, "You ride with us, little mother." Hem then began running back toward their Jeep. Hector led the way. He grabbed their dead driver and tossed his body into the road. Hector was about to swing into the driver's seat when Hem said, "No, Lasso, I know the roads. I know the closest way to the hospital."

Hector nodded and took the boy in his arms and climbed in back — Hem steadying him with a firm hand. The woman climbed in up front with Hem and they tore off.

A block from the first blast site, Hem frowned and yelled over the freezing wind shear, "Duck low, not that it'll help."

Another shell whined overhead then blew the front off a café. More screams.

5

Hem frowned and said, "I don't like this sobriety stuff on you. Makes you more suspicious, somehow."

Hector laughed. "Alright, I'll fucking have one, my poor kidney be damned."

Hem beamed and called out, "Another whiskey soda!"

The writers were both wrung out now, and their pants and shirts were soaked through with the boy's drying blood.

True to his word, Hem had gotten the boy to the hospital within four minutes of the kid's leg being blasted off. The doctor's seemed quite hopeful.

The boy's mother had kissed their bloodied hands. Most of her attention had been lavished on Hem, whom she seemed to recognize — unbidden, she had called him "Papa" over and over. That punted Hem into something like a state of ecstasy, Hector had thought. But Hector had to smile. In such situations, Hem was the best man to have at your side...and impossible not to love.

Hem said, "Back to this other thing. These murders — I have a theory."

"I can guess. Quentin Windly."

"Exactly," Hem said. "That cocksucker! I know it ain't you or me. Bishop's on his last legs. But Quentin was there in Miami, Matecumbe and Key West."

"Also in Mexico," Hector said. "While back, Orson told me some stories about strange murders down there. Sounded like these things all over again."

"Orson? Welles? Funny, he's supposed to do the narration of my script for *The Spanish Earth*. God willing he won't fuck it up."

"I told the secret police what I thought about Windly," Hector said. "They won't touch him."

"That doesn't surprise me," Hem said. "He's too connected, too prominent...and his fucking family is richer than God. They buy ambulances for one side and rifles for the other in this god-damn cluster-fuck."

Hector searched Hem's brown eyes. He decided to confide it to Hem: "I've been given permission to handle it myself."

"Good," Hem said, meeting his inquiring gaze. "That's good. We clean up after our own, Lasso. I want a piece. I liked Rachel...I liked her fine."

"I don't want to put you at risk."

"Fuck off, Lasso. What do you need? I know there's no way you got your Peacemaker here — you couldn't have gotten that old Colt across the borders."

"That's exactly what I need: ordinance."

"Done. And you've got yourself a wheelman." Hem checked the clock behind the bar. "Just time to get you back to your lady. By the way, does she know what's on with Wind?"

"No," Hector lied. "No."

"Good. Two can keep a secret..."

"If one is dead," Hector finished for him.

"But we two are the exceptions that prove that sorry rule. When do you want to do this, Lasso?"

"Tomorrow night. Then I leave the following morning. I'm promised safe passage back to France. Then I'll likely be sentenced to death, *in abstentia*."

"At least it's publicity," Hem said. "Hell, it may goose some book sales for you."

*"There is perhaps no finer defense
of surrealism's central theme of transgression
via eroticism than Man Ray's wanton nudes,
who point more to death than to sexuality."*

— WERNER SPIES

CHAPTER 23

PARLEZ-MOI D'AMOUR

BISHOP BLAIR SAID, "Quite an exceptional, developing talent — quite a talent in one still so young. A painter isn't really whole until they're in their thirties. They do not reach artistic maturity until they're in their forties or fifties. Mastery can be a decade beyond that. I can't fathom what you'll be then, Alva."

She kissed the old man on both cheeks. "Thank you, Maestro," she said.

Maestro? Hector wasn't liking this at all — it seemed to him to further dim his prospects of getting Alva to move to Puget Sound.

Frowning, Hector helped Alva on with his given-away leather coat. He said to her, "Where's your portfolio? I'll carry it for you."

"No need, Hector," Bishop said. "I've just shipped the paintings Alva brought on to a gallery in Paris. I had just the dealer in mind. I can guarantee the first of many sales. I'm sure of that."

"Sounds like you and me better really seal that deal on those works of yours I want," Hector said to Alva. "I'm getting this sense that in a few months, I won't be able to afford you anymore."

Alva rolled her eyes and Bishop smiled. She looked again at Hector — at his black corduroy pants and black flannel shirt. She

narrowed her eyes and said, "Have you been rolling in the mud?"
She sniffed a few times and then leaned in closer. "Good Lord,
Hector, is that blood?"

He explained then what had happened to Hem and him since
dropping Alva off at Bishop's studio.

The old man nodded gravely, then squeezed Hector's arm. It
was meant as a comradely gesture, Hector figured, but there was
no grip there at all. Bishop said, "But the boy will live?"

"The doctors said so."

"Good work…good work, and just what I'd expect from Hem
and particularly from you," Bishop said.

"I just feel sorry for that poor kid," Hector said. "Probably has
been walking less than a year or two. Now he's a cripple for life.
Sorry little bastard."

"These creatures on the other side," Bishop said — real
venom in the old man — "their ceaseless shelling is monstrous.
Sometimes I think they deserve the cruelest things we can conceive
for them in the darkest corners of our imaginations. And we have
darker corners than most."

"On that note," Hector said, "I heard the most incredible
thing today." He first told the old painter about the killings that
had been occurring in and around Madrid — the ones echoing
those in Key West. Blair said, without hesitation.

"We should look to this critic, Windly."

"*We* are," Hector said.

Alva seemed to be made uncomfortable by the drift of the
conversation. She said:

"We should get home, Hector. Get you out of those clothes
and get you into a bath."

"Soon," Hector said. "There's something else, Bishop…have
you heard word of some, well, we'll call them 'experiments' involving psychological torture using surrealist imagery as a weapon?"

Alva said, "You sure you weren't hit on the head when that

Jeep nearly blew up under you, Hector?" She took his arm. "Let's get you home where I can watch you for a while, mister. I'm even more worried about you. I'm worried you have a concussion."

Annoyed, he pushed her hand away. "Just a minute, Alva. Does this sound like anything you've heard whispers of, Bishop?"

"I'm not even sure I understand what you're suggesting," the old painter said.

Hector pressed ahead, again shrugging off Alva's hand. "I'm told there are hidden prison camps strewn around Barcelona. They are full of little rooms with curved and crooked walls...tilting beds and benches. Vertigo-inducing forced perspectives and blocks — like something torn from Escher — strewn glued to the floors. The rooms are said to drive men mad."

Bishop's eyes widened. He wet his lips, looking furtively at Alva. He said, "I'll make some inquiries, my friend." He handed Hector one of his cards. "Assuming the fascists don't hit the telephone exchange, call me later this evening. Or I will call you. Perhaps we can meet, just the two of us, for a drink. I may know more in a short while." He nodded again at Alva. He said softly, "Your work, my dear, is more startling, more revelatory, the more I think on it."

He shook Hector's hand — another damp handshake. "We'll talk in a few hours, Hector. Please watch after yourself until then."

"Always," Hector said, taking Alva's arm. She looked a last time over her shoulder at Bishop, so Hector did that, too. The old man was standing there, his hands clasped in front of him, looking like Hector thought he might have looked when Harriet died — lost...terribly alone.

5

As they stepped out of the studio, a horn honked. A man waved at them from a cab. Hector frowned: Quentin Windly. When the critic saw who was with Alva, he quickly dropped his hand.

Alva said, "I hate him, now."

"Put on a brave face for a few more hours, darling," Hector said. "Take solace from this fact — the bastard's living on my clock."

5

Hector was in his third bath. He finally felt clean. And he must finally have come clean enough to meet Alva's standards. She put on some music — "Parlez-Moi D'Amour" — and then smiling, slowly stripped off her clothes and climbed into the claw-foot tub with Hector. She lowered herself slowly, saying, "You really do like it hot, don't you?"

He watched as she eased into the tub. He noticed for the first time that her pubic hair was several shades paler than the short hair framing her face. Usually it ran the other way — darker down there than on top. Hector realized he must have misunderstood what Alva had told Bishop about keeping herself brunette: it must be Alva who dyed her hair, not Rachel.

Smiling and scooting around until she found a comfortable position, facing him, he said, "Cold baths are only for Key West in the summer and early fall."

"I'll never know," she said. "How's your kidney?"

He had excused himself to the water closet down the hall before getting in the bath. While he was there, Alva had gone downstairs to arrange to have someone knock on her door if a call came from Bishop Blair. With a shrug she explained before going downstairs, "I haven't had a phone of my own since my husband…"

When she returned from her landlord's office, she had found that Hector was still in the water closet. When he finally returned to her loft, she had commented upon how pale he looked — how wrenching his expression was. "Kidney pain is a remarkable thing for a man," he had said.

Now, stroking his chest with her bare foot, she said, "Is the kidney getting better at all?"

"It'll take a few days," he said, fishing around for the big sponge at the bottom of the tub and then soaping her long legs. "The bleeding is weakening. The pain comes and goes. Heat helps."

"Then we'll keep you warm. I'm not letting you out of this apartment again until…" It hung there unsaid: *Until you go to kill Quentin Windly.* "When will that be?"

"Tomorrow night," he said. "I'll have to leave the next morning. Cross into France. I'll be safe there."

"But unable to come back here?"

"That's right. Maybe not in this lifetime. Certainly not if Franco wins and can hold power. And Franco has won. It's just an undeclared victory."

"So you keep saying," Alva said. "I've been thinking about Paris. You used to live there — Rachel noted that in her letter. Maybe in Paris, we could…"

Hector was beginning to think that Rachel must have written her kid sister a novella. He said, "I like Paris fine, but not to ever live there again. And with this coming war, well, my sense is, if Hitler wants Paris, Hitler will have Paris."

"So it's really the thing to come — your island out West?"

"I've bought the house. Papers are all signed. Just have to move in." He smiled. "It has a third floor — a finished attic, with big dormers on all four sides. There'll always be light there. It could be a fine studio."

"What are you saying?"

"I'm saying again — come to my new island."

"But I have so much to move," she said, going along as if she thought he was joking about moving in with him. "I can't part with the furniture…shabby as it must look to you."

"I'll see it's all moved. Attic's square footage is about the same as your place here. We can recreate this room there, if you want. Hell, I'd insist upon it. I love this place."

Her smile went away as she saw that he was serious. "It really is very tempting to come. As you say, this city is becoming like a tomb. I think of that little boy you saved this morning…out for a walk with his mother, then mutilated, just like that." She tried to snap her fingers but they were too wet to make much sound.

Hector picked up the straight razor resting on the stool by the tub. "You sure you trust me to do this?"

She winked. "Trust me to shave your face?"

"Sure," he said.

"Your throat?"

"It's connected to my face. Sure."

"So you can shave my legs," Alva said.

It seemed a pointless gesture — her legs were covered with a fine blond down he could hardly see. He said, "So, you're *really* a blond?"

She shrugged. "Sure."

"I'm trying to imagine you with blond hair."

"That shouldn't be hard," she said…acid there. "And *I'm* trying to imagine you didn't just say that — that you didn't wonder aloud how I'd look looking like my sister. You almost had me swayed to run west with you."

"I didn't mean it like that, Alva. Hell, I love dark hair…prefer it, really. This is about you and me, not your sister."

"You swear?"

He held up three fingers. "Scout's honor."

"Don't be flip, Hector."

"I didn't mean to be…I swear. It's you and it's me."

She was quiet for a time. "I couldn't come with you on that train," she finally said. "It would take time for me to pack — to prepare paintings for shipping. Except for whatever else I turn over to Mr. Blair."

"Or sell to me."

She smiled. "Or sell to you."

"How long would it take you to prepare — how long will I

have to wait?"

"Some weeks, probably. Then I could follow you. You sure you want this…this with *me*?"

He set the razor aside. "Come here, Alva — I'll show you."

5

They were again on the carpet next to the fireplace. Hector said, "Have you ever painted anything you don't display?"

She shrugged. "You ever write anything you don't publish?"

"I used to, when I was younger. Before I found my voice."

"Why do you ask that question, Hector?"

"I was thinking of Hem. He wrote a story once and showed it to Gertrude Stein. Because it described a woman's first sexual experience, old Gert said it could never be published. She likened it to something that an artist paints, but can't hang. Said it was 'inaccrochable.'"

Alva said, "A few months ago — when I was beside myself — I painted a few things that were kind of a response to Man Ray's photos of naked women. The women all looked dead to me in his photos. So I painted naked men with their eyes closed. The men all looked dead to me. Too disturbing. Transgressive."

Her *inaccrochable* paintings sounded macabre enough. "You still have them?"

"No," she said. "Money was tight. So I painted over them." She looked at him, this strange smile on her face. "If I move in with you, I'm going to expect modeling time out of you. You know that, don't you?"

"Do I have to play dead?"

Her hand drifted down there. "Only from the neck up."

"When man commits a crime,
God will find a witness."

— ORIGIN UNKNOWN

CHAPTER 24

MUERTE

ABOUT FIVE O'CLOCK, Hector began to wonder why he hadn't heard from Bishop Blair. He'd dressed and gone downstairs twice to try to phone the surrealists' shared studio, but nobody answered there.

Hector was sitting at Alva's desk, trying to do some afternoon writing — a rarity for Hector. He was a morning writer and for whatever reason, more prolific then. And he kept finding himself distracted. Alva was painting, using herself as a model again. She sat at her easel, nude, referencing herself in a floor length mirror that she had leaned against the wall.

He shook his head and turned back to his Underwood. He'd never be able to write like this — not with her close by, naked like that. He thought he was lucky his new house had three floors.

There was knock at her door. Alva put down her brushes and reached for a robe. Hector said through the door, "Yes?"

"There's a phone call for you *Señor* Lassiter," the landlord's wife said in Spanish.

Hector excused himself from Alva. He trotted down the steps and scooped up the candlestick phone. He said, "Bishop?"

A gruff, vaguely familiar voice: "How interesting you answer that way. It's Captain Barrera. We met the other night."

"Oh, I haven't forgotten, *Jefe*. Neither has my kidney."

"I call with bad news. You were expecting a call from *Señor* Blair?"

"That's right."

"You can stop waiting, hombre. *Señor* Blair was killed about an hour ago. I thought since you knew him, and since he was around the fringes of this other — I mean his having been in Key West during the time of the other killings — you would want to know."

Hector was reeling. He leaned on the counter of the landlord's front desk. "Dead? Killed? Like the others? You mean he was murdered?"

"Nothing so…exotic, Mr. Lassiter. His throat was cut. Mr. Blair's wallet was taken. His watch, too. It looks like robbery…maybe he resisted so the man cut his throat."

"Witnesses?"

"Just a couple of fellow artists who saw just the end — the slice and Mr. Blair falling, clutching his neck."

"What did they see of the attacker? I don't suppose the 'thief' in any way resembled our friend Mr. Windly?"

"Quite the opposite. A dark-haired man with a thin dark moustache and rather prominent ears. But since you invoke the name — it happens soon for QW, yes?"

"It happens tomorrow night."

"Any notions of how you'll…?"

"I'm contemplating something that might be construed as a tragedy of war."

"Better and better." He hesitated. "Then you leave. It's harder for me to protect you on this other — this of the spying. There has been another denunciation, you see."

"Windly again?"

"No, a woman. Don't ask me who. I did not take the complaint. But I'm told it was a woman. Tall…perhaps orange-haired, according to a clerk who may have seen her chatting with my lieutenant."

5

Alva turned at the sound of the door opening, then closing. Sitting naked again at her easel, she said, "Word from Bishop?" She was very casual in her nudity…comfortable. She had one foot on the uppermost rung of her painter's stool, the other on the floor…her knees slightly apart. She was wearing big woolen socks, but that was all. She'd stoked up a big, crackling fire.

"No more word is to come from old Bish, not ever," Hector said. "Sorry honey — sorry if it has any effect on your future in terms of that gallery in France."

"What are you saying, Hector?"

"Bishop was murdered a bit ago. It looks like a robbery. His throat was slashed."

"*Robbery?*"

"So the police say."

"You sound unconvinced."

"Don't I?"

"There is no such thing

as an exact synonym

or an unmixed motive."

— KATHERINE ANNE PORTER

CHAPTER 25

RIFTS

HEM SENT A JEEP around to pick them up at Alva's loft. They were to dine at Botín's.

Hector asked that they first be taken to the Hotel Florida. He left Alva in the hotel bar with a drink and promised to rejoin her in a few minutes.

She arched an eyebrow. "Where are you going?"

"To see if I can find a friend."

Hector checked with the front desk and was told Dos Passos was still in room 89, but he had just requested a porter.

Hector found Dos' room and rapped his knuckles on the door in a playful rhythm.

Dos called, "Friend or Hemingway?"

"The former," Hector said.

"Former friend?"

"You'll have to tell me," Hector said. "I still like *you* fine."

Dos opened the door a crack. Through the gap, Hector could see his luggage on the bed, opened.

"You're packing?"

"That's right," Dos said. He opened the door wider for Hector to pass through and then closed it behind him. Dos was fairly tall in stocking feet, but Hector towered over him.

Dos said, "You heard?"

"Yeah. I'm damned sorry, buddy. It's terrible."

"How long have you known what happened, Hector?"

"It's not like that, Dos. I heard after you. Hem came by Alva's after he broke the news to you. Guess he wanted to put his own face on it. Guess he wanted get his version out first."

Hector planted his ass on the bureau's corner. Dos pushed aside a suitcase and took a seat at the foot of the bed. There was a deep rumble from the direction of the front. "Guess the Republic is finally shelling back," Dos said.

"For all the good that will do."

Dos shrugged. "It wasn't news, not really, of course — about José, I mean. I figured José was dead and had been for some time. It was Hem's tone in telling me that set me off. He managed to be at once condescending and imperious. Too knowing."

"He'll get over it," Hector said.

"Doubtful. Hem nurses his grudges. And he did it in pub-lic…at a party. And *I'll* never get over it. We're quits. He's been tire-some for a long while. He used to be such an intense listener and learner. Now he pulls on the white whiskers and issues pronounce-ments. Demands to be believed. That air of superiority was all over *Death in the Afternoon*, and it's all over *Green Hills*, too. And all his shots at the critics — he was begging for a backlash from them. If you lob grenades at critics, you have to expect retaliation."

"Unless you hit 'em square," Hector said, with a crooked smile. "With the grenades, I mean."

Dos said, "Katy calls Hem the Mahatma, now. She's known Hem longer than any of us, since they were kids, really. She sees drastic changes in him. She thinks about another ten years and he'll be — her term, not mine — 'imminently nettable.' Really thinks Hem'll be in a mental institution."

"That's a happy thought."

"Hem's very forgiving of the communists."

"They didn't kill *his* old good friend," Hector said.

"What about you, Hec? You've been here in Spain a few days...close to the ground. Got yourself arrested and out of it, like José evidently couldn't. Hem told me, 'You're either with us, or against us.' You've met some players from both factions. You taking sides yet?"

"Not even leaning," Hector said. "In fact, I'm getting out of Dodge. Come morning, this shithole country won't see me for my dust." Hector pointed at his friend's bags. "What about you? Heading home? I hope so...this 'war' isn't for shit. I think it's really being run by Stalin."

"I'm just moving across town," Dos said. "At least for a few more days. Need to get some distance on the Mahatma and his sycophants. And you're right, maybe, about the wrongness and futility of all this. Like I told Hemingway, what's the use of fighting a war for civil liberties if you destroy civil liberties in the process? Like José: arrested by God knows who for God knows what and shot without a trial. Now I need to get a death certificate for José. For his wife and kids, I mean. That's the only way they can ever collect on his life insurance policy. So this isn't over for me. Fuck Hemingway. And fuck Martha fucking Gellhorn." Dos shook his head. "What are you really here for, Hec? Not just to say goodbye, right? Got an audience with the great man?"

"Little of both," Hector said. "Wanted to see how you're doing...and there is a dinner tonight. So far as the social event goes, I'm there for the just desserts."

"Serving them I suppose. I know you well enough to know not to ask for more."

Hector winked. "Wise course in this dusty land of dread and fear, my brother...this fucked up country full of snitches and spies."

"So what's your next stop, Hector?"

"Paris. Then home. Found a new house on Puget Sound.

Whidbey Island." Hector stood and put out a hand. Dos shook it firmly. "You come by the new island, you and Katy," Hector said. "We'll go fishing for the kind of fish you don't have to club to death, or to machine gun."

"That sounds real good. Watch yourself, Hec." Dos thought about it, then said, "Hem's done with all of us I think — all us old guard, I mean. He's committed to moving on to the next phase of his life, and old friends aren't going to be asked along for the ride. You're about the only one left, and I don't think there are any rewards for being last man standing in this match. He'll find an excuse to cut you out, too. He'll find one, or else he'll manufacture one."

"No saying I won't do it first," Hector said. "Not intentionally, of course…it's just you can't tell what might set Hem off these days."

5

As he approached the bar, Hector saw that Hem was sitting with Alva. He heard her say, "It's yummy."

"Well, they're even better back home," Hem said. "There you can have them with mint, as they're supposed to be made." He picked up her drink and sipped some. "Only about 80 percent there," Hem said. "And it really needs to be made with Bacardi rum." Hem saw that Hector had arrived, and smiled at him. "Hey, Lasso. Just been introducing Alva to the miracle of the mojito. Or as close as they come to one in these parts."

Hector waved off the bartender and said, "No, nothing for me."

Hem frowned. "Still trying to change your way of living? This late in life?"

"No, I'm pacing myself, because I'm still pissing blood from that kidney punch," Hector said. "I drink much of anything stronger than mineral water, I feel like I'm being knifed in the back."

Hem sipped his drink; Hector thought he smelled Scotch. Hem asked, "How's Dos coping?"

Hector said, "Do you really care?"

"Up to a point, sure," Hem said. "But not enough to go to the source. That door is closed and barricaded."

"That door's barricaded on both sides, then. Damn shame. At least there'll be more room down below on the *Pilar*. It wasn't what you said, you know. Dos had already reconciled himself to the fact that Robles was likely dead. It was the way you confirmed his suspicions. The way you said it."

Hem sipped his cocktail. "Everyone is a critic."

Hector shook his head and spun his chair around. He straddled the chair, his arms crossed atop its back. "You thought anymore about your future, Hem?"

"I have."

"Does that future find you in Key West?"

"Not Key West. Not sure where yet, but not there."

"Alright then."

Hem said, "Alva tells me you're headed west and trying to drag her along."

Hector shot her a look.

"That wasn't my word, Hector," she said. "I didn't use 'drag.'"

"Puget Sound," Hector said. "FDR and company hasn't fucked up those environs yet."

"And you're going farther and farther from the action," Hem said. "Farther from the fight. Was a time, a man was supposed to ride to the sound of the cannons, not away from them."

Hector took a breath, thought about it, then decided to go ahead with it. Hem was on poorly chosen ground, needling him over military service. Hector decided to remind him of that fact. First he looked at Alva, searching her face. She looked away. Hector's blue eyes narrowed. He carefully chose his words, placing

the emphasis on just the right ones. He saw his one true sentence
in his mind's eye — as it would look typed on his Underwood,
underlined to indicate the italics:

```
"I have fought in war."
```

Hector said his one true sentence aloud.

Hem actually flinched, clearly feeling every word and all the
other ones that Hector's five, carefully chosen, *stated* words
implied. Hector's one true sentence, stretched out to a paragraph
with its between-the-lines sentences made explicit would have
gone more along the lines of:

```
"I have fought in war. I fought in Mexico with
Black Jack Pershing, Hem. I fought in the
trenches of Europe, and I did it as an armed
combatant. I was wounded in battle. I wasn't
injured and then given disingenuous medals for
being blown up passing out chocolates in a place
I had no right or authorization to be. You know
— the way you sustained your war injuries in
Italy . . . the unnecessary wounds that have been
twisted by Scribner's publicity department to
make you look like a soldier in arms. I have
killed men in Mexico and I have killed men in
France and Italy. In Cuba and Canada, and points
in between. I will kill one tonight, here, in
Spain. So far as I know, Hem, you have never killed
another man. You have never fired on another man,
or been fired upon by one — not with intent."
```

That was all unsaid, but Hem got the message as clearly as if
it had been said aloud by Hector.

Alva, on the other hand, did not grasp the dynamic or the dangerous subtext. Sensing an alliance with Hem that might somehow sway Hector to some undefined end, she said, "Some things are worth fighting for, Hector. Some things are worth dying or even killing for."

"That's right," Hector said evenly. "And I've done all of those things but the dying, Alva. And that one I expect I'll get around to, particularly if I stay in this goddamn country much longer. And I expect to kill again, and quite soon, as you well know."

So now Hem would know that Alva knew what was on for the night. Hector didn't care anymore. Fuck him. Or *Hem*. Fuck Alva. Fuck them both.

Alva said, "I'm sorry, Hector. I didn't mean to anger you. I didn't mean to insult you. It's just that you have these skills — martial and otherwise. To remain passive in this fight? To do nothing at this time? I can't grasp that."

Hector shrugged. "We fight the battles we can win. I ain't playin' crusader rabbit for a lost cause. I invest my capital more wisely than that. I don't do the Don Quixote number."

"But to stand back…to watch this all unfold and do nothing?" *Alva just didn't know how to let it go*, Hector thought. She said, "Do you know the line by Donne, Hector? Do you know it, Hem?"

Both writers shrugged. Hector said, "I'm not one for poetry, much. 'Specially those great dead white writers we're all supposed to dote on. I might read some Robert Service…a little Yeats when St. Patrick's Day rolls around and I feel like getting all wet about Ireland, but that's it."

Alva sipped her mojito and said, "Donne wrote, 'No man is an *Iland*, intire of its selfe; every man is a peece of the Continent, part of the *maine*…any man's death diminishes *me*'."

"Sentimental bullshit," Hector said. "Donne's a joke."

Hem was watching her with his brown eyes. "I do recall that passage, now," he said.

Hector lifted Alva's glass. The rim of her glass was stained with lipstick. She'd dressed and primped for dinner — the first time he'd really seen her wear make-up and assume airs. He missed his lusty bohemian with her careless, gamine hair and unvarnished nails. He tapped glasses with a wary Hem and said, "Here's to diminishing ourselves this evening." He sipped the mojito and made a face. "This is no mojito."

"It's sweetened with honey," Hem said. "You know I can't abide sugar."

"But you weren't the one that was going to drink that drink, *Papa*." It was the first time that Hector had used the nickname Hem had generated for himself. Hector wasn't sure why he kept provoking Hem this way — trying to beat him to the punch in instigating what Dos had predicted was an inevitable rift between Hector and Ernest? *Maybe…*

Hem smiled. Hector almost shivered, knowing him well enough to know the smile was full of menace. Hem reached over and took the glass from Hector's hand. "It wasn't made for you, either, Hector." They stared at one another.

Hem blinked first. "No, not like this, Hector. Not *now*. We have something to do tonight, remember? *Rache*."

"*Rachel*," Alva said softly.

"No, he means *r-a-c-h-e*," Hector said, not looking at her. "It's the German for 'revenge.'"

5

Hem had invited his new cronies for pre-dinner drinks at Chicote's. The cronies invited cronies who invited their friends and so on. The result was a sodden clot of suck-ups and syco-

phants and hangers-on who tried to cadge drinks and bum cigarettes or get their ashes hauled by camp followers who were themselves drunk enough to engage in discounts or to barter for more
drinks and smokes.

Hector thought he glimpsed George Orwell, his head bowed,
moving to get the hell out of the place now that Hem and company had arrived in force.

It was deafening with the overlapping, drunken conversations.
Two gypsy singers were practically screaming to have their *cante
jondo* heard over the buzz of voices. In another corner, some
drunken communists were singing a sloppy but enthusiastic version of the "International."

Alva had been pulled away for conversation with an intense,
hawk-faced man with slicked-back dark hair, a pencil-thin moustache and very prominent ears…some presumed painter Hector
thought might be Salvador Dali.

For his part, Hector drifted away to a table close by the
door…drawn to a small band of charismatic men and women who
claimed to be attached to the Abraham Lincoln Brigade. Hector
sat chatting with one of them — an older woman named Roslyn.
Her strawberry-blond hair was streaked with gray. She had lived
for many years in Alaska before eventually finding her way to
Spain. She spoke of Alaska and of having met Kafka and Houdini.

After about an hour of chatting with her, Hem and Alva
found Hector. Hem said, "Our reservations, Hector — we have to
get to Botín's."

"All critics should be assassinated."

— MAN RAY

CHAPTER 26

BANDERILLAS DE FUEGO

THEIRS WAS A PARTY OF EIGHT: Hem, Martha, several members of the crew of *The Spanish Earth*, Hector and Alva…and Quentin Windly.

While Martha and Alva went with the film crew to claim their table, Hem and Hector hung back at the Jeep. Hem pulled a rucksack from under the backseat of the Jeep. Hem said, "Mausers…a Mannlicher. What's your pleasure tonight?"

Hector thought of Dos Passos and his aside about Hem and the critics. He said, "Got any grenades?"

Hem smiled crookedly. "Going to give as bloody as his victims got, huh, Lasso?" He rooted around the bag to show Hector. "Just three — 'Potato Smashers,'" he said, pulling one from the bag to give Hector a better glimpse. The grenade's nickname said it all — a square container of explosives with a stick for a handle. "They're of German-manufacture," Hem said.

"Fuse length?"

"Five seconds, give or take."

"Just want to make sure there isn't time for the bastard to catch it and pitch it back."

"How do you want to do this, Hector?"

"You've indicated Quentin's a poseur…talks a big game but avoids the front. Certainly isn't fighting for either side."

Hem nodded. "Certainly isn't. He sucks up to both sides and plays a wheel because of his family's investments on either side of the war. Covering their asses, you know. He trades on their largesse. I've tried to get him to ride along for some filming expeditions, but he demurs. Cocksucker's a coward."

"So I figure we shame him into a reckless drive up nearer to the front," Hector said. "Play drunken louts and go at his manhood, do it in a merciless way, if we have to. Get him up there by the front and then…"

Hem winked. "Then the unlucky Wind gets hit by a fascist shell."

"Fascist?"

"Sure, you keep insisting you've got no politics," Hem said. "So I get to construct this narrative. Wind gets shelled by Franco. The Republic can use the money the Windlys will invest to avenge their dead son."

Hector shrugged. "So everybody wins."

ฌ

Hector couldn't tell if Hem was truly drunk or faking it.

Either way, Hem's boorishness had proven too much for Martha. She said something about cramps and excused herself shortly after the main course of *cochinillo asado*. That was okay with Hector — he was tired of Martha's incessant and portentous staring at him. He kept thinking of the tall, strawberry-blond woman who had supposedly denounced him. But he couldn't venture that supposition to Hem…not cunt-struck as Hem had become.

For his part, Hector was forcing himself to drink more than his body could stand. It wasn't really affecting him in terms of impaired judgment or a loose tongue. His kidney pain gave him a point of focus that cut through the dulling effects of the Rioja Alta. Hector helped himself to one of the roasted potatoes arrayed around the suckling pig and took some more bread. He tore off a chunk of bread and stirred it around on a small saucer covered with olive oil.

He sipped some more wine, watching Alva chat up Joris Ivens, the director of *The Spanish Earth*. Hector didn't trust Ivens; he thought if anyone was a spy or a communist tool, it was the Dutchman. Ivens had thick black hair, good looks and dimples. Hector hated him.

Hem checked his watch and said, "Soon you and me have to make that run, Lasso."

Hector looked cagily around and said, "Sure. Yeah. Just let me finish this drink."

Joris said, "Something I should come along for? We could bring some lights if it is somewhere that might not draw fire."

"No, this isn't like that, Ivy," Hem said. "This is some unfinished business Hector and me are eager to tie off. And it is going to require a trip near to the front. Need to get up by the lines so a Nationalist can slip across to give us the information."

Joris said, "So the rumors are true — Hector *is* a spy!"

Hector almost came out of his chair.

Hem held up a hand. "No, Hec is most goddamn certainly not a bloody fucking spy, Jor." Hem drank some more wine and said, "There were some killings in Key West a few years ago. Alva's sister was one of the victims. The killer seems to be here in Spain, working again. So we owe the cocksucker. Tonight we get some information that may let us repay the debt. We mean to take this bastard down and stop him from killing any more women." Hem narrowed his eyes. He said, "Wind, you were there, in Key West, I mean. You know what I'm talking about."

"Crazy as it sounds," Quentin said, "Hem is telling the truth, Joris."

"As a man, you must want a piece of this, too," Hem said to Quentin. "I was thoughtless not to have asked you along. You knew Rachel just as well as I did. You seemed to like her very much. You'll come along, of course. I'm sure Alva will be grateful. You and Hector will just have to play nice. This is about honor after all, about avenging a friend."

"It's okay, Hem," Quentin said, shifting in his chair. "Hector's stake is much larger than mine. I don't want to intrude. Wouldn't want to spoil it for him."

"It's no intrusion, and in fact I insist," Hem said. "We could use the extra hand and muscle, if needed. We'll leave now. Have to drive without the headlights the last part of the way, so it'll take a bit of time. I'll drive of course."

Quentin tried a last time. "I really don't want to get in the way of anything. And, as you point out, this is Hector's show, and me and Hector—"

"No hard feelings, Q," Hector said, putting out a hand. "You come on along. As men, we know what we have to do...can't let personal bitterness or drunken spats get in the way of getting Alva's sister here justice. Come on, old pal."

5

It had taken fifteen more minutes of needling to get Quentin in the Jeep. Eventually, Alva implored him to go. That seemed to tip him over — at least in front of the filmmakers. The Dutch director and his crew actually cheered Quentin when he agreed to go along.

Hector sat up front with Hem, nervous this time to be at the mercy of his driving talents. Pauline Hemingway had rightly claimed Hem had no reliable night vision — and that was two years ago...Hector figured Hem's vision could only have weakened since.

It was the bumpiest ride of Hector's life — there was so much debris that Hem's weak night vision insured they hit every chunk of concrete and every shell crater on the road down from Madrid toward the decimated outskirts and the front. Hector thought it a strong possibility Quentin might be killed as a result of bouncing out of the Jeep on the drive out of town.

The last quarter mile Hem drove without headlights. He pulled over alongside a row house of apartments reduced to rubble. "Here we are," Hem said.

Nervous, Quentin jumped down out of the back of the Jeep and looked around. He was about to pull his cigarettes and lighter from his pocket but Hector took his arm. "No, Q, you'd be a target for snipers, buddy."

"Thanks, Hector," Quentin said nervously. Hector pulled a bag from under a front seat. He took something from the bag in the low light. Quentin said, "Who are we meeting? Where is he?"

"We're not meeting anybody," Hem said. "This is about you, and what you did to Rachel and the others."

Quentin's eyes widened. "Are you fucking mad? You're certainly fucking drunk, but are you mad, too?"

"Miami," Hector said, pointing a Mauser at Quentin. "You were there, and a woman was murdered and her torso left on a park bench. Matecumbe Key. You were there, and there at the same time as a woman named Beverly, Rachel's friend, was gutted and turned into a work of 'art' with another woman in a shack on that godforsaken island."

"Then Key West," Hem said. "We all know what you did there."

"And then on into Mexico," Hector said. "You said in Key West you were going to go to Mexico to start your study of the bullfight. While you were in Mexico, the surrealist murders moved down there. Now, they're underway in Spain. And here you are. You saw me leaving Bishop Blair's the other day. Did Blair know something? Is that why you had Bishop killed? Why you had his murder disguised as a robbery?"

"Coincidence," Quentin said. "That's what it is, pure accident. And Matecumbe, when I was there, that other was there, too. That cock-tease—"

Hem lashed out with a right hook. Quentin fell…spit out a tooth. Blood was running down his chin. "You two *hear* me out *goddammit*! I said—"

"This isn't a trial," Hem said. "This is an execution. I remember in Pamplona, in the old days, you ran pretty fast. Start running now, Quentin. You're running with the bulls again, tonight. So move your ass. Run to the sound of the cannons."

"You fucking cowards," Quentin spat, "you'd shoot me in the fucking back?"

Grim-faced, Hector held up the grenades.

"The trick is to outrun Hector's arm," Hem said. "Lasso's a righty. His right kidney took a shot the other day, so I figure his throwing arm is impaired. That's your sporting chance," Hem said.

"You don't understand," Quentin said. "Rachel was—"

Hem said, "Shooting him now would at least end this blather."

Quentin scrambled to his feet and began running down the darkened street, screaming for help…glass crunching under his feet. He slipped once on the glass and fell. He held up bloodied hands, and then began running again, looking back over his shoulder.

Hector triggered the fuse of the "potato smasher," counted to three and then lobbed the grenade at Quentin's running silhouette, remembering the old line about horseshoes and hand grenades.

He heard the grenade smack the pavement and more broken glass tinkle.

There was a flash. Hector saw Quentin's body lifted from the ground and sent cartwheeling into a stack of metal drums. Hector felt a spasm of guilt and nausea. Pitching a grenade at the back of a running man just didn't square with whatever was left of his con-

science. Then Hector flinched as there was a second explosion —
a massive fireball. Hector figured there must have been some kind
of fuel oil in the metal canisters that the critic's body had been
blasted into.

Hem coaxed a second grenade from Hector's hand, twisted
the handle and lobbed the grenade at the flaming metal drums.
There was another small, primary explosion from the grenade, followed by a larger, secondary blast.

Hector shook his head. Hem's pitch had been meanly gratuitous — killing a corpse, really.

But Hem was grinning — euphoric.

Hector sensed that by the time they returned to Botín's, Hem
would have himself convinced that he had thrown the first
grenade. He hoped Hem got his high spirits under control soon
— they would have to return to Botín's looking shocked and grief-
stricken in order to sell their agreed-upon lie…that Quentin had
fallen prey to a fascist shelling.

As they walked back to the Jeep, Hem slapped Hector's back
and said, "That's how you deal with a fucking critic!"

"There is no logic…

The acts of life have no beginning and no end.

Everything happens in a completely idiotic way."

— TRISTAN TZARA

CHAPTER 27

PARTINGS

HEM HAD TOLD HECTOR, riding back from Quentin's execution, that he planned to leave Spain in a couple of weeks. He needed to get to Key West, he said, "to square accounts with Pfife. Get things rolling." Hem spoke of taking a last fishing trip — a couple of days at sea with Hector. Sullen, strangely empty-feeling, Hector had said, "Sure, sounds swell, Hem."

Driving back to her loft, Alva was also quiet…not pushing Hector for details. She just sat quietly by him in the backseat of the Jeep, shivering, despite having Hector's big leather coat with its sheepskin lining pulled close around her.

Hector saw her shaking and pulled her closer to him, wrapping an arm around her shoulders. "I'll be better in a bit," he said. "It was just like shooting fish in a barrel, that's all. Not that you want such a thing to be 'sporting,' either."

"Don't say anymore," Alva said. "We won't talk about this, not ever again. We'll end it this way: thank you so much for what you did to avenge our Rachel."

ᔕ

Hector got the fire going then checked his watch. "Only six hours until the train. It's not enough time."

Alva kissed him. "Can't you stay? Can't you work it out with the captain?"

Hector traced her jawline with his thumb. "There's been another accusation against me. So no, I can't stay. And I want to go home. Want to enjoy life the way it is there in the time that is left before all this here reaches there. Are you still coming, Alva?"

She dipped her head. "I'm sorry for what I did earlier today. Trying to shame you into staying and fighting."

"It's not to be," he said. "And my heart isn't in the fight. Are you coming home with me?"

She smiled up at him. "Yes. Yes, Hector. But it will take time to ready everything so I can leave."

He hugged her. "I'll leave you the money — for the train and the boat. I have to close out my own business in Key West. Have to pack the things in my house that I want to take with me and have furniture shipped. When you get New York, wire me, and we'll work out the logistics for getting you down to Florida. We'll go on together from there to the Sound. Maybe see Yellowstone… I love parts of Idaho. We'll travel along Route 66. Make an adventure of it."

"Sounds wonderful, Hector. Are you *sure* you really still want me there?"

"Sure," Hector said. "Sure I am."

He pulled her closer to the fire and began to undress her.

ᔕ

Hector spent a week in Paris — catching up, finding old friends. He stopped by Shakespeare and Company to gossip and flirt with Sylvia Beach. He filled her in about the rift between Dos and Hem. She caught Hector up on the latest about Jim Joyce…about Gertrude and Alice B. Toklas. Sitting by the fire with Sylvia, Hector said, "Are you and Adrienne still thinking about parenthood?"

Hector had always been attracted to Sylvia, and liked her lover, Adrienne. In his unworthy youth, he had imagined wild couplings with the two women. He winked and said, "Because, if you are still thinking that, I could help…help you both with that. You know that we grow 'em tall in Texas." Sylvia blushed and laughed and punched his arm. "Always the rogue, aren't you, Hector? God I miss having you around. You and Hem coming in together, that was always the best."

On his last day in Paris, Hector was feeling sentimental and rang up the surrealists' shared studio in Madrid. He asked to be given the address of the gallery in Paris that Bishop Blair had shipped Alva's paintings to shortly before his murder.

It was raining and he ducked under the canopy of the gallery, closed and shook out his umbrella, and stepped into the warmth of the art studio. The proprietor, a wan, thin woman with glasses, offered Hector a glass of Burgundy. His kidney was improving so he accepted the wine and began browsing around the studio.

From across the room, Hector recognized Alva's distinctive, photo-realistic style.

He walked to her canvasses hanging there.

The first painting was a nude self-portrait, but in the picture, Alva had painted herself with small drawers and compartments in her arms and legs and belly — she looked like a sexy sideboard. Between her breasts, one of the drawers was opened and her heart was on display inside the drawer.

The next painting gave Hector pause. A man was stretched out naked on a bed. His arms were stretched above his head, in the pose of the "Minotaure." His head was turned and his eyes closed. A nude woman was standing at the foot of the bed.

She had been painted with her back to the viewer. Her hair was long and blond and she was hovering above the naked, sleeping man. She was clutching a long butcher knife behind her back. The painting was entitled, *In Perfumed Night, Choice Come Courting on Pink Toes*.

The more Hector stared at the painting, the more he began to think that the sleeping man on the bed resembled himself. The man even had a scar above his right knee, very much like one on Hector's leg. The room, too, reminded Hector more than a little of his bedroom in Key West. And the woman? Why, she could easily be Rachel.

The third of Alva's paintings deeply unsettled Hector. In that one, another man lay screaming on a bed. He was naked, and the bed was set on an angle. The walls of the room in which the bed rested were also crooked and curved and covered with crazed designs. The floor of the room was strewn with strange blocks of varying sizes. The painting was titled simply, *Barcelona, 1937*.

Hector bought all three paintings, arranging to have them shipped to his new home in Puget Sound. He left the gallery shaken…trying to make sense of what he had seen.

ʊ

The passage back to New York was uneventful…calm weather, no one interesting on the ship. Hector spent most of his days in his room, typing. He had a new novel underway. It pitted his Key West private eye against a beautiful con artist. He was calling it *Bait and Switch*.

He had completed half of the first draft by the time his ship reached harbor.

5

A knock sounded at Hector's hotel room door. He opened it and a youngish, well-groomed man in an understated blue suit smiled and stepped in. "Hello, Mr. Lassiter, welcome to New York City."

"Hello, Agent Tilly. How's J. Edgar? How's that Clive? How are the dogs?"

The FBI agent tossed his hat on the table and pulled out a notebook, smiling. "Time is short. Let's talk about Spain, and what you learned there, Mr. Lassiter."

"Fine," Hector said. "But you just remember the other part of our agreement. You bury any record of my participation in this — bury it even within your own fucking bureau."

5

Hector stood in the center of his living room and looked around. Some of the furniture he was leaving behind for use by the vacationers who'd be leasing his place. The rest had already been shipped west. Hector had even sent his bed ahead — he was planning on spending his last night on Key West in the Colonial Hotel.

His phone rang. It was Andy Haden, at the telegraph office. "I have a wire, for you Mr. Lassiter."

"I'll drop the tip by your office later today, just go ahead and read it to me, Andy."

"I'd rather not, Mr. Lassiter. I'd...I'll send a boy by with it. He'll be there in five minutes."

It was eighty-two degrees in Key West, and probably closer to ninety degrees inside Hector's house. Yet Hector felt cold all over. He said, "At least tell me who sent the damned wire."

"A Mr. John Dos Passos, writing from Valencia, Spain."

$$5$$

Hector sat on his front step looking at the telegram:

```
Hector, terrible news my friend   stop   I did-
n't know how best to reach you and didn't want
Papa  to  be  the  one  to  break  the  news   stop
There was a denunciation stop Alva Taurino was
arrested  and  charged  with  participation  in a
plot  to  torture combatants,  some of them Soviet
advisors, using some form of psychological tor-
ture based on surrealist imagery stop I know it
sounds  mad,  but  that  is  what  I've  heard stop
They say she was shot, Hector stop Katy and me
are  so  sorry  stop  If  there  is anything we can
do, you know we will stop Stay strong, my broth-
er  stop  I'll  send  more  by  letter  or phone you
as I know more stop Again, I'm so sorry, Hector.
                                             — Dos
```

Dazed, Hector crumpled up the telegram and began walking. He was on his third cigarette, wandering aimlessly around the Key when he heard someone calling his name:

"Hector! I didn't know you were back!"

He glanced around and realized he was on Whitehead Street, across from the Hemingway house. Pauline was standing at the gate. "Come over here, Hector," she said. "Talk to me." He crossed the street, a bit shakily. She said, "My God, what's happened?"

5

Hector had talked out Alva…talked out the split between Dos and Hem. And he'd been frank but gentle in describing the status of Martha's and Ernest's love affair.

"This one isn't like Jane Mason, or some of the others," Hector said. "He's plunging ahead."

"And leaving me behind," Pauline said. "Me and our boys. I should sue him for support."

Hector didn't have anything to say to that. Pauline rose from the couch, patting his thigh as she did. "Guess neither of us will forget this sorry day."

"No."

She said, "It's funny…well, not funny. But Papa wrote a long letter that arrived the other day. Posted from Paris…I guess he's heading back to tell me face-to-face. He wrote about this woman, Alva…and about you having been arrested. Charged with spying. Seems everyone in Spain thought you were spying for Hoover."

"It didn't start that way."

Pauline paused. "So, it's true." She said, "We need a drink for this, I think."

She came back with two glasses and a green bottle. Hector said, "Oh Jesus, absinthe?"

"Yes," Pauline said. "You said it tastes of regret. I want the taste now. The numbing. And it'll infuriate Papa…he's been sparing in using it. This is bottle number two of three."

Hector said, "Let's at least do it right." He went to the kitchen and got the drip spoons and glasses.

Watching him, Pauline said, "So you were really were there as a spy, then?"

Hector shook his head. "That's vastly overstating it. I was stopped by the feds in New York. It's supposed to be illegal to travel to Spain now. I got caught. I explained I was going over to kind of stand watch on Hem and maybe to gather material for my own novel. I insisted I wasn't going over as a combatant or because I was a communist. That's all true. Then a nice young man in a blue suit told me what fate I might expect when I came back. They've already decided on the terminology they'll use to discredit the Americans over there. They'll be called 'premature anti-fascists.' They'll be blacklisted…treated as communist fifth-columnists back here. They won't be permitted to fight in the coming war. Their careers — be they literary, journalistic or cinematic — will be over when they get back to America. I figured by agreeing to come back and report what I've seen, I could at least protect Hem and Dos. Insulate them from the ostracizing to come for the rest here at home."

"Have you? Have you done that?"

"I think, like me, that they'll be alright. But many of our other friends won't be — not because of me. There are other, real FBI spies over there to see to that." Hector drank some absinthe, still hating the taste. He said, his voice raw, "Alva would have been alright."

They sipped their absinthe and Pauline hugged Hector, long and hard. "I'm so sorry for you. First Rachel, and now this…"

"I'm sorry for you too," Hector said. He untangled himself from her arms and sipped more absinthe. "Where are Patrick and Gig?"

"The boys are out with Toby, fishing for the day."

"Place is sure quiet."

"Quiet, and quite empty. Especially upstairs. It's a very big bed for one person." She hesitated, then said, "You didn't approve of me, and what happened, I knew that. You took Hadley's side."

Hector wanted to say, *Somebody had to.*

He said, "Hadley was my friend. She treated me like a kid brother. I was dreadfully fond of her."

"Now here I am, right where she was. Probably the same reasons, too. We have the child…gain weight…stop being seen as a sex partner…as a bedmate. As a *chum*. Look at me — I'm a mother, twice over. Terrible scars from the Cesareans…"

Hector wasn't liking the drift of the conversation. He drained his absinthe and poured himself some more. Pauline slammed hers back and slapped her glass down on the table. "See, I can still be a chum…can still drink like a *chap*. But Ernest doesn't see that. He hasn't slept with me in two years."

Oh God. Hector wanted to check his watch — make some excuse to leave. Go home with his absinthe buzz and mourn Alva. Or maybe go to a sporting house. Find himself some hot little Cuban whore who'd scar his back with her nails…bite his shoulder as she was peaking.

And he certainly didn't need this insight into Ernest's most private life.

"For what my opinion's worth, I don't think it's about you, Pauline," Hector said. "You're still an attractive woman," he said it more than a bit disingenuously. "Scott has a theory. I think he might be right. He told me that Hem needs a new wife for every big novel. He had Hadley for *The Sun Also Rises*. He had you for *A Farewell to Arms*. I suppose he'll have Martha for his Spanish Civil War novel. Then, when it's time for the next big novel after that, I suspect we'll start getting inklings of the fourth Mrs. Hemingway."

Pauline nodded. She looked fairly smashed…even blowsy.

She prepared them both some more absinthe.

"Go easy on that for me," Hector said. "It hits me hard and wrong and with my head like it is now, after Alva…"

"I'm going to get drunk," Pauline said. "Well, I'm already drunk. But I mean to keep drinking a while longer. I shouldn't drink alone, should I?"

"I do it all the time."

"Fine, so we'll drink alone together."

She got up and put on some music: Marlene Dietrich singing "La Vie en Rose."

She pulled her frock away from her breast with a fluttering motion a few times. "So hot. Well, at least when he gives me the heave-ho, I'll have reason to leave this damned oven of an island."

Hector nodded. "Where will you go? Back to Arkansas? Maybe back to Paris?"

"Arkansas is no place to live after the life I've had with Ernest," she said. "And Paris? Hadley is still there. Can't have the City of Lights becoming a repository for former Mrs. Hemingways."

"I suppose not."

Pauline sat back down next to Hector. Very close. She said, "So you think I'm still attractive?"

Christ. Hector put his drink down. He was about to stand up when she threw a leg over him. Her mouth found his. He didn't really respond, and she began dry humping his thigh. Her hands found his and she lifted them to her breasts...pressed them there.

Hector was trying to disentangle himself when he sensed motion in the hall — saw Hem standing there with his suitcases, watching them.

Pauline looked over her shoulder, drunk, and said, "Don't stop, Hector. Please. Don't mind Hem. He doesn't love me anymore. You know better than anyone. Don't stop — it's been so long. You're 'the man who writes what he lives and lives what he writes.' You've written about things like this. Don't stop now, Hector."

Hem just stood there, watching them. Hector pushed Pauline off his lap. Hector stood up, shakily. He said, "Sometimes we bin what we write, Pauline. When it's not right. I'll leave you two to talk."

Hem stood in the middle of the doorway to the hall. He wouldn't step aside and Hector had to squeeze past, brushing shoulders. Hem hesitated and said, "You should know something, Hector."

"I already know it, Ernest. Dos wired me."

"You going to do what Dos did? Go back there and try to find answers?"

Hector shook his head. "Dead is dead. What's the point?"

5

Hector was continuing packing when he heard the knock at the door. He opened it and Ernest caught him on the jaw, just below his left ear, sending him to the floor.

Hector struggled up onto one elbow, massaging his jaw. "Christ, I'm sorry, okay," Hector said. "I didn't do anything, not really. She was high on that damned absinthe…feeling rejected. I'm not attracted to her."

"Guess that makes two of us," Hem said, red-faced. "Hell, I'd probably be grateful if you two did end up together. Like Hadley and Paul Mowrer…good to know she's found a good man."

"Not this man," Hector said. "Jesus, Hem."

Hem glared at him. "Well, anyway, that was for the other — this spying shit. You goddamned traitor."

"Did Pauline explain *why* I was 'spying' for the FBI?"

Hem said nothing. So Hector explained again. When he was finished, Hem said, "Don't do me favors like that ever again. And you know what, the more I think on it, that slug was for insulting my wife by not sleeping with her. It's been fun, Hec. Sorry about Alva and all that, but you know, you're just bad news for me, Lasso."

Hem slammed the door behind himself.

Hector lay on his floor, rubbing his jaw and trying to make sense of the logic of insulting a man by refusing to fuck his drunken wife.

PART THREE

FILM NOIR

(1947)

"The enemy of art is the absence of limitations."

— Orson Welles

CHAPTER 28

THE LADY FROM SHANGHAI

HECTOR WAS AT THE WHEEL of his new blue Chevrolet Fleetmaster convertible. It was raining hard and the wipers were slapping…the only real noise in the car.

Conversation had been stingy for miles, so Hector turned on the radio. He was captured by Billie Holiday's moody, even sinister cover of "Deep Song."

It was January. Shivering, Hector clicked the car heater up a notch.

Orson promptly wiped his forehead and turned down the heater. He lit a cigarette. Welles was not much of a cigarette smoker, but his current on-screen character was and Orson seemed to be getting the habit. The butt of the cigarette jittered in the dark…hinting of shaking hands. Orson, in rumbling voice, finally spoke from the darkness. "Thank you again for coming to help, Hector, old friend. My nerves…"

Invisible as he nearly was next to Hector, and with that famous voice, it made Hector feel a little as though he was giving a lift to one of Orson's famous radio characters, *The Shadow* — "Never seen, only heard. As haunting to superstitious minds as a ghost; as inevitable as a guilty conscience."

Hector shook his head. "Nerves" was a face-saving euphemism

on Orson's part. Near as Hector could tell, Orson was stretched to the breaking point by all the "pep" pills he was popping to keep his weight down. Orson had resorted to amphetamines to keep himself trim enough to be convincing in the role of "Michael O'Hara," a two-fisted "Black Irish" sailor and wanted man in Spain for killing a Franco spy during the Spanish Civil War. O'Hara was conceived as a scrappy, lonely, haunted man and struggling novelist.

Orson had lured Hector to Hollywood in late December for $300 a week to serve as a kind of off-screen consultant for his new thriller, *The Lady From Shanghai*. Orson had feverishly made the pitch, citing parallels between Hector's picaresque biography and that of the fictional O'Hara.

In addition to his wife, as he often did, Orson had salted the cast with old friends from his Mercury Theatre Days. But even Orson's band of friends was in near revolt, too. The production was frenetically moving north and south of the Mexican border and back again — zigzagging between Mexico, San Francisco, Acapulco and the studio lot. Nearly all the cast and crew members had contracted various intestinal diseases or other exotic maladies during one or another of the trips south.

Perhaps most devastating of all, a union strike was threatening completion of a set critical to the film's climax — a surrealistic boardwalk "funhouse" that looked, at least on paper, to evoke something closer to images ripped from Bosch than Barnum and Bailey...a surrealist nightmare.

Pressed for time, unable to sleep from the mixture of anxiety and all the pep pills and gallons of black coffee sustaining him, Orson was risking a union backlash spending nights at the studio painting his own lurid images on the walls of his funhouse.

It was vintage Orson: trying to do it all — turning limitations and setbacks into inspired innovations and ingenious solutions. But this time, Orson seemed to Hector in danger of hitting the wall. Orson must have sensed it, too, because he'd actually signed on some hired hands, out-of-pocket: Hector as undesignated batman, and a couple of young women to help with the painting of the funhouse set.

Orson had personally recruited the "girls," one "a serious if unknown painter in her own right," Orson insisted, who was helping him create the funhouse's lurid wall illustrations. The other was an "aspiring, no-talent wannabe actress" as Orson described her, some Massachusetts girl come out to Hollywood named Beth, or Betty, or some such. He was using the second young woman to mix paints, clean brushes and to fill in the monochromatic backgrounds — what Orson, sniffing, declared "the drudge painting."

"Invisible" Orson gestured at the radio with the glowing end of his cigarette. "Billie and me, we used to date, did you know that?"

"No," Hector said. Given the racial backlash that might have resulted, Hector wasn't surprised their affair came as news to him. "When was that?"

"During *Kane*...the filming and a bit after the release."

Billie Holiday's tune ended; Jo Stafford was crooning "Haunted Heart", "backed by Paul Weston and his fine fine orchestra."

Hector said, "Painting this set yourself — all night, every night — it's going to kill you, Orson."

"But I have my help now, Hector," Orson said. "And the whole film turns on the climax, as it should. And I have my pride. Hitchcock hired Dali to formulate a key sequence in *Spellbound* a couple of years ago. I mean to out-Hitch Hitchcock...to out-Dali Dali."

Hector slowed and a studio guard checked his Chevy's license plate, and then waved them through the gate.

"I'd sure like to get a look at this funhouse set," Hector said, steering onto the studio's back lot.

"Not yet, Hector. I do crave your take, but only when my vision is closer to complete. Another day, two at most. You'll pick me up at six tomorrow?"

"Whatever's left of you, sure," Hector said. "Six a.m. it is. You've got to sleep sometime, you know. And these women? You've got something going with them?"

"Not yet, not both."

"Well, there's still time," Hector said dryly. Then, "I thought you and Rita had moved back in together."

Orson shook his head. "Only for the duration of filming. She talks of going longer, of trying to patch things up, but the essential problems between us remain. Living together again has only reminded me of all that. But until the filming is over…"

"Sacrifices must be made for art?"

"Always." Orson laughed and slapped Hector's knee. "God, it's good to have you seeing me through this. This is the critical one, Hector. It can turn it all around for me."

"So meet me halfway and don't make my caretaking impossible," Hector said. "Go easy with these women tonight."

"Of course. We're racing a deadline prepping the set. Two more days, and much of the pressure will be off. I'll see you in the morning, Hector. Oh, and bring plenty of coffee."

"It's your funeral," Hector said. "You might as well be awake for it."

Orson opened the door of the Chevy and the interior light came on. Hector got another look at Welles in the unflattering light and shuddered: Orson looked bad.

Hector watched him run hunched through the rain into the studio warehouse in which he was fashioning his hellish sounding funhouse. With some deft editing, the ersatz amusement attraction would appear to be located at Whitney's Playland in San Francisco.

A woman dressed in black opened the soundstage door for Orson. She had long blond hair and looked to be tall, athletic. Built like a dancer, maybe. Orson was quite tall by Hollywood standards, and she stood up well against him. She also looked pretty enough, but Hector couldn't see much more than that through his Chevy's rain-streaked windshield. Hector saw the other woman, smaller, strangely pale and raven-haired, embrace Orson.

Hector shook his head, checked his wristwatch, and then got his car in gear. He turned around and drove down out of the studio, waved back through the gates by the old, bored-looking guard.

Hector fiddled with the radio and found Billie Holiday again, this time crooning "Lover Come Back To Me."

The past six years had found Hector drifting away from screenwork and back to writing novels — a string of increasingly successful thrillers that had found their own way to the screen.

As he half listened to Holiday's haunted tune, Hector thought about his latest gig as paid babysitter to Hollywood's hopped-up *enfant terrible*. He was increasingly tempted to leave Los Angeles. He had recently divorced and was weighing going back to his new home in New Mexico. His big hacienda shouldered right up to the border and Hector yearned to stray across that line. He could spend some time in Mexico. He'd find himself some dark-haired, dark-eyed *señorita* who had never heard of Hector Lassiter, author and screenwriter. He could reinvent himself for a wanton weekend. He'd maybe pretend to be a merchant marine with a dark secret. Or perhaps, like Welles' Michael O'Hara, he'd be a soldier of fortune, running from something ominous tied to the Spanish Civil War.

It was tempting…

Cracking his window so he could smell the winter California rain, Hector turned the wipers up a notch, and then shook loose a cigarette. He pushed in the car lighter and twisted the radio tuner, waiting for the lighter to prime and pop out.

Fiddling more with the radio, he settled on an instrumental version of Cole Porter's "Ev'ry Time We Say Goodbye." The lighter clicked and Hector pulled it out and held the glowing orange coils up to his cigarette.

Hector had been invited to the home of some art collectors

in Laurel Canyon. The party promised to be mix of other art collectors, on- and off-screen Hollywood movers-and-shakers, free-
thinkers and Bohemians. There would also be the requisite suspect writers and actors and artists being badgered by the House
Un-American Activities Committee. As a result of those party
guests, there would also probably be some snitches and spies for
HUAC and for the FBI — a designation Hector, happily, could
no longer claim.

But there would be women there, too. Probably young and
available, free-thinking women of forgiving morals.

The latter prospect decided it for Hector. He checked his
scribbled-down directions and headed toward Laurel Canyon.

"If the crowd really knew
who we were and what we represented,
we'd probably be lynched."
— MAN RAY

CHAPTER 29

CADAVRE EXQUIS

THE HOUSE WAS BUILT onto a cliff side and was reached by a steep, zigzagging driveway with several switchbacks and hairpin turns. Hector thought of all the drinking that was probably well underway and wondered how many guests wouldn't be coming back for return engagements once they tried to navigate that steep driveway back *down* — squinting into darkness and three-sheets-to-the-wind.

Hector reached the top and rolled slowly by the house. It had been designed by some protégé of Frank Lloyd Wright's and looked like nothing so much as a Mayan temple fused to a prototypical Hollywood rich man's pad.

Hector pulled alongside the temple-cum-house, backed up, and turned around so he'd have an easier time leaving. Not that Hector intended to be drunk — his most recent ex-wife had at least convinced him to taper off on the booze during their last days together and he was still enjoying near-sobriety. Hector just liked the option of quick exits.

A swarthy man in a white jacket put a hand to Hector's chest as the writer stepped up onto the porch out of the rain. He spoke in lightly-accented English. Not Mexican, but perhaps Spanish…maybe a Moor. "You have an invitation?"

"I'm here as a guest of John Huston. Name's Hector Lassiter."

The man checked a clipboard and said, "Right. Good. Go ahead."

Hector scoped the main room: very swanky. The Mayan motif carried on through the interior of the house. The place was packed with pre-Columbian art and artifacts, interspersed with cubist and surrealist paintings, photographs and sculptures. Hector perused Picassos, Miros and Man Rays…several Magrittes and a couple of works by Salvador Dali.

Another swarthy man with jug ears, also dressed in a starched white jacket, sidled up next to Hector with a couple of trays. Hector helped himself to some champagne and a couple of *hors d'oeuvres*. The hosts seemed to favor Billie Holiday, too. Her recording of "Lover Man" played low under the buzz of the guests.

Roaming, he saw bug-eyed Man Ray in spirited conversation with a couple of men whose backs were to Hector. Hector had always thought the little photographer, whose given name was Emmanuel Radnitsky, from Philly, of all places, to be quite mad. In those long-gone Left Bank days, Hector had invested much more of his interest in Man Ray's then-lover, the sleek, blond model-turned-photographer Lee Miller. Lee was Man Ray's muse become *bête noire*…a woman Hector had not succeeded in catching on the bounce, despite a few tries.

When Lee had left Man Ray to pursue her own photographic career, Man had unleashed a flurry of pieces that literally deconstructed Lee Miller, entitling one "Object to Be Destroyed."

By a tall sculpted stone fireplace, Hector spotted Vincent Price — something of an art collector himself, Hector had heard — chatting up John Huston…two gaunt and imperious men with world-class voices, passionately going at it over something regarding the Marquis de Sade.

Hector was headed their way when a pair of arms slipped

through his. "You're Hector Lassiter, aren't you?" It was the voice of a little girl.

Hector looked over the young woman hanging on his "gun arm." He switched his unsampled drink to his left hand, so she wouldn't jostle it, and said, "Howdy, honey. Yeah, I'm Hector Lassiter."

"I've read all your books…I just loved *Satan's Daughter*. It was a gas."

"Great. But aren't you a little young for that book? I mean, what are you? Sixteen, certainly not seventeen?"

"Fifteen."

Hector smiled and slid his right arm free. She was tallish, buxom. Enough drinks and enough impaired judgment — the right low light — and a man might convince himself she was a newly minted eighteen. She struck Hector as disturbingly worldly. He said, "What's your name, angel?"

"Sarah."

"Got a last name to go with 'Sarah'?"

"Sarah Marshall."

"Ah. Daughter of the hosts, yes?"

"That's right. Mummy sent me to fetch you."

"Yeah? How'd she say to do that?"

"Left it up to me."

"So where is Mummy?"

"Right there," she said, pointing. "When she's through with you, find me again. I want to talk more about your books."

"Sure. Sure…if it's not past your bedtime."

Her cheeks flushed. Sarah stuck out her tongue, tossed her hair…and headed toward Man Ray.

Hector watched her go — all bouncing brown hair and wagging hips. *Jesus.* Man Ray smiled at her and slipped an arm around her shoulders. The photographer stopped one of the interchangeable, white-jacket-clad swarthy men and grabbed some champagne. The photographer handed the glass to Sarah.

Hector was quickly losing his taste for the party. Another arm slipped through his. The woman was a taller, legal version of Sarah Marshall. The woman said, "I'm Mercedes Marshall, Mr. Lassiter. I was thrilled to hear it when John mentioned you were coming as his guest."

Hector smiled, all innocence and bonhomie. "You read my books too? Just like your little girl?"

The woman tilted her head; a sly smile. Her eyes were big and blue with violet highlights. Her eyes unsettled Hector: she didn't seem to blink. "Sarah's not so little, as I noticed you noticing. And we're both avid readers of yours, yes."

"That's…real nice," Hector said. "Quite a collection you and your husband have amassed." He waved a hand at the paintings and sculptures surrounding them.

"Me, mostly. I don't think Raymond really cares a toss for art, Mr. Lassiter. Other than as an investment, of course."

"One of those, eh?"

She winked. "As I said, I was thrilled to hear you were coming. I'm told you know, or knew, a particular painter. I've been able to purchase some of her works, which are quite rare, given her terrible and early end. I'm told you might have some more of them in your own collection. I'd like to buy them from you. I'll pay you quite handsomely. What I'm prepared to pay you will more than return your investment in them."

Hector's mouth was suddenly dry. Already fairly certain of the answer, he said, "Who is this painter?"

Mercedes took Hector's champagne flute from his hand and drained it to its dregs. Hector looked at her lipstick stain left on his emptied glass. She smiled and said, "Alva Taurino. I have many of her works. She was a genius. What a tragic waste. What a terrible and senseless loss. I mean, her being executed in service to a lost cause like that."

"She wasn't the only one." Hector motioned around them with his left hand. "I don't see any of her paintings here."

"They're in my private study. I'll show you." She took his hand.

He followed her down a long hallway, the walls covered with more geometric patterns contrived to evoke the sense of an ancient temple. Hector looked her over as he followed. Mercedes wore a clingy black gown with no back. She had lush hips that Hector figured the vixenish daughter had studied to master her own slink. Mercedes had long legs, one of which was visible through a dramatic slit up the left side of her gown. Good shoulders, too: she wore her hair up to showcase her fine shoulders and long back. Mrs. Marshall opened a door at the end of the dimly lit hallway and Hector followed her in. Low bookcases ran around the perimeter of the room. A massive, hand-carved desk dominated the study. The walls were filled with canvasses; nearly all of them were signed "Alva."

Hector walked around the room, lips parted and heart racing… moving dumbstruck from painting to painting. "I was in Alva's loft, in Madrid, and saw many of her works," Hector said. "But I don't remember any of these. Never saw anything like these, there."

Many of the paintings were essentially nude, surrealist self-portraits. Hector was nearly stricken to see Alva staring back at him, and in such dark contexts. In some of the paintings, Alva had made herself a redhead, or a blond — the latter reminding Hector of Rachel. But the paintings were stark and brazen…some verging on the pornographic. Others were almost offensive in their blunt, lovingly-studied depictions of violence.

"*Inaccrochable*," Hector caught himself whispering.

"Yes, you can see why these are hung in my most private area," Mrs. Marshall said, taking Hector's arm again. "Nobody can really tell me just how many of her works exist. Each time I think I've hit bottom, another painting or two of Alva's seems to surface at some gallery in Paris…maybe in Milan or Barcelona. They aren't for every taste. But they are brave, you must admit."

"I suppose you could call them 'brave.' There's also something almost jaded or debauched about these," Hector said. "They smack of a kind of dark glut. The ones I own are nothing like these. These hint of a side of Alva that I never saw."

She leaned her head against his shoulder. "A fact made more striking because you and Alva were lovers…or so I've heard."

Hector made a sour face.

"I've offended you," she said. "How strange. I mean, based on your books, I thought you more the man of the world than perhaps you are. I at least expected you to be a man who would be more frank and open."

Hector continued frowning. "I can be those, in the right company. Being open right now, let me be frank and say I frankly don't know you, lady."

She said, "You don't strike me as a champagne drinker, Hector. What can I make for you?"

"Whiskey and water will be fine."

"A serious drinker, after my own heart." As he continued studying the paintings, she poured them both cocktails from a sideboard bar. She tapped glasses with him and said, "*Los toros dan y los toros quitan.*"

"Right." Hector sipped his whiskey, staring at Alva's depiction of a bull raping a woman who looked uncomfortably like Alva. The woman's expression was something between terror and a sensual snarl. The bull seemed aloof…but hung.

"What was Alva like, Mr. Lassiter? I confess, I'm utterly fascinated by her. By her vision and by her life…what little I've been able to learn about it."

Hector sipped his whiskey. He thought awhile and then he said, "She was very passionate about her painting. Very free spirited. Unfortunately, she allowed politics to begin to impinge on her work, both on and off the canvas. It was the same trap that befell many creative types in the 1930s — writers, painters and actors. She had the misfortune of doing it in Spain…and of choosing losing sides. I tried to warn her off."

Mrs. Marshall was still hanging on Hector's arm, her head tilted against his shoulder and her piled-up brown hair tickling his neck. "Is it true what they say about what led to her shooting? That she was using surrealist art as a means of torturing fascists to secure intelligence?"

"That was the story out of Spain, and last I heard, those on the scene seemed to be sticking to it," Hector said. "Not that those are sources to be trusted. Nothing was what it seemed in Spain. Nobody was who they seemed in Spain."

"And Alva?"

"A casualty of war. What was that phrase of Auden's that Orwell so hated? Oh yeah, Alva became some son of a bitch's 'necessary murder.'"

"Ten years, and you're still very bitter." She squeezed his arm. "The memories must be terrible. They say 'out of sight, out of mind.' So in that spirit, you would consider selling me your paintings of Alva's?"

Hector shook his head. "No, I wouldn't. Unlike your husband, I don't buy art for investment's sake. I liked the art, and, as you've said, I had a very close connection to the painter. They're mementos to me, not collectibles."

"You haven't heard my offer, Hector."

"Money isn't the issue."

This look in her eyes. He said, "Sex isn't the issue either."

"I haven't offered that."

"Well, now it's out of the way, either way," Hector said.

Mercedes said, "I saw you with my daughter. Sarah seemed to like you. And I could tell, in some ways, you liked Sarah, too. Like Alva, you and your books fascinate me. I've heard stories about the tension between what you write and your own life. Sarah's fascinated by all that, too. Perhaps you could explain in more detail to both of us…"

Hector shook loose his arm. "Twenty years ago, I'd probably have followed that conversational thread all the way to a sweaty, panting, limb-tangled end. But now I'm just going to follow that path back down that hallway of yours and back to your damned fine party."

"Think some more about it, Hector. I really mean to have your paintings."

"I'll think about it," he said.

"Think about all of it."

"Oh, I'll do that, too. Filthy thoughts about all of that will probably eat at me for the rest of the night…maybe longer."

Hector stepped back into the hubbub of the party. He thought he smelled marijuana. A back slap. "Hector, I saw you, then I lost you." Director John Huston…slender, slope-shouldered…bushy eyebrows and *the voice.*

"I was getting a private showing," Hector said. "Mrs. Marshall was showing off her collection of Alva Taurinos. You asked me here, John. Did you do that so she could make a pitch to buy my 'Alvas'?"

"Partly, Hector," John said. "I also don't see you often enough, and caretaking Orson as you are, I thought this was a rare chance to catch up."

"Quite a crew," Hector said. "I was looking around and counting communists."

"It's a real concern for the artists, particularly, Hector," John said. "Many have quite overt communist connections. The city of Los Angeles has actually passed an ordinance, Hector, banning modern art. Particularly, *surrealist* art. Bastards have banned it from public spaces, declaring it all to be 'emblematic of communist enterprise and philosophy.'"

Hector smiled. "They all got painted with the same slanted brush, eh? Ironic fate for a bunch of lefty, loony artists."

"You were in Spain in 1937, Hector," John said. "How have you eluded a subpoena from HUAC?"

"I was in Spain babysitting another friend," Hector said. "I didn't choose sides. Just ate and drank and caroused and watched Hem's back for his second wife."

"I'll spread that word," John said. "Because you see, Hector, some people are talking. Some are wondering how you've avoided the House subcommittee hearings."

"Well, fuck 'some people,'" Hector said.

John changed topics. "Orson was supposed to be here tonight. What's he up to now, Hector?"

"He's wired and working on his own sets. He's painting up some funhouse for the climax of his latest film."

"Ah, yes. I guess I have heard something about that. Mercedes scrounged up a painter and some young would-be actress to help him."

Hector realized he was still carrying his glass of whiskey. He sipped a little more. A couple of years of near-abstinence had taken away his taste for the stuff. He dropped his glass on the tray of a passing, swarthy waiter and pulled off a fresh glass of champagne...something he could nurse, if Mercedes Marshall didn't take it away and drain it again. Behind him, Hector heard two women discussing some work of Dali's, something titled *Dream Caused by the Flight of a Bee around a Pomegranate a Second Before Awakening*. Hector said, "I overheard you talking about De Sade to Vincent Price a bit ago. Didn't realize you were all so steeped in De Sade's works."

"We all are," John said. "As a man who favors strong sensations, I'm frankly surprised you aren't as well, Hector. Of course nobody else is quite so devoted to Sade as Man is."

"Man? Man Ray?" Hector sipped champagne. "Makes sense in Man's case. I mean, old Man's more than a bit of a misogynist, isn't he? Strikes me as very sadistic."

John brushed back an unruly forelock of brown hair.

"How so?"

"It's always been there in his work. I attended a showing of some of his photographs a few years back. The Fantasies of William Seabrook, it was called…naked women in chains and ropes, gagged…their privates on display. They looked like the stuff that crazy killer Barney Waxmiller shot of his victims before he raped and then killed them."

"By God, you've grown stodgy in your forties, Hector," John said, laughing. "Pardon me, I've got to go chat-up Fanny Brice. We're negotiating a trade of some pre-Columbian pottery."

Hector drifted around some more, increasingly eyeing the exit. He also was aware of Mercedes Marshall and her saucy, jailbait daughter, eyeing him. Some artists were gathered around a table with a long strip of paper. Hector leaned over for a look and Vincent Price whispered, "It's a game of *Exquisite Corpse*. Quite an intense one." Their game was also highly pornographic, from what Hector could see of the lower-most portion of the sketch, now well underway.

One of the artists, a short fat man with bucked teeth, said, "We need a model for round two!"

Sarah Marshall obediently put down her drink and, looking more than a bit drunk, tugged her blouse from her skirt. She began fiddling with the buttons. Several of the artists moved to the couch for a better view. Hector drifted over to Mercedes and said, "You don't seem to be moving to stop this."

Sarah's mother shrugged, reminding Hector of her proud, bare shoulders. She said, "Why would I? They're artists. I collect surrealist paintings. Those artists I collect used live models. I'd be a hypocrite to buy their art and then rebel at the elements critical to its creation."

"Even if one of those 'elements' is your lushed-out, underage daughter?"

"I really did badly misjudge you, Hector," Mercedes said. "I guess that just like you can't judge a book by its cover, you can't judge an author by his characters."

"Maybe," Hector agreed. "And 'artists' do evolve."

"So where have you 'evolved' to? What are you working on now, Hector?"

From the corner of his eye, Hector could see the young girl struggling with her brassiere. He made a conscious effort not to look there again. Riffing, Hector lied, "It's a literary thriller. And a bit of a *roman à clef.* It's based on the premise that a collection of libertine artists have moved through several phases of creativity. Because they have functioned with utter abandon, and with no restrictions on their behavior nearly all along the way, they have escalated in their debauchery. So they try to redeem themselves with abstract notions of politics, then social commentary. But jaded as they are, they eventually sink into complete decadence, and murder…reaching for increasingly bloodier places, just to *feel.*"

Mercedes was pure ice. "Really." Hector heard wolf-whistles behind him.

"Yeah," Hector said. "Really. Thanks for the evening, Merc. It was swell."

Hector drifted over to a couch where John Huston was still "chatting-up" Fanny Brice. "You best clear out," he whispered in the director's ear. "I scent raid…*Confidential Magazine*…morals charges and lawsuits. Stir in a little statutory rape."

John quickly rose and took Hector's arm, walking him out of the house and onto the front porch. It was raining and drops dripped from the eaves of the porch. "I guess I miscalculated asking you here, Hector," John said, his sonorous tone now terse. "I guess I misjudged you."

"You wouldn't be the first tonight."

John wagged a long finger in his face. "Well, Hector, leave if you must. But don't do something precipitous. These people aren't to be trifled with, Hector. They're not to be crossed. And they have friends who are even less to be trifled with."

"Why, hell, is that a threat, John?"

The director patted Hector's cheeks with both hands. "Threats are for people you're willing to act against. That was advice, Hector. Advice is for those you wish to keep around. The world's more interesting with you in it. Really: don't go getting your cock up to fuck with these people."

"You should take your own advice, John. There's a minor in there about to be corrupted all over the place."

"Who? Sarah? That girl's well beyond corrupting." The director smiled, hesitating. "You should come south of the border with me, Hector. Bogie and me, we're going to film *Treasure of the Sierra Madre* in Mexico later this year. Damn near all of it will be shot on location. Isn't that something? Come down for the party, yes?"

"Tempting," Hector said. "The novelist who wrote the book, he's kind of a mystery man, isn't he? I hear nobody knows who he really is."

"German, they say. But that could be a lie," John said. "Others say he's Polish. Or maybe just from Chicago. He doesn't put a premium on self-identity. Hell, he could be a woman. They say he has ten or more identities he uses. Some think he's the bastard offspring of the Kaiser. Isn't that marvelous? For my money, well, I think 'Bruno Traven,' our mystery novelist, was actually posing as his own agent — as the man I had to cut the deal with for the film rights to the novel. That's marvelous, too. I hope it's true. We all strike poses...put on masks. But who reinvents themselves like that?"

Hector watched John's back as the gangly director went weaving back inside. An old man was standing out on the porch, smoking a pipe. He said, "Hear the game is in session...*The Exquisite Corpse*. I need to get back inside for that. It's just that it's so damned crowded."

Hector said, "Well, a space just opened up. I'm out of here."

The old man wrinkled his brow. "It's still early. You're already leaving?"

"Yes." Hector couldn't place it...something familiar about the old man's eyes and their color...something about the shape of his ears. Hector shook out a Pall Mall. "You've been coming to parties like this one for a long time, Pops?"

The old man smiled. "Hell, I used to throw parties like this one."

Trailing cigarette smoke, Hector trotted through a light rain back to his Chevrolet. He heard someone else running up behind him, overtaking him. Passing him by, squinting into the rain, Vincent Price said to Hector, "So, the only other prudent man at the party. Like you, when the orgy starts, I flee."

Hector decided right there to be a Vincent Price fan. He called, "Any films coming up?"

"Two thrillers," Vincent called back, smiling and blinking in the rain. "*The Web* and *The Long Night*."

Hector gave him a thumbs-up. "I'll look for 'em."

Sinatra on the radio: "Everything Happens to Me." Hector began the long, zigzagging drive down from the Marshall house, following Vincent Price's coupe from a respectable and safe distance.

He was still toying with finding a payphone and dropping a dime on the surrealists, despite John's warnings.

Or, he could simply go home and make it an early night. Maybe get some of the sleep Orson was sacrificing.

Hector was enjoying the cleaner life…enjoying a quiet, steady routine with no drama.

He didn't need to go kicking cabals of flaky painters in the balls. Or so he told himself.

Hector was halfway to his rented bungalow when he realized whom the old man's eyes and ears reminded him of. His epiphany almost sent him into a skid and back to Laurel Canyon:

The old man's eyes and ears were just like those of Rachel Harper, and of her sister, Alva Taurino.

*"The approval of the public
must be avoided above all.
The public must be forbidden
to enter if confusion is to be avoided."*

— ANDRÉ BRETON

CHAPTER 30

THE COLLECTOR

HECTOR ROLLED UP alongside his rented bungalow and idled into the carport. He locked up his Chevy and trotted through the harder rain up to his front door and groped in the dark with the keys. Safely inside, he shrugged off his trench coat and turned on some lights and fiddled with the radio...dialing past various dramas and comedies and quiz shows until he found some music: Jo Stafford and "Haunted Heart."

He looked at his typewriter, standing at the ready, half-a-page of the opening of the last chapter of his next novel already there, the last paragraph ending in mid-sentence, as was his custom.

Hector figured he should probably just knuckle down and finish it now. But he was tired and his mind was weighed down — besieged really. He was swarmed by all the memories of Rachel and Alva and the surrealist murders in Key West and Spain that the party and seeing Alva's paintings — and, perhaps, actually seeing Rachel and Alva's hated *father* — had triggered.

He thought he had put it all away...put it behind him. It had been ten years after all, just as Mercedes Marshall, his fetching, slutty host had said. But it was like that poem, *The Hound of Heaven*: a sense of still being dogged by all of that, ten, no, really twelve years on.

If Rachel was still alive, she'd be perhaps thirty-five…still young enough…ripe. By now she would have found her true voice as a writer or painter. And if they'd gone the distance, Rachel might have saved Hector from some go-nowhere marriages.

And kid sister, Alva? She'd be thirty-three, Hector reckoned — a resonant age for poets, writers, artists and martyrs.

Screw it. He needed to get his head into something else. Hector turned up Jo and "Haunted Heart" a little louder. He sat down at his typewriter and lit a Pall Mall. He pulled out the page of manuscript there and rolled in a fresh sheet of paper. He started banging away at the keys, thinking of the Keys — Key West in the middle 1930s. He was thinking of Rachel, too. He typed:

> You know how it is in August on Bone Key when the night doesn't take off the heat and the wind from the Gulf just pushes around the heavy stale air without cooling anything down.
>
> I was stretched out there naked on top of the sheets until two, unable to sleep, just watching the sheers billow inward with the dead warm rushes of air, my skin beaded with sweat. I could hear the wind chimes hung out back of the widow Jackson's house, and from far away, I could hear the horns of the ships out on the Gulf. The ships' horns and the wind chimes were the last sounds I remembered before awakening, squinting in the orange light through the window, torn from sleep by the caws of Nigger Peru's fighting cocks.
>
> Now there was a woman on the bed next to me, naked and sleeping.
>
> I stroked her cool back. I shook her once.
>
> She wasn't sleeping.

Christ. He *hated* it. Hector tore out the sheet of typing paper, crumpled it and threw it at the empty waste paper basket sitting alongside the desk. He rolled back into the typewriter the chapter-in-progress of his current novel. He tried to line the unfinished sentence up with the keys to continue on.

A knock at his door.

Hector flipped on the porch light, stepped alongside the door and cracked it just enough to peek through the slit, the chain still on the storm door.

"Hey, Cowboy."

It was against his better instincts, but Hector was suddenly tired of his better instincts. He closed the door enough to slip loose the chain and then swung it wide for Mercedes Marshall.

"You left your own party," he said.

"That party."

"Not exciting enough?"

She shrugged. "Not different enough. I think we're in a rut."

Hector shook his head. "Jesus. If that kind of thing becomes rote or routine, what's left you?"

She smiled. "Maybe tall, attractive Texans who have their own creative streaks and who know surrealist art," she said. "What do you think?"

"I don't know. Maybe we should ask Mr. Marshall, first."

"Mr. Marshall is otherwise engaged. He's back at the party, playing host with his good friend, Randolph Scott."

"Oh." Hector had heard the rumors for years. The lanky, laconic cowboy hero was light-in-the-loafers. Well, light-in-the-Justin-boots.

Hector said, "Thanks for not bringing your daughter along. I do have some careworn scraps of scruples to which I stubbornly cling."

"So you say."

She shrugged off her fox coat. Mercedes was still wearing her slinky black dress. She opened her purse and took out a long cigarette case. Hector fetched his Zippo from the writing table and fired her up. Mercedes looked at the inscription on his lighter as he sat it down on the table. She said, "So it's true. John said you and Hemingway used to be tight. He said you two fell out when Hem came back from Spain and caught you with his wife. Guess your scruples don't run in that direction."

Hector shrugged. "Old John, he's a motor mouth of the first water, isn't he? And he's not got it quite right."

"Care to elaborate?"

"Ancient history," Hector said.

"You should make me a drink, Tex."

"Afraid this place is dry."

"Good thing I brought provisions then," Mercedes said. "There's a bag on the porch step."

Hector sighed and fetched the bag. He pulled out six bottles of booze: rum, scotch, vodka, Kahlúa, bourbon and tequila. He poured some scotch and a little water into a juice tumbler and handed it to Mercedes. He poured himself a few fingers of tequila. It had been a while. It hit the spot. He said:

"I guess John with the oral dysentery told you how and where to find me."

"Sure."

"Bless John again. Here to continue negotiations?"

She smiled. "You amenable?"

"Maybe more than I was earlier this evening."

"What changed your mind? Maybe us being here alone?"

"Maybe your party. Particularly, a particular guest."

That got her attention. "Who was that?"

"I hope you'll tell me."

"Then let's talk business," she said.

Hector sat down on the couch and she sat down next to him, very close. She crossed one leg over the other, and the slit in her dress spread, affording him a generous view of her pale slender thigh.

"I have six Alvas," Hector said. "Three are early self-portraits I won't ever sell. I selected them for myself from her loft in Spain. The other three, well, they're a bit more in the direction of your collection. They disturb me sufficiently that I don't even have them hanging where I can see them. One actually depicts one of those surrealist torture cells you said you heard Alva was executed for having helped to design. I'll sell you those three paintings, but apart from cash, I want some information."

"Sounds fair. You really don't care for Alva's transgressive paintings, do you?"

"No, I really don't," Hector said. "*Inaccrochable*, like I said. What's the point? Even you can't hang them in public — hell, you hide 'em from your sleaze ball guests."

"You really are very bourgeois, aren't you?"

Well that was hurtful. Hector said, "I'm just a lapsed Baptist from Texas — a converted Catholic of convenience and a pulp writer. What do you expect of me?"

She smiled up at him from under long, carefully tended lashes. Her eyes were fogged with drink…her lips full. She had a dimple in her left cheek when she smiled. The daughter hadn't inherited that trait from her mother. But that seemed to be the only thing that Mercedes hadn't handed down to daughter Sarah.

Thinking of her daughter, Hector said, "You're here. Your homo husband is presumably playing Cowboys and Indians with randy Randy Scott. Who's minding the kid? Don't you worry for her, even a little, back home in the hands of that misogynistic, woman-exploiting crowd of partying drunks and hopheads?"

The art collector wrinkled her nose…this strange little pout. "That's the pot calling the kettle black, isn't it? John said you're quite the womanizer yourself, Hector. And there's a misogynistic streak in all womanizers. John said you're very promiscuous. How'd he put it, in his crude but charming way? Oh, he said, that you 'get more ass than a toilet seat.'"

"As much talking as John, does, he really needs a new dialogue writer to punch up his repartee," Hector said.

"Well, anyway, he says you're a womanizer too, Hector. He says you're crazy for women. But that's fine — I like that in a man."

"But not in a husband."

"There are the men you marry," Mercedes said, "and the men you enjoy."

"And daughter Sarah, too? Alone with those surrealists? Think she's really enjoying that?"

"At this point, there's nothing they can teach her."

"That wasn't really my question." Hector shook his head his again. "Alright, so forget the plight of Sarah. How much are you willing to pay for my paintings?"

"Two thousand dollars each."

"No. Three thousand each for the two smaller pieces. If you want the painting of the Spanish torture cell, which is much larger — at least twice the size of the others — that one will be $5,000."

"Seems too much."

"It's a one of a kind. I could make it $6,000, but you're going to get the dealer's discount because you're going to tell me about an old man I met on the porch of your house this evening."

"Okay. Agreed." She stuck out a hand.

Hector didn't accept it. "We'll shake after you tell me about this guest."

"What's your interest in him?"

"I think he might be related to or have known someone I knew."

"Another alienated friend like Hemingway?"

"More like a lost friend." Hector described the man he'd met on Mercedes' porch.

Mercedes listened, flirting with her eyes…tracing the outline of his mouth with a long, polished nail as he talked. She said, "That's Bernard Harper you've described."

Hector tried not to react visibly to that last name. Ironic: Mercedes Marshall's favorite painter's father was a friend of hers — at least a social acquaintance — and Mercedes didn't even seem to know it.

"Bernard's a surrealist photographer, though middling if you ask me," Mercedes said. "He's never really been what you'd call significant. He supports himself as a studio photographer. You know, those publicity shots you see of George Raft in a double-breasted suit, posed at some off-kilter angle and smoking…glamour shots of Rita Hayworth. That kind of thing."

"You have to have his phone number or address to have invited him to your decadent little soiree," Hector said.

She nodded and picked up her purse. She pulled out a small address book, flipped pages and then said, "Here it is." She looked around, uncrossed her legs and stood up. She swayed over to his writing desk, selected a sheet of typing paper and a fountain pen. She scribbled down Bernard Harper's address and phone number. Then she looked at Hector's typewriter and read what was there. "It's wonderful. Is this from your next novel?"

"Looks to be," he said.

Mercedes smiled. A pretty enough smile. He was enticed. "Maybe you'll make me a character," she said.

Hector winked and pointed at his own head with his index finger. "Maybe I already have."

She smiled slyly. "Speaking of movie stars, you're really like a taller, beefier Bill Holden. God, you're my type."

Hector didn't take that as a compliment.

Still…

She walked back to him, ground out her cigarette, and standing in front of him, slipped off the straps of her slinky black dress. "Let's work on my character." Her dress slid to the floor.

Nude, she pulled him up to her.

Hector said, "You think we need to revise your character?"

Mercedes hand strayed between his legs; felt him there. "Maybe not," she said. "I mean, you don't feel like I need revising."

"I have an unfortunate personality."

— ORSON WELLES

CHAPTER 31

CRAZY HOUSE

HE PUNCHED the car's horn again: still no response. Hector slipped out of his Chevy, walked around to the passenger side, and opened the door. He took out the cardboard carton with the four coffees resting there on the seat. He locked his car, then banged on the door of the soundstage with his fist.

The door opened following Hector's third round of pounding. Orson stood squinting in the doorway, one hand held up to shield his bloodshot eyes from the sun. Black rings lay heavy under Orson's eyes and his wavy dark hair was askew — full of cowlicks, like some overgrown kid.

Hector held up the cardboard carton containing the four large, Styrofoam cups of piping black coffee. Hector said, "As promised."

Orson took the container of coffee. "Fabulous. Did you get some for yourself?"

Hector eyed the four large cups of coffee. He'd figured one for himself, another for Orson, and the remaining two javas for Welles' "helpers." Hector said, "Uh, I've had my fill this morning."

Orson said, "Suppose this will be a good enough start for me." He squinted at Hector again, eyeing the marks on the crime writer's neck. Orson said, "What, Hector, did you shag a bobby-soxer?" With his free hand, Orson tugged Hector's collar back from his neck for a closer look. He said, "Haven't seen the likes of those since grade school."

"Actually, I passed on the bobby-soxer," Hector said. "These were given me by her mother."

"Some mother," Orson said. He smiled wickedly. "You want to see the set?"

"Of course," Hector said. "I'd love to. But I thought it wouldn't be done for at least two more days. That's what you said last night."

"Funniest thing…you dropped me off last night, and my helper, the real painter, Rhonda, she and me started talking about you, and how you collect paintings and what not. She's a reader of yours and was fascinated. Asked all about you. You probably could have bedded her. Anyway, we just got on a roll. Got inspired. The set is wonderfully dark and surreal. We finished it all up about an hour ago."

"Great," Hector said. "This puts you ahead of schedule for filming, right? That should please Harry Cohn, shouldn't it?"

"Fuck Harry," Orson grumbled. "Fuck all producers. And Rita is ill again."

Hector smiled. "Right. So am I going to get to meet these helpers of yours?"

"I would have liked for you to meet Rhonda…Rhonda Horton is her name. Unfortunately, she just couldn't function any longer. Just exhausted to the point of a breakdown, I think. I put her in a cab an hour ago. Given those marks on your neck, it's probably just as well you didn't meet her this morning. Betty is still here, but sleeping. She's actually been practically living here at the set the past few days. I think she has boyfriend problems or something. This is like a sanctuary for her. A hiding place. So, as we move through the set, keep your voice low. It was an intense night…Betty needs the sleep."

Orson suddenly stumbled, like he'd lost his balance…perhaps overcome briefly by vertigo. Hector took his arm, steadying him.

"Maybe we should delay the tour."

"No, I'm alright now," Orson said. "Just stay close…the pills, the coffee…the too-little sleep. And I think I have sinusitis, too. My God, the headache I have got now is indescribable."

Turning and holding the door open with a foot for Hector to step through, Orson sat his carton of coffee down along the wall just inside the door. He took a cup of coffee in each hand. Rising, his tired eyes twinkling, he said, "Let's explore, Hector."

Hector followed Orson into the dimly lit soundstage, letting the door close softly behind them. They took a few steps in, and Hector was seized by the sense of being surrounded on all sides by a crowd of strangers. Startled, he then heard the slurp of hot coffee being sipped and realized the dimly-visible crowd around them simultaneously appeared to be drinking coffee with Orson — right arms crooked and heads tipped back. And they all looked just like Orson.

They were in a hall of mirrors. "I should say at this point, we're moving backward through the funhouse set, or the 'Crazy House' as I call it," Orson said. "Well, we're sort of moving backward. The slide is just off a ways over there…that's really closer to the beginning of the maze that I — I mean, *Michael* — must explore at the climax. The slide is the way that I — Michael — gets into the Crazy House."

As his eyes adjusted to the light, Hector could just make out the dim outlines of the zigzagging slide. It was nearly 130-feet long. Orson saw Hector examining the slide and said, "It had to be built extra wide because I want to get some subjective camera shots on the thing. I have to send the cameraman and his rig down the slide to get my — Michael's — point of view, going down the bastard."

Orson — all the Orsons — drank more coffee and waved at the mirrors. "This is the big thing…here for the finale. We'll have the final shootout between Rita and me right here," Orson growled, clearly delighted with the prospect. "Eighty mirrors, Hector, and sixty grand to build," Orson said. "I told you this was a big picture, Hector. We'll break every one of these mirrors."

"Sounds like a lot of bad luck," Hector said, smiling. "But how will you use a camera in here with all the reflections?"

"That's what will make it so striking and so wonderful… bravura, even. It will perhaps be my greatest scene, ever. And that's where the magic comes in." Orson handed one of his coffees to Hector to hold and then produced a coin from behind the writer's ear, then another. "Magic, like I said."

"Always with the magic," Hector said, handing the coffee cup back to Orson. Welles was as an avid amateur magician, though calling him an amateur was understating it quite a bit. Orson maintained a collection of full-scale magic tricks and illusions and props. He had famously sawn in half Marlene Dietrich and wife Rita, among other pretty stars. He sometimes did so in Asian make-up, billed as "Orson the Great." A couple of years back, he had even mounted a full-scale magical review called *The Mercury Wonder Show* to entertain troops — a magic show-cum-carnival set up in a lot on Cahuenga.

Orson, coffee cup clutched in either hand, again said, "Follow me."

They left the mirror maze and moved into a room filled with skeletons severed at the waist. The severed arms of hundreds of mannequins projected from the walls.

And those walls — some were curved, others crooked or set at jagged angles. Spirals and crazed designs covered the walls. Hector was irresistibly reminded of Alva Taurino's painting, *Barcelona, 1937*.

Orson stumbled again. Sleep-deprived as he was, Hector couldn't see how Orson was keeping upright in the disorienting room. He took his arm again. "Surreal, you said, Orson. You weren't blowing smoke."

"Never," Orson said. "But it is a little much for me in my present state, maybe. I mean, I'm getting catnaps here and there, but when I do, I just dream about filming or about tackling some logistical problem tied to the film. My day-to-day duties and my dreams have become almost one. It's hard, now and then, to distinguish between what I do and what I dream that I do."

Hector squeezed his arm. "Congratulations — what you've achieved would be bliss for some I've known. I mean, isn't that the surrealist ideal — dissolving the membrane between our world and that of our imagination?"

"A worthy ambition for a shaman perhaps," Orson said, "but I have a big budget film to bring in, on time and under budget, if I can."

Hector frowned as they walked by numerous mannequins, many cut in half, all of them with their arms positioned above their heads, *a la* Man Ray's "Minotaure." "This is playing with my head, Orson," Hector heard himself say in a funny voice he almost didn't recognize. "I really need to get out of here."

"That's terrific," Orson said. "I mean, terrific it's working on you. I'm delighted — it's supposed to do that."

"I don't mean just like that," Hector said. "I come to this set with some unusual baggage."

"What baggage?"

"Tell you outside," Hector said, then, reacting again, he said, "Whoa!" He pointed at a steer's skull, or the skull of a bull, hanging on the wall. He said, "This piece here, Orson, this bull's bones — this your touch?"

"I like to think I'd have thought of it," Orson said, "but Rhonda, my budding surrealist, she scrounged it up from some Western prop room. It's perfect, really. It will be one of the first things the viewer sees in the final film as Michael enters the Crazy House. It's perfect in that I was going for that surrealist-nightmare feel and the bull — *el toro* or *le Minotaure* — is the prime surrealist symbol. But all this," he waved his coffee cups at the surrounding funhouse, "all of this is also really the labyrinth, and Rita will be the Minotaur at its center that I — that Michael — must vanquish. So the bull's skull is the perfect touch, yes?"

Hector looked around. "Right." Then he found himself startled again. The figure of a pale-skinned, black-haired woman was laying on her back on an altar. She had a longish face and high cheekbones. Her arms were stretched above her head in the pose of the "Minotaure," and her legs were stretched out straight and slightly apart. But unlike the other mannequins or statues, she was clothed and not cut in half at the waist. Her hands and black hair were flecked with paint. Her toenails were painted pink.

Hector pointed at her and said, "Very realistic."

Orson winked. "She should be. That's my other helper, Betty. I told you, she sleeps — practically lives — here at the set. Or she has for several days." Orson said softly, "We'll let her sleep." He jerked his head for Hector to follow. They stepped up to a giant web filled with severed arms that looked like some enormous spider's leftovers. Suspended in the web were the words, "Stand Up Or Give Up."

They both squinted and stepped into the California sun.

"This is how the picture will end," Orson said in normal speaking voice once the door of the soundstage closed behind them. He tossed aside his empty coffee cup and started in on the other. "At the climax, I — I mean, Michael — will step out of the ruined mirror maze, out through a turnstile and onto the boardwalk in San Francisco. I'll wander toward the ocean, and in voice-over — I'm adopting an Irish accent, by the way — I'll say, 'Maybe I'll live so long that I forget her — maybe I'll die trying.'"

"Great stuff," Hector said. He shook loose his day's first cigarette and lit up. "Betty back there — is it a good thing for her to wake up alone in there?" Hector frowned. "I know that I'd hate to come to in that place."

"She's exhausted," Orson said. "She'll sleep until late afternoon, probably, as is her custom. As I've said, I think she might be hiding from a boyfriend. She wants to be an actress, but it won't happen...not with that voice. And her teeth are quite bad. She plugs the holes with candle wax."

Hector winced. "How in God's name do you know that?"

"She told me," Orson said. "She confides everything to me, and to Rhonda. Such stories. Bum a cigarette?"

Nodding, Hector passed Orson a cigarette and lit it. Orson held Hector's hand so he could read the engraving on his Zippo. "You and Papa still not speaking?"

"No. You and Hem on speaking terms again yet?"

Orson and Ernest had had a falling out over the narration of *The Spanish Earth.* Orson had criticized Hemingway's script; Hemingway had mocked Orson's delivery. In the final cut of the film, Hem had narrated from his own script.

"We're still on the outs, too," Orson said. He nodded back at the warehouse. "We were speaking of Betty's bad teeth. That's the least of what she tells me. She tells me everything. About lost husbands and babies…about engagements with vets and entanglements with mobsters. I can't tell most times if they are lies, dreams or dearest wishes, but I sense they have no foundation in our reality."

"If that's true, she's a surrealist's dream…like she walked right out of central casting for your movie."

Orson smiled, blew smoke. "You know, I should give her a walk-on. Can't trust her with dialogue, poor thing, but we'll give the folks back home in Medford a little thrill by getting Betty up there on the big screen. Maybe that will take her own mind off things — her fingernails are chewed to the quick."

"That would be a real nice thing to do," Hector said.

"What day is it, Hector," Orson suddenly said. "Is it the weekend?"

"No. It's Tuesday, January 14," Hector said, frowning. "You look like hell, pal. Let me take you to a hotel."

"No, we resume filming tomorrow. I have a lot to do." Orson paused. "You said my Crazy House unsettled you for a particular reason. You were going to tell me about all that."

"Make you a deal," Hector said. "Ride back to my bungalow with me. I'll tell you about all of that on the drive there. Then you sack out at my place for a few hours. I've got to call on someone.

I'll wake you when you I get back. We'll grab some healthy food and I'll have you back here by four. Hell, that's an early start for a night-owl like you."

"I could use the sleep," Orson said. "Don't know how I'll function tomorrow without some. Yes, let's go."

"What about Betty?"

"She's slept here the past few days," Orson said. "I've gotten her a commissary food ticket. She'll be fine."

"After all, crime is only a left-handed form

of human endeavor."

— JOHN HUSTON

SHUTTERBUG

"IT'S A FANTASTIC STORY," Orson said. They were still sitting in Hector's Chevy, parked under the carport roof attached to Hector's rented bungalow. "We could do a hell of a story-treatment, you and me. It's like something Ben Hecht would concoct. Phantasmagoric. We'll do it as a Mercury Theatre production. Joe Cotton will play you, of course."

"I wouldn't turn this into a novel," Hector said, "let alone a film."

"Forget about token naps," Orson said. "We'll talk about the screenplay later. I want to come along with you to confront the father of these two women. I want to be there."

"I'll be fine," Hector said.

"It's not that," Orson said. "I'm afraid you'll kill the son of a bitch. Deservedly, but still…"

"I'm not going to murder the old bastard."

"Maybe not," Orson said, "but you might go right up to the edge. And I really want to hear this wicked old man's story."

"I promise to give you the full account, Orson. Now get your ass inside and turn in. We're neither of us kids anymore. Heart attacks, nervous breakdowns — you're a candidate for either one, pushing yourself like you are."

Hector let Orson into his bungalow. "Treat the place like your own, pal," he said. "I'll see you in a few hours."

As Hector stepped back out onto the front porch to lock up behind himself — effectively locking Orson in — he caught sight of a black Ford sitting across the street. It was an older model — a '36 or '37 sedan. The driver was female — blond, or so it appeared. Hector couldn't make out much beyond that. She wore a black hat with an attached black mesh veil that obscured her face. She wore a big-shouldered black dress and matching black gloves. She appeared to be studying a map.

Hector climbed into his Chevy and twisted his mirror around to where he could watch her. She was still fiddling with a street map, struggling to fold it. It all seemed innocent enough.

Yet there was something almost familiar in her movements. Before he had gotten in his own car, he might have just walked over and offered her directions. But he'd squandered his chance for that pretext: hauling himself back out of the Chevy to head her way now would telegraph the fact he was suspicious of her.

Hector started up his car, backed it out onto the street, shifted gears and rolled slowly past the black car. He figured he might smile at the woman, get a better look at her face. But now she was twisted around in her seat, like she was rooting around in her purse or a bag, the back of her head facing Hector.

Even as he rolled by, picking up speed, Hector couldn't let it go. He turned right, and then made a sequence of further right turns, essentially circling the block. When he drove past his bungalow again, the old black Ford was gone.

Not yet satisfied, Hector took a longer lap around the neighborhood, but the car still wasn't there when he passed by his rental again.

Hector turned on the radio — "Strange Fruit." He checked his directions, then headed off to ambush Bernard Harper.

ഗ

Hector was wearing a dove gray trench coat and matching fedora. He'd even taken the trouble to put on a necktie. He had an honorary badge given him a few years back by an LAPD chum. Flashed at the average citizen, the badge was convincing enough to open doors.

It certainly worked well enough on Bernard Harper. At least that was so until Hector got inside and cast off his hat. Then Bernard bit his lip and said, "You're that man from the party. Are you really a detective?"

Hector locked the door behind himself. He slipped off his trench coat and tossed it over the back of a chair and threw his hat atop it. Then he drew his Colt. The old surrealist's eyes widened as Hector leveled the long barrel of the Peacemaker at him.

Hector said, "You here alone, Pops?"

"Yes, but I can scream and the neighbors will hear," Bernard said.

"And I can shoot you before you finish drawing breath for that scream. The folks around here, the folks up on the hill, have probably never heard a gunshot. They won't know what they heard. Probably mistake it for a car backfiring. But it doesn't have to play like that. Park your scrawny ass on that sofa, Bernie, won't you."

Careful to keep his Colt trained on Bernard Harper, Hector shook out a cigarette from his pack and drew it out the rest of the way with his mouth. He opened his Zippo with a one-handed flick and lit up. Inhaling deeply, he cast a glance at the fireplace mantel. There were numerous photos of Rachel there — little girl through her late teens and into her early twenties. Hector didn't see any photographs of Alva. He was flustered to see the photos of Rachel.

They were the first real images of her he'd seen since he left her alone in his Key West house in September 1935 to strike off for Matecumbe with Hem. There had been echoes of Rachel's features in Alva's self-portraits, but these were photos of the real, still-living Rachel Harper, and they unsettled Hector.

All the unexpected feelings he'd come to have for Rachel flooded back over Hector. *And that was bad news for her old man*, Hector thought.

Bernard said, "That's my daughter, Rachel. She passed away more than ten years ago."

"Twelve years ago, in Key West," Hector said, his voice raw. "That's where I met her."

The old man looked authentically startled. "You knew my Rachel?"

"That's right," Hector said. "If you smoke, now would be the time."

"No, I don't want my pipe."

"A pipe. Of course." Hector remembered now seeing the old man smoking his pipe, staring off through the rain from Mercedes Marshall's front porch.

"How did you know my daughter, Detective?"

"I knew her, but I'm no detective," Hector said. "I'm not a cop. My name is Lassiter."

"How did you know my daughter, Mr. Lassiter?" He wet his lips and his eyes darted. "You're not the man who…who did that to her?"

"Murdered her? No." Hector shook his head. "No, as nearly as I can tell, the man who did that was a 'professional' critic, a man named Quentin Windly."

"Where can he be found? I want the police—"

"Too late," Hector said. "He died in Spain, in 1937. He was on the wrong end of an explosion."

"At your hands?"

"Or another's who knew your daughter. But that doesn't matter anymore."

"My daughter, Rachel and you, were…friends?"

"Friends. Yes." The radio was on low in the background. Hector recognized "I've Got My Love to Keep Me Warm." He said, "I met your daughter in Key West in 1935, just a few days before the Labor Day hurricane that swept through the Keys. I saw her through that Blow. She seemed to have a great fear of storms. I hear you're responsible for that phobia. But we'll get to that in due course. As I said, I helped her weather that storm, then I was called away to aid in recovery and rescue on the most affected Key. I left Rachel alone in my house in Key West. That's when this critic—" Hector left it hanging there.

"And now you've had your questions answered," Hector said. "This is my meeting. I have my own questions, old man, and you're going to answer each and every one of them. Understood?"

"Who exactly are you, Mr. Lassiter?"

Hector suppressed a smile. Evidently, Bernard wasn't one of his readers.

The crime writer said, "Who am I? I'm the guy who just said you don't get any more questions. This party last night…you're a fixture at these things. You move in these surrealist circles. Do all of their get-togethers play like that one? Lots of politics and art talk between games of *Exquisite Corpse* and gangbanging underage girls?"

"That's a rather charged and distorted description."

"But essentially accurate."

The old man shrugged. "I believe I will have my pipe."

"Do it," Hector said. "But again I ask, is that how all these parties play?"

"I don't agree with your characterization of last night, or of our other social gatherings, but I can see, you being the man you appear to be, how you might view them that way…as sordid affairs."

The old man got his pipe going. Hector always hated the smell of pipes. He said, "How, Bernard, do you justify all those things that happen at your 'parties'? Particularly the abuse of some pretty young thing like Sarah Marshall?"

Bernard shrugged and sniffed. "In some states Sarah would be of age. In some countries, Sarah would be considered an old maid."

"Relativism doesn't cut it, old man," Hector said sourly. "Not even in Los Angeles. At least not here in this room and not now."

"Certainly not for the likes of you," Bernard Harper said.

Hector snorted. He thought, *That's it: dig your own grave deeper.*

Bernard continued, pointing a finger at his own head. "We all share the belief that our created life eclipses, trumps, the lives we're forced to lead out here. So, in safe zones, like the party last night, we attempt to actualize our interior lives together. To forge what Breton calls, 'a shared Surreality.' In that context, anything is acceptable, 'Do what thou wilt shall be all the law.'"

"I know that last line," Hector said. "Aleister Crowley said that. I knew that cocksucker back in Paris."

"I envy you his association," Bernard said, puffing on his pipe.

"I nearly beat him to death."

"Oh."

"You said at these parties, 'Anything is acceptable.' Up to, and including, murder?"

"That's crazy talk," Bernard said.

"Not so much," Hector said. "No I'm afraid it isn't crazy at all. On the porch last night, I asked you if you attended many parties like that one. You said you used to throw them. I guess that was in Paris, and here in Los Angeles."

"That's right."

"When I met Rachel in Key West, it pretty quickly became clear she was damaged in some ways. She told me about those parties you threw. About the naked pictures you insisted upon taking of her. And she confided to me about the two of you, together, after her mother died."

The color went out of the old man's face. "Well, that last was wrong. It only happened a few times. I tried to make amends."

"Once was too many times," Hector said, hearing his voice now, and scared by what he heard there. He suddenly wished he'd brought Orson along for restraint. "Once like that — doing that sick bad thing to your own child — would be an unthinkable crime," Hector said. "Twice is perversion beyond possibility of redemption. And 'several' times? I'm a crime writer and I come up dry for terms to characterize that."

The old man's head was bowed.

"And the parties," Hector said. "Did you pass Rachel around to your surrealist friends like Sarah was being used last night?"

Bernard Harper kept staring at his hands. His pipe, trailing smoke, was clutched in his trembling right hand.

Hector said, "In Key West, I saw, first-hand, what your 'attentions' and what your parties did to Rachel. So I look at last night and Sarah Marshall and I wonder what kind of casualty she's being made to be every time Mummy and Daddy Marshall decide to ring up their surrealist pals for another orgy. What kind of mess or monster are they creating?"

Hector realized his finger was sweaty and twitching at the trigger of his Colt. The gun had a hair-trigger. Hector aimed it away from Bernard Harper and slowly lowered the hammer. He holstered the gun. It was overkill: Hector could easily subdue Bernard barehanded. And if he wanted to kill him, well, he told himself he'd do that barehanded, too. Slowly. Surgically.

"How do you live," Hector said, "having done all that to Rachel? Jesus. And Alva, trying to rape her, too…"

The old man was still staring at his hands.

"Alva said you didn't touch her because she wouldn't let you,"

Hector said. "I was told that Alva scared you. Rachel said you and
Alva had a split that I assume you couldn't forgive. I mean, I see
you have no pictures of Alva on your mantel. Don't even have one
of Alva's paintings."

The old man looked up, his eyes now red-rimmed and his
chin trembling. He said, "What? Who? Who is 'Alva'?"

"Your youngest daughter, asshole, I—"

"No," Bernard said, "I don't know who this Alva is, but
Rachel was our only child."

Hector felt cold all over. He saw black spots. The enormity of
Bernard's simple statement and all its implications ripped through
Hector — it was nearly insupportable. He heard it again in his
head: *Rachel was an only child.*

"You're a goddamn liar," Hector said, hearing his own voice
from far away. He had the old man by the collar now.

The old surrealist screamed, "You're insane. I have only one child.
I don't who this Alva is, but if you don't let go of me right now…"

Hector shook the old man again, raising a fist. He held it
there, trembling, then swung past the old man's head, narrow-
ly missing his face. "Don't you fucking lie to me you evil old
bastard!"

"Why would I lie?" The surrealist's old hands clutched at
Hector's wrists. "There were problems…Rachel had problems,
yes. But she was my daughter. My only daughter. I tried to get her
help…doctors. I loved her. Loved her as a father loves his only
daughter. But the damned psychiatrists, they said my poor
Rachel's mind had fractured, that she 'divided inside' and…"

Hector remembered reading about something like that…he'd
even used it in an early short story once. The damage done to
Rachel's mind, first by her incestuous rape by her own father, then
being used as a party favor by all those sadistic surrealists had
caused Rachel to "split"…that's what the evil old bastard was
claiming.

That was what the headshrinkers called it.

Hector had seen intimations of it during the Great War, and again during World War II — soldiers or nurses whose minds splintered under the insupportable pressures of combat and its bloody results. The victims created new identities for themselves and sometimes permanently retreated into those identities.

Alva must have been something like a kind of "imaginary friend" of Rachel's...a tough, mythical little sister who became Rachel's protector and eventual avatar. In time, Rachel actually recreated herself as Alva and presumably found her "voice" as a painter.

Hector stood and picked up his coat and shrugged it on. He picked up his hat. He walked over to the fireplace mantel and stared at one of the pictures. He found the one in which Rachel looked the most like he remembered her: probably twenty-one or -two in the picture, and said, "I'm taking this. I'm owed it. You keep your other pictures of her you evil old cocksucker. You keep the perverted photos you took of her...the ones that took so much from her."

"Who is this Alva person?" Bernard Harper shook his pipe at Hector. "I demand answers."

Hector pivoted. He placed the framed photo of Rachel on the chair where he'd been sitting and dropped his hat atop it. Then he shrugged off his trench coat and drew his Colt and put it on the chair, too.

He strode over to Bernard Harper and punched the old man in the mouth. Hector continued hitting the old man, not as hard as he could, but hard enough.

Drawing back for a fresh blow, Hector caught sight of himself in a mirror — this crazed-looking guy whaling on a rickety old libertine. It didn't square with any image Hector had of himself.

The crime writer stood up and massaged his fists. Bernard Harper lay on his couch, bleeding from the mouth and nose. A few teeth lay scattered on the hardwood floor. Hector said, "You asked who I am. Well, tell your friends: I'm the man who's come to destroy them. I mean to burn their surrealist circle down. Starting today."

Blood bubbling from his mouth, Bernard Harper said, "They'll burn you down…you and yours."

"There's just me," Hector said. "I'm a lone wolf. I have no second heart to aim for. There's nothing you can use to distract me from my task. I'm going to cut through Hollywood and your surrealist circle like Sherman moved through Atlanta. You spread that word, old man."

"We have powerful friends," Bernard Harper said, coughing up blood. Hector figured he must have broken one of the old man's ribs, and the rib must have found a lung.

"I have powerful friends, too," Hector said. "That party last night was full of communists. Like I say, I have powerful friends, too."

Hector holstered his Colt and put on his hat and coat. He picked up his photo of Rachel.

Her father said, "I need an ambulance."

"You sure do. Phone's still right there on the table, just where you left it. I've taken my share of beatings so I know: the bad news is, you're going to live, you diseased son of a bitch."

ഗ

Sitting in his Chevy, Hector stared at the photograph of Rachel. She hadn't died in Key West.

Maybe she hadn't died in Spain, either. But if she hadn't been murdered on Bone Key, then she had faked her own death, or at the very least, Rachel had participated in its staging.

What did that say about Quentin Windly's connections to the surrealist murders?

What did that say about Rachel/Alva's connection to the crimes?

"Every man I knew went to bed with Gilda...

and woke up with me."

— RITA HAYWORTH

CHAPTER 33

SIREN

HECTOR KEYED HIMSELF into his bungalow. As he did that, he cast a last glance over his shoulder: no black Ford sedan loitering out front. There was no blond spying on him from across the street.

But there was a blond on his couch — a freshly minted blond, curled up on the sofa with the manuscript of Hector's almost finished novel, *Squeeze Play*.

"You haven't seen the new 'do, Hector," Rita said, pulling at her shorter hair. "What do you think of my reinvention?"

Welles had created a tabloid scandal by having Rita Hayworth's long, trademark red hair cut short and died platinum blond. Orson and Rita had invited the world press to observe her dubious transformation. Orson's obvious aim had been to gen up publicity for their film. He'd certainly achieved that objective, but he'd badly underestimated the backlash to be suffered for tampering with a screen icon; most agreed Orson had mutilated their favorite screen siren.

One of those who was most upset — and in a unique position to do something about it — was the film's producer, Harry Cohn.

Cohn had initially been impressed by the film's central twist: the villain of the piece would be revealed to be a woman. Cohn also had designs on Rita...until he had seen her as a short-haired blond.

And Welles' efforts actually represented Rita's latest "reinvention." Hector had known Rita for many years. He had known her in Mexico, long before Hollywood got its hooks in her. Rita Hayworth, performing under her real name of Margarita Carmen Cansino, was then dancing at the Mexican gambling resort of Agua Caliente. Margarita was being chaperoned by her mother, Volga, herself a retired Zigfield Follies performer.

At Agua Caliente Casino, in the mid-1930s, vacationing Hector met Margarita, not too-terribly long before he met Rachel Harper.

It was at Agua Caliente that an enamored Winfield Sheehan, Fox Film chief, later met Margarita Cansino and signed her to a film contract. Louella Parsons, omnipotent Hollywood gossip maven — the woman who pissed all over Orson's *Citizen Kane* — witnessed that meeting and was incredulous when told of the contract. Raven-haired Margarita was, Parsons sniffed, "too fat."

Sheehan remained firm, above and below the belt.

The Hollywood studio system worked its magic.

Plump and dark-haired Margarita Carmen Cansino was transformed into svelte/shapely, redheaded Rita Hayworth.

Hector smiled at Rita and said, "You look dynamite, sweetheart."

Rita shook her head, and pulled again at her bobbed, platinum hair. "I think I actually miss the red hair."

"You know me, I'm a brunette man. I'd like to see your hair that way again."

"Well, it won't happen," Rita said. "Harry Cohn is furious at Orson for my hair. Soon as filming wraps, I'll be out of the public eye for a couple of months, growing it back out and dyeing it red. Crazy: dye and cut your hair, and get treated like a whole different person."

Hector said, "Orson said you were feeling badly."

"Feeling badly for Orson, is more like it. I'm trying to make this reconciliation work, but he isn't. Or if he is, I'm sure not seeing it."

Hector nodded. "He in back, out cold still?"

"No, Orson flew the coop. Studio tracked him down. He's gone back to the set."

"Jesus, he should be asleep." He figured Orson must have called and left word where to find him after Hector dropped him off and locked him in. It would explain what Rita Hayworth was now doing on his couch.

"He left me to explain and defend his decision to run off without sleep," Rita said. "So now I've done that. Orson also said that you told him to treat your place like his own. So I've done that, too. Also helped myself to your bar. Hope you don't mind."

"Not at all," Hector said. "I'm cutting back, in fact. The booze was a gift from a visitor."

"Girlfriend?"

"Not more than last night."

"I helped myself to your manuscript, too," Rita said. "Hope you don't mind that, either. I love it. The tension is wonderful, and the way you've closed the net around the hero, Owen Walters, squeezed between these two crime families, that's marvelous and tense, too. Can't wait to see how it comes out. To see how he gets out."

"If he does. And it may be a bit of a wait," Hector said. "The last five or six chapters are only up here." He tapped his forehead.

Rita was certainly a nice distraction…a pleasant surprise to come home to find stretched out on your couch. But Hector was still turning over the revelation of Rachel/Alva. He was still trying to sort it all out in his own mind. He'd intended to come home and stack on some records and close the drapes and sit in the dark, listening to torch songs and thinking.

Rita put down the manuscript and stood and hugged Hector. "You're looking well, if a little shaken up. Tell me it isn't my hair."

"It isn't your hair," he said, kissing her cheek. He fetched himself a glass and poured himself some tequila. She grabbed her own glass and offered it for refill. Hector did that and they tapped glasses. "To absent friends," he said.

"Sure," she said a bit uncertainly. "I came to talk to Orson and he promptly fled of course. He's going to move out again after we finish shooting, I know it."

Hector took a breath. He poured himself another shot of tequila, drank it down, then poured another. It was almost too harsh. He went around the counter and opened the refrigerator and got some orange juice and poured it into his tequila. Rita said, "You're a genius," and held up her glass for some juice to be poured in on top of her tequila.

Rita flipped on the radio: "I'll Be Seeing You." "You're his friend, Hector. Orson confides in you. He's not committed to reconciliation, is he?"

Rita sat down on the couch and patted it for Hector to join her. He did that. "I'm his friend and I'm not certain that Orson is committed to anything," Hector said. "He's a big one for grandiose schemes and unfinished projects. Not finishing equates with no risk of failure in Orson's mind, I think. He'll take a picture 90 percent of the way and then let the studio hacks hijack it and mutilate his 'masterpiece.' Gives him something to bitch about."

"It's a harsh assessment," Rita said. "And you think that philosophy extends to his women, too?" Rita sipped her drink. "You think his relationships are run the same way?"

"Maybe," Hector said. "You should think about what you want to do next, M. I think you're right about Orson not hanging around much after this film wraps."

She shook her head. "Right. They all see the woman on the screen, you know. Orson was the only one who saw through it. He really talked to me…engaged me as person, not as that damned 'Gilda.' Engaged me in every sense, I mean. He was the only one to ever do that. Other than you of course — the only man who knows Margarita."

Hector smiled and squeezed her hand. "Gildas make for jazzy weekends, honey. Margaritas are the ones you marry."

Hector and Rita seemed to end up in bed every few years…not lovers in the purest sense, but more like one another's safest harbor. He felt himself drifting that way now, and could tell she was, too. "The Man I Love" played low in the background.

"What is it with men?" Rita posed that question and offered Hector her glass for a refill. He realized his was empty, too. He got up and mixed two more drinks — deep ones this time.

He said, "What do you mean, 'What is it with men?'"

Rita said, "There are sure no happy, or even enduring marriages in this sorry town. And you — how many times have you gone to the well, Hector?"

"Marriage? More than once."

"Did you love them?"

Hector handed Rita her fresh drink. This time he'd used some ice, too.

Rita said, "You didn't, clearly. Not all the way. Were there ones you loved and who got away? Ones you wished you'd married?"

He'd loved his first two wives very much, but said, "Funny you should ask."

Rita took it the wrong way. "Me and you, Hector…"

"No, I wasn't talking about us."

She smiled. "That's a relief." She checked the wall clock. "Orson said if you were back in time — say, two or three — you should bring me along and meet him at the soundstage where the 'Crazy House' is set up." She checked the clock again. "There is still time before we have to do that…" She stroked his thigh.

He smiled. "Sure."

She fiddled with his tie. "God, I've never seen you in one of these. Seems wrong."

"I was playing police detective."

"You've taken up acting?"

"Only around painters and photographers."

She frowned as she loosened his collar and saw his throat. "Lord…someone sure has been here first."

"It was nothing, but if it bothers you…"

"No, it's just…you're such a man." Some of her Spanish inflection crept in there.

Thinking of Mercedes Marshall, Hector said dryly, "Some women like that in a man."

"Some, yeah." Rita took his hand and led Hector back to his own bedroom.

"Artistic imagination must remain free.
It is by definition free from any fidelity to circumstances,
especially to the intoxicating circumstances of history."

— ANDRÉ BRETON

CHAPTER 34

STRIKE

HECTOR SAID, "DAMMIT!" as they reached the door of the soundstage.

The door was slightly ajar. The door's handle was mangled and askew — nearly sheared off.

"Maybe Orson forgot his key," Rita said.

"But he remembered his sledge hammer?" Hector toed the door open further, simultaneously drawing his Colt. "This is trouble." He said, "Stay behind me, M. If things go wrong, get bad or I go down, you run back out here and scream like Fay Wray."

Powerful friends, Bernard Harper had said. Powerful enough to afford studio access.

They edged into the darkened soundstage, the light through the door glancing off all those mirrors, flooding the soundstage with natural light. Hector tried to see past the dozens of himself in the mirrors; past all the hundreds of stunning blonds dogging his heels.

Hector said softly to Rita, "Your first time on this set, M?"

"First time seeing it," Rita said. "Orson has described it. He didn't do it justice."

"It gets worse…more frightening, I mean."

They explored the entire, lurid set and found nothing — no signs of a struggle and no signs of Orson. They didn't even come across a sleeping, pale-skinned, henna-haired painting assistant named Betty.

Hector was about to take Rita and leave the set when he saw an envelope skewered on the horn of the bull's skull mounted on the wall. Rita was examining the lurid wall paintings, her back to Hector. He took down the envelope and slipped it in the pocket of his sports coat.

Rita said, "I'm going to check the commissary. Maybe he's grabbing some food."

"Do that," Hector said. "Also look for a young girl, probably in her early twenties. She has pale skin and longish black hair. Her name is Betty. She and another woman helped Orson paint all this. She might know where to find him. While you do that, I'll hang around the soundstage here, outside, just in case he shows up. You look for me here."

He watched Rita cross the lot, gorgeous in a tailored gray dress and pumps, then Hector sat down on the step of the soundstage's front door and ripped open the envelope.

It wasn't a handwritten letter, but something that looked more like someone's notion of a ransom note taken from pulp magazines or B-movies — a collage of letters and words clipped from disparate magazines and newspapers…a riot of fonts and point-sizes. The letter said:

F u c k with A R **t** ,
and
A R**T** will
F u c k **with** Y O U **!**

Hector folded up the note, put it back in the envelope and slipped it into his pocket.

So much for his lone wolf theory for himself.

The surrealists were striking at him through Orson…and maybe through this "Betty" friend of the wired *auteur*.

5

Rita found him still sitting on the step of the soundstage. The stubs of three cigarettes lay at Hector's feet. She said, "You're burning through those."

"Thinking," Hector said. "Plotting." He stood up and brushed off the seat of his pants. "Nothing?"

"*Nada*," Rita said. "Not of Orson, or that girl you told me to look for. Nobody in there has ever seen her, near as I can tell."

"They didn't come back here, either. Not Orson, and not Betty." Hector took Rita's arm.

She fell in step alongside him. She said, "So what next?"

"We get you somewhere safe."

"You think something has gone that wrong?"

"I have reason to think so."

Rita scowled. "What, you think this could be some kind of kidnapping thing? Orson's a publicity fiend, but even he wouldn't try that old dodge. The staged-Hollywood kidnapping was stale twenty years ago…"

"It wouldn't necessarily be staged," Hector said. "And I'm not even thinking that way, not yet."

"I'm staying with you," Rita said. "I can't be safer than running around with a man carrying a six-gun. How do you get away with that, anyway?"

"I wear big coats."

5

Hector drove downtown. He parked next to a pay phone where he could keep an eye on Rita and fished coins from his pocket. He called the operator and got the number for the Marshall house.

Mercedes answered. Hector said, "Alright, toots, you've got my attention."

"I don't know what you're talking about, lover," she said.

"Sure you do."

"No, I don't. And I don't have important conversations over the phone. Not anymore. Wire taps, you know. HUAC, and the like. Several of my friends have warned me about talking over phones. Oh, but did you hear the terrible news? Someone beat up poor Bernard Harper. Nearly killed him. Bernard's old, so it wouldn't necessarily take a tough guy, a man, to hurt him. They say whoever did it probably has bruised knuckles, though."

Hector looked at his own hands. He'd seen worse.

"Just let Orson and the girl go," Hector said. "We'll call it even."

"I really don't know what you're talking about, Cowboy."

"If I have to come over there…"

"You'd be trespassing, Hector. I've already called the police and asked for a watch on my house. We're going to be traveling, you see. Maybe go to Canada. Maybe to Europe, or down to Mexico. My lawyer will be in touch about Alva's paintings…about shipping and the like."

Hector said, "If anything happens to Orson or that girl, there's nowhere you can run to get far enough away from me."

He could hear Mercedes' sneer in her voice. "Hector, the definition of insanity is doing the same thing over and over in hopes of obtaining a different result. Haven't there been enough destructive threats? And did you feel better, after — a big strong man like you — beating the stuffing out of an old man like Bernard?"

Hector slammed down the phone. He called the LAPD and was connected to his friend, Russ Evans. He chatted him up a bit and then asked for ways to contact Russ in a pinch. Russ said, "Something big shaking?"

Hector hesitated. "Not yet. But I have a feeling."

Rita eyed him suspiciously when Hector climbed back behind the wheel of his Chevy. "You look shaken up, Hector," she said. "Has something happened?"

"Not yet." He started up his Chevy and started rolling. They'd traveled four blocks when Hector steered toward Brentwood. He was watching the mirror: a 1936 black Ford sedan back there, several car lengths behind. He thought about forcing a confrontation. Then he rethought that strategy. He said, "Where's Huston live?"

Rita scowled. "Huston? John Huston, you mean?"

"Yeah. You know the place?"

"Been there once or twice with Orson, so yeah, I can find it."

"Let's go there now," Hector said.

"The bullfight itself has a religious origin.

Its ancestor is the Minotaur.

The bullfighter is something of a priest."

— JOHN HUSTON

CHAPTER 35

COUNTERSTRIKE

HUSTON KEPT horses at his ranch. Hector hadn't been on horseback much since he'd ridden behind Black Jack Pershing in search of Pancho Villa in the run-up to the Great War. It came back easily enough, though Hector felt foolish to be riding a horse while wearing dress slacks and a sports jacket...wing-tips and black sunglasses.

John's wife had loaned Rita one of her riding outfits. John was dressed in jodhpurs, calfskin boots and a riding helmet. Hector was very much the odd-man out.

Rita and John's wife were riding some distance ahead. John's and Hector's horses were plodding along at restrained reign.

"I foreswear any knowledge of this, Hector," John said. "You have to believe that. I really know nothing, and I'm committed to knowing nothing. I will endeavor in the days ahead to maintain that blissful — and safe — state of ignorance. That said, I think Orson is simply too big, too famous for them to harm in any real way."

"But they are capable of harm," Hector said thinly. "That's implied in your phrasing."

"God preserve us all from close listeners," John said.

"Where might they have taken them, John? Too that damned 'temple' in Laurel Canyon?"

John shook his head. "No, there last of all. Probably somewhere more squalid and out of sight. If they have done what you propose. Frankly, I can't see them kidnapping those two. It's daft, Hector. They're intellectuals…dilettante artists and art collectors. They kill with words and brushes. They slander with reviews and slash with their tongues. I don't think it within their purview to commit acts of enduring physical violence." He cast an eye at Hector's barked and swollen knuckles, then ducked low for a low-hanging branch. "Only crime writers do that. Men who live what they write and write what they live."

Hector was growing very tired of that line and its incessant application to himself. What, had some publicist placed an ad, or something? Where was that coming from?

"Well, I suspect you're in a position to send a signal back," Hector said. "So you tell them I'm issuing a new ultimatum. If Orson isn't delivered safely back to my bungalow by this evening to report to the studio for filming *mañana*, I'm delivering on all threats. I'm going to become an enthusiastic snitch for HUAC. Hell, I may even go on camera. I'm told I look like a taller, beefier Bill Holden." Hector winked and smiled. "In other words, John, I think I'm ready for my close-up."

"You bear a passing resemblance to Holden, to be sure, though I think Bill has a nicer smile," John said.

"That's because old Bill maybe has nicer friends," Hector said.

John frowned; his right eye twitched. "I'll make some calls…try to pipeline your threat. But I do it under duress, Hector. What you propose is essentially the same as giving them 24 hours' warning to kill you. You know that don't you?"

"Bring 'em on," Hector said. "What can a bunch of intellectuals and dilettantes, as you characterize them, do to lay a glove on the likes of me?"

"I told you, they have powerful friends."

"And I told you that I do, too."

5

Hector hit another payphone and contacted another of his Left Coast chums — Arnold, "Packy" Thompson, an Angelino heavyweight with a thirty and two valley record — the undisputed champ of California water-tank towns. Packy was between bouts and sacked out in his swanky Brentwood apartment. When he heard he'd be standing watch over Rita Hayworth he waived Hector's offered fee for protection.

Rita balked at staying with the boxer for the afternoon, but when Hector explained his next stop was a federal office to make an overture to HUAC she acquiesced. Rita said only, "You'd really sell out to those bastards?"

"No, I'd really use those bastards."

Hector left her in the hubbub of a bus station to be picked up by Packy. Then he drove to a diner and ordered himself eggs, toast and coffee. While he waited for his food, he called Washington, D.C. and Special Agent Edmond Tilly.

Tilly said, "Christ, Hector, it's been a long time."

"Ten years."

"Well, as you see, with all these subpoenas flying around you, but not at you, I was good to my word."

"I know," Hector said. "That's why I'm calling you now. I have some more dope for you. Same terms. You protect me now, use me silently, and you hide my participation within your own department's archives, now to forever."

He could hear the zeal in Agent Tilly's voice. "What do you have?"

"You sitting down, Agent? You might want to pour yourself a drink, too. It's a long, crazed story and there are a lot of big names…artists, photographers, sculptors and art collectors. And now that we're done using my name, you might want to put me on speaker and shag yourself a steno. Oh, and get yourself a Los Angeles federal judge in cue. You need to file subpoenas an hour ago — some of these cocksuckers are almost in full flight."

ꙅ

Hector spent an hour on the phone with Agent Tilly. He told him about the killings in Key West, and in Mexico and Spain. Hector mentioned "a suspect the Spanish authorities" had at the time, one "presumed killed" soon after. He didn't tell him that he thought Rachel Harper/Alva Taurino might still be alive. If Rachel was still alive Hector wanted to confront her directly…he wanted some options.

Then Hector ate his cold, late-afternoon breakfast, picked up some newspapers and headed back to his bungalow.

As he approached the house, he saw that the door front had been forced. He quickly surveyed the living room, but saw nothing out of place; nothing obviously missing. The pages of his manuscript were still sitting stacked on the couch, just where Rita had left them. The intruders were creative types themselves, Hector guessed — they couldn't countenance destroying even an enemy's creative endeavors.

Gun-in-hand, Hector continued combing through his bungalow.

He found Orson stretched out on the bed, fully clothed and bathed in blood.

"The only difference between myself and a madman

is that I'm not mad."

— SALVADOR DALI

CHAPTER 36

OUT OF THE PAST

HECTOR WAS A BIG MAN, but so was Orson: it was hard work getting Orson up off the bed, stripped naked and into the shower. Hector first took off his own shirt and coat to avoid ruining it with all the blood on Orson's clothes. He got the bath water warm, then he got Orson up and across his back and shoulders in a sloppy fireman's carry. He lugged the director into the bathroom and muscled him into the tub. Hector stripped him, then turned on the shower, leaving Orson unconscious in its needle-spray.

After he did that, Hector grabbed an empty, aluminum trashcan, placed it in the middle of his backyard, and stuffed in some old newspapers. He then wadded in Orson's clothes — suit, socks, underwear, belt and shoes. He covered those with his own bloodied sheets. Hector poured in some starter fluid stored in the carport next to a portable barbecue and he set fire to the trashcan's contents.

While all of that burned, Hector phoned Packy's apartment and asked that the boxer bring Rita by his place.

As he hung up, he heard Orson's distinctive voice over the shower spray, ringing off the tiles. "Jesus fuck, where am I wounded?"

Hector grimaced and hung up the phone.

He found Orson still sitting in the tub, looking vaguely drunk, holding up his hands, now pink with water-diluted blood. "Good Christ, Hector, what has happened to me?"

"Jury's out on that front, Orson. I found you on my bed, covered in blood. But not your own blood." Hector narrowed his eyes. He stooped down and grabbed Orson's arm and turned it in the light. Needle-tracks. "They shot you up with something. Dammit."

Orson shook his head. "They? Who is they?"

"The surrealists."

"What?"

"You've been missing, all day. Betty is still missing. I'd say we should file a report with the police about that, except I think it might put you in more danger to do that."

"What in God's name are you talking about?"

Hector nodded at the soap dish. "Use that, Orson. Wash off, get all the blood off you. Don't know what's coming next, but we can't have the cops or their like suddenly turning up here and finding you covered in blood, right?"

"Well, no. But, whose blood is this, Hector?"

"I'd rather not think about that now."

Orson said, "What about Rita? I don't remember anything except being here with Rita."

"You left here," Hector said. "I found Rita on my couch. She's safe with a friend of mine. She's on her way here, now. When she gets here, I think you two should find a good hotel with some top-flight security. Lock yourselves away until the next shoe drops."

"Next shoe?"

"That's right." Hector nodded. "I'm afraid it might be a big one."

"I can't just wait," Orson said. "Jesus, I'm covered in blood. What have these bastards done?"

Hector lit a cigarette. He handed it to Orson and then lit one for himself. "I don't think we have long to wait to find that out. Do you remember anything? Anything at all?"

"No," Orson said, scowling. "Images...bodies and severed torsos. Blood. But it could be the set I'm remembering. I told you, Hector, dreams...my waking hours...it's all a blur this past week."

"Well unblur it...or construct an airtight narrative that locks in every movement you've made for the past 48 hours," Hector said. "If you can't do that yourself, then allow me."

ഗ

Orson was dressed in a pair of Hector's pants and a shirt. "Good thing we're nearly the same size," Orson said. Hector thought, *Yeah, so long as you keep popping those pills.*

The director was sitting on the couch with Rita, who was rubbing his back. Hector said, "You're going to have lie for Orson, M. Are you prepared to do that?"

Rita nodded. "Of course. What's my lie?"

"You two've been together all day and all night. Somewhere. Something like that. Somewhere where there could be no witnesses."

"But people saw me at the commissary looking for Orson and this girl, Betty," Rita said. "The studio guard waved you and me through the gate earlier this afternoon."

Hector dismissed that. "The guard is old and wears glasses...he sees stars every day. He can be discredited. The studio hash-slingers are wage slaves. Their testimony won't hold water either — not up against some shark lawyer."

Rita nodded. Then she said, "And John and his wife?"

"John is like Sweden," Hector said, "John is gloriously neutral. He's playing both ends against the middle and covering his own ass. He's no danger to us."

Hector's phone rang. Hector scooped it up. "Lassiter."

A long pause. This voice: alto...female — it cut through Hector. "You need to get your friend out of there, now. The police are on their way."

Hector could hardly get the word out. He rasped, "*Rachel?*"

"Get your friend out of there now. And you go somewhere safe, too. Take anything you value, Hector, but run, please. Now!"

Frantic, Hector said, "In two hours I'm going to be at the Pacific Dining Car. Call me there, won't you?"

The line went dead.

Hector swallowed hard and said to Rita, "M, call a cab, now. You and Orson need to get out of here, pronto. I've got to pack and then I need to split, too."

Orson looked shaken. "That was someone calling with a threat?"

"More like a warning."

5

Hector was on his third margarita when the waiter carried the phone over and deposited it in front of him. He took a deep breath and said, "Rachel?"

A long pause, then, "Murder. That's the frame they've set for your friend. You'll start to see it unfold tomorrow."

Hector winced. "Who's dead? The girl, Betty?"

"Sure. Yes, she's dead. They tortured and killed her...all of them. They play their game with real people now. With real women."

Hector said, "Game? What game?"

"*Exquisite Corpse*. They collaborate on women they find at bus stations...on prostitutes and orphans. Betty's not the first...just one of the first that they'll put on 'display.' I'm afraid there might be more. They like it."

Hector's jaw tightened. "And you helped?"

"No, I don't...I mean now..." Another long pause. "It doesn't matter anymore. But I saw it — saw what they did to Betty...not while they were doing it, but what was left. I'm trying to get loose from it all, I swear to you, but it's too late as far as Elizabeth — or Betty — is concerned. You'll hear in the morning. Everyone will hear. Some will even see."

Hector said, "Orson...they drugged him...you say they mean to frame him."

"Or come close to that. They're really just trying to neutralize you. Tie your hands. You terrify them, Hector. You're like a 'rogue elephant' they say. They think you're actually capable of worse than they are. If only..."

"Did Orson really do anything to Betty, Rachel? Was Orson made to do anything to her?"

"No. But her blood..."

"I saw."

"I'm going to have to go soon," she said. "They're watching...we're all being forced to stay close...to watch one another."

"I need to talk to you again, Rachel. I need to know things. I need to know what's happening with you now. I need — I want to see you."

"It doesn't matter, Hector. And it's too late. The things I did years ago...even sick as I was... Just please try to forget it all. I am still dead. That's how you should think of me. In many ways it's true, you know."

Hector said, "You were 'Rhonda Horton' — Orson's painting assistant, weren't you? Those initials — deliberate on your part?"

"More like uninspired on my part," Rachel said. "I'm no writer, like you. Not clever about inventing names."

"I don't know, 'Alva Taurino' is pretty clever," Hector said. "Very unusual and distinctive. You took 'Alva' from Salvador Dali's name, is that it?"

"No, it's Spanish for 'white.' And Taurino—"

"Is a derivation of *toro*...for bull," Hector said. "The White Bull. Just like the myth Mrs. Blair told us about back in Key West. God, how'd I miss it?"

"It was unconscious on my part...I only figured out what I'd done later."

"How...surreal. I need to know more...I need to know about Key West and Mexico...about Spain and why—"

"They're coming Hector, coming across the parking lot to the phone booth where I am now. They'll be able to hear me in just a moment. I have to go."

"Do they know who you really are, Rachel? What you've...done?"

"No. They don't know any of that. The old crimes they've heard of...but they don't know I'm responsible for them. They don't know I was their inspiration for their own set of murders."

"Call me here tomorrow, this time, Rachel. I'll be waiting."

"Please don't bother, darling. There won't be a chance for that, Hector. Not for me, and come morning, you'll be preoccupied. I'm so sorry, for everything. This is likely the last time we'll ever speak. Please take care to protect yourself."

Another dead line. Hector went in search of a hotel in which to spend the night, knowing he would never be able to sleep.

"(Art) is about as outrageous and murderous

an act a person can do

short of really doing one physically."

— STEPHEN WRIGHT

CHAPTER 37

JANE DOE: NUMBER ONE

THE NEWS REPORTS were breathless — long on innuendo, hysteria and hyperbole, but short on useful facts.

Between the papers and radio, Hector had distilled it down to a few agreed upon, chilling particulars. The nude, bisected body of a young, dark-haired woman had been found in an empty, weedy lot on Norton Avenue, close to 39th Street, her body just a few inches off the sidewalk.

A mother walking her young child had found the body, at first mistaking it for a mannequin.

That image resonated for Hector.

And although she was unidentified — temporarily dubbed "Jane Doe, number one," Los Angeles' first unidentified homicide victim for 1947 — Hector was pretty sure he knew who she was.

Hector phoned his LAPD detective friend Russ Evans.

Russ said, "Gotta keep it short, Hec. Things are shaking — we're all being mobilized over this murder this morning."

"Got an I.D. on the victim, Russ?"

"Nah, but the papers are working with us," Russ said, "and hand in glove. We've got her fingerprints. The *Examiner* has agreed to let us use their wire photo gizmo to send the prints to Washington for identification. It's all pretty technical, and nobody knows if this will even work, but if it does, we could have her name by lunch tomorrow."

"Wow, that's great news," Hector said.

It was also potentially terrible news for Orson.

"Tell me a little about this — about the state of her body," Hector said.

Russ said, "Haven't the time, and you and a thousand others want info on this, Hec."

"It's not like that," Hector said. "I'm not hoping to 'use' this. I told you the other day that something big might be up."

"And this is it? Hector, if you had foreknowledge of this murder…"

"Not this, specifically Russ," he said. "But something maybe like it, from before. Just tell me about the state of the body…how it was arranged…what it looked like, generally."

"Hector—"

"Two minutes' description, Russ, that's all I ask."

The detective sighed. "I hope you haven't eaten."

The mere description of Betty's body made Hector nauseous — left him shaking. It sounded more terrible than anything he'd seen in the Keys or in the photos of the murder victims in Spain in 1937.

Betty — for Hector was sure that's who the victim was — had been cut in half at the waist.

That had apparently been done by someone with at least a modicum of surgical ability. That was the other thing — the girl's body was a strange mix of seemingly surgically executed mutilations and forms of torture counterpoised with raw, unfettered brutality.

Betty had endured a mastectomy and a hysterectomy. Deep hollows had been cut into her thigh and upper torso — mutilations echoing the "compartments" Salvador Dali etched into the bodies of the dissected women in much of his art.

In addition to being cut in half, Betty's mouth had also been sliced ear to ear — cut into a "terrible smile."

"It's almost like there might have been more than one bastard going at her," Russ said. "That's a terrible thought, but it's the one I have. Almost like a surgeon and a boxer went at her in tandem."

"Maybe there was more than one killer," Hector said. He stopped short of saying what he truly thought — that there might be as many as a dozen who'd directly participated in Betty's torture and murder. Hector shook his head — to think that he had scoffed at Agatha Christie and her "solution" for a killing in one of her mysteries. Dame Agatha had had nearly every ticket-holder on her damned train plunge a knife into the corpse. Hector had howled when he read it.

Hector said, "So what killed her exactly? She choke on her own blood from the mouth wound, or…?"

"Blunt force trauma to the head and face killed her, they think," Russ said. "Probably, she died of a brain hemorrhage. God, I hope so, anyway. I'd hate to think she was alive when he started cutting her in half."

"Can't argue with that," Hector said.

"What 'big thing' do you have, Hec? Does it touch on this?"

"No, I'm so sorry to have wasted your time, Russ. You're right, this is beyond anything. Sorry again."

"No using anything I told you, right, Hec? I don't want to go to some bookstore or open up *Ellery Queen Mystery Magazine* and find some short story…"

"Never," Hector said. "I'm too dark and real for that rag. Now you go and nail the son of a bitch who did that to that poor girl."

Hector's next call was to Aggie Underwood, the reporter for the *Herald Express*.

Aggie said, "Listen you good-looking son of a bitch, I can't talk now, I'm on deadline with this murder."

"Right," Hector said. "File your story, then meet me at the Pacific Dining Car. My treat."

"When?"

"Whenever you get here," Hector said. "I'm holding down the bar. Hiding out, sort of. But I may know something you can use."

"See you in two hours. Try to stay sober, Hec. So we can get drunk together, I mean. I really need it."

"Bring some of your crime scene photos, would you?"

"You a ghoul?"

"I call with reason. And I've heard descriptions from the cops. I need a first-hand look."

"Don't order food then — stick with a liquid diet," Aggie said. "I know that's my plan."

She hung up without saying goodbye. Hector's next call was placed to Agent Tilly.

Edmond said, "You weren't kidding about 'em being in full flight, Lassiter. A few have already escaped the net. But we've nailed a number of the smaller fish. We'll at least get 'em deposed, and maybe even get a few of them before the committee."

"Couldn't happen to a nicer crew. You pick up Mercedes Marshall and family?"

"Still among the missing, but we closed down the borders on them — except to the south. I mean, if they want to go to Mexico, we can't really seal that border. And from there they can go anywhere."

"What about the painters?"

"They've made some runs of their own, Hector. Most are trying to get to Paris. One or two are en route suddenly to Spain. You name it. John Huston's name came up as an art collector, but he's suddenly in Mexico, too. Scouting locations for some film he's doing with Bogart. Or that's the story, anyway — can't use him for information on these bastards."

Hector said, "You hear about a murder in Los Angeles, Agent?"

"It's the news everywhere…'cause it's so grisly, I guess."

"Those people you're trying to serve to get their testimony? Well, they're tied into this killing," Hector said. "Again, this is off the record, and you didn't hear it from me. But there's a connection. You should call an LAPD detective named Russ Evans. You two should kibitz."

"Detective Evans is a friend of yours, Hector?"

"Overstating it more than a little, but he's okay. And he shouldn't know I effected the introduction. But trust me, this thing in Los Angeles is tied to those killings I told you about in Key West — in Mexico and Spain."

"What the hell are you up to, Hector? How do you know all this stuff?"

"Just comes of traveling in the wrong circles, I reckon."

"Had a counter-charge I've got to follow-up on," Edmond said.

"Oh? A HUAC kind of thing?"

"Yeah, on Orson Welles, if you can believe that."

"Commie stuff?"

"Yeah."

"I know him pretty well," Hector said. "Orson isn't. Oh, he's left as can be, but Orson's a limousine liberal. Not worth your effort. You've got bigger fish to fry."

"We'll see. Save me some trouble, Hector?"

"Sure, if I can. What?"

"Shoot me your buddy's number at the LAPD."

A small, redheaded woman zeroed in on Hector as he sat at the bar. He saw her coming in the mirror — Agnes Underwood.

"Buy me that drink, Hector."

He waved at the bartender. Hector said, "Whatever the lady wants."

Aggie handed Hector a manila envelope. "Turn this so I don't have to see those photos again. I had to stand up on the car roof to really get much of a look at that kid and I wish I hadn't. Then, seeing the photos up close, at the paper…I don't know how I'll sleep. I didn't know people could do such things to one another."

A harrowing admission to come from a veteran Los Angeles crime reporter.

Hector twisted around in his seat and opened the file. He was aware of Aggie watching him closely…waiting to see how it would hit him. Hector had braced himself for what he would see. He had already turned his mind loose to imagine it as bad as it could be. He almost scared himself at how close he'd come in his mind's eye to the actual images.

Aggie slugged back her drink and said, "You're a tough guy, okay. Frankly, I'd have forgiven you for throwing up all over the bar."

Hector said, "Her arms were bent above her head, just like they appear in this photograph?"

"Sure, nobody's touched her. She's like the murderer left her. She was washed clean. Some think that may mean it was a cop or cops — knowing enough to destroy evidence."

"What's the theory on the arms above her head, Ag?"

"That she died that way. With her arms tied over her head. Also, her lower torso is tilted upward a bit — like maybe she died in a seated position…maybe in a bathtub."

"How long do they estimate she was dead when she was found?"

"At least ten hours."

"So that puts her time of death sometime in the afternoon of January 14," Hector said.

"That's right, sometime yesterday afternoon."

Hector finished looking at the pictures. He handed the file back to Aggie.

She said, "Much as I appreciate the offer for a meal, I'm not up to eating."

"Me either, now. So we'll drink."

"I need to get back to the paper," Aggie said. "I have some research I want to do. I don't think this girl is the first to be murdered by this bastard. I have some old pet unsolveds I want to look at. Ever hear of the 'White Gardenia' murder?"

"Nah. Done here in Los Angeles?"

"Yeah, a woman named Ora Murray, in 1943. Maybe the Georgette Bauerdorf murder, too."

"That one got by me, too," Hector said. "But I'm in and out of Hollywood, you know — a script here or there. Taking a meeting. I don't like this town."

"What's your interest in this, Hector?"

"That's a different story," he said. "That's one that takes more time than I have now and involves some real risk for a reporter who might want to chase it. Let me just suggest this to you. You get a chance, get yourself some art books. Get a stiff drink, then lay out those photos you've got there against some prints of Salvador Dali's *Art of Radio*. See if you can shag a copy of the now defunct surrealist magazine *Minotaure*, particularly Issue 8. Dali did that cover, too. Check out a photo by Man Ray called "Minotaure." And there's another work, it's called "Anatomie als Braut", by Max Ernst." Hector had taken out his own subscription to *Minotaure* after the Keys hurricane...never quite able to put it all behind him in 1935.

Aggie scowled. "God, you're weird. Are you telling me this killing has something to do with art?"

"Maybe. It wouldn't be the first, either."

"What the hell are you talking about?"

"I heard a story once," Hector lied. "Heard it from a federal agent, based in D.C. Guy named Tilly. You should call him. But don't mention my name. He hates me."

Aggie smiled crookedly. "Was it money or a woman?"

"I have to choose?"

5

The radio on low: "Ghosts of Yesterday."

The Christmas trees were still lining Hollywood Boulevard and the city must have had some post-war mad money because it was still paying to keep them lit.

Hector pulled into the lot of the hotel and tossed his keys to a bellhop. "Point her nose out," he said.

The kid shrugged. "Don't like backing out, eh?"

"I like fast exits," Hector said.

The elevator operator looked to be a vet — he was missing his left arm. Hector went to reach for the gate, trying to be helpful, and drew a scowl. "Sorry, partner," he said.

"That's my fucking job," the vet said, pulling the gate shut.

Rita answered Hector's knock. She opened the door and hugged him tightly. "We've been worried."

"Me too."

Orson emerged from the bedroom. He was wearing a smoking jacket…puffing on a pipe. Very Hollywood. Orson finally looked reasonably rested. "I closed down the set today," he said. "I couldn't go in now. What have you learned, Hector? Say that poor woman isn't Betty."

Hector walked to the wet bar and poured himself a Scotch. He drained that and poured another. "Afraid I'd be lying, folks. It was Betty. I've seen the pictures."

Orson looked stricken. "As bad as they say?"

"Beyond your darkest dreams."

Orson collapsed onto the couch. "She was really cut in half then?"

"Yes," Hector said. "She looks like something pulled from your Crazy House set. And I expect that's deliberate."

"Probably in many ways," Orson said. "The Mercury Wonder Show used to be set up right there in almost the same place she was found. I used to saw women in half there — maybe on that very lot."

"And the victim has direct ties to you," Hector said. "She actually helped you create a set full of mannequins that predict her own mutilation."

"I should leave the country," Orson said. "I could call Darryl Zanuck. He'll help me out — find me work overseas."

Hector considered that. "Might be the thing to do. I had a tip HUAC may be coming after you, too. How much of your picture is left to film in the States?"

"Just the shootout...the Crazy House scenes, in other words," Orson said.

Rita was watching them, chewing her nails. Hector said, "How quickly could you do that?"

"If we started tonight, and shot through the day tomorrow, I could get it done," Orson said. "Then we were headed back to Mexico for some last things down there, now that the weather is better."

"Then that's what you have to do," Hector said. "Get your crew going on that showdown. Do it off the books, if you can, Orson. Let the suits and the cops think that the set is still closed. Do it with a skeleton crew — guerilla-style. While you do that, I'll run interference and keep digging. I'll do what I can to deflect attention from you. I figure late tomorrow, day after at the latest, the cops are going to identify Betty. Then they'll get scrambling. That's when your name and your ties to Betty could enter the investigative stream."

Rita poured herself a drink. "What about you, Hector? Who protects you?"

Hector shrugged. "I'm not sitting still, M. I'm banking on the axiom a moving target is harder to hit." Hector checked his watch.

"That said, I've got to get back to my favorite bar."

He spent two hours in the Pacific Dining Car's bar, waiting for a phone call that never came.

Sighing, Hector settled up and slipped out the back and navigated alleys until he found a cab to take him to the hotel where he was hiding out.

"A good artist should be isolated.

If he isn't isolated, something is wrong."

— ORSON WELLES

CHAPTER 38

SQUEEZE PLAY

HECTOR CALLED Agent Edmond Tilly at six in the morning, Los Angeles time. It was nine in the District of Columbia. "This is all insane, Hector," Edmond said. "I've confirmed your reports of the murders in Key West in 1935, and of the ones in Spain. The stuff in Mexico? Well, the records are spotty."

"Well, the other two should be enough," Hector said.

"Enough to convince me, but I don't have any authority over this murder case in Los Angeles," the agent said.

"So Russ wasn't going for it, huh?"

"He's at best a functionary — in no position to do much that's useful," Edmond said. "And he strikes me as unimaginative. So no, your LAPD buddy didn't go for it. He thinks this Elizabeth Short was a sex crime victim."

"Short? Elizabeth? You've identified her, then?"

"We haven't told LAPD yet," the agent said. "That'll happen by noon, your time. But yes, she's Elizabeth Short of Medford Massachusetts. Age twenty-two. She was five-six, 113 pounds...black hair, green eyes. Pretty enough. Last seen leaving the Biltmore Hotel on the night of January 9. She has a missing 'week' between the ninth and the morning of January 15, when she was found cut in half on Norton Avenue."

Hector knew where she'd been — crashed in Orson's Crazy House set on the studio backlot...arranging mannequins and painting the faces of mutilated clowns on the walls of Orson's indefensible set.

Almost as if it was on cue, Agent Tilly said, "We had another tip on your friend Orson Welles, Hector. Oddly enough, it ties to this case. Someone has accused him of Beth Short's murder. Seems she was allegedly seeing a man named George. Seems Welles' real name is George Orson Welles. Hear Welles also used to do magic shows for servicemen on the site where Beth Short was found. He used to cut women in half there. Damning stuff."

"Wild stuff," Hector said. "Fanciful stuff. Bullshit."

Edmond said, "Like surrealist artists killing ingenues, you mean?"

"Yeah, like that."

Edmond wasn't finished. "I hear also that Welles actually filed an application a few days ago — an application to serve as a morgue assistant. He did that just a few days before the body was found. Figure Welles either wanted to look at his work a last time, or have a last shot at destroying evidence."

Hector said, "Well, that one is hard to explain."

"LAPD made a run out to your rented bungalow last night, Hector. They had a tip that Welles might be found there, covered in blood."

"I skipped on that place yesterday afternoon," Hector said. "Getting ready to head home to New Mexico. What'd you find?"

"A big empty," Edmond said. "You wouldn't know where to find Welles, would you?"

"Why?"

"We're hauling him in for a deposition. In the course of discussing some political matters — some leftist fundraising issues —

we may want to ask him some questions about Beth Short. I mean, Director Hoover would certainly not balk at the notion of solving what's shaping up to be California's most infamous murder. The 'Crime of the Century' they're calling it."

"I thought the Lindbergh baby's kidnapping was the 'Crime of the Century'," Hector said.

"That was last decade's crime of the century," Agent Tilly said. "Where can I find Welles?"

"I don't know," Hector said.

"Did I mention production of his latest movie, *The Lady From Shanghai*, was shut down yesterday — the day the body was found. I'm told it's shut down today, too," the agent said.

"Interesting…"

"If you know anything, Hector…"

"I'm fresh out of revelations, Agent."

"I had a call last evening from a reporter — some woman named Underwood. She knew some things I can't figure out her knowing unless she's one of your broads. Or someone else you're using toward your own still mysterious ends."

"Jesus, you give me way too much credit," Hector said. "You arrest Mercedes Marshall yet?"

"No, but the stuff with her daughter is a wonderful cudgel," the agent said. "You have no idea what an effective motivational tool it is to haul in some lefty degenerate painter or photographer and be able to level a statutory rape charge at them — quite a motivator."

"I'll bet."

"If you were Welles, what would you do, Hector?"

Hector thought about it. "First, I'd have to know I was a suspect to know to run," Hector said. "Then, not being savvy about these things, but knowing I was being looked at for a murder, I'd probably make a run for the border. Mexico, probably."

"You think he'd be dumb enough to fly down?"

"He's a genius," Hector said. "Everyone says so. But that doesn't mean he's smart."

"If you get a line on him, Hector…"

"You'll be my first call."

"You being a friend and all, I wouldn't be upset if you were to tip him to our interest in the murder…"

"What? So he can 'fly'?"

"That's right. But only tip him to our interest. You wouldn't want to become an accessory, after all, would you, Hector?"

"No, I wouldn't want that."

"And you wouldn't want HUAC taking an interest in you, would you?"

"Not that, either." He hung up. To the phone Hector said, "Asshole."

ی

Hector had kept the call to the FBI agent short, so he didn't think it could be traced. Nevertheless, he drove around for an hour until he was sure he had no tail. Then he drove to the studio.

He knocked on the door several times before a dwarf — a longtime gopher of Orson's named "Shorty" Chirello — let Hector in.

Orson was seated in a chair, smoking a cigarette. He smiled thinly when he saw Hector. "More news?"

"None of it good," Hector said. "Did you really apply to be a morgue assistant?"

"Yes."

"In God's name, why?"

"Verisimilitude, for my Crazy House set."

Hector sighed. He said, "I saw some real painters out there moving around on the lot. The labor strike is settled?"

"So I've heard," Orson said.

"You finish the Crazy House scenes?"

"Yes," Orson said. "We still have the mirror scene to finish —
we're about three-quarters through that."

"But the Crazy House set could be struck?"

"Torn down, you mean?"

"More or less," Hector said.

"Yes."

"Then I suggest you throw a tantrum," Hector said. "Pitch a
bitch about how shitty it looks. Get the real painters in here and
let them go to town to their own inspiration."

"Wipe out the evidence, you mean," Orson said. "I suppose
I'll have to cut the material from the film, too."

"That's months down the road. And with some careful editing..." Hector shrugged. "But that's thinking too far ahead. Right
now, you need to transform that set. You need to move it away
from the crime photos I've seen. And another thing, when could
you leave for Mexico?"

"Tomorrow afternoon? Say, early evening?"

"Perfect," Hector said. "The feds are close to moving on you,
for HUAC stuff, but also for the murder, maybe."

"Oh, good Christ."

"We still have some cards to play," Hector said. "Have Shorty
make your arrangements. You'll want to make it look like you're
flying to Paris."

"But if they are looking for me...trying to keep tabs...I mean,
if I fly, Hector, they'll know before I ever get on that plane...to
Mexico or France or wherever."

"That's right," Hector said. "We're going to count on them
knowing."

Ꞅ

Rita Hayworth was standing by the door, smoking. She said,
"I've been thinking about your novel-in-progress, *Squeeze Play*,

Hector. Do you know yet if your hero, Owen Walters, survives his predicament? Does he get the girl and walk away clean?"

"Nobody's ever clean in my books, and I don't write many, if any, happy endings," Hector said. "But I'm leaning toward Owen at least getting out with his life."

"And the girl?"

"Jury's still out on her."

ת

Hector had taken up station at his usual stool at the Dining Car's bar. For the hell of it he dialed the Marshall house — the number had been disconnected.

He called John Huston's place: a servant said John and his family were in Mexico with the Bogarts, scouting film locations.

Hector walked outside and bought an afternoon paper and read about "Elizabeth Short" and her "werewolf" murderer and brought it back in to read more while he drank.

Breathless stuff — even Aggie's reportage rubbed Hector the wrong way.

Motion behind him in the mirror behind the bar — a busty blond in a black dress and hat…her face covered by a black veil. She pulled off black gloves and raised her veil to kiss Hector on the cheek.

"Hello, Hector," Rachel said.

"In bullfighting there is a term called querencia.
The querencia *is the spot in the ring to which the bull returns.*
Each bull has a different querencia, *but as the bullfight continues,*
and the animal becomes more threatened, it returns more and
more often to his spot. As he returns to his querencia,
he becomes more predictable. And so, in the end,
the matador is able to kill the bull because
instead of trying something new,
the bull returns to what is familiar. His comfort zone."

— CARLY FIORINA

CHAPTER 39

FEMME FATALE

RACHEL'S HAIR was again its natural blond, grown out long and wavy. She had some laugh lines now — at least she'd found reason to laugh. Her full lips were painted dark crimson and her eyes shadowed umber. Her tailored jacket and skirt emphasized her bust and long slender legs.

"You've hardly changed," Hector said.

"You haven't either," Rachel said.

"You're abilities as a liar seem to be waning." He held up his pack of cigarettes. "You still smoke?"

"Only with friends."

Hector lit two cigarettes and placed one between her lips.

"You're torn, aren't you?"

Hector shrugged. "How so?"

"Between kissing and killing me."

"Why not do both?"

A sad smile. "You sound like one of your characters."

"Or all my characters sound like me."

The bartender said, "Anything?"

Rachel thought about that and said, "You know how to make a mojito?"

"Sure," he said.

"One of those, then." She smoked her cigarette, then she said to Hector, "I hear you met my father...and that you beat him nearly to death."

"I'll get it right next time."

"There won't be a next time," she said. "He's past your punishment for what he did. It was so many years ago."

"He destroyed you from the inside out," Hector said. "He's not through paying yet."

Rachel shrugged. "I'm the one who cracked inside...twisted into something terrible. Something destructive and inhuman."

Hector looked away...then looked at his drink. "You killed Beverly, by yourself? Is that what you're saying?"

"Yes, Hector. I killed them all. I was sick, but I was rational. I could reason, in my own way. Bev was someone I met on the boat...a fellow traveler to use a phrase that used to be innocent. I was trying to make art — I had myself convinced of that. I did what artists do, copied the works of others. Or so I told myself."

She sipped her mojito. "Nobody makes them as good as you do."

"Because I use more liquor." Hector wet his lips. "Artists put down a copy of a drawing or painting next to a pad of paper or an easel, and they draw or paint that, Rachel. Maybe they even trace it. Writers retype or hand-write another writer's short story to get a feel for doing it...for putting the words together, just so. Maybe they break down the plot of a novel and then rewrite that book to the other author's plot outline as an exercise."

Rachel nodded. "I know. But I used real people. I suffered for my father's notions of art. It seemed everyone else should suffer for mine."

"That's a little pat, isn't it?"

"Well, I was more than a little insane, Hector. Criminally insane."

"And now?"

"I got help...saw doctors. Jung himself in the late 1930s. I became a case study of his. And the painting...I began to follow my own muse...I became my own muse. As Alva, I was able to paint. As I did that, I was able to move away from the bloody destruction that fed my art. You were a big part of that change in me. In Key West, when I was with you, I tried to be — I was — just what I said. I was Rachel Harper, a fashion journalist. I was your girlfriend. I started thinking I could be her, indefinitely. I wanted to be her. But I knew I was on borrowed time with you. Quentin Windly saw me on Matecumbe Key. I was afraid he would tell you."

Hector suddenly remembered something that Quentin had said in Spain, before his execution: "That other one was there, too...that cock-tease..."

"I thought Quentin would put it together first," Rachel said. "Then Hem came and dragged you away to Matecumbe. Goddamn Hemingway. I blame him for costing me you, time and time again. I knew how small Matecumbe is. I thought there was a chance that even if you didn't come across evidence of what I did there on that Key, that you'd hear things. That someone might have survived the hurricane and would remember me and describe me to you. So Rachel had to die."

"Who did the dying for you?"

Rachel couldn't look at him. "That woman I met in the Electric Kitchen with you," Rachel said. "The waitress, Karen. She had about my figure…she was blond."

Hector's knuckles were white around his glass. He thought it might shatter in his hand, and let go of it. "And you cut off her head," Hector said. "Slashed her belly open and shoved in a dozen roses. Jesus Christ."

"I was sick," Rachel said, "but something in me began to change then, to curdle. I went to Mexico. I kept doing it, but to men. To me, in my state then, that seemed like a step toward improvement."

Hector snorted and drained his drink; ordered another.

"Then came Spain," Rachel said. "I became Alva, the bohemian widow and painter. The activist. Buried myself in the part, you might say. I began to see how what I did, what I couldn't quite yet stop doing, could be used toward an end…to discredit the Franco forces. Then I got involved with the other surrealists and with Alphonse Laurencic. I helped him with the design of his psychological torture cells…helped him shape his concepts of 'psychotechnic interrogation.' As I did that, I found I was able to hold the other — the killing — in check. My own painting began to go down original paths, at last. I wasn't just copying, or re-imagining or answering the works of others. I was my own painter. It was intoxicating."

"And us?"

"As Alva, I first met Hem," Rachel said, "as you know. Hem was fooled. Hem was prepared to accept me as my own younger sister. I couldn't get you out of my head. When Hem said you were in Spain, and that you wanted to meet me, I was thrilled. I decided to risk it all, to see if I could make you believe I was Alva."

"And you did. And then you let me and Hem kill Windly. You let us continue to think Quentin was the killer. You helped us lure Quentin out to his own execution."

Rachel ran her hands back through her pale hair. "I still had some arrogance about all that," she said. "It was a kick to have taken in a literary writer and a crime writer — the two great macho men of American literature. As Rachel, when I first met you two, I played with you both…played to your biases. I dropped those little clues at you just to see which way you would jump. You might as well know I came to Key West planning on meeting you both. I thought I might even kill the two of you — Hemingway, the great prose modernist who based his famous style on paintings he studied in Paris…and Hector Lassiter, the crime novelist who found his own lauded, laconic American writer's voice in Paris. I thought you two — your deaths — might be my kind of announcement as an artist, so to speak. My first great 'public works.' So I arranged to have that telegram sent to Key West just to dangle it in front of you, Hector. Setting up the patina of a conspiracy by telling you Beverly was headed to Cuba and then having a telegram arrive from Matecumbe. And misspelling my own name — another 'clue'. I'd made a study of your books…I was a fan. And you exceeded my wildest expectations. You were like your characters…seizing a thread in that telegram and constructing your own narrative right in front of me. It was delicious. And Hem? Hem was much easier to play to. And it was a laugh to me — to the calculating mess I was — to see you two writers immediately leap to the conclusion that the killer you were seeking had to be a literary critic. Too perfect."

"It's a knee-slapper, to be sure," Hector said, his voice flat.

"But I fell in love a second time with you," Rachel said. "Even deeper and harder than the first time. And I was going to come to the States and live with you, as Alva the painter. I had the other under control, you see. Not put away yet, but in check. I haven't killed another person since Spain. I thought I could live as Alva and I was really going to try."

"What happened?"

"Bishop Blair was the first complication," she said. "You blundered into his studio with that story about damned Alphonse Laurencic and his surrealist torture chambers. You did that five minutes after poor old Bishop had shipped my painting of just such an interrogation cell to Paris. Along with that other painting I'd done of you, in your bed in Key West. I watched him put it together, right there. He was going to get you alone and tell you. Bishop had figured it all out. He knew I was the killer."

"So you had him killed."

"To protect me, and the others, I thought I had to. Another painter, quite a famous one now, he actually cut Bishop's throat. Made it look like a robbery. But I didn't do it. To my mind, at the time, that was an important thing for me...even a kind of affirmation I was getting better."

Hector just shook his head.

"So I got to Paris, Hector. I was following you back, just as I'd promised. But you — you and your goddamn sentimental streak... I went to the gallery to see my three paintings that Bishop had shipped there, and the proprietor told me they'd been sold. She described you quite wonderfully and accurately. Obviously, she'd been attracted to you. She remembered your accent and smile. When I knew you had those three paintings, I knew I couldn't face you again. So I spread word back to Spain that I'd been denounced and executed. In the to-and-fro of all that in Spain in 1937, it was an easy and potent lie to plant."

Rachel signaled for another mojito. "Here's the funny thing, Hector. Once Alva was dead, presumed posthumous, I — *she* — became insanely collectible. Like that horrible woman, Mercedes...several others...they tried to snatch up all there was of my work. Prices of my paintings spiraled upward. But the best market is here in Los Angeles, here in my father's town. So I'm careful. I stay here for now...hidden from him...from his friends. A faceless name."

"And all the while you keep feeding the collecting beast," Hector said, a crooked smile on his face. "*That* I can admire. Creating a never-ending flow of posthumous works and making a bundle in the process. Mercedes said that every time she thought she'd collected all you had done, another painting or two would surface."

"And they always will," Rachel said. "For Mercedes and for half-a-dozen rich others I can never meet face-to-face, for obvious reasons. So I'm a successful dead painter now," Rachel said, rueful. "Some fine joke."

"This one painting of yours I own," Hector said, lighting a cigarette, "you titled it, *In Perfumed Night, Choice Come Courting on Pink Toes*. That painting that tipped Bishop. That was really me there, naked on the bed, and you standing naked at the foot of the bed with a knife, contemplating killing me? That really happened, didn't it?"

"Our first night together," Rachel said, cheeks red. "But I made my choice. And I've never wavered from it. I keep coming back to you. I hear about you here or there, and I have to make the connection, or try. There have been other overtures you missed, or maybe messages that didn't reach you. But the fact is that I want to think we can still be together some day. I still love you, Hector."

"In bullfighting there is a term, it's called the *querencia*," Hector said. "Hem said it's the place in the ring where a particular bull feels at home. He returns there again and again, and eventually, it gets him killed. I guess maybe I'm your *querencia*."

Rachel's eyes were wet. She said, "There was a time, before I 'made my choice,' and even sometimes after, when I viewed the two of us as a kind of game. I thought of you as the bull — you and Hem, really — and of me as the matador."

"Sometimes these things are a matter of perspective," Hector said. "And sometimes the bull kills the matador."

Rachel nodded. "A lot has happened to you since 1937. I've heard stories about you. And you've killed people, too, Hector, justly or unjustly. Some would say you and me are more alike than different. You murder and then you write about it. You're the man who writes what he lives and lives what he writes. Isn't that what Quentin said, before you eventually blew him up?"

"I've killed...in combat," Hector said. "I've killed for revenge, or to stop other killings. But you killed for aesthetics...for pleasure. You killed for *art*."

"You told Alva — told me — that you loved Rachel."

"I loved Alva, too."

"And now, Hector?"

"I still love them. But you? I don't even know who you are. I can't grasp what you are. You're sublime beyond all my understanding. Do you understand yourself? I mean, who are you now? Are you Rachel? Are you Alva? Are you Rhonda? Which do you prefer to be called?"

"Whatever name you prefer is fine with me," she said. "I'm not doing that other anymore. I've beaten that. I've killed it in myself."

"But you're still tied to it," Hector said. "You're running with this sick crowd that just killed an innocent young woman."

"They do what I did, yes. But I'm trying to get free of them. I wasn't *of* or even *with* that crowd, not really. They were clients... people I had to keep some contact with to continue to sell my paintings." She took a breath, then said, some bitterness there, "I hear that Mercedes is boasting she slept with you. How was she?"

"Enthusiastic. Enthusiasm will carry you a ways, all on its own."

"And she's beautiful. And you're a man. How could you say no?"

"Where is the bitch now?"

"In the Yucatan...headed to parts unknown."

Hector nodded. "And the others?"

"They're all running. You haven't destroyed them, Hector, but you've ended what they had here on the coast, and in the United States. Man Ray, Dali, all of them — between you and HUAC they've all left the country in the past few days or will by month's end. Their circle is destroyed in this country. Their underground is wiped out, largely thanks to you."

"And you? Where do you go next?"

"I'm not sure," she said. "But I have to leave here in a few minutes. There are a few of them at a bar just across the street. They're enjoying their last drink in the States. We have one last stop first, then we're headed to the airport. I figure once we're in the crowd, I'll slip away. Go my own way. Maybe I'll go down to Mexico. Maybe just across the border from La Mesilla. How would you feel about that?"

Hector shrugged. "You don't even seem to know who you are anymore, Rachel. How can I think about trying to pick up things with you when you don't even know who or what you really are? I'd go to bed every night imagining waking up with you standing over me with a fucking butcher knife. And maybe you're really better, just like you say you are, but I can't quite shake images of you sawing off Karen's head. I see you gutting that poor girl Beverly and scooping out her organs and shoving in cogs and wheels. Jesus Christ."

Rachel stood up, smoothed out her dress and picked up her purse. "This was a mistake. You're right...I keep coming back and I should know better...should stop chasing memories. But know this: I do love you, Hector. I love you and understand you more than any other woman is capable of — I truly believe that."

"I do too." Hector ground out his Pall Mall. "You've really not killed anyone since Spain?"

"No, though I'm sorely tempted to kill my father. And to kill Hem, too. You know it was that bitch Martha Gellhorn who denounced you for spying, don't you? After you left Spain, there was a party at Chicote's. Martha was boasting about how she knew you were a spy for Hoover and how she'd gotten you run out of the country. She laughed and said what a shame it was that you escaped without being shot. Hem laughed right along with her."

Rachel suddenly leaned in for a kiss. Hector hesitated, then kissed her hard, and long. Surprising himself, he said, "Don't go to the airport. My car's out back. We'll get in it and we'll just start driving...talk some more. Try to figure things out."

She shook her head sadly, her hand on his cheek. "That's my Hector — at once forceful and conflicted. You have your friend who's in trouble. You have to help Orson. If you left him in this mess you'd never forgive yourself and you'd always resent me...resent me more than I can see you already do. And you're right to feel that way. And you're right about something else. You asked me a simple question. Am I Rachel, Alva? Who am I? And I don't have that answer. Not yet. Please stay well, Hector."

He turned and watched her walk out of the bar. He saw her silhouetted a last time against the sun, then she disappeared as the door closed behind her.

Dinah Washington on the jukebox: "My Heart Cries for You."

"It's taken me a lot longer than I hoped
to grow up to be a magician."

— ORSON WELLES

CHAPTER 40

ABRACADABRA

AGENT TILLY picked up on the first ring.

Hector said, "Citizen Welles is leaving on a plane tomorrow for Europe, Agent. I thought you might want to know."

"I do," Edmond Tilly said. "And I appreciate it, but I thought you two were friends. This is a pretty brazen sell out. I mean, I thought you two were close friends."

"So does Orson," Hector said. "Orson still thinks that."

"Jesus, what happened?"

"He bounced a check he wrote to me."

"Remind me never to lay bad paper on you, Hec. You'll be with him at the airport?"

"Just to see him off there. It's my last shot at getting my money. I would prefer it if you didn't arrest him within my sight."

"What, you'll trip him, but you don't want to see him fall?"

"Something like that," Hector said.

"Well, we've got a federal warrant out on him now," Tilly said. "But if you can deliver him without harm to us, I can sit on that. Rather do this safely and quietly as possible."

"Tomorrow then," Hector said. "Ten in the morning at Los Angeles airport. You said you're thinking of doing this quietly?"

"Subtle," Edmond said, "yeah. Just in case nothing sticks. He's big and famous and the bureau doesn't need a black eye."

"This could be a bit tricky then," Hector said. "He's working overtime to drum-up press for his movie that he's close to wrapping. He's invited the press to see him off tomorrow…promising them a shot at Rita and him together, though I don't think she's really coming along."

"What's Welles' eventual destination?"

"Paris," Hector said, "by way of New York."

"We'll grab him quietly as he boards," Tilly said. "That way, the other passengers who stand to witness anything will be on the plane for hours before they can talk to the press."

"That's clever," Hector said.

"So, what's your own plan? You're going to drop the bastard off at the airport and then take a powder?"

"Not at all," Hector said. "No, since the other stuff is going to go down on the runway, I think I'll hit the airport lounge. See if I can't pick up a comely hostess."

Agent Tilly said, "Are all you novelists degenerates?"

"All us good ones."

§

It was cold but the sky was clear — a sharp, sunny California winter morning.

Hector sat in the backseat with Orson. Welles' dwarf man-Friday was driving. The limo was equipped with special hand accelerators and brakes. Orson was wearing a black wool cape and scarf and a big floppy black slouch hat worthy of the pulp magazine version of Orson's old radio character *The Shadow*. Hector was wearing his dove gray trench coat and matching fedora. Both men wore dark blue suits and black-lacquered sunglasses.

As they rolled to a stop in front of the airport, Orson lit up a long fat cigar.

Hector said, "Remember — no showboating."

5

The first out of the limousine was a small man who ran around to the back of the car and began fiddling with the trunk.

Field agents Larry Rice and Carl Reed moved behind a pillar. They exchanged nods as Orson Welles stepped from the back of the car and raised both arms above his head, hands grasping one another and pumping up and down like a heavyweight fighter entering the ring.

Hector stepped out after Orson, nearly invisible behind the great director.

Flash bulbs began popping and a rush of newsmen and women crowded the limo.

The two agents briefly lost sight of Orson, then the reporters began to disperse and the agents spotted Orson's broad back and flapping black wool cape. Their quarry waved with a desultory hand over his shoulder at the reporters. A blue-gray haze of pungent smoke trailed from his cigar.

The agents followed at a respectable distance, hesitating as their man entered the public restroom.

A few other men shuffled into the restroom behind their target. The agents exchanged glances, then positioned themselves on either side of the men's room door.

A minute passed, then a small skinny blondish man with wall-eyes and a big nose emerged from the men's room. He had a black wool coat or cape draped over one arm and a briefcase clutched in his other hand.

The agents both took note when the broad brim of large black slouch hat emerged through the door, but the man wearing the hat was an elderly Negro dressed in a double-breasted gray suit.

Another tall man soon followed that one of out of the bathroom. That man was slipping a cigarette between his lips and he flicked open a silver Zippo with one hand and held the lighter up to his mouth. He closed the lighter as he passed Agent Rice, nodding at the agent.

Three more minutes passed, and there was still no sign of Orson Welles emerging from the men's room. The agents nodded at one another. Agent Rice took off his hat and glasses and slipped through the door.

There was nobody standing at the urinals. The stall doors were all ajar, as well. The FBI agent moved from door to door, confronted by empty stall after empty stall.

The men's room stank of urine and disinfectant and cigar smoke.

Agent Rice stared at the blue-gray smoke from the cigar left resting on the marble ledge above the sinks.

5

Hector was sitting in the airport lounge, engaging in some serious eye-contact with a redheaded stewardess — furthering his cover story in case he was also being watched. He heard a crackle over the loud speaker and then a request that "Michael O'Hara" should "please pick up the courtesy phone."

He grabbed the bartender and was directed to a red phone mounted on the wall kitty-corner to the bar. Hector scooped up the phone and said, "Can't let go of that character, can you?"

Orson was deploying his Irish accent. "I'm just glad you remembered the name and made the connection." Hector had heard better assumed Irish accents, but he wasn't about to say that to touchy Orson. Welles said, "I'm taking your advice, Hector. We're going to cross over from Arizona. Be a few more hours before we reach the

California border."

Hector said, "Where'd you scrounge up all the reporters? Particularly with this 'Dahlia' madness. I figured they'd all be spoken for."

"A little last curtain call for the Mercury Players," Orson said. "The woman with the Graflex, the one who helped you and me swap coats and hats, that was Agnes Moorhead."

"God, I didn't even recognize her," Hector said.

"That's the beauty and talent of Agnes," Orson said.

"What will you do now?"

"Stay in Europe," he said. "Finance my films from there. They appreciate me. I want to film *Don Quixote*, and to do it in Spain. I'd like to take another stab at *Heart of Darkness*."

"Conceivably, this could all blow over by year's end," Hector said. "The LAPD isn't on to you yet as a suspect for Betty's murder. Only the Feds were thinking that way. And if I succeed in hanging her killing on some surrealists who can be made to flip on the others…"

"I'd have left the country anyway, Hector. And this facilitates things with Rita. She insists on staying in Hollywood. Who can blame her? She's a movie star. The only thing that upsets me is not getting to finish *The Lady From Shanghai*. Cohn will probably fuck it up."

Hector bit his lip: thus was another of Orson's mutilated masterpieces being born.

"If I can shake loose soon here in Los Angeles, maybe I'll catch you in Mexico," Hector said. He was thinking again about journeying to Mexico…about straying over that border from his hacienda in La Mesilla.

"Just mind your own back, Hector, please," Orson said. "Think of what they did to Betty, and she was an innocent in every sense. You're actively engaging them. I'd hate to think what they'd do to you if they got their hands on you."

"They've got their own problems now," Hector said. "And I've got a long memory and short temper…loads of imagination, too. We'll see what that trifecta maybe buys those cocksuckers. They're my new hobby."

Hector had just hung up the phone when another page came over the airport's intercom system for him — this one paging Hector by his real name.

Edmond Tilly said, "What the hell happened?"

Hector said, "What the hell are you talking about? And thanks so much for broadcasting my fucking handle all over goddamn Los Angeles airport, dumbass."

"Welles! Fucking Orson Welles has fucking disappeared!"

"Disappeared?"

"Yeah, fucking literally disappeared. My guys followed him into the men's room. They stood guard outside the door. Only one way in or out of the fucking room. Time passed. They went in, and they found just his fucking cigar. Just his goddamn cigar!"

"These boys of yours maybe closet hopheads, Agent?"

"What did you see, Lassiter?"

"I saw nothing. Hell, I didn't even see your boys, and I've got the eye. I got out of the car with Orson, then I moved my ass away…just in case your boys got jumpy and decided to arrest the poor bastard on the spot. Orson went one way, and I went another. As I speak, I think you're queering my shot at nailing a redheaded stew."

"I don't understand this," Tilly said.

"I'd kick your boys' asses," Hector said. "I'd see if they were really even here. Orson's hard to miss. Sounds to me like they did just that, though. Maybe they showed up late and so they concocted this crazy-ass tale about him pulling a Houdini in the crapper."

"Maybe."

Hector said, "How are we doing on the surrealist front?"

"More bad news," Agent Tilly said. "We got some more small fish, but the big targets seemed to have slipped our nets. At least we've dispersed them, anyway."

"Maybe here," Hector said, "but they'll reconstitute in Europe."

"So let France and the Brits cope with the bastards."

"So Mercedes and her family walk?"

"I can only arrest the ones I can find."

"Damn." Hector said, "You ever get your hooks into an old bastard named Bernard Harper?"

"Never even heard of him — the name's never come up."

"He's connected to all of them," Hector said. "But he's old and just enough out of the loop to maybe have gone unwarned. He might still be in Los Angeles...off everyone's radar but my own."

"Sounds worth a try," Tilly said. "I've got to have something to take back to the director after this fuck-up. Where do I find this Harper guy?"

"I'm going to head over to his place now," Hector said. "Have one or two of your boys meet me there, won't you?"

"I've already got the two guys there at the airport, Hector. You could hook up with them and ride out together."

Hector couldn't risk being recognized by one of the agents as one of the men who emerged from the men's "restroom of mystery." And Hector's hand still stank of Orson's cigar.

Feigning indignance, Hector said, "You keep those two incompetent sons of bitches away from me. After the way they fucked up with Welles, why would I want them having my back? And I mean, Jesus — how does the bureau expect to win the war against communism fielding dumbasses like those two?"

5

The field agents dispatched to meet Hector at Bernard Harper's house finally agreed to force the front door.

They did that and then kicked the broken door open. The smell of blood was thick on the stale air that burped from the house as the door slammed back against the interior wall.

The younger of the agents — a gung-ho, blond, former-All-American — edged through the door, then came stumbling out backward, doubled over and vomiting uncontrollably.

The other agent, an older guy named Fletcher Long, edged in, gun out. This choked voice: "Holy Christ!"

Frowning, Hector edged through the door, a hand already covering his nose and mouth from the stench.

Bernard Harper had literally been taken apart.

The old man's living room looked like Orsons' Crazy House set recreated with real body parts.

Every one of Bernard Harper's digits, limbs and extremities had been disarticulated and arranged around the living room.

Ropes of intestine were coiled around banisters and curtain rods.

Painted in blood on the wall was the title:

OLD MAN EXPLODED OUT TO ALL POINTS PAST REDEMPTION OR REASSEMBLY

The photographer's severed head sat on the bottom step of the stairs leading to the second floor. An envelope was balanced against the head. On the envelope was written "Hector."

Arching an eyebrow, Hector said, "May I?"

"Use a handkerchief to pick it up," Agent Long said, his face white. "And I'll read it with you."

Hector opened the envelope and unfolded the note with his display handkerchief. It read:

This time I almost helped them.

But in the end, I just gave them ideas.

For what he cost me.

For what he cost <u>us</u>.

— R/A

Fletcher Long's voice was raw and cracking. "What's it mean?" He waved his arms around at the bloodied room. "What does any of this mean? What do you even call something like this?"

Hector said, "A masterpiece."

PART FOUR

HOW THE
GHOST OF YOU CLINGS
(1959)

"The attitude that nature is chaotic
and that the artist puts order into it
is a very absurd point of view, I think.
All that we can hope for
is to put some order into ourselves."

— WILLEM DE KOONING

CHAPTER 41

LIONS IN WINTER

TWO PRINTS of Salvador Dali's hung on the wall of the travel agent's office: *Young Virgin Auto-Sodomized by the Horns of Her Own Chastity* and *The Ghost of Vermeer of Delft Which Can Be Used As a Table.*

Hector hoped it wasn't some kind of omen.

ᴎ

Hector still doubted the wisdom of his trip to Cuba.

It was all Marlene Dietrich's fault...he bitterly blamed the Kraut.

The German chanteuse's siege had been focused and forceful and it was waged over many months. She'd finally appealed to Hector's conscience — never an easy target, but all too effective when struck.

Hem, Marlene confided, was sliding into some sustained state of paranoia. Hem had become increasingly suicidal, she sobbed.

Hem's current wife, Mary, had confided to Marlene that Hem was convinced he was under perpetual FBI surveillance, even in Cuba...that he was being stalked by unnamed enemies.

"He probably is under Hoover's flunkies' watch," Hector had told Marlene. "I had him all but cleared of communist suspicion in Spain, then he started his crazy stuff about hunting Jap submarines with his drunken Cuban buddies on the *Pilar*. That earned him the kind of attention from J. Edgar nobody needs. Now the story is Hem's getting cozy with Castro — even offering him publicity advice."

"You're truly the last of Hem's old friends," Marlene insisted. "You know one another best and you're the only one either of you has left from the old days. Living as you both do, how long can you two have to fix it? How long can either of you have left to enjoy the other's company before it's too late?"

Repeatedly shamed by Marlene, Hector had eventually relented and agreed to be the one to reach out.

He'd called Hem at the *Finca Vigía* — the "Lookout Farm" — and they had shared a cordial, almost sentimental thirty-minute phone conversation...all the while Ernest holding the phone too far from his ear and shouting into it, as was his custom.

Hem said that he and Mary had just returned from wintering in Ketchum, Idaho.

They had returned briefly home to Cuba for a few weeks before pushing on to Spain, where Hem planned to follow a series of pivotal *mano a manos* between Antonio Ordóñez and Luis Miguel Dominguín.

Hem was going to observe the *corridas* in order to update, or perhaps even to write a sequel to *Death in the Afternoon*.

Hector would be welcome to come down for a few days. He could bunk in the Finca's guesthouse and they would continue to patch things up, to catch up.

And Hector suddenly had some time on his hands.

He'd taken a meeting with Alfred Hitchcock, ostensibly to discuss a film project, but it had gone very badly.

When Hector had gotten to Los Angeles — and gotten there on his own nickel (*That cheapskate limey son of a bitch, Hitch!*) — he found he had really only been invited to receive a punishing lecture from Hitchcock for having dropped out of participation in the bloated director's latest film, *Vertigo*.

"I'm frankly still miffed, Mr. Lassiter," Hitch had said.

Months before, Hitch had sat behind the same desk, his short, fat fingers interlaced over the immensity of his potbelly, his lips puckering, as he described the central conceit of his next thriller. An everyman man — Jimmy Stewart, Hitch's favorite doppelganger — would fall in love with two women. But perhaps they would be the same woman. "There'll be delicious kink, a whiff of necrophilia, even, underlying all that of course, dear boy," Hitch had told Hector.

But Hector had begged off the screenwriting chores.

Angered, Hitch had blustered, and pouted, and accused. "What, you think the concept is too preposterous, Mr. Lassiter?"

"Quite the contrary," Hector had said. "The son of a bitch has too much verisimilitude for me. I've lived that sucker."

"Then you're perfect to write it, dear boy."

"Too perfect," Hector had said, begging off.

So all of that had conspired to send Hector on to Cuba.

But in the end, a rather chilling revelation had truly tipped Hector over into making the trip.

Hem had been receiving anonymous, menacing letters...letters filled with ranting death threats over some unspecified injustice allegedly done the anonymous author by Hem.

That wasn't particularly unusual in itself — Hem was famous and so he was bound to attract his share of kooks and cranks... mentals, all.

But a body had also recently been found not far from Hem's rambling home and hilltop grounds — a woman's disarticulated torso.

Hem had shrugged it off on face — dismissing it.

Ernest, Mary told Marlene, figured the torso was the handiwork of adherents to some secretive cult called *Abaqua* — an offshoot of the Santeria religion — some mystery cult centered around Havana.

But Hem had written the murder into a passage of one of his several novels in progress, *Islands in the Stream*. The mutilation murder had clearly made an impression on Hem. He kept bringing it up in odd moments of conversation with Mary — the fourth Mrs. Hemingway, and the one now looking to be Papa's last wife.

For his part, Hector had made an instinctive linkage between the threatening notes and the mutilated corpse that reminded him too vividly of another torso of a murdered woman that had been left on display on a park bench along Miami's South Beach decades before.

The last time Hector had seen Rachel, she had expressed a desire to kill her father and perhaps even to kill Hemingway, whom she most blamed for keeping her and Hector apart.

Since then, Rachel had certainly seen to — or helped to shape — the bloody murder of her own father.

The horrific destruction visited upon Bernard Harper had been so extreme that Hector had often wondered if Rachel's fragile equilibrium had been compromised witnessing it.

He wondered if standing by and watching her own father's dissection — even offering tips if her last note to Hector was to be believed — had tipped Rachel back over into committing murder herself.

For a dozen years, Hector had kept his ear to the ground… watching for news reports or wire stories that might indicate the surrealist murders had resumed somewhere else…maybe in Mexico where Rachel had said she might head next. Maybe in California, where he had last seen her.

But there had been nothing in North or South America until the revelation about the torso recently found near Hem's house in Cuba.

Hector had immediately put out some feelers to some old Cuban friends and learned of two other mutilation murders that had occurred in recent days in and around San Francisco de Paula, where Hemingway lived. Both the victims had been prostitutes, and both of them had been "linked" to Hem during his randier late-forties and early-fifties.

When Hector determined to go to Cuba and visit Hem, he took the unprecedented step of first tipping celebrity gossip columnist Leonard Lyons to his pending trip: "I'm going down to Cuba to see my old friend Hem and fish and drink and maybe take Castro's measure myself. Maybe get a crime novel out of that revolution. Can't see why I should let Graham Greene have Havana all to himself."

Hector figured the resulting blurb in Lyons' widely distributed and wildly popular gossip column might draw Rachel out…draw her to him in Cuba, if she was indeed there…if she had broken inside again. If she had begun killing again and had now set her sites on Hem.

The door of the plane opened and passengers began deboarding. Hector was seated near the rear of the plane and so had to await the departure of the other passengers. As he sat there, he could feel the heavy tropical heat creeping into the plane.

Hector stood and shrugged off his pale sports jacket and draped it over one arm. He slipped on his black sunglasses before stepping out into the harsh sunlight.

It was windy and the palm trees around the terminal were whipping furiously, their bending trunks creaking in the wind.

Ernest was standing by a red Chrysler, perspiring and grinning. A small thin Cuban in a gray chauffeur's uniform was standing next to Ernest. Hem's fourth wife, Mary, stood on the other side of Ernest…small and blond.

Hem was wearing a starched white guyabera shirt, khaki pants and brown moccasins without socks. He had a full beard now, snow white, and his white thinning hair was carefully parted at the back of his neck and combed forward in long strands.

Though there was less than a year or so between them, Hector thought Hem might have passed as Hector's father. Hem's magnificent, once-imposing musculature had all but collapsed and he had an enormous gut.

As he approached Hem, for the first time Hector realized how much taller he was than Ernest and he was shocked by the difference in their height. It was like Hem's charisma and actual stature were bleeding away from him at the end.

Hem opened his arms and gave Hector a bear hug. "Christ, it's good to see you, Lasso."

"You too, Hem." Even as he said it, Hector was surprised by how much he meant it.

Hem's small, blond, sun-wizened fourth wife smiled at Hector — a smile that showed no teeth and made her pointed chin more pointy. She said, "Jesus Christ, I've heard all about this big handsome son of a bitch." Mary hugged Hector and feinted one up at his chin and said, "Anyone ever tell you that you look like Billy Holden?"

"Not today."

Mary punched Hector in the gut and winked at Hem. "Fuck, but I like this one."

"Women always do," Hem said. "You ride up front with Juan, Pickle. Me and Lasso, we've got twenty-two years of catching up to do."

"Art evokes the mystery

without which the world would not exist."

— RENEE MAGRITTE

CHAPTER 42

FINCA VIGIA

THEY WERE SITTING by the pool. Hem said, "Ava Gardner used to swim naked in there."

Hector smiled and accepted a mojito from one of the servants. He nodded at the long pool, the sun glistening on its wind-rippled surface and said, "You change the water since?"

Hem winked and pulled on a pair of sunglasses. He scooted his chair into the shade. He moved like an old man now.

Hector had given his own body no quarter over the years. He had recently been diagnosed with a mild form of diabetes and needed glasses for anything involving real seeing, but he felt positively spry set against Ernest.

By all accounts, successive plane crashes that Hem had suffered in Africa during his last safari had nearly killed him. Hem had played tough for the world press, even drinking while in the throes of a concussion…next trying to put out a brush fire while severely incapacitated with his plane injuries. That had resulted in Hem actually falling into the fire and sustaining more injuries. Those who knew him best claimed that Hem had aged many years in a period of just days in the aftermath of the crashes and the fire.

Hem sat back down and pulled on a white, long-billed fisherman's hat — probably to keep his thinly covered scalp from sunburn Hector guessed — and wincing, crossed one leg over the other. The old scars from Italy and "the Great War" were still prominent on Hem's calves and shins. As if he was reading Hector's mind, Hem said, "I still have some metal work itself to the surface now and then. Hardly a month goes by I'm not at my legs with tweezers, trying to dig out some shard of kraut shrapnel. How you doin', Lasso?"

Hector shrugged and hoisted his glass. "Gotta keep these to a minimum," he said. "Blood-sugar. And I can't see for a damn. Feel like the two Jimmys — Joyce and Thurber — when I'm without my spectacles."

"Me too…wingshooting's gone to hell," Hem said. "Can't drink like I want. Have to watch my eating. Can't fuck at will. Can't…"

He didn't say "write," but Hector figured that's where Hem was headed when his voice trailed off.

"It's a beautiful place," Hector said, nodding at the magnificent, old white hilltop house, built in 1887 by some long-dead wealthy Catalonian. Martha had found it for them. Hector figured he couldn't hold that fact against the Finca — he loved it on sight.

"I'll have to leave it forever soon," Hem said. "Since Batista fled on New Year's Eve, it's been dicey. All the property confiscations, the shootings. And now with Castro's crowd…one of his guerilla's shot Black Dog. So, we're going to buy a house in Idaho. Move there after Spain. Try to get the paintings and books and other things out of here before Castro seizes the place like he has nearly every other damn thing on this island. My public stature is the only thing standing between me and losing all of this to that son of a *puta* and his bloody revolution."

"Yeah, things back home are deteriorating fast in terms of relations with Cuba," Hector said. "We may be headed for an embargo."

"That'd be seen as an act of war down here, if the sons of bitches could wage a war on anything other than one another." Hem sipped his own drink — a daiquiri — and said, "You married currently?"

"Nah, between wars," Hector said, smiling crookedly. "I may even be done on that front. Four's probably enough."

Hem waved a hand. "*No hay quinto malo.* No prospects?"

"I had a damned fine one," Hector said, thinking of the woman he had met two years before, a young unwed Mexican mother named Alicia. "But she was too fine for the likes of me."

Hem smiled. "Back in the day, I'd have made odds you would have ended up with that woman you were bedding during the hurricane. Or with her sister, the painter. A bloody fucking crime what happened with those two."

"Yeah — either one I could have gone for," Hector said. "Might even have lasted."

There was no percentage in telling Hem that neither Rachel nor Alva had died all those years before. It was enough for Hector to soldier on alone knowing he and Hem had killed an innocent man — a critic, but an innocent man — for Rachel's crimes.

And in Hem's present state, Hector feared that confiding to Ernest that they'd conspired to unjustly murder Quentin Windly might push Hem over some precipice.

"Those murders were maybe the oddest thing I was ever party to," Hem said.

"Me too," Hector said. "You know, I had some more brushes with all of that back in 1947. Out in Hollywood. A whole crew of killer surrealists. The parties that bunch threw would make Sodom and Gomorrah look like an Amish mixer."

"I hear they're all back in Europe, now," Hem said, sipping his drink. "Hell, ain't many of us from back then left around. Fucking Dos'll outlive us all, I'm convinced of that. But Max, and Scott…that old cunt Gertrude, all gone. And more passing on every week…people dying this year who've never died before."

"Tell me about Mary," Hector said.

"She's…fine. Hell, it's too late to find another. Not who'll take me on as I am now."

And…

But there was no more to come.

And then Mary was suddenly there, wearing a terrycloth robe.

"It's sweltering you two lugs," she said, beaming again, her tiny eyes hidden behind big round sunglasses. "How about a dip?"

"Didn't bring a suit," Hector said.

"We don't use 'em," she said, dropping her robe. She was small and busty…a drinker's gut of her own. She dove naked into the pool. Hector shifted in his chair, trying to focus on Ernest, who seemed unconcerned.

A small elderly Cuban woman sidled up to Hem and whispered something into this ear.

He looked up sharply. Hem said to her in Spanish, "Fetch me a gun."

Hector said, "Trouble? Castro's crew?"

"No, something else," Hem said, putting down his drink and struggling up. Hector put down his glass and followed him off a ways down a path toward the driveway.

Another of Hem's servants trotted up behind them and passed Hem a double-barreled shotgun. A few neighborhood children were standing at the wrought iron gate at the end of the Finca's driveway, standing in the dusty shade of the many mango trees that bounded the property on Hem's side of the wall.

As he had in Key West, Hem kept many cats on the property …more polydactyl pussies.

One of his mutant cats had been tied to the front gate. Its belly was slit open and its tiny lungs and innards had been thrown over its shoulders in the manner of some miniaturized Viking blood eagle.

A slip of bloodied paper was jammed into the cat's mouth.

Hem was visibly unhinged — spitting iron.

Hector reached out and took the slip of paper and unrolled it. Scrawled in Spanish on the note:

Ultimo

In a postscript it read:

P. S. So much for pussy's eight other lives, eh?

"'Último,'" Hem said, "the *last*...the final third of the bull-fight, when the bull is killed. And to fucking kill a man's cat this way..."

Hector almost said, "At least you've got four or five dozen more," but held his tongue. Hem so loved his fucking cats.

Hem borrowed a pocketknife from one of the Cuban kids and started to work cutting down the corpse of his murdered cat.

Hector watched him, then looked around — just kids...a few peasants...some burned hunchback with a badly broken nose in a worn guyabera shirt. A couple of old men with less than half-a-mouthful of teeth between them, loitering...watching.

Gawkers and beggars.

No pretty blonds; no striking brunettes.

Not a surrealist in sight.

"Art should give us back the world
that our living confiscates."

— JOHN WILSON

CHAPTER 43

POSTHUMA

HEM AND MARY had gone down into Havana to finalize some
details for their pending trip to Spain. Hem had left Hector alone
in the Finca's sitting room.

The sitting room had a high ceiling and tall, open doors on
one side. A couple of floral-print chairs faced a long, matching
sofa. There was a table placed between the two chairs with a serving tray on top. The tray was burdened with liquor bottles —
Hem didn't even have to stand up to mix himself any conceivable
drink...unless he wanted ice.

Low bookcases ran around the sides of the room and the walls
were covered with paintings and trophy heads from Hem's first
safari.

It was very much a "writer's house" and it was strikingly rem-
iniscent of the house that Pauline had maintained for Hem in
Key West.

Hector was sitting in Hem's own favorite chair, a TV tray set
before him. On the tray sat three stacks of typed manuscripts.
These included what had come to be known among the
Hemingway cognoscenti as "The Big Novel," Hem's novel of a

painter coping with the effects of World War II. The second was *The Garden of Eden*, a kind of *roman à clef* about a couple of young artistic men, each caught in the throes of a tawdry *ménage à trois*. The third was what Hem was calling the "Paris book." This last was essentially Papa's memoir of his apprenticeship in the City of Lights in the 1920s.

Hector had read deeply enough of all three manuscripts to settle on the memoir as his favorite.

Somewhere off in the Finca, Hector heard the phone ring, then a servant came in and turned down the stereo: Hem had stacked on several discs of Bach before leaving.

The servant said, "It is the phone for you *Señor* Lassiter." Then she led Hector to that phone.

It was odd to be receiving a phone call at Hem's.

The world knew of course, thanks to Leonard Lyons' column, just where to find Hector, but he didn't expect anyone to actually try to call him at the Finca.

Except maybe for Rachel.

Hector picked up the phone, half expecting a female voice on the other end.

It was a man speaking — guttural…a voice filled with hatred and violence.

"I'm going to kill you, *Lasso*. I'm going to fucking kill you, and I'm going to kill Hem, at last, now that you're both together. I'm going to do that soon. I just wanted you to know that, so you don't have any peace. You're both dead…and very soon."

The caller hung up.

Hector stared at the phone, trying to place the voice.

Hector, who hadn't yet told Hem about the phone call, thought they should perhaps hang around the Finca…at least be reasonably safe, or well-armed there — there in proximity to Hem's impressive arsenal of weapons.

But Hem was adamant they go to his favorite bar. "We can't drink 'em like the old days, maybe," Hem said, "But we can drink a few like the old days."

တ

The chauffeur let them out of the big red Chrysler and climbed back behind the wheel with a paperback novel…not one of Hem's, but some pulp Western from the looks of the thing.

Hem and Hector walked through dirty streets by a few ancient, crumbling facades, then Hem said, "My oasis."

It was one of Hector's axioms: *It's always a dangerous prospect to really know or to be known by a world-class bartender.*

Hem had barely parked his broadening ass on the stool when the first of several of Papa's peculiar and potent daiquiris were plunked down before him. It was made to Hem's own idiosyncratic, alcoholic tastes: no sugar and a double portion of rum.

Things were slow in the Floridita bar. An old man with a hunchback and ancient scars from some terrible burns was mopping the black and white tile floor. The man made funny noises as he walked — his right leg turned out at some crazy angle from some long-ago injury.

Hector looked up at the ceramic statue of a fighting cock set on the top shelf of the bar — the cock depicted in mid-crow. He said, "You get out on the *Pilar* much?"

"Not as much these days," Hem said. "Bad weather, all the time it seems. And the quality of the fishing in the Gulf has been tapering off for years. What are you drinking, Lasso?"

"Kind of enjoying mojitos now that I'm back where people know how to make them. I'll stay with those boys." Hector shook loose a cigarette and fished out his Zippo.

Hem grunted and took the lighter from Hector's hand. "You carried this all these years?"

"Sure."

"You're a sentimental sort, aren't you, Lasso?"

"You're not the first to say it," Hector said.

Hem handed the Zippo back to Hector. "Who knew? So, Lasso, no lies now, kind or otherwise. I can take an honest shot from my oldest friend. You read all three, or at least good bits of all of them, yes?"

The manuscripts. Hector took a deep sip of his first mojito. "Yes."

"What are your thoughts, Lasso? I want your honest thoughts. If you think they're shit, and you say it, I'm not going to lose my temper or get my fucking nose out of joint."

Hector didn't believe that. He sucked down smoke to buy himself a minute. He expelled that in a slow, thin stream, then sipped more of his rum. He was honest, but selective:

"They've all got stretches of absolute brilliance. Description that can stand up to the best stuff you've ever done," Hector said. "The memoir is the best, and it's brilliant and funny and mean. It's good a thing that so many in it are dead — and thanks, parenthetically, for giving me a pass."

Hem seemed very pleased but said, "No saying the manuscript is done, yet." He sipped his daiquiri. "And the novels? What about those?"

"*Islands in the Stream* has wonderful moments...but purely on a plot level, I think it has one major issue, and that's at the end. It's too close to *To Have and Have Not*. For me, Harry Morgan's and Thomas Hudson's ends are too close...the circumstances too similar. It doesn't play as an homage, or echo, or something inviting reinterpretation, or an attempt at recontextualization. It just seems the same."

Hem shook his head. "You're right. I knew it, but I didn't know it, until you just said it. You're right. I need to put a new ending on that bastard. Kill him differently."

Or maybe for once, Hector thought, *not kill "him" or "Hem" at all*. Hem had famously remarked that all stories followed far enough end in death, and since *A Farewell to Arms*, in every one of his novels, Hem had driven each book right to that end. Only poor, dickless "Jake Barnes" had ever gotten out of a Hemingway novel alive. Oh, and Santiago...the old man in *The Old Man and the Sea*. But Hector had heard Santiago had survived only at Mary's begging.

Hem said, "And *The Garden of Eden*?"

"Brave. Even fearless and naked in some ways. Self-aware, often. But to borrow Gertrude Stein's old word to you, for the moment, maybe even for many years to come, that novel is *inaccrochable*. Even as the work of Ernest Hemingway — as a work the world would pant for after *The Old Man and the Sea* and all the big awards, the Swedish thing and all that — even with your clout, Scribner's could never put that book out, not in our current climate."

"Exactly. I'm writing for the long game now," Hem said. "The legacy. I see all three of these as posthumous works. Maybe in the 1970s, or the 1980s, the world will be ready for *Garden* and *Islands*. And they'll ensure I'm still out there — still the champ. Like I told that bitch Gellhorn — they'll be reading me long after the worms have finished with her."

Brutal.

But Hector was no fan of Martha's, so he shrugged. He said, "Hem, you had a passage in *Islands*, about a murdered woman's body," Hector said. "It's based on a real killing, I hear."

Hem toyed with Hector's lighter left on the counter atop the crime writer's pack of Pall Mall cigarettes.

"Yeah, I finally told Mary it was some voodoo nonsense," Hem said. "She thinks I'm crazy, anyway. There's no denying I go through phases of Black Ass that defy description, Hector. Days without sleep that leave me buggy…wondering what I've actually done and what I've only dreamed. But I know some things — can still sense a real threat. I made the mistake of being too honest with Mary about that dead woman's body and what it might mean for me…and about J. Edgar's boys stalking me. Mary doesn't believe any of that, either. She says I'm paranoid. I may be, but that doesn't mean that sometimes I don't have reason to be."

"No. It surely doesn't." Hector ground out his cigarette's stub and lit another. "I believe you."

"You'd know, especially about the FBI maybe, I guess."

Hector let that one pass without remark. He said, "If not a cult, or not just some psycho boyfriend or husband, what about this murdered girl?"

"I'm getting letters, too," Hem said. "I haven't shown Mary the worst of those. They reference that murdered woman's torso. That murder, and a couple of other murders…killings of working girls from around here committed over the past few days. And now this cat of mine…gutted like that. The handwriting on the letter shoved in the cat's mouth looks like the handwriting in the death threats I've been getting. It's almost like living in one of your novels."

Hector said, "A call came for me at your house today, Hem. It was a male voice. I almost thought I knew the voice, but I couldn't quite place it. The caller threatened us both. Said he would kill us both, and soon."

Hem said, "So some cocksucker really does have a hard-on for me. For both of us, I guess." Hem frowned. "But how'd this son of a bitch know you are here?"

"I gave Leonard Lyons a heads-up," Hector said carefully. "I asked him to put a note in his column, advertising my visit to you.

I told you — in Los Angeles, in 1947, I crossed this thing again. Something tied back to Key West...to Spain and the murders there linked to surrealism."

"So you're trying to draw fire?" Hem accepted another daiquiri. "Don't tell Mary any of this about the Keys or Spain or L.A. or now, Lasso, or she'll think you're buggy like me."

"I heard about the murders here," Hector said. "And being here, seeing your cat, and taking that call and hearing about your other letters, well, there's no question in my mind anymore. Someone means us both dead. And that someone is tied to the murders we both saw in '35 and '37...to what I saw in 1947."

Hem pulled off his wire-rimmed glasses and squeezed the bridge of his nose. "Hell of it is that your coming here makes it easier for this killer, Lasso. Us together means an easier target for him."

"From a different perspective," Hector said smiling, all bluff, "now the son of a bitch has the pair of us to deal with. He's the one should be sweating just about now."

Hem thought about that, then said, "At least that makes the two of us sound like forces to maybe still be reckoned with. Still, I'd like to be home, where I have guns. We should drink up and go there, pronto. Hunker down for a fight."

"Agreed," Hector said. "But between here and there, I have your back, Hem." Hector pulled back his white sports coat to reveal the butt of his old Colt. "Smuggled it in past security," Hector said.

"How'd you do that?"

"Tricks of the trade."

Hem smiled and slapped Hector's arm. "That fucking bitch Martha. It's another thing to hate her for...making you and me piss away twenty-two years. Jesus, the good times we've missed together."

"Surrealism: An archaic term.

Formerly an art movement.

No longer distinguishable from everyday life."

— BRAD HOLLAND

CHAPTER 44

THE WIDOW-IN-WAITING

HECTOR HAD PROMISED himself one thing: there would be none of his own writing undertaken at the Hemingway house. The notion of two typewriters firing away down the morning-quiet halls of the ancient Finca struck Hector as a kind of risk in itself — it could descend into competition. It would be a one-way competition, but no less dangerous for that.

Hem would maybe want to start comparing daily page or word counts...wanting to remark on things in progress. Hector only shared full first drafts, and he wouldn't do that with Hem, not ever. And Hector knew too well Ernest's attitudes toward "genre" fiction.

So Hector sat out by the pool in the early morning cool with Mary, watching all the cats prowl.

The island's heat hadn't come on yet and he was wearing khaki slacks, decks shoes, a long-sleeved white shirt and a nylon wind-breaker — the last something that would allow him to hide his big Peacemaker.

It was just past eight and Hector was drinking orange juice. Mary was savoring a screwdriver. Hector figured the morning chill must be keeping Mary from thoughts of a swim since she was wearing clothes — a baggy sundress and sweater.

She said, "You've read his three books in progress. What did you really think, Hector?" Mary smiled and winked. "This is just between us — what did you really think?"

It sounded to Hector like his stated opinions to Hem had already been made known to Mary. So he reiterated, "The memoir is brilliant, if mean, and it will further restore his reputation…build on what *The Old Man and the Sea* has started."

She nodded eagerly. "And the other two, the novels?"

"Both show great promise. When Hem starts to pare back, to cut back toward the bone and bring them down to the length of his first two novels, they'll strengthen, maybe become brilliant. Hem always writes a good deal more than he uses. I read *The Sun* and *Farewell* in their original drafts. I know how he works."

Mary shook loose a cigarette and Hector leaned over with his Zippo to light it. She took his hand to hold the lighter where she wanted it. Puffing away, she said from the side of her mouth, "The memoir is drawing on notebooks from the old days that Hem found a short time back. Some are fragments cut from *The Sun* — evidently from some version you never saw. Because he won't show me the old notebooks, only Ernest knows how much of the Paris book is writing or rewriting. The new novels are a mess."

Hector said nothing.

"When the self-destructive son of a bitch finally takes himself down, it'll fall to me to whip those in shape," Mary said. "Probably the Paris book, too. Hem won't finish 'em, mark my words. He'll leave that for me. And the other books he's left? Well, it's a big job ahead of me."

Hector sensed he was frowning. He covered his mouth by hoisting his glass of orange juice. The notion of someone like Mary presuming to edit Hem horrified Hector. The expected thing when it came to editing a major author's posthuma was to entrust the task to the author's best scholar, or critic. The man for the job, in Hector's estimation, was Edmund Wilson. Edmund was Hem's best and most astute critic. And he was one of the few critics that Hem — the über hater of all critics — held in any regard.

Then a voice suddenly bellowed from inside the house, "You goddamn well did bump my head! I don't like my head touched! Fucking do it again and I'll blow your fucking head off. Now get your ass out of here and dust later. I'm fucking trying to write."

"That's what life with Papa has become," Mary said. "That's the Ernest most of us get now, dawn to dusk. Paranoid and mean. That poor little bitch Consuelo must have touched his hair…what's left of it. I should go talk to her. Calm her down." But Mary made no move to do that. Borrowing Hem's nickname for Hector, she said, "You know, Lasso—"

Mary stopped, staring at her suddenly broken juice glass, its jagged-edged bottom still tumbling to the ground. Orange juice and vodka was pouring out of the broken glass and onto her lap.

Hector was stung by something that just nicked his cheek. He saw splinters of wood falling from the wooden pillar about a foot from his face. He screamed, "Hem, we've got a shooter!"

He threw down his own drink and cigarette and grabbed Mary's rocking chair, pulling it over onto its side, rolling Mary to the ground and sprawling half atop her. The juice pitcher exploded on the table above them, peppering Hector's face and hair with glass and orange juice.

Brushing glass from her bleach blond hair, Mary said, "What fucking maniac…?!" Trying to stand up, she said, "Castro! I bet it's those chickenshit Castroties."

Hector had never heard the Cuban revolutionaries called that.

He said, "Stay the hell down, sweetheart." Then, his knees cracking, he struggled up onto his feet and said again, "Just stay down there, Mary." Hector pushed aside a big fern and vaulted off the patio and began running down the hill, thick with overgrowth, drawing his Colt, in the direction he guessed the shot must have been fired from.

Whoever the shooter was, Hector seemed to be gaining. Then he tripped, tumbling down the sudden-steepening hill, slamming into the wall that bounded Hem's property. From the other side of the wall, Hector heard a car door slam and an engine fire…tires squeal.

He heard someone else coming down the hill from which he had just fallen. Hem emerged through the shrubs and ferns, barechested and clutching a Mauser rifle. Hem said, "Did you see him? Did you see the car, Lasso?"

Hector struggled up and holstered his Colt. "No, dammit."

"So we've got nothing."

Hector was squinting at the ground, still wet from the overnight dew. There were footprints in the mud — heading up the hill toward the Hemingways' swimming pool.

Looking at the footprints, Hem, the hunter, said, "Still not much."

"Check out the right foot," Hector said. "Sucker is twisted out at nearly a right angle to the left foot. Not club-footed…worse than that. A badly set leg from a break, maybe."

Hem grunted. "Yeah. So he's a limber gimp. What's that get us?"

"An identification," Hector said. "This is all we need. I need to borrow your car."

"Where are *we* going, Lasso?"

"The Floridita, to ask about a custodian — a man I saw there and who I think I saw in the crowd that morning your cat was killed."

"Surrealism is merely the reflection of the death process.
It is one of the manifestations of a life becoming extinct,
a virus which quickens the inevitable end."

— HENRY MILLER

CHAPTER 45

"PURSUIT AS HAPPINESS"

"HE'S BEEN WITH US, oh, two weeks at most, Papa." The bartender handed Hem one of his *daiquiris à la Papa.*

Hector said, "This fella who cleans for you, what handle did he give you?"

The dapper Cuban blinked a few times, handing Hector an unasked for *daiquiri à la Papa.* He said, "*Handle?*"

"Name," Hector said. He warily sipped his drink. It was not to his taste at all. It struck Hector as a woman's drink — though the kind of woman's drink that might sneak up on you, particularly with that double dose of rum.

"He said his name was Ernesto," the bartender said. "The name he gave was Ernesto Lassiter."

Hem snorted. "Least our quarry has a sense of humor."

"Yeah, and he's laughing at us," Hector said. He said to the Cuban man, "He seems badly injured, this 'Ernesto.'"

"From the war," the bartender said. "From Hürtgenwald he said, where he was blown up and badly burned. His face and hands are very scarred. He's missing an ear that was burned off.

His hair grows in patches on one side, around the scar tissue. He's quite disfigured. Quite ugly."

Hem had been at Hürtgenwald. Hector said, "An address — how do you reach him?"

"He merely shows up."

"How's he know when to come?"

"He comes each morning. Late morning, perhaps after ten. He comes in again about seven in the evening."

Hector turned to Hem, "That cover your usual drinking hours here?"

Hem shifted uncomfortably. "Roughly."

"This 'Ernesto,' he show up for his shift this morning?"

"No, he did not," the bartender said. "The first morning he has missed since he started two weeks ago." Two weeks. That would have been shortly after Leonard Lyon's column appeared advertising Hector's trip to Cuba to visit Hem. "Perhaps tonight he will show up."

"We'll be around to see," Hem said. "Don't tell him we were asking after him. Don't tell anyone, okay, Norberto?"

"*Sí*, Papa."

Hector watched Hem as he drank his namesake daiquiri then eyed Hector's nearly untouched drink. "A shame to waste," Hem said.

"Kill it off, old pal," Hector said, pushing the glass toward Hem. He watched Ernest watching two men at the back of the bar. They were obviously American. One was about fifty. Hector guessed the other might be about twenty-eight. Probably father and son.

His eyes narrowing, Hem said loudly, "No, I'm driving — better call it quits."

Hector followed Hem out of the Floridita. Someone in an old Buick honked and yelled, "*Hola*, Papa!" Hem waved absently back at them. He said, "Did you see them there at the back of the Floridita, Hector?"

Hector reached for his pack of cigarettes. "The older guy and the younger one? Sure, Hem, tourists."

"Fucking FBI," Hem growled.

The hairs stood up on the back of Hector's neck. Hem's eyes were hard and crazed looking. It had come over him all at once.

"A father and son," Hector said. "That's all they were. At worst some chicken hawk and his 'boy.'"

"FBI," Hem insisted. "I can spot 'em every time. Trying to get me on taxes, or for Spain. For trying to get crazy old Ezra out of the bughouse, and the like. They'd love to catch me on a drunk driving charge — make me look like a rummy. Like a Faulkner."

"Tourists," Hector said, again, gently. "Some father who probably thought it would be a kick to bring his son down to sinful Cuba for a last blast. Probably hopped a dayboat from Miami or Key West and they came down here to old Havana hoping to see one of Castro's guerillas. Maybe share some cute little Cuban whore…find themselves some *gachis*."

"FBI."

Hector didn't want to waste breath or risk a fight. He said, unconvinced, "Maybe. Guess old J. Edgar might be wising up to the fact he shouldn't dress his minions in matching blue suits and give them all the same haircut."

"FBI," Hem said again. He suddenly smiled and then slapped Hector's back. "So what's the plan, MacDuff? We sit out here tonight and wait out this boy?"

"Not in your pretty red Chrysler, no, Hem. And I don't discount he's watching us, maybe right now."

"'He'? You think he's operating alone?"

"Could be a 'she' in the mix," Hector said. "Could be more than one. But as ugly as this bastard sounds, I'd doubt it — doubt there's a woman at work, too."

"I think I know who this bastard is."

"I have a thought on that, too, Hem."

"Want to elaborate, Lasso, or do I have to drag it out of you?"

"I ain't sharin' yet. Don't want to look like an idiot if I'm wrong."

Hem shook his head. "We both know who it is — it's fucking Windly. We should have checked the body that night in Madrid…should have shoved the last grenade up his ass."

5

Hem called back to the Finca to make sure that Mary was okay. A couple of Hem's stooges were standing sentry. Hector could hear Mary's end of the exchange as Hem held the phone away from his ear, screaming into it…like he thought he had to push his voice across the distance.

Mary said, "What is this nonsense, Ernest! This old friend of yours, this Lassiter, he seems crazy as you…seeing enemies everywhere. It was probably just some kid screwing around — some wingshooter who got reckless, Papa."

Hector frowned and Hem made a face and said, "Hey Pickle, fuck you and your slut Gellhorn mouth!" He slammed down the phone. Hem said to Hector, "About now, I'm thinking you're thinking twice about having pushed Mary to the ground after that first shot. Now she thinks we're both *decompuesto*."

"We'll explain it to her later. I'll make her see how it was," Hector said.

"She thinks I'm buggy, like Ezra," Ernest said. "She's trying to railroad me into the crazy house. Keeps pushing at me to go to the Menninger Clinic. She blames all my concussions. Says I can't distinguish between reality and fantasy. She says I can't write anymore."

Hector said, "She says that?" Hector figured Mary for a destructive, hardhearted bitch, but that last was beyond the pale. He said again, "Mary says that to you?"

"Sure," Hem said. "She says I only write myself now. And she's always quoting Edmund Wilson back to me — about how I'm my own worst character."

Hector said, "Man once said, 'Be careful what you dream: soon your dreams will be dreaming you.'"

"You agree with Mary?" A real edge there in Hem's voice.

"No," Hector said firmly. "I don't. I've read your Paris sketches. And I read *Across the River and into The Trees*. When I read that one, I read the novel you wrote, not the novel the critics tried to make it. I saw what you did with Cantwell…your portrait in self-contempt. I admire what you did."

"I hear stories about you, Lasso. Even during the 1940s, I heard 'em…and about your wife and little girl a few years back. I've heard dark things. The distance between you and your own books ain't all that great either, and never has been, but in the past three or four years, particularly, I hear that there's no distance at all. Sounds to me like your dreams are dreaming you."

"Maybe."

"Very surreal," Hem said.

Hector said, "You were around in the '30s. You saw what happened in Key West and in Spain. Like that hurricane in '35, and Rachel Harper and those murders. Trouble finds me."

"Chicken and egg stuff," Hem said. "Your dreams are dreaming you. Or both of us, now. Either way, guess we're just fucked. Like Yeats said, we're old men now, 'fastened to a dying animal.'"

"Maybe," Hector said. "But I'm not prepared to check-out just yet. At least not until we put this murderous bastard down first."

"You think it's Windly, too?"

"Sure," Hector said.

"Well, one thing's sure," Hem said. "This cloak and dagger stuff that 'finds' you sure beats all hell out of writing."

*"Surrealism in painting amounted to little more than
the contents of a meagerly stocked dream world:
a few witty fantasies, mostly wet dreams
and agoraphobic nightmares."*

— SUSAN SONTAG

CHAPTER 46

THE HUNTERS

THEY PASSED the day into evening roaming Havana, visiting old
haunts and taking drinks in bars they had shut down as young
hell-raisers. As they moved from one watering hole to the next,
Hector began to rue the fact that so many bars insisted upon hanging mirrors. He liked to think of himself as he saw himself in his
own dreams — as a perpetual thirty-five. The man in the mirrors
of the bars of old Havana had brindle hair and deep lines around
his eyes and mouth. Not a welcoming sight. And Hem — Hector
never once saw Hem look in a mirror. Hem tended to stare into
his cups.

Now they were sitting in a café across from the Floridita,
drinking strong Cuban coffee and watching the bar.

A black and white, 1959 Chevrolet convertible rolled to a stop
a block from the Floridita, across the street from where Hector and
Hem watched from the café.

A man struggled out of the new-model Chevy. The man had a
humped back and his right leg was twisted out at a severe angle. He
didn't use a cane and he actually seemed to move with some speed
once he was out of the car. Hector guessed that shouldn't surprise

him too much: the shooter had escaped Hector down that steep hill at the Finca, after all. The shooter had clambered over the wall bounding Hem's property. The man had graying-blond hair and would probably have been tall if his backbone wasn't so twisted.

"We get him now," Hem said, "right?"

"Not yet. We settle up, get your car and move it around where we can see his car…follow him after he's done mopping up and probably asking Norberto about you."

ဟ

An hour later, they were sitting outside an apartment building in northern Havana.

"Upscale," Hem said. "Wind could afford it."

"Hi-tone," Hector agreed.

"We confront him inside?"

Hector shook his head. "No, I'd like to get a look at his digs, first. There's a bar right there. You should go in and phone the Floridita, Hem. If you can trust your friend the bartender, Norberto, you should see if this character made inquiries after you, or after us."

While he waited, Hector smoked two Pall Malls, tapping the ashes out the open window into the street. A couple of Cuban kids begged him for money — for American coins. Hector paid them to move them along.

Hem leaned in through the open passenger's side window. "Norberto said our friend left a phone number where he can be reached. He asked he be called next time I show up at the Floridita. Something about getting a copy of *The Old Man* signed for a sick nephew."

"Touching," Hector said. "Have Norberto make that call," Hector said. "Won't give us much time, but it'll have to do. When our boy gets to the Floridita, Norberto should shrug and say we pushed on. You give Norberto the name of some specific other bar, at some distance from the Floridita and here, ideally. Buy us some more time. While you do that, I'm going to move your Chevy out of sight. I'll meet you in the bar. Don't leave there until I come for you, Hem."

∽

Hector and Hem crossed the street to their stalker's apartment building. Hector was struck again by how much smaller Hem seemed now. Hem said, "How do we know which apartment to search?"

Hector winked. "While you made your phone calls, I watched lights go on and off inside this flophouse. I'm banking on the third floor, southwestern corner. Lights came on in that pad shortly after our buddy entered the building, and went off shortly before he left."

"How do we get into that apartment, Lasso?"

Hector smiled and held up the thin leather case with lock-picks. "Always be prepared," he said. "You know, like a good Boy Scout."

"I never got past Weblo level," Hem said.

"Hell," said Hector, "I didn't even get that far."

"Surrealism can only deliver a reactionary judgment;

can make out of history only an accumulation of oddities,

a joke, a death trip."

— SUSAN SONTAG

CHAPTER 47

ÚLTIMO

HECTOR STOPPED fiddling with the lock long enough to pull on his glasses. He shrugged and said, "I told you, Hem, it's come to this…blind as a bat without 'em." He began juggling the pick again and the lock finally popped.

"Just like your books," Hem said. Hector wished Ernest would give that one a rest.

The apartment was neutral; anonymous. There was an old sofa and a couple of matching chairs. A tube-radio the size of a small icebox. Stuff that probably came with the place.

Hector checked the bathroom. He found no pill bottles with useful names on the prescription labels. A couple of tortoise-shell brushes lay on the sink. They were monogrammed: *QW*. Their theory was holding, but it didn't make it any less disquieting for Hector.

Hem had drifted into the bedroom. It had been quiet for a while. He called out suddenly, "Jesus Christ! Goddamit, I knew I should have shot the cocksucker back in Spain."

Hector followed Hem's rants to the bedroom. It was another anonymous room: a bureau, a couple of sidetables on either side of a Marlowe bed with a chenille coverlet. An undistinguished painting of Havana's skyline hung above the bed.

Hem was sorting books: some bullfighting manuals, a copy of *The Old Man and the Sea* and a Badekers of Cuba. He handed those volumes to Hector. Hem held up a leatherbound journal, again bearing the initials *QW.*

Hector said, "So it is Quentin Windly."

Hector tossed the other books on the bed.

"So we wait for him, is that it, Lasso?"

"Huh-uh. Get on that phone there by the bed, Hem. There should still be time to call that bar we sent him to from the Floridita. Doubt Windly's reached it yet. Have the bartender at that second bar tell Windly we left there, as well. Have him say that we were drunk as hell and talking of going back to the Finca for a swim to sober up."

"Make us sound like sitting ducks, eh?" Hem smiled. "This time we shoot that cocksucker. We see the body. I shoot that son of a bitch."

Hector wasn't about to let that happen. But he said, "Hurry: you make that call. And toss me that journal."

"We're taking it?"

"We are. I think we are decided on what happens next. If all goes according to plan, Quentin won't be coming back here, ever. He won't be needing this." Hector held up the journal.

"Oh, we're agreed," Hem said.

"Then make that phone call."

‿

Hector drove fast back to the Finca, following Hem's directions. Hector took it as another ominous sign of Hem's deterioration that he'd been permitted to drive. Hem's night vision had evidently declined to the point that Ernest couldn't bluster through it...Hem seemingly feared his own weakness behind the wheel.

As they approached the Finca, Hector saw Quentin's Chevy sitting across the street from Hem's front gate.

"Pretty brazen of him...pretty reckless," Hem said.

"Quentin doesn't know we know who he is, or what he drives," Hector reminded him. "I just can't believe he got here first."

"I know," Hem said, voice thin. "God, poor Mary. I may have gotten her killed doing this."

Hector didn't tell Hem that he had seen the driver of the Chevy duck down as they approached. *Let Hem be afraid and protective of Mary*, Hector thought. It would keep him out of the way and safely from the mouth of Windly...give Hector time to put him down first.

Shifting into park, Hector said, "I'll get out and open the gate. You take the wheel and drive through. I'll close the gate behind you, then I'll open and close the passenger door again — make him think I got back into the car. Then you drive on up to the house and I'll make my way up the hill on foot."

Hem licked his lips, nodding. "Squeeze him, you mean?"

"That's the plan I have."

Hem smiled. "Good. I'd feel better having a gun when I get up there, though. What about you, Lasso, you carrying your Colt?"

Hector smiled and said, "Yeah. And I put a back-up under your seat. Military issue .45 with extra clips."

Hem beamed.

Hector opened the gate and Hem drove through. Hector locked the gate and trotted around the front of the red Chrysler. He opened the passenger side door then slammed it loudly. "See you up top," he said softly through the opened window, then slid off into the overgrown brush.

As Hem drove up to the Finca, Hector watched Windly's black and white Chevy through the bars of the gate.

Quentin struggled out of the car, bent over…running like some wounded crab over to the wall. Hector crept along the interior side of the wall, crouched down and gun out, waiting for Quentin to drop over the wall.

Hector was determined to keep it short — no chitchat…no chance for Quentin to tip Hem to any of the facts surrounding those old murders and Rachel/Alva.

Two feet, one of them twisted out at an angle, were dangling over the wall — Quentin was sitting on the wall, preparing to drop down.

The crime writer shoved his Peacemaker into the waistband of his pants and grabbed both of the critic's legs, just above the ankles. He jerked hard, then stepped out of the way, again.

Quentin landed on his face. Hector pulled the critic's coat down over his hump and around his arms, constricting his movement, then picked up the rifle the critic had been carrying — a Heckler & Koch with a now-damaged scope. Hector slammed the butt of the H&K against the wall, breaking its stock, then tossed the ruined rifle off into the undergrowth. He drew his own Colt.

Hector stomped hard on Quentin's right kidney, and said, "That's for denouncing me in Spain for a murderer, you son of a bitch. You nearly got me killed before I tried to kill you." Hector got down and pressed one knee to the small of Quentin's back. He pressed his Colt's barrel to the back of Quentin's head.

"Just do it, Lassiter," Quentin snarled.

"Sure. We have nothing left to say to one another."

"No," Quentin said. "You and Hem picked the wrong killer, that's all. You missed the fact that Rachel, then 'Alva,' was the real killer. That crazy, bloodthirsty bitch. Or she was."

Hector got in close. "Why the past tense?"

"I got to know those people over the past few years," Quentin said. "Those surrealists — I got inside their circle in Europe after the war…after they all left the States to duck the HUAC subpoenas and warrants you helped bring against them."

"Birds of a feather…" Hector said.

"I pierced the inner circle. There are two women it all revolves around, now. Name of Marshall. They're coming for you, too. Some others. They have long memories, Lassiter. I tipped them to Rachel…let them know that she was really this 'Alva' whose paintings they all covet. I figured all that out back in Spain, while you two had me down there on my back, getting ready to blow me up. To do this to me." Hector guessed he meant his injuries…his burns. Hector could really only see the left side of Quentin's face, and he'd be hard-pressed to recognize anything of Quentin other than his eyes. "You ever feel bad about that, even for a moment, *Lasso*? Blowing up an innocent man?"

"I've learned to cope," Hector said.

"Stop talking like one of your goddamn hard-case heroes," Quentin said. "Jesus, look at it like a normal human being just once. You two dragged me out for something I didn't do, and you tried to murder me. Jesus."

"You denounced me as a murderer to the Spanish secret police," Hector said. "Given the possible consequences to me, that alone justified killing you."

"Well, I'm taking some back," Quentin said. "They're all hunting this Rachel, or Alva, or Rhonda or whatever she calls herself, now. They'll find her. Probably already have. And they're going to kill you, too. They're patient, and committed."

"Me too," Hector said. "You're the one who killed these three women in Cuba — made it look like those other killings back in the Keys and Spain?"

"I had to get your attention, make you think Rachel was back at work. Did it as a lure, because I wanted you to die with Ernest — wanted you two to die together, like you tried to kill me together."

"You enjoy it? Killing those women…cutting them up. Was it a sexy kick?"

"It was terrible."

"But you did it anyway, 'innocent man.' You became what

Hem and me thought we beheld in you in '35 and '37. It's a terrible thing, to be tangled up in the creativity of another, isn't it?"

Hector heard rustling behind them. It was Hem, making his way down the hill. Hector couldn't risk Quentin calling out, so he kicked Windly again, hard and in both kidneys. He kicked him in the stomach. The critic curled up in a ball. Hector kicked him once more in the crotch, robbing Quentin of all wind. "That's for killing those women," Hector said, loudly, so Hem could hear, "and for killing Hem's cat!"

Hem finally reached them.

Hector almost shot Windly then — before the critic could maybe say something...something about Rachel or Alva that would tip Hem to the mistake that he and Hector had made so many years ago when they had wrongly judged and tried to execute Quentin the first time.

"Fucking Windly," Hem said, panting. "Fucking lousy kraut grenades. I knew I should have shot this son of a bitch all those years ago in Spain. Should have shot him when I had the chance." Hem was holding his arm, massaging his forearm. "Tripped and lost my goddamn gun," he said. Hector winced: back in the day, Hem would never have fallen, and even if he had, he would never have lost his gun.

Quentin was up on his knees, still panting and clutching his stomach and between his legs. Hector was standing behind him, his antique Colt pointed at the back of the disfigured critic's head, just below his mutilated ear.

Hem said suddenly, "Pass me that goddamned gun of yours, Hector."

"No way," Hector said. "I'll do this. His finger twitched at the trigger of the old Peacemaker.

"Give me the damn Colt," Hem said. "*Dame aca, con que a los mios los mato yo.*"

As Hector started to say, "What was that?" Hem suddenly tried to twist the old Colt from Hector's hand. "I said give it to me, damn it, I kill my own," Hem said. Hector was almost depressed at how easily he staved off Hem's attempt to take the gun. He shifted the Colt to his left hand and fired twice.

The critic tumbled to the ground.

Hem crossed himself and gestured at the old Colt.

Hem said, "Blessed are the Peacemakers."

"I believe in the future resolution of...

dream and reality, which are seemingly so contradictory,

into a kind of absolute reality, a surreality."

— ANDRÉ BRETON

CHAPTER 48

RECESSIONAL

"YOU SHOULD come to Spain with us," Hem said, "or meet us there along the way. It'll be just like old days, Lasso."

Hector smiled and shook his head.

It might be a lot of things, but it would never be like old days.

It was obvious to Hector that Hem was dedicated to chasing memories straight into his unquiet grave. Hem had done it with Italy in the run up to the writing and aftermath of *Across the River and into the Trees*. Hem was doing it presently with his Paris memoir.

And Spain? Hem was chasing the ghosts of the time of *The Sun Also Rises* and *Death in the Afternoon*.

And Hector and Hem couldn't maintain the pace of their twenty-six-year-old selves, though it was clear to Hector that Hem aimed to try to do just that.

"Too much to do," Hector said, trying hard to sound regretful. "There's the other thing, too: Franco is still north of the dirt. He might decide to exercise that still-standing death warrant against me. Maybe I'll catch up with you in Idaho. Always liked that part of the country. We'll murder some bottles of Rioja Alta in the Ram."

They hugged and Hem said, "It was good we did this. Good that we leave it like this."

"Yeah." Hector started up the gangplank, then he turned and yelled back, "Hemingstein! One true sentence: 'A best friend—'"

Hem chewed his lip and said, "'—one day stands alone.'"

Hector boarded the plane, found his seat, then stared out at the old, white-haired man with the big beard waving at him. It would be the last time he saw Ernest.

ഗ

Hector was sitting in the lounge of the Miami airport. Someone slapped him on the back. Agent Edmond Tilly took up a chair across from him. The crime writer smiled and said, "Jesus, when did you get to be so old, G-Man?"

"Going to retire at the end of this year," Tilly said. "How about you, Hector?"

"Writers never retire."

"You don't have much time, so let's get down to cases." Tilly plunked a wire recorder down on the table between them. "What are your thoughts on Cuba and the state of things down there? And please, keep it clean — this tape goes straight to the director and to Ike."

Hector shook his head. "In that order?"

ഗ

The wire recorder had been turned off. Agent Tilly drained his drink and Hector said, "Your boys still watching Hemingway?"

"Sure," Tilly said. "He's one of the director's obsessions. Hemingway's made a lot of cracks about the agency over the years, and about her agents. Papa seems to delight in tweaking Mr. Hoover."

"People around him increasingly think Hem's crazy because he says your folks are watching him all the time. Can't you do something to pull them off him? He's harmless. Hem's in steep decline. He should be given quarter."

"Mr. Hoover will never let it go," Tilly said. Hector rose with the agent and they began walking back through the terminal.

Hector said, "How's Agent Kenneth Brown doing, by the way? He recover from his injuries in '57?"

"He's doing pretty well," Tilly said. "And he strongly warned me away from any field action with you." Tilly paused as they reached the restrooms. "Gotta hit the head first. Damned enlarged prostate. Wait for me, yeah? I'll walk you to your plane."

Hector found a pay phone and called his answering service while he waited for Agent Tilly. He had a few messages from various directors offering screenwriting opportunities...Sam Ford...Hitchcock again. Hitch had some project in mind about a noted crime writer suspected of killing his own wife. *Fuck that.*

There was an urgent call from his Key West property manager. Hector scribbled down the number and called. Probably the old house had finally gotten termites...maybe burned down.

"So sorry, Mr. Lassiter," the property manager said, "but the party currently leasing your Key West home was adamant that you'd be furious if I didn't get word to you about her being there.'"

"A woman? What's her name?" Hector's stomach felt sour...he was swarmed by visions of paternity suits or the like.

"Harper," the man said. "She said her name is Rachel Harper."

Shaken, Hector hung up the phone.

"The imagination is perhaps

on the point of reasserting itself,

of reclaiming its rights."

— ANDRÉ BRETON

CHAPTER 49

RACHEL

SHE WAS STANDING on the front porch of his old Key West house. She was wearing a white dress...the blast furnace wind fingering its hem and her long blond hair.

Hector guessed she was in her mid- to late-forties. Still beautiful, if a bit pale looking...a little tired looking, too. He figured that was probably from the running and the hiding from the other surrealists.

Rachel smiled. "God, it's so good to see you, Hec." She spread her arms. Hector dropped his bags on the porch and hugged her back.

"Let's go inside."

"This place is still my favorite place," Rachel said. "My *querencia*, like you said."

"Or maybe just your safe harbor," Hector said.

The house was cool inside. He'd sprung for window air conditioners a couple of years before — trying to goose sagging rental traffic.

"You look wonderful," he said.

"Yeah...?" She said, "I was poking around in here...trying to see if I might find something of yours still here. I found a little storage closet and those blank canvasses you bought me so many years ago. I bought some fresh paints to go with them. You said I owed you some paintings. I'm working on them. And I want to paint one of you. Maybe you can put it on a book jacket."

"So you do still paint?"

"Sure. It's all I do. Even a few more posthumous 'Alvas' now and again. Just to make the crust. Not everyone knows the story about Rachel and Alva — Quentin Windly's reach didn't extend that far beyond the Marshalls."

"On that note, have there been many close calls, Rachel?" Then Hector frowned. "What am I calling you, by the way? Rachel, or...?"

"Rachel is what you call me," she said.

Hector shook loose a cigarette and offered one to Rachel. She shook her head. "No, thanks." She took the lighter and his unlit cigarette from his hands. She hugged him close again, her mouth finding his.

ꙅ

They had been lolling in bed together for a couple of hours. "The ones who don't create," she said, "what sustains them?"

"Maybe the simple fact they're spared the compulsion," he said.

"That's a terrible thought." Rachel got up to go to the bathroom: a long back with the sheet slipping free. He watched her naked body...still fit...still voluptuous...though thinner than she had been in Key West. Now she looked more like her undernourished self in Spain.

Hector tried to get a cigarette going, but his Zippo's flint seemed to have died. He reached across to the nightstand on Rachel's side of the bed; opened the drawer looking for matches.

Inside the drawer was hidden a long knife...honed to razor sharpness.

Going cold inside, Hector picked up the knife. He slid the blade under the sheets on his side of the bed.

ら

They were still in bed together, well into a second bottle of wine. Billie Holiday on the phonograph: "That Old Devil Called Love."

· Rachel said, "We're really something aren't we — the three of us?" They had been talking about Hem. Talking about how Hector had found Ernest in Cuba and his resulting pessimistic thoughts for Hem's future.

"I was insane, so badly damaged, doing what I did to find a path to my own art...my own artistic voice," Rachel said. "As I became a painter, I healed...put the past — the need to destroy in order to create — behind me. Now I've evolved further — no longer even paint anything I can describe as surrealist. I mean other than the increasingly rare, tossed-off 'Alva' to pay the bills."

"I want to see that art," Hector said. "I want to see your new stuff."

"You will, when I finish my new paintings for you, and no peeking," Rachel said, smiling. She said, "And then there's Hem. I always figured Hem could only write what he figured he could live. Now the distance between himself and his macho subject matter is tearing him to pieces — he's incapable of maturing as an artist. He rode his style into the ground. I still hate Hem, still feel a need to punish him for keeping us apart. But I wouldn't wish his present life on him. How terrible it must be for him."

"And me?" Hector wasn't certain he really wanted Rachel's assessment.

"I think your books have gotten richer as you've gotten older and as you've used more and more of yourself," she said. "Maybe that's because unlike Hem, you're not your own number one fan. I read a piece someone wrote about crime writers. They said Chandler wrote the man he wanted to be. I guess that's why I can't read Chandler — too sentimental. This writer — this critic — said Hammett wrote the man he feared he was. And you, Hector, you increasingly write about the man you don't want to be anymore. I've heard the stories like I guess everyone has. About your last wife, Maria, about your little girl and why you maybe did that to your wife."

Now Hector felt very cold inside. The topic of his daughter's death, a death precipitated by her mother's hidden drug addiction — and what Hector had done to Maria when he'd learned the true cause of their daughter's death — was one of Hector's only *no-go* areas.

Rachel said, "When I heard the rumors about your wife's death, and thought about the blurring of the lines between yourself and your characters, and about my own path to becoming a painter, I felt a strange kinship with you. You — always writing with regret about the man you've made yourself become. The thought that you might have killed your wife — for 'revenge,' of course — but the thought of you committing crimes like that and then writing about them…confessing in print and being rewarded for it… I thought that maybe meant we're the same. We both destroy to create. Or I used to. And I thought that now, with all of that bloody business behind both of us, that we could really be together. That we could trust one another."

Hector bit his lip. "Funny you should say that." He pulled the knife from under the bedsheets and then moved it quickly between Rachel's bare breasts, the knife's tip pressed there, just breaking the skin.

Rachel searched his eyes, scared-looking, frowning deeply.

Her arms were stretched above her head, poised in the position of Man Ray's "Minotaure." It was all too perfect.

All he had to do was press down. Hector dipped his head so he didn't have to look at her face, or even to see Rachel's head. He narrowed his eyes until she was just the Minotaur — her arms its horns, her breasts its eyes...the hollow of her flat belly the bull's maw.

The knife there between the "eyes" was like the matador's *estoque.* The sword was poised high up on the bull, for the *estocada* — the killing thrust.

Billie was crooning "You Better Go Now."

He sensed Rachel's hand drifting. It happened fast. She pulled his Colt from under his pillow and pushed it to his throat. "I remembered," she said. "Remembered where you keep your gun from the old days. Take the knife away, please."

Sick inside, Hector said, "I remembered you might remember. The bullets are under your pillow."

Rachel looked like she'd just failed some test. She dropped the Peacemaker atop his pillow and said, "I don't know that I deserve to live after all I've done, Hector. I probably don't. But I am better, and I have been for a long time. Like that painting of mine you bought all those years ago in Paris, I've made my choice, Hector. I made it years ago, my love. I've been in this house for two days. I put the knife in the drawer that first night for self-defense — in case the others found me before you did. I'd forgotten it was there. I could never hurt you...not more than I already have over the years, by running from you and making you think I was twice dead. I just wanted to have a few last weeks with you, Hector. Try to have a last good time together. So it's your turn to decide." She looked down at the knife between her breasts. "You told me long ago that your father said you have to 'find what you love and let it kill you.' Guess maybe I've done that."

Hector thought about that. He raised the knife and said, "Me too...and I've made my choice as well."

He put his weight behind the thrust.

They both watched the knife's blade quiver after it sank into the wall above the bed.

Rachel wrapped a leg around his. She said, "I'm very sick, Hector. All the cigarettes… The doctors say I can't be fixed. They say for six or seven weeks, maybe nine at most, I'll have what they describe as 'a quality of life.' After that, it will go very quickly, they say. So I've rented this place of yours for the next two months. But I won't have you see me sick, Hector. I'll never have you watch me waste away and die. As soon as I know the end is beginning…"

There were tears in her eyes. Hector wiped them away with his thumbs. Rachel said, "So you see, in some ways, it would have been better for me to let you use that knife. But you've suffered enough for me…and because of me. So you have another choice to make, Hector: eight weeks, or should I leave now?"

He'd never consent to her going off there at the end, never consent to Rachel crawling off to die alone. Though it nearly killed him, Hector had stood vigil over his dying daughter. He'd do it again for Rachel.

Rachel lay there with her arms over her head, searching his blue eyes. "What are you thinking?"

Hector stroked Rachel's torso, wiping away the droplets of blood from the small pinpoint wound between her breasts, his hand moving further down her belly.

He said, "I'm thinking of all we've been to one another. Thinking of the things we've shared and done to one another in the last twenty-four years. And yet, in all that time, we were really lovers for maybe less than a week, total."

Rachel nodded. "*And…*"

Hector was bending his head toward hers for a kiss. He said, "And so, for the likes of us, eight weeks could maybe feel like forever."

EPILOGUE
(July 2, 1961)

"The artist is his own most severe judge."

— MAN RAY

CHAPTER 50

REMATAR

AT FIRST Hector wasn't sure to whom he was talking.

The newly minted widow started simply: "Well, Lasso, Papa finally got the job done."

It dawned on him slowly who was calling and Hector, living one time zone behind Idaho, said, "Mary?"

"He shot himself this morning," Mary Hemingway said. "Papa got up early, found the key to the place where the guns were locked away, and he killed himself. As you're his oldest remaining friend, I wanted to call personally. Wanted you to hear it from me...the world will be told it was a gun accident. You are hearing it first from me, aren't you, Hector?"

"...Yes."

Hector realized he was sitting down. He'd been standing when he picked up the phone.

It felt like the world had suddenly tipped on its side.

Hector said thickly, "I knew Hem had been sick. Dos had somehow gotten word, and then got word back to me. I know about..." Hector hesitated, then said, "I know about the Mayo Clinic, and the electroshock therapy."

"That damned chickenshit voodoo," Mary said. "That killed him. That put Papa under."

"Did he leave a note?"

"No," Mary said quickly. "No, he didn't. That was the real problem, don't you see? He couldn't write anymore. After the shock treatments, Papa's long-term memory was scrambled. And he couldn't put words together on the page. They said it would come back, but Papa didn't believe the doctors...or he didn't have the patience."

"I'll see if I can catch a plane," Hector said.

"No, it's all fine so far as that goes," Mary said firmly. "Family is coming. It'll be a family-only affair."

"How are you then, Mary?"

"I'm not sure yet. Numb."

"If there's anything..."

"Maybe one thing," she said. "It's strange. I didn't find a note with the envelope, so I assume Ernest must have torn it up or burned it. But Papa's memory was scrambled, like I said. He forgot to get rid of the envelope. I found the envelope in the pocket of his robe...the robe he was wearing this morning when he..."

"What envelope? Who was it from?"

"That's the thing, I don't recognize the name," Mary said. "It's funny. There was a lot of mail delivered to the Finca just after we left Cuba that last time, and left so quickly. We'd finally just had a bundle catch up to us here in Ketchum a couple of days ago. A big bundle — some of the mail in it many many months or even years old. This letter must have been among that batch, I guess. Looking at the date of the postmark on the envelope I have to guess that. It was mailed from Key West in 1959."

Hector said softly, "Who was the sender?"

"That's just it. Do you know, or did you know, a woman named Rachel Harper?"

Hector was tingling. He said simply, "She was someone I knew quite well, in Key West in the old days. A woman I loved. Hem met her once or twice. But that's all so far as those two go. She died the year that letter was sent."

"How strange for her to write Papa after so many years," Mary said. "I wonder what was in this Rachel's letter?"

Hector said, "Me too." He had, he supposed, badly underestimated her grudge against Hem.

"Maybe this Rachel was trying to reach you through Papa."

"That's probably it," he lied.

"Sure," Mary said. "It must be. That must be how it was."

Mary and Hector talked for a few more minutes and he wished her well again and promised to check back with the Widow Hemingway in a few days to see how she was faring.

Shaken, Hector walked to the bar in his library-office and poured a glass of Rioja Alta. Then, smiling, he poured a second glass and set it out for Hem's maybe thirsty spirit.

Sipping his wine, Hector wondered what Rachel had written in her letter to Hem.

Had she told Hem the truth about what she had been…about what she had done?

Had she sneered at Hem and taunted him with the knowledge that he'd been complicit in the murder of an innocent man in the person of Quentin Windly?

Had she twisted the knife and mocked half-crazed Hem for being manipulated into helping to commit an unnecessary murder?

Scrambled as his memory was, would Hem have even remembered Rachel, or Alva? Would he have remembered what had happened in Spain with the critic, or later, in Cuba? Hector didn't think so. Hector didn't think Hem could have brought any useful context to anything that Rachel might have written.

And, more importantly to Hector in some ways, he wondered if Rachel had written and mailed the letter to Hem before or after she had confronted Hector in his own Key West house that last time when he returned from Cuba.

The crime author sipped his red wine and shrugged.

What had Rachel written to Hem?

Hell. It didn't matter now, Hector tried to convince himself.

Either way, with or without Rachel's possible push, Hem had judged himself.

"Papa" just didn't measure up to his own standard for a man, Hector figured.

Writers don't retire and Papa couldn't write anymore.

And knowingly, or unknowingly, deliberately or accidentally, in her long, crazed bloody game of 'last tag' with Hector, Rachel might just have scored the last and most devastating touch.

But in a way, given Papa's state, maybe Rachel had done Hem a favor if she had in some way firmed his resolve for the last of it.

Viewed in that light, it might almost be regarded as a gift.

Hector raised his glass to one of Alva's, or rather Rachel's self-portraits, hanging there on the wall above his fireplace mantle.

Toasting and winking at the painting, Hector said, "*Olé.*"

ACKNOWLEDGMENTS

Thanks again to Svetlana Pironko, Michael O'Brien and Bleak House publisher Ben LeRoy. A very special note of gratitude to my editor, Alison Janssen: every author should be so fortunate to have such a remarkable and gifted editor.

I also thank my parents, Betty and James McDonald, my wife, Debbie, and our daughters Madeleine and Yeats, for making room for the writing.

For special help with obtaining permissions for the Diego Rivera painting that graces the cover, grateful thanks to Alexandre Civico and Metze Mur Effing, Rubén Marshall and Erika Hernandez-Sanchez. Also, special thanks to Amy Lyle and Erin Holl.

Toros & Torsos is a work of fiction but it rests on a foundation of unsettling historical fact and informed supposition and scholarship, nearly all of which is based on official documents and public records.

Many nonfiction books were consulted during the writing of this novel. Among the most useful were *Exquisite Corpse: Surrealism and the Black Dahlia Murder* by Mark Nelson and Sarah Hudson Bayliss; *Orson Welles, Volume 2: Hello Americans* by Simon Callow; *The Breaking Point: Hemingway, Dos Passos and the Murder of José Robles* by Stephen Koch; *Black Dahlia Avenger* by Steve Hodel, *The Lives of Lee Miller* by Anthony Penrose; *The Best Times, An Informal Memoir*, John Dos Passos; *Running with the Bulls: My Years with the Hemingways*, by Valerie Hemingway and *Hemingway's Hurricane: The Great Florida Keys Storm of 1935* by Phil Scott. Also consulted were *Hemingway: The 1930s* and *Hemingway: The Final Years*, both by the finest of Hemingway's biographers, Michael Reynolds.

I am indebted to these and the other authors, memoirists and biographers whose scholarship contributed to the tapestry of *Toros & Torsos*.

ABOUT THE AUTHOR

Edgar®-finalist Craig McDonald is an award-winning journalist, editor and fiction writer. His short fiction has appeared in literary magazines, anthologies and several online crime fiction sites.

His debut novel, *Head Games*, was selected as a 2008 Edgar® nominee for Best First Novel by an American Author. It was also nominated for Anthony and Gumshoe awards.

His nonfiction books include *Art in the Blood*, a collection of interviews with twenty major crime authors which appeared in 2006, and *Rogue Males: Conversations and Confrontations About the Writing Life*, a second collection of interviews to be published by Bleak House Books.

McDonald was also a contributor to the NYT's nonfiction bestseller, *Secrets of the Code*. He recently won national awards for his profiles of crime novelists James Crumley, Daniel Woodrell and James Sallis.

He is a member of the Mystery Writers of America, and the International Association of Crime Writers.